Kathy
REICHS
& Brendan Reichs
TERMINAL

1 3 5 7 9 10 8 6 4 2

Young Arrow
20 Vauxhall Bridge Road
London SW1V 2SA

Young Arrow is part of the Penguin Random House group of companies whose
addresses can be found at global.penguinrandomhouse.com.

Penguin
Random House
UK

First published by Young Arrow in 2015, and published by arrangement with
G.P.Putnam's Sons, an imprint of the Penguin Group (USA) LLC

www.randomhouse.co.uk

A CIP catalogue record for this book is
available from the British Library.

ISBN 9780099567271

Printed and bound by CPI Group (UK) Ltd, Croydon, CR0 4YY

Brendan Reichs would like to dedicate this book to his mother:
I couldn't ask for a better mentor and writing partner. You gave me
the opportunity of a lifetime. I owe you more than one.

Kathy Reichs would like to dedicate this book to her son:
Without you, the Virals series would not have happened, a tragedy
too awful to contemplate. Great things await you!

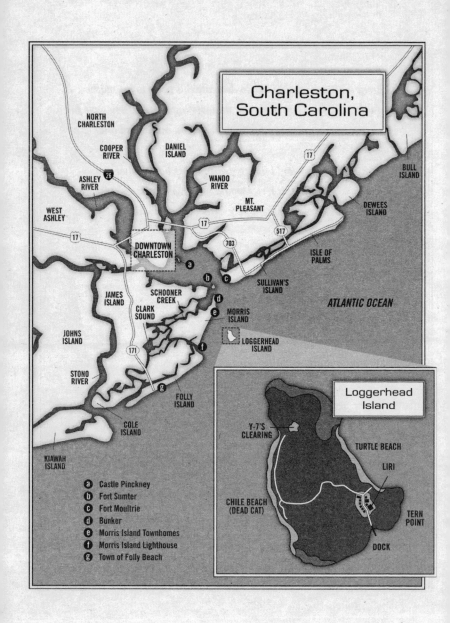

Charleston, South Carolina

NORTH CHARLESTON

COOPER RIVER

DANIEL ISLAND

ASHLEY RIVER

26

WANDO RIVER

WEST ASHLEY

MT. PLEASANT

BULL ISLAND

DEWEES ISLAND

17

17

DOWNTOWN CHARLESTON

703

517

ISLE OF PALMS

SULLIVAN'S ISLAND

JAMES ISLAND

SCHOONER CREEK

CLARK SOUND

ⓐ

ⓑ

ⓒ

ⓓ

ⓔ MORRIS ISLAND

ATLANTIC OCEAN

JOHNS ISLAND

171

ⓕ

STONO RIVER

ⓖ

FOLLY ISLAND

LOGGERHEAD ISLAND

COLE ISLAND

KIAWAH ISLAND

ⓐ Castle Pinckney
ⓑ Fort Sumter
ⓒ Fort Moultrie
ⓓ Bunker
ⓔ Morris Island Townhomes
ⓕ Morris Island Lighthouse
ⓖ Town of Folly Beach

Loggerhead Island

Y-7'S CLEARING

TURTLE BEACH

LIRI

CHILE BEACH (DEAD CAT)

TERN POINT

DOCK

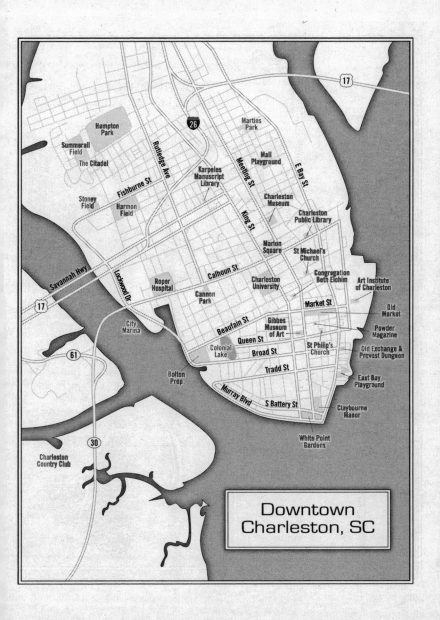

Downtown Charleston, SC

ATTENTION: DIRECTOR WALSH ["EYES ONLY"]

FILE STATUS: TOP SECRET [LEVEL 5]

CASE: #34687 (AKA—PHOENIX INQUIRY)

FILE TYPE: SURVEILLANCE REPORT (CONVERSATION RECORDED WITHOUT THE SUBJECTS' KNOWLEDGE UNDER THE AUTHORITY OF INFORMATION CONTAINMENT PROTOCOL 12.C ("ICP 12.C-1.1").)

DATE: APRIL 8, 2014

SUBJECT(S): BRENNAN, VICTORIA G. ("VB"); CLAYBOURNE, CHANCE A. ("CC")

PRINCIPAL INVESTIGATING AGENT(S): J. SALTMAN, B. ROGERS

RECORDING AGENT(S): J. SALTMAN, B. ROGERS

RECORDING LOCATION: 74 BEE STREET, CHARLESTON, SC

HEADQUARTERS—CANDELA PHARMACEUTICALS, INC.

ADDITIONAL NOTE(S): INVESTIGATING AGENTS BELIEVE THE PHOENIX INQUIRY SHOULD BE ELEVATED TO ACTIVE-MISSION STATUS. REQUESTING OPERATIONAL RESOURCES AND FIELD PERSONNEL.

TIME: 10:34 AM

VB: When did you learn how to flare, Chance?

CC: Over the last few days. Though "learn" is fairly generous. I have almost no idea how it works. My powers can snap on without warning, or fizzle in seconds.

VB: Still, that's . . . incredible. It took me weeks to gain even that much control. [PAUSE] How'd this happen? How'd you suddenly become . . . Viral?

CC: I was careless. Didn't take proper precautions in the lab. Then, last week, I got terribly sick. Could barely function. Strange things started happening to my body—unnerving side effects you won't find on WebMD. By that point, I no longer had any illusions about the cause.

VB: The weird sensation I've been experiencing lately—an odd kinetic force, like my mind is connecting to things around me—it spikes around *you*. *Because* of you, I'm sure of it now. How can that be?

CC: Don't ask me. I'm new to the species, remember? [PAUSE] Maybe it involves whatever sets you apart from normal people. Sets *us* apart, I should say, now. Perhaps your unconscious mind innately recognizes the presence of another Viral.

VB: That can't be it. I've had this feeling for months now, off and on, since right after the hurricane. I noticed it at least a half-dozen times before last week.

CC: Yeah. Um, about that. [PAUSE]

VB: Yes?

CC: Well. You know I've been following you. [PAUSE] But you probably don't know for how long.

VB: What . . . for months? [PAUSE] Months!?! Seriously? Are you saying you were in Charlotte after the storm?

CC: Had to go somewhere.

VB: What about Morris Island?

CC: I've visited a few times, unannounced.

VB: Even to our . . . *private* retreat?

CC: You mean that hill bunker? [LAUGHTER] Nice place. I love the décor. How'd you get all that stuff in there?

VB: *Jesus.* [PAUSE] How'd you find it? Because of me?

CC: I don't pretend to understand any of this. But sometimes, if I concentrate really hard, I can pinpoint exactly where you are. I sense your presence, perhaps in the same way you detected mine. I can't explain it, either.

VB: I . . . that's . . .

CC: Also, I'm fairly certain I've been infected for a while. Months, most likely, probably since the first few days of the Brimstone experiment. What you just said—that you've been sensing my presence for some time—all but confirms it.

VB: How is that possible? How could you carry a supervirus that long and not . . . change?

CC: I have a guess. The parvovirus strain used in Brimstone was slightly different from the one that infected you. Better, we thought, though we obviously had no idea what we were doing. I think our pathogen has a longer incubation period, which would explain the course of my infection. This viral deviation must've caused other differences, too.

VB: Your eyes glow *red,* Chance. Not golden. Why?

CC: [PAUSE] I don't know. I wish I did. I'm just glad I stopped puking all day.

VB: How do you feel now?

CC: Great. My fever broke yesterday. The chills and sweats are finally gone. I can actually stand without feeling dizzy. But I have no idea what's happened to my body.

VB: Yesterday? [PAUSE] Interesting.

CC: Why?

VB: Because our flares were a mess last week. Erratic. Unstable. Mine backfired more than once. We couldn't understand why, but it seems like the trouble occurred during your worst symptoms.

CC: You think *my* sickness was somehow related?

VB: I don't know. But our powers stabilized at the same time you recovered.

CC: Could be a coincidence.

VB: Maybe. [PAUSE] Or maybe your . . . transformation was disrupting whatever shared mind-space Virals inhabit. We don't really know how any of this works either. Perhaps your evolution created a ripple in the telepathic framework of our pack. That makes as much sense as anything.

CC: *Our* pack? Does that mean I'm one of you?

VB: I . . . I don't know. That's not up to me alone. It might not even be something we can choose.

CC: Well, I hope we *can* choose, Tory. I hope your friends will accept me.

VB: I'll try to convince them. I promise that much.

CC: Good. Because I . . . I . . . [LONG PAUSE][MUFFLED NOISE]

VB: Chance?

CC: I haven't told you everything yet. [PAUSE]

VB: *Oh my God.* [PAUSE] The night on the beach!

CC: I was wondering when you'd remember.

VB: When I was attacked on Morris Island, afterward I saw *three* sets of red eyes in the dunes. Three, Chance!

CC: Yes. I'm afraid you did.

[END TRANSCRIPT]

PROLOGUE
(FIVE WEEKS LATER)

The Trinity peered down from atop a church tower.

They sat stone still, watching the sleek black skyscraper across the street. Brilliant white lettering along its apex labeled it the world-wide headquarters of Candela Pharmaceuticals.

The Four had entered hours ago. The sun had set, yet they remained inside.

Night blanketed the city. Cloaking the figures in darkness.

A low growl floated on the wind.

The largest turned bloodred eyes on two companions.

A jerk of the head motioned them to follow.

They were ready. Determined. But it would have to be another day.

As one, the trio crept across a narrow ledge, ignoring heart-stopping drops to either side, and vaulted gracefully onto a lower roof. Moving like ghosts, they leaped to a willow tree in the yard below, then dropped into a small cemetery.

The smallest hissed softly.

The largest grunted in agreement.

Soon.

The Four lived on a remote island.

The Trinity had observed their alpha there once before.

She and her mixed-blood beast.

Rivals.

A second growl escaped, louder than the first.

Soon.

With preternatural grace, the figures melted into the shadowy field of tombstones.

Three haunting calls echoed down the streets of Charleston.

Soon.

PART ONE

CHALLENGE

CHAPTER 1

My adversary charged at full speed, intent on running me down.

Not this time.

I nudged the ball left, deftly sidestepping the girl's clumsy challenge. Keeping my head up, I spotted Ella twenty yards ahead, streaking for the corner. The field opened like a book, and for once, I knew what to do.

I booted the ball into Ella's path, then cut behind her, racing to a pocket of space across midfield. As a fullback I rarely ventured forward, but I was tired of playing it safe. The game was deadlocked at zero, and goals don't score themselves.

Plus, the blonde, ponytailed freak who just missed spiking my ankle had been attacking relentlessly all game. Four hard fouls were enough. Time to put *her* on the defensive.

Ella corralled the ball, dancing between two hopeless opponents before noticing my run in support. She pulled the ball back, drawing the defenders closer, then lofted a cross over James Island Charter's entire back line.

I experienced a brief moment of panic as the ball arced toward me.

Don't embarrass yourself, Brennan.

Thankfully, I didn't. Chesting the ball down, I was shocked to find myself completely unmarked. Thirty yards of open grass separated me and the opposing goalie.

"Push forward!" Ella shouted.

Oh crap oh crap oh crap. But I drove the ball ahead.

To say I lacked confidence in my soccer skills is an understatement. I'd only been playing a few months, and charging the other team's goal without support, during the biggest game of the season, was not something I'd planned.

Please, God. Don't let me trip over the ball.

As I neared the eighteen-yard box, a defender barreled over. I tapped the ball between her outstretched legs and raced around the awkward slide tackle, nearly stumbling in surprise when the move actually worked. The keeper charged, a look of desperation on her face.

Chip it over. Score. Win!

But before I could exploit the opening, my legs were ruthlessly hacked out from under me. I fell forward, slamming into the turf with a groan. A cleat dug into the small of my back as someone flopped over me from behind.

My head spun. The whistle blew.

I heard Ella shouting. What sounded like shoving.

I looked up.

Blonde Ponytail was standing astride the ball. She and Ella were nose to nose, and they weren't discussing favorite boy bands. The harridan even had the gall to protest when the official showed her a yellow card. Unfortunately, Ella got one, too.

I rose unsteadily, wiping dirt from my purple Bolton Prep uniform. The official stepped between Ella and Ponytail and signaled a free kick for our side.

"You okay?" Ella was staring at my tormentor, face red with anger.

"Never better." Gulping air into my lungs. "She seems nice."

Ella laughed, but the humor didn't touch her eyes. "That bitch knows you're better with your feet, so she's bull-rushing the ball, trying to intimidate you. Don't let her."

The official placed the ball fifteen feet beyond the edge of the box, then paced off ten yards. He glanced at his watch. There were only moments left in the match.

As the James Island defenders formed a wall, I began to retreat to my fullback slot.

Ella grabbed my arm. "Want this one? You definitely earned it."

A generous thought, but Ella was worlds better than me. And everyone else on the field.

Not to mention that taking a game-deciding free kick was too terrifying to contemplate. I'd probably find a way to knock it into our own goal.

Ella frowned. "Well, at least get up there. Look for a rebound."

Before I could react, Ella cupped her hands to her mouth. "Maddy!"

Madison Dunkle turned. Ella pointed at me, then at Madison, then jerked a thumb over her shoulder. Madison nodded without hesitation, jogging back to cover my position.

"Take her spot in the middle." Ella's rope of black hair brushed the ground as she knelt to position the ball on the grass. We both knew it'd take a miracle to score from this distance. "If the ball bounces your way, just blast it on goal."

"That I can do."

I think.

Joining the line of players jockeying for position, I felt an elbow dig into my back. Right where the cleat had struck.

I spun, knowing who I'd find. My temper slipped a notch.

"Be careful, ginger princess." Ponytail's eyes glittered with malice. "No more dancing. Things can get rough up here."

My anger was reaching a boil. "Thanks. I'll be fine."

The hateful girl shouldered into me, forcing me outside the eighteen-yard box. "Even without your mommy to protect you?" She nodded toward Ella, who was lining up her strike. All eyes were on my friend as she prepared to take the free kick.

Maybe it was ninety minutes of abuse.

Or Ponytail's smug attitude. Or the hard foul. Or the fact that I was hungry.

Maybe it was her referencing my mother.

SNAP.

I felt a rush of adrenaline.

A thousand suns torched my skin, followed by an ocean of freezing rain.

Energy poured into my muscles. My senses blazed with hyperacuity. Smell. Sight. Sound. Feel. Taste. Each shifted to superhuman clarity and perception.

Golden fire ignited in my eyes.

I *flared.*

In public. In the open.

In the middle of a freaking soccer game.

I quickly averted my eyes. Thankfully, everyone was watching Ella.

This is crazy. CRAZY.

But I ignored common sense. I was going to show this bully what's what.

Head lowered, I was about to push back into the scrum when a message winged into my brain.

I was wondering when you'd go wolf style on that beast.

I stopped short, gaze darting to the sideline.

To where Hiram, Shelton, and Ben were lounging on a grassy hill.

Hi! You shouldn't be flaring in public!

Oh, you're one to talk. Hi tapped the sunglasses covering his eyes.

Like Shelton, he still wore his Bolton Prep uniform, though he'd ditched the jacket, loosened his tie, and removed his shoes and socks. *Which of us is standing in a group of strangers?*

Okay. Fine. And I'd connected our pack mind without thinking.

I lost my cool, but—

Shh! Just listen. Hi pointed a chubby finger. *There's no one on the back post.*

I glanced to my left, pretending to shade my eyes from the sun. He was right—expecting a direct shot, the James Island defenders were clogging the middle of the box.

No one was guarding the flank.

You're welcome. Hi's message carried a distinct note of smugness.

Ella was lined up over the ball. I had only seconds.

As casually as possible, I moved along the wall of defenders until I stood farthest right. Then I stuck an arm behind my back, waggling frantically for Ella's attention.

At the last moment, she spotted my signal. Her eyes narrowed in confusion.

I nodded right. Spun my finger in a circle. Tapped my head.

Ella dipped her chin, then took two steps to the left.

What am I doing? I can't pull this off!

Noticing Ella's shift, Ponytail glanced down the line. Spotting my position, her eyes widened. She surged toward me, barreling over a teammate in the process.

Too late.

Ella shot forward and struck the ball.

At the same moment, I spun, looping around the wall and behind the defense.

The ball arced through the air—not toward goal, as everyone expected, but to where I waited at the corner of the six-yard box.

The goalkeeper tried to adjust, scrambling off her line with a muffled curse. Ponytail backpedaled desperately as the ball cut across the clear blue sky.

I leaped high, my flare-powered muscles firing me up with ease. The black-and-white sphere seemed to hang forever. I could smell yesterday's rain on the wind, could see the cross-stitching on the ball. Heard a collective intake of breath.

I rose. The keeper rose. Ponytail rose.

Then I rose higher still.

I headed the ball as lightly as a feather, directing it into the open net. Goal.

My first ever.

I landed less gracefully, since both James Island girls slammed me in midair. I hit the ground hard, jamming my knee and tumbling backward, flipping ass over teakettle before rolling to a stop. Then my teammates mobbed me in a giant dog pile.

In the confusion, no one got a good look at my face.

The official consulted his watch, then blew the whistle three times. Game over.

Nice one, Pelé!

Thanks, Hiram.

SNUP.

As the crowd went nuts, Ella dragged me up and smacked my butt. Hard.

"Ow!" Woozy from the loss of my flare.

"You have more hops than any girl I know!" Ella shot a nasty look at Ponytail, who was chewing out her teammates. Catching the girl's eye, I winked. She practically snarled in frustration before stalking away.

"That was awesome, Tory!" Madison beamed at me as she shook out her wavy auburn hair. We exchanged an awkward hug. I tried not to cringe.

Things were different now—Madison and I had become friendly over the last few weeks—but old habits die hard.

"Thanks, Maddy. And thanks for letting me get forward."

"When my captain commands, I obey." Madison squeezed Ella's arm before trotting toward the sideline. We watched her go with matching headshakes.

"I'm sold." My shoulders rose and fell. "I can't explain it, but she really *is* different."

"Or she's after something. But I can't for the life of me guess what."

"Maybe she finally had enough of Tripod life."

Ella grunted noncommittally, eyes heavy with skepticism as she began unstrapping her shin guards. "In my experience, girls like that *never* change."

I didn't respond. Honestly, I felt the same.

Madison and I had history. A dangerous one, for me and my friends. She'd seen things I fervently wished she hadn't.

Afterward, Madison had spent months avoiding me. Terrified of me. Scheming against me when she could. But now she'd simply let it all go, just like that? It didn't seem possible.

Ella nudged me, crashing my train of thought. "Look alive, Brennan. Your cheering section is in full effect."

Hi and Shelton were standing shoulder to shoulder, clapping and chanting my name. In response to my wave, Hi attempted a running cartwheel, only to stall halfway and flop on his back. Shelton leaned over his prone form and began an exaggerated ten-count. Ben—lying on the grass with his legs crossed—just shook his head at the two of them.

I snorted, pawing through my tangled red hair. "That's my fan club, huh?"

"Better than not having one."

"Like you'd know anything about that." Ella was one of the prettiest girls in school.

"True." My friend grinned wickedly—she'd recovered her spark since last month's ordeal, something I was extremely happy to see. "But your followers will have to be patient. Our fearless leader wants us. He looks like he might propose."

I glanced at our sideline. A grinning Coach Lynch waved us over to where the rest of the team huddled. A look back at the hill. Hi and Shelton were dousing Ben with water bottles as he howled in protest.

My eyes rolled. "Doofuses."

Ella hooked her arm through mine. "Come on. Time for a well-deserved bow. After all, you're the man of the match."

A smile spread across my face. "I am, aren't I?"

Not bad.

CHAPTER 2

"Flaring! On an open field! With dozens of people watching!"

Shelton Devers shivered as if spiders were crawling down his spine. Boxy, black-framed glasses nearly tumbled from his nose. "That's not like you, Tor. To be so *reckless*. So *irresponsible*. Thank God no one saw!"

I dodged his eye as we strode along the sidewalk. Azaleas, dogwoods, and long-limbed willow trees shaded Gadsden Street, tucked close to the historic homes lining both sides. Warm May sunshine had Charleston's gardens looking and smelling their finest.

Not that Shelton could be distracted.

He was right, and we both knew it.

"It was stupid." I wilted under my friend's unrelenting scowl. "I don't know what came over me."

"More than stupid." Shelton tossed his uniform jacket over one bony shoulder. The heat had cranked up to match the humidity, reminding everyone that summer was nearly here. Shelton's dark skin glistened with sweat as he lowered his voice. "I know our powers are humming right now, but that doesn't mean we should get crazy."

"*I* thought it was awesome."

I glanced over my shoulder. Ben Blue's dark eyes twinkled as he flashed a rare smile. "You shot up like a kangaroo. That James Island troll nearly lost it."

I smiled, but quickly looked away. Ben's compliments had the tendency to make my pale, freckled skin burn like a supernova, matching the shade of my unruly hair.

Things had been awkward between Ben and me since that night at the police station, though I tried not to let it show. Still, at times his mere presence could fluster me. Conflict me. Pull me in different directions.

Ben was a packmate, practically a blood brother.

But, lately, there were times when I thought of him differently.

Not now, you moron.

"Thanks to *me*." Hiram Stolowitski was plodding along at Ben's side, his Bolton Prep uniform unbuttoned to the maximum extent allowed by public decency. He toed the line between chubby and portly, a red-faced jokester with sharp chestnut eyes, wavy brown hair, and a wickedly sarcastic tongue. Hi reached over and patted his own back. "I should get an assist. Or at least an assistant coach gig. Although the girls wouldn't be able to concentrate once they saw me in my game shorts."

Ben smacked Hi's head without breaking stride. "Dope."

"Jealous."

The four of us were walking north, up the peninsula, bound for Charleston's cozy medical district on the eastern edge of downtown. A trip we now took three times a week after school.

We had an appointment, though we couldn't tell anyone about it.

"*You* shouldn't have been flaring either," Shelton grumbled, unwilling to let it go. "Things are getting way too loose around here. Too casual. We're still genetic freaks, remember? Dog-scrambled mutants, one step ahead of the Man, trying to keep a low profile?"

"You're right." My palms rose in surrender. "Unacceptable risk. Won't happen again."

Though, being honest, I felt less guilty than I should have.

Flaring came so easily now. So smoothly.

These last few weeks, our powers had been responding as if we were born to them. I could sharpen my senses in a blink. Linking with another flaring Viral—a struggle for so long—now came as easily as closing my eyes. Telepathy worked without a hitch. As if a storm had passed, leaving behind blue skies and clear sailing.

The odd *connected* feeling I'd been experiencing had disappeared as well.

None of us knew what to make of things.

Was the viral transformation complete? Had our hybrid DNA finally stopped churning?

Or was this simply the prelude to some new phase? A pleasant spring sojourn, before the wolf came back with a vengeance. The final pit stop on our evolutionary roller coaster.

I didn't know. But I was damn sure going to find out.

And finally, maybe, we had someone who could provide us with concrete answers.

At Calhoun Street we turned left, then took a quick right onto Courtenay Drive. Three more blocks brought us to our destination on Bee Street—the gleaming headquarters of Candela Pharmaceuticals.

"He better not make us wait again." Ben's customary scowl was back in place. Freed from school uniforms—Ben had been kicked out of Bolton Prep, and now attended Wando High in Mount Pleasant—he wore his typical black tee and jeans. A brooding, muscular boy with copper skin and shoulder-length black hair, nearly everything about Ben was dark.

Except his heart, of course.

I tried for diplomatic. "Chance is under a lot of pressure. He's in the same boat as we are now, and running a covert medical experiment can't be easy."

Ben snorted. "Why not? He owns the damn place."

"And did it once before," Hi quipped.

"He's just a stockholder, yo." Shelton peered up at the black-windowed monolith looming before us. "Chance Claybourne might own the biggest chunk—which scores him a nice gig at his father's old company—but Candela is run by a board of directors. We're lucky he's in charge of special projects, or Chance probably couldn't help us at all."

"'Lucky'?" Ben crossed his arms, making no move to cross the street. "The whole reason we're stuck with that douchebag is *because* of his 'special project.' And his father's *special project* before that, which is what infected us in the first place!"

"That's not Chance's fault." Unsure why I was defending him.

"Without Claybourne, we don't have access to a medical lab." Hi shrugged, indicating the conversation was pointless. "We need his fancy machines to find out what's wrong with us."

"Nothing's *wrong* with us," Ben snapped. "And we could've used LIRI to run the tests. We don't need Claybourne for anything."

"LIRI?" I gave Ben an exasperated look. "My dad's realm? Not a chance. We'd never get within ten feet of the necessary equipment. Like it or not, using Candela's resources is the only way we'll ever get answers. You *know* that."

Ben shook his head but didn't reply, his jaw tight with frustration.

Ben *hated* needing Chance. Or anyone else, for that matter, but especially Chance.

But this was a tired argument.

"We can't just stand here." Hi stepped into the crosswalk. "We're supposed to be keeping a low profile, remember?"

The Candela building rose thirty stories, with shiny glass doors accessing a marble lobby patrolled by security guards. Not good for our purposes. Too public. Therefore, upon reaching the opposite curb, we glanced both ways, then slipped into a narrow service alley running alongside the office tower. Halfway down was an unmarked steel door.

Hi dropped to a crouch and spun a quick 360, shading his eyes while humming the *Mission: Impossible* theme. "The coast is . . . clear!"

"Hush." Removing a key card, I swiped it through the attached security box and typed a ten-digit number. A soft beep. The door swung open. We hurried down an empty hallway to a service elevator, then rode to the twenty-fifth floor.

Chance was waiting when the doors opened.

Tall and lean, with a strong chin and dark, piercing eyes, Chance Claybourne was as close to perfect as a guy could look. My stomach flipped upon seeing him, just as it always did.

Without speaking, Chance turned and strode down the hall, moving with the effortless grace of a jungle cat. I couldn't help watching him the whole way.

Beside me, Ben's shoulders tensed. I could practically hear his teeth grinding.

A sigh escaped. Was today the day they'd finally come to blows?

Chance occupied a corner office on a corridor that was empty most days. He'd chosen the twenty-fifth floor for that very reason.

Chance waved us inside, locked the door, then lowered the shades facing the hallway. We took seats on a couch and chair set surrounding a glass coffee table, waiting with varying degrees of patience. Chance always conducted the meetings.

"All right, then." Chance clasped his hands before him, not deigning to sit. "News?"

"Nothing to report, captain." Hi snapped off a mock salute. "The enemy is quiet."

Chance shook his head wistfully. "Our enemy has already stormed the gates, Hiram. He's inside our cells, wrecking shop. It's just damage control at this point."

"Speak for yourself." Ben leaned back and placed his feet on the coffee table. "*You* might be damaged. For all we know, you're barely Viral. A newborn pup, all alone, with silly red eyes."

Ben waved a lazy hand at the rest of us. "My pack is just fine."

Chance's coal-black brows dipped in mock consternation. "You sure of that, Benjamin? I'd *love* to see your research. The medical tests you're basing that opinion on."

"You can shove your stupid tests." Ben flashed an icy smile as golden light exploded from his eyes. "*This* is all the proof I need."

"Ben, enough!" I slapped my knee in irritation. "Quit acting like a child!"

Ben's neck flushed red. His glare slid to me for an instant, then he jerked his head away, scowling at the window. In the reflection, I saw the yellow fire fade from his irises. "Whatever."

"We need to know what's going on in our bodies." Shelton spoke softly but firmly to Ben's back. "If only to understand what happens next."

"A few tests can't hurt," Hi seconded, hands locked behind his head as he lounged on the couch. "If Chance wants to give us superduper secret physicals, we should let him. Don't punch gift horses in the face, and all that."

Ben didn't respond. Continued staring out the window.

For his part, Chance didn't seem to care. "Moving along. I was able to slide our blood samples onto the DNA-sequencing schedule. I marked them as urgent for Special Projects, under Candela's strictest proprietary R&D protocols, so I'll be the only one to see the results. We should have them back sometime this week."

"So nothing new," Ben muttered. "Wonderful."

"What blood tests did you order?" I asked Chance, in no mood for another round of bickering.

"A full battery." Chance raked slender fingers through his dark hair. "I didn't want to tip my interest in the DNA sequencing."

I nodded. "The other tests might tell us something anyway. Our blood chemistry. Antibody loads. White and red blood cell counts. I just wish we'd thought to flare before giving the samples." I was still kicking myself over that oversight.

"Next batch," Chance promised. "First we need baseline results."

"It's all about the DNA." Hi steepled his fingers as he spoke. "That's where the wolf is hiding. That's where the changes are buried."

Shelton, Chance, and I nodded in unison. We knew the supervirus had scrambled our genetic material—Karsten had said that much, before he was gone. But we'd never gotten any specifics. I'd never imagined we ever could.

Then, suddenly, Chance Claybourne opened a door.

In a few short days, we'd learn the truth. For the first time, we'd have an accurate picture of what the virus had done to us. Maybe even catch a glimpse of what we'd become.

Maybe find a way to stop it.

I stood abruptly. Crossed the office. Tested the thought.

Was *that* what I wanted? Was that the point of all this?

Distracted by the unsettling notion, it took me a moment to notice what was sitting on Chance's desk. When I finally saw, my hackles rose. Goose bumps covered my arms.

"What is this?" I demanded.

"*That* is what we need to talk about today." Chance rubbed his eyes with both palms before continuing in a tired voice. "It seems our new friends paid Claybourne Manor a visit last night. Left me gift."

I swallowed, mouth suddenly dry.

Oh no.

Oh no no no no no no . . .

CHAPTER 3

They looked like crime-scene photos.

Three hi-res, glossy eight-by-tens, recently printed, spread neatly across Chance's otherwise empty desk. Each provided a different angle of the same subject: a frowning marble statue on a raised dais.

I recognized the setting immediately. "This is inside your house."

"The grand foyer," Chance confirmed, joining me by the desk. "The beating heart of Claybourne Manor. You remember my great-uncle Milton, don't you?"

The room in the picture was like something out of the Italian Renaissance. Murals covered the walls, bordered by ornate frescoes and exquisitely carved crown molding. A grand staircase circled the airy chamber, which was capped by a seventy-foot stained-glass dome high above.

The room's centerpiece was an eight-foot chiseled representation of Milton Ignatius Claybourne, the mansion's original architect. He scowled down from his perch, face bandaged and dressed for war, an ancient musket clutched in one hand.

The pictures triggered a flood of emotions. The first time I encountered this statue, I'd broken into Claybourne Manor to spy on Chance's father. In the process I'd learned that Chance was playing me for a fool. The memory still burned.

That was back when Chance had been an adversary. Before he'd become Viral, like me.

So what was he now? What were *we* now?

Things change so fast.

But the familiar statue wasn't what had grabbed my attention.

"What happened here?" I whispered, shoving my nose close to the first shot.

The other boys shuffled over, forming a loose circle around the desk as we tried to make sense of the images.

"As you can see, my ancestor was painted red." Chance frowned, thumb-scratching the side of his nose. "Except for his eyes, which are blacked out with shoe polish." He reached under the desk and pulled out a grocery bag. "And if that isn't delightful enough, I found *this* hanging around Uncle Milton's neck."

Chance removed a torn cardboard square, punctured on both ends by a knotted shoelace. Painted on its face were three black wolf heads—red eyed and bordered in white—hanging over a single word.

Simple, direct, and to the point.

TRAITOR

"It's them." I could barely breathe. "Virals."

Chance laid the sign beside the photos. "We don't know for sure there's more than one."

"Maybe *you* don't." I hugged my arms to ward off a chill. "But I know what I saw on the beach that night, Chance. There were *three* sets of red eyes in those dunes, not just yours."

Ben glared at Chance. "And you know nothing about that, huh?"

"I've told you a dozen times," Chance snapped defensively, "I was there on Morris Island that night, but I didn't see the attack. Then a flare erupted out of nowhere and I could barely control it. By the time I spotted Tory, it was just her and the wolfdog. She looked right at me, so I bolted."

"You were there all right," Ben growled. "Stalking Tory like a psychopath."

Chance's tone grew sarcastic. "That morning I'd discovered I possessed mutant superpowers. Excuse me for thinking I had a right to pry." Then he shot me a guilty look. "But I didn't see anyone else that night, and no one was with me. If you saw other eyes in the dunes, the bastards must've been following *me*. And avoiding me."

"Like your buddy Speckman?" Ben needled. "Was your partner in crime in the bushes, too?"

"He's not my buddy!" Chance snapped. "And I told you, I don't know."

I held up a hand. "Enough."

Chance had explained this all before, and I'd accepted his story. More or less.

Ben, however, likely never would.

"I saw three sets of red eyes," I said firmly. "You make one pair, which means there were two other Virals in those dunes."

Hi pointed to the primitive symbols painted on the cardboard. "The vandals painted *three* wolf heads on this sign. Seems specific. I'm guessing a trio of bad boys."

Chance shook his head reflexively, but didn't respond.

The chill in my arms spread throughout my body.

Besides Chance, how many new Virals were out there? How did they catch the virus?

We only know of one.

Shelton tapped the nearest photo. "This all went down *inside* your house. Don't you lock your doors at night?"

"Locked and dead-bolted, with the alarm engaged." Chance blew out an exasperated breath. "My security system is *military* grade, with motion sensors, cameras, even laser harmonic sensors. Good enough to protect a freaking bank. And yet . . ."

"What do you think the message means?" Hi tapped the lone word on the sign.

Chance snorted. "It means, Hiram, that whoever did this thinks I'm a traitor."

"Join the club," Ben said.

"We *know* who did this," I cut in, unwilling to endure another macho pissing match. "It's obviously Will Speckman. Who else but the lab tech that worked with you?"

Chance nodded unhappily. "He's the only person that makes any sense. But it's been months since we accidentally infected ourselves. Why he would suddenly make such an elaborate . . . whatever this is . . ." Chance trailed off, waving a hand at the photographs.

"Months since Speckman was infected," Ben pressed, refusing to let up. "Yet *we* first heard about him a few weeks ago."

"I didn't know before then," Chance shot back. "I'm not psychic!"

Shelton tugged his earlobe, a nervous habit. "This isn't a love note, y'all. It's a warning. Maybe even a challenge. Why would this dude—and who knows who else—break into your palace and vandalize a damn statue? How pissed was this guy when you fired him?"

Chance's expression soured. "Extremely."

"I'm no psychologist," Hi said, crossing his arms, "but this seems like the actions of someone both super-pissed off and not right in the head. That's a bad combo, especially if he can sneak into your house like a ghost."

"Not just Speckman," I repeated. "There are at least two of them."

"Well, I can only identify one," Chance replied irritably. "Will Speckman worked for me at Candela. I knew him from Bolton Prep. When

I began Brimstone I was trying to keep the project quiet, and wanted to use only outside people. Speckman was at Charleston University by then. He seemed perfect, so I hired him part-time. He was the only person besides me who came into direct contact with the new supervirus. No one else touched it. No one."

"Which means Speckman must've infected someone else." I caught and held Chance's eye. "Maybe more than one person. For all we know, *lots* of people could've accidentally caught the bug. You could be spreading it, too."

Chance shook his head firmly, but his eyes were troubled. "It's not possible."

I didn't let him wriggle off the hook. "There are at least *two* others out there. Red-eyed Virals, just like you. I *saw* them. *Coop* saw them. It happened, Chance. You need to accept the truth."

"If Will were . . . if *we* were . . . *contagious*—" Chance grimaced, barely able to say the word, "—there'd be more evidence of it. People getting sick. Patients going Viral. I've been monitoring the hospitals every single day, and nothing like my symptoms has been reported. Our experimental parvovirus strain was specifically designed to transmit only through blood-to-blood contact."

"I think we can safely dismiss whatever you guys 'designed' at this point," Hi countered. "Things clearly didn't go as planned."

Chance gave him a hard look. Then he seemed to fold, slumping back in his chair with a frown. "We tried a different formulation than Karsten's. Our experiment still used Parvovirus B19, the human form, but we tweaked the canine strain slightly. We thought the newer hybrid would be more stable, and more palatable to a host's immune system. Of course, we didn't know what Karsten's creation actually *did*. The odds of *two* different designer viruses, both suddenly capable of making the jump to human hosts . . . it . . . it boggles the mind."

Chance took a deep breath, then met each of our eyes in turn. "I screwed up. I admit it. I didn't know what I was dealing with and jumped in too soon, with too little caution. But I knew *something* was wrong with you guys. After everything I'd seen—everything you'd done—Karsten's experiment was the only thing I could guess at." His lips tilted in a sheepish smile. "You have to give me a *little* credit for making the right connection."

Ben rolled his eyes. "Idiot."

Chance half rose, but I waved him back into his seat.

I wheeled on Ben. Spoke calmly and coolly. "We are trying to solve a problem right now. Either help, or leave."

Ben flushed scarlet. His jaw worked, but he only nodded.

"Good." Turning back to Chance. "We need to focus on finding Speckman."

"I haven't been sitting around playing Candy Crush." Chance yanked open a drawer and removed a dog-eared folder. "William Thomas Speckman. Born in Goose Creek, attended Palmetto Scholars Academy, a local charter school for gifted children. Transferred to Bolton Prep his junior year to join our lacrosse team." Chance dropped the folder onto his desk. "He was a year ahead of me, but I knew Will was studying molecular biology and had the rep of a computer whiz. When I decided to investigate Karsten's files, I hired him in Special Projects as my primary lab tech on Brimstone."

"Great screening work." Hi flashed a thumbs-up.

"I *knew* Will," Chance replied flatly. "I wanted a tight ship, was new to Candela, and figured I'd better limit the number of Candela personnel who could figure out what I was up to. Hiring an old teammate part-time seemed perfect."

Shelton sighed. "Until he got infected."

Chance nodded. "It must've happened early in the process. I didn't experience symptoms until much later. By the time I suspected the virus, Will was already gone."

"You mean fired," Ben said.

"Yes." Chance shifted in his chair. "Will became unreliable near the end. He stopped coming to work on time, but would appear at odd hours, acting strangely in the lab and attempting to access files he wasn't cleared to see. I had to let him go. A few weeks later, when I realized I'd been infected, I tried to contact him. By then he'd stopped answering my calls and texts. He'd even moved out of his dorm. Will never contacted his parents—I inquired discreetly, not wishing to set off any alarms. But as far as I can tell, he just blew town."

"But now we know different." My eyes strayed to the vandalized statue.

Ominous, empty black eyes. And why paint the rest red?

What happened to Will Speckman?

"Too true." Chance laughed without humor. "It seems Will paid me a visit, while I slept."

I arched a brow. "Or the other did. Or both."

Chance said nothing. Silence stretched as I considered our next move.

"The lab work will be ready this week?" I said finally.

Chance shrugged. "I had to be cautious, but that's my best guess."

"What does that matter?" Ben sneered at the photos. "Obviously, we have to deal with this nonsense first, thanks to our master scientist."

"Enough!" Chance shot to his feet. "If you four hadn't lied to me at every turn, messing with my head, making me think I was *crazy*, this never would've happened." His voice went ice cold. "Would *you* have let it go, Blue? Would you have walked away?"

Ben looked away. Then, ever so slightly, he nodded.

"Okay, then!" Hi flashed a used-car-salesman smile. "So we'll look into this little piece of modern art. Suggestions?"

Eyes slid to me.

Of course, I *have to figure it out.*

"Take samples of the paint," I said. "And bag the cardboard."

Chance nodded.

A thought struck me. "You said Speckman was enrolled at CU?"

"Up until a month ago." Chance opened the folder and shuffled through papers until he located a student transcript. "That's where I convinced him to come work for me."

"Then we start there." Spoken with more confidence than I felt. "Let's meet after school tomorrow and check out his dorm room."

"Do we need disguises?" Hiram's eyes sparkled with anticipation. "I've got one of those sweatshirts that just says 'College,' and we could buy some croakies or something."

"Street clothes will be fine, Hi."

Shelton's hand fluttered nervously. "And what do we do if we find him?"

Great question.

"We need to know who broke into Chance's house." I crossed the room and scooped up my backpack. "And why they called him a traitor."

I brushed hair from my face, steeling my voice.

"We need confirm that Speckman is Viral. Identify the others."

"And if these puppies make trouble?" Ben asked. "If they want to play loose with our secrets?"

I looked him dead in the eye. "We persuade them otherwise."

CHAPTER 4

Coop was up on his hind paws, wet doggie nose smushed against the glass.

"Back it up!" I pushed inside and closed the front door behind me. Then I wrapped my arms around the frisky wolfdog. "I missed you, too, dog face. But Whitney'll freak when she sees that snout print."

Ben had driven us the thirty minutes home to Morris Island. Thankfully, that night he was sleeping at his dad's place, just seven doors down our lonely block of townhouses. Most nights Ben stayed with his mother in Mount Pleasant, a trip of almost an hour.

Shelton had just gotten his license, but didn't have a car. Hi had yet to take the test. Still only fifteen, I didn't even have a learner's permit. So we relied on Ben to cart us around—either in his beat-up Ford Explorer, or across the waves in a sixteen-foot Boston Whaler runabout currently tied up at the neighborhood dock.

"That you, kiddo?"

I climbed three steps, found Kit lounging on the couch, watching *Through the Wormhole* on the Science Channel. Muting the TV, my father patted the spot next to him. "Come veg out with me. Morgan Freeman is explaining how aliens might think."

A last scratch behind Coop's ears, then I dropped my bag on the floor and flopped down beside my father. Coop trotted to his doggie bed, circled three times, and lay down. In seconds he was sound asleep—a light-switch napping ability I thoroughly envied.

"Everything good on Loggerhead?" I asked.

My dad is director of the Loggerhead Island Research Institute, one of the world's most advanced veterinary research facilities. I loved visiting the place, but hadn't been out there in weeks. Loggerhead Island is even more remote than Morris, and lately I'd had less than zero free time.

"Same old," Kit replied lazily, eyes on the screen. "We had a weird rash break out among the rhesus monkeys, but it seems to have tapered off. The wolves got into a storage shed and ruined the seed for the bird feeders, but I blame myself for relying on an old padlock."

Outside of the fenced LIRI facility, Loggerhead Island is a giant nature preserve. Birds. Alligators. Sea turtles. Rhesus monkeys living free in the interior forest. It's as close to paradise as you can find.

I was about to follow up when a singsong voice floated from the kitchen. "Dinner's ready! I made enchiladas."

My eyes rolled. Then darted to Kit, but he hadn't noticed.

Kit paused the DVR, popped up from the couch, and hurried to the table. "Looks like we're the big winners tonight!"

"Oh yes," I muttered. "Big winners."

Whitney DuBois glided into the room, a serving tray effortlessly balanced on her slender arm. She wore a springy tangerine sundress that complimented her figure. Perfect blonde curls formed a bun that appeared casual, haphazard, and insanely complex all at once.

My father's girlfriend was undeniably beautiful. A woman of impeccable Southern taste.

She drove me bonkers. We couldn't have been more different.

"Welcome home, darling." Whitney flashed a megawatt smile. "Did you have a productive study group?"

Was there the slightest whisper of a doubt?

Kit never asked questions about my after-school SAT prep course. But Whitney did.

Can't say I blame her. When it comes to accounting for my whereabouts, I don't have a great track record. And, being honest, I'm always slightly disappointed in Kit for being so gullible.

"Yeah." Taking my seat. "We covered analogies, which I'm already good at."

This cover story was airtight. The class existed. I was enrolled. There was no method of taking attendance. Perfect.

"Of course you are," Whitney said agreeably.

"I'm really waiting for the math portion. Need to brush up on my geometry."

"Side-angle-side," Kit announced, draping a napkin across his lap. "A squared plus B squared equals C squared. That's all you need to know, right?"

Whitney giggled as she finished setting the table. "You've lost me already."

I plastered on a smile. Gotta make the best of things.

"I just hope it's worth three afternoons a week," Whitney murmured, her tone carefully neutral. "We've missed you here at Casa de Howard."

"I'm a Brennan anyway," I quipped, but the joke fell flat, even to my ears.

I'd come to live with my father a year ago, after my mother was killed by a drunk driver. Prior to the accident, Kit Howard and I hadn't known the other existed, but fate can deal strange hands. Before I could process the loss of one parent, I learned of the existence of another.

Good-bye, Massachusetts. Hello, South Carolina.

Moving to Mars would've been less of a culture shock.

After some initial disasters, Kit and I had settled into routines that

worked. We'd grown to like each other, and to enjoy spending time together. The faint tinglings of family began to flourish. To my continual
surprise, Kit and I actually see most things eye to eye.

Except Whitney. On that point we did *not* agree, and having my
dad's ditzy gal-pal force me into debutante life hadn't improved the situation. Even so, over the previous year we'd managed to strike a balance.

Until Hurricane Katelyn destroyed Whitney's home and moved her
into mine.

I now had the pleasure of her company 24/7.

Joy.

Kit broke the awkward silence. "This looks delicious, honey. You've
done it again." Grinning, he raised his fork in a mock salute.

My dad, the dork.

I suppressed a sigh. If this silly, white-gloved dingbat made my father happy—and I knew she did—it was my solemn duty as his progeny
to suffer it.

"Now, Tory," Whitney began, distributing salad with giant metal
tongs, "your committee assignment for the Magnolia League came in
the mail today. And I have good news!"

But sometimes it's so hard . . .

"Yes?" Voice level.

"You've been selected for churchyard floral arrangement!" A near
squeal.

I stiffened. "But that's—"

"That's right!" Whitney smiled in triumph as she set down the bowl.
"*My* committee! I pulled a few strings so we could work together this
year. Isn't that fabulous?"

I didn't trust myself to speak.

Why dost thou test me, oh Lord?

Whitney misread my silent horror. "I'm excited, too! And don't worry, I snagged your friend Ella Francis as well. We can all *hang* together." Emphasized in that clueless way adults speak when trying to sound hip. "Like girlfriends."

I found my voice. "But I signed up for Habitat. Home building, for homeless people. Not decorating wreaths and bouquets for . . . whatever."

"We put them in historic graveyards, and adorn soldiers' tombs, of course." Whitney reached over and squeezed my hand. "It's a *highly* sought-after committee. There will be many disappointed girls tonight, I can assure you. But not you!"

Shock gave way to anger. I'd only agreed to join this stupid organization because it was charitable. Though riddled with frivolity and wasted time, there was good, honest community service buried within the Mag League's endless catalog of parties, committees, and bureaucracy.

But she *had* to butt in. The tactless dolt interfered with the most basic of my choices. Now I was stuck with the least useful nonsense imaginable. In a way, it was perfect. Whitney, to a T.

I put down my utensils. Sucked in a breath.

Kit caught my eye. I saw the pleading there.

Sorry, Dad.

Floral arrangements? This time, I had no intention of holding back.

At that moment, Kit's program ran out of "pause" and blipped from the TV screen. A reporter's breathless voice interrupted our meal. "Park officials say it's the first reported case of vandalism in decades at the venerable island fortress, one of Charleston's most visible landmarks."

I twisted in my chair for a better look.

The image shifted to an elderly park ranger frowning in disapproval. "It's a despicable act, and no mistake." The furious senior pointed to a stone wall behind him. "I don't know what kind of sick mind would do this, but they have no respect for history."

I rose and crossed to the living room. Was surprised when Kit joined me.

"That looks like Fort Sumter," he muttered.

The camera zoomed in on the stonework, which was slathered with paint.

An electric jolt traveled my spine. My hand flew to my mouth before I quickly snatched it down. Kit grumbled under his breath, eyes on the screen.

Chiseled into the rock, and daubed jet black, was a trio of wolf heads. Each was outlined in white, with bloodred eyes.

My mind shot back to the pictures on Chance's desk. These carvings matched.

Unbidden, I thought of that night not long ago, on a beach less than a hundred yards from where I currently stood. Three sets of red eyes, watching me in the darkness.

The other Virals.

Will Speckman? Someone else?

The camera panned up to a single line painted above the wolf heads.

ONE TERRITORY. ONE PACK.

The newscaster returned, but I barely heard.

What did *that* mean?

A taunt? A warning? A challenge?

I heard a low growl.

Cooper was standing by the window, golden eyes staring eastward across the island.

To where Fort Sumter rose from the harbor like a shark's fin.

I walked over to my wolfdog. "What is it, boy?"

Coop's head whipped to me, then back to the window. The growl repeated.

A buzz in my pocket startled me. I pulled out my phone to find a text from Hiram.

As I read, two more messages arrived. Shelton. Ben.

Then my ring tone sounded an incoming call. Chance Claybourne.

Seems everyone had caught the news.

"Gotta take this call." I was already hurrying upstairs. "I'll eat later."

Ignoring Kit's and Whitney's protests, I locked myself in my bedroom.

As I answered, three wolf heads danced in my brain.

I felt a sudden urgency. A need for action.

Whatever was happening wouldn't wait until tomorrow.

ATTENTION: DIRECTOR WALSH ["EYES ONLY"]

FILE STATUS: TOP SECRET [LEVEL 5]

CASE: #34687 (AKA—PHOENIX INQUIRY)

FILE TYPE: INTERVIEW TRANSCRIPT

DATE: APRIL 11, 2014

SUBJECT(S): WHYTHE, HANNAH M. ("HW")

PRINCIPAL INVESTIGATING AGENT(S): J. SALTMAN, B. ROGERS

INTERVIEWING AGENT(S): J. SALTMAN ("JS"), B. ROGERS ("BR")

INTERVIEW LOCATION: LEATH CORRECTIONAL INSTITUTION

WOMEN'S LEVEL 3—MAXIMUM SECURITY

GREENWOOD, SOUTH CAROLINA

ADDITIONAL NOTE(S): UPON ADVICE OF CORRECTIONAL FACILITY PERSONNEL,
SUBJECT WHYTHE WAS CONFINED TO THE INTERVIEW TABLE THROUGH USE OF
RESTRAINTS.

TIME: 8:17 AM

JS: Please explain the nature of your past relationship with Chance Claybourne.

HW: The *nature* of it? He's my fiancé, you dolt. We're going to be married in the fall. It's
all settled.

JS: Miss Whythe, are you aware that your commitment to this facility is open-ended,
pending a review by the South Carolina state mental health board?

HW: *Pssh.* Details. Chance and I are meant to be together. It was written in the stars.
He'll come for me as soon as he's able. Chance can take care of *anything.* Even that
silly little review board. You'll see.

JS: Okay. Right. [PAUSE] In your dealings with Mr. Claybourne, did he ever exhibit any
characteristics that were . . . unnatural?

HW: Of course.

JS: Please elaborate. In detail, if you could.

HW: Chance is the most honorable, gallant, wonderful man on planet Earth. That's why I agreed to marry him. He's better than anyone else alive. Sure, he can be a touch squeamish about the nastier bits of business that need taking care of from time to time, but I'd expect nothing less from such a pure heart. That's why he chose me. To take care of those ugly things, so that he doesn't have to. We're the perfect team.

JS: Um, yes. Of course. But I was referring more to . . . physical attributes. Have you ever witnessed Mr. Claybourne exhibit extraordinary athletic abilities? Unnatural acuities? Has he ever displayed a preternatural sensory awareness? Things of that nature.

HW: Chance is a *phenomenal* athlete. He was the best player on Bolton Prep's championship lacrosse team, by far. I should know, I never missed a single game.

JS: I'm not referring to normal abilities, I want to know—

BR: Let's change gears here, shall we?

[AGENT ROGERS REPLACED AGENT SALTMAN AT INTERVIEW TABLE]

BR: I'd like to discuss a different subject. You're familiar with a former classmate named Victoria Brennan? Goes by Tory?

[PAUSE]

BR: Miss Whythe? I'd like to know more about Tory Brennan. [PAUSE] I shouldn't need to remind you that she's one of the four Bolton Prep students you were charged with attempting to murder.

[PAUSE]

BR: The length of your stay in this facility is, at the moment, undetermined. The people we work for could help you, but only—

HW: How *dare* you question me about her.

BR: Miss Whythe, we need—

HW: That . . . *tramp.* I was so nice to her. I tried to *help* that snotty, hopeless, spineless little ingrate. And how did she repay me? By trying to steal Chance away! By ruining everything I'd planned!

BR: What do you—

HW: Tory just *had* to stick her nose into everything. Couldn't leave her betters alone. She and her ghoulish nerd friends. I *hate* them!

BR: You said *ghoulish*. Why? Explain that word.

HW: You want 'unnatural'? Take a look at those sneaking, thieving brats. They jumped Chance and me in the dark. Attacked us! Moving like shadows, or some band of underworld demons. There's something *wrong* with them. *All* of them! Tory most of all. She moved so . . . too fast . . . too much . . . I could barely follow . . . they came from *everywhere* at once . . . glowing yellow eyes . . . I . . . I . . .

BR: Miss Wh—

HW: That grubby, meddling little nobody *hurt* me.

[PAUSE]

BR: Miss Whythe? Are you okay?

HW: You're working for *her,* aren't you? Both of you.

[PAUSE]

BR: Miss Whythe, I can assure you we aren't—

[BACKGROUND NOISE; UNINTELLIGIBLE]

HW: [SCREAM]

[BACKGROUND NOISE; UNINTELLIGIBLE]

BR: [MUFFLED] JESUS! Get her off me!

JS: Rogers, you're bleeding. It's . . . oh man, it looks bad. [BACKGROUND NOISE] Guard! Guard! Get a medic in here!

[ALARM SOUNDS]

HW: *Tory* sent you, didn't she?!? I'll rip out your throats! *No one will stand between me and Chance! NO ONE!* We're meant to be!

[END TRANSCRIPT]

SPECIAL NOTE(S): IT IS THE OPINION OF BOTH INTERVIEWING AGENTS THAT SUBJECT HANNAH WHYTHE IS HIGHLY UNSTABLE AND OF LIMITED USE TO THE INQUIRY.

CHAPTER 5

I can't believe you invited Chance. Here, of all places!"

Ben paced the bunker like a caged animal, anger and frustration etched on his face. Coop watched him with narrowed eyes, his bushy tail tucked tightly to his body. After two more circuits, my furry companion rose and slunk into the back room, preferring the comfort of his doggie bed to the crackling tension filling our hideout's main chamber.

Eight forty-five p.m. The earliest we could all escape. The sun had already sunk behind Schooner Creek, forcing us to light the bunker's three floor lamps.

Hi was sitting at our drawing table in the chair farthest from Ben's path. He wore khaki shorts and a jarring red-and-orange floral shirt. "How could we exclude him? Plus, Chance already knows where this place is."

Shelton slouched beside Hi, eyes on his tennis shoes. He'd changed into a navy polo and white basketball shorts, but didn't look comfortable. I sat cross-legged at our computer workstation, sporting brown shorts and a LIRI tee, trying to think of ways to calm Ben down.

"'How could we exclude him'!?" Ben's eyes nearly popped from his skull. He hadn't changed from his usual look. Never did. "We've *never* invited an outsider here. *Ever.* This place is secret! Our *oldest* secret. A *Virals* secret, for God's sake!"

Our bunker is a two-room dugout tucked into a sand hill at the northern end of Morris Island. Overlooking the entrance to Charleston Harbor, the ancient defensive work had long been abandoned by the time we converted it into a secret clubhouse. Funds acquired during a previous Virals adventure had paid for stunning upgrades, including a solar power array, kick-ass computer and AV hardware, and enough amenities to outclass your average college lounge.

No one, not even our parents, knew anything about it.

Until Chance found the place while spying on me.

"Chance isn't an outsider." My words stopped Ben in his tracks. "Not anymore. Not in this, anyway. He's the one who tipped us to the wolf-head vandals in the first place!"

Ben's dark eyes smoldered. "Chance Claybourne is *not* one of us."

"Thanks for the vote of confidence."

Chance emerged from the bunker's narrow crawl entrance, began wiping dirt from his shiny black Hugo Boss sweat suit. "I know more about Will Speckman than anyone. He's already paid me one visit."

"So you say." Ben's shoulders were taut as bowstrings. "For all we know, *you're* responsible for this wolf-head nonsense. A bored little rich boy, playing some pathetic game to worm your way into our pack. Well, it's not gonna happen."

Hi frowned, then stroked his chin.

Shelton continued a meticulous study of his footwear.

I could feel an avalanche about to shake loose, but was powerless to stop it.

"I desecrated my own house?" Chance snorted in disbelief. "Then swam out to Fort Sumter and played paint-by-numbers on the walls, all to make Benjamin Blue like me? Don't flatter yourself, kid."

Ben's eyes cut like diamonds. "You act like such a big shot. But you don't fool me. Do you have *any* friends, Chance? Is there a single person who cares where you are right now?"

"Ben!" I blurted, horrified. "That's not—"

"You're one to talk." Chance stepped closer to Ben and matched him glare for glare. "I've never *betrayed* my friends. Not like you, eh, Benjamin?"

Ben's whole body went still. "What did you say?"

"Guys, guys!" Hi half rose, palms up. "There's no need for anyone to get upset. I've got Go-Gurt in the mini-fridge. I know when *I* get hungry, my manners can—"

"Shut up, Hi." Ben and Chance, in unison.

"Okay, then." Hi flopped back into his seat, a sheen of sweat glistening his brow.

Chance's face was granite as he stared down my friend. "You may not like me, Benjamin. You might not consider me one of your pack. But *I'm* Viral, too. I can show you, if you'd like."

The dam burst.

Before I could speak, golden light ignited in Ben's eyes.

"You're a newborn puppy," Ben hissed. "Not even housebroken."

"A puppy?" Red fire infused Chance's irises. "You're nothing but a mangy, sullen stray. But come on then, if you want to test my claws."

The air left the room as both boys teetered on the brink of violence.

I hurried between them. I'd never seen flaring Virals fight—couldn't imagine it, really—and had no intention of witnessing such a display now.

"Stop it, both of you!" A hand shot toward each of them, though neither was paying me the slightest attention. Their eyes were locked. Neither would look away first.

The situation balanced on a knife's edge.

"Ben!" I squared my shoulders, forcing him to look at me. "*I* invited Chance here. *Me.* Chance is Viral, just like us. Like it or not, he's involved now. If you've got a problem with that, take a swing at me."

Ben's face blanched. "I would never—"

He backed up a step, then spun to stare out the cannon slit.

I wheeled on Chance. "And you! I expected better, Claybourne. What happened between the four of us is *our* business, not yours. It's in the past, and that's where it's going to stay. If you can't act like an adult, just crawl right back out of here, and deal with your problems alone. Understood?"

Chance's lips quirked. "Understood."

I nodded curtly, heart beating like a drum. "Then stand down. Both of you."

Chance closed his eyes. His body shuddered, then sagged. Face pale, Chance wobbled to the table and sat. "I still don't quite . . . can't control . . ."

He began coughing so violently that Hi reached over and pounded his back.

"That happen every time?" Shelton asked.

Chance nodded, still hacking into his fist. "I can turn it on easy enough . . . but shutting down a flare is a . . . it can be tough." He wiped tears from his eyes. "Floors me sometimes."

Ben's back was to me as he stared out at the Atlantic.

"Ben?"

He glanced over his shoulder, brown eyes filled with poorly concealed hurt. "What?"

"Why don't we discuss what we came here to?" Trying to banish the storm clouds still darkening the room. "Let's focus on Will Speckman. Do we think he's responsible for what happened at Fort Sumter?"

I joined Chance, Shelton, and Hi at the drawing table. Ben held back, eyeing us from across the bunker. Finally, he sat down on the window bench and crossed his arms.

Detached, but listening. Best I was going to get.

I sat back in my chair and looked to Chance. "Did you find out anything else about Speckman? Why he dropped out of school? Where he might be now?"

Chance shook his head. "I know where Will's parents live, but he's not there. They still don't know anything's wrong, as far as I can tell. We can check his dorm room, but his roommate said Will packed up and left weeks ago."

Hi tapped his bottom lip thoughtfully. "Where would he go without telling anyone?"

Chance shrugged. "Who knows? We weren't close, even when he worked for me. I just knew him from Bolton. He could be anywhere."

"Come on, y'all. Seems obvious to me." Shelton slipped off his glasses and wiped them on his shirtsleeve. "He's probably with whoever else has flaming red eyes."

My thought. "That makes the most sense."

Chance shifted uncomfortably, but said nothing. Disbelief? Or something else?

"We don't know anything about these other Virals," Shelton grumbled. "Not even how many there are."

Ben's voice arrowed across the room. "Three."

We all turned. Even Chance.

"They drew three more wolf heads on the wall at Fort Sumter." Ben stared straight ahead at nothing as he spoke. "Just like the sign around that jackass statue's neck. Hi was right—if they keep drawing three figures in their stupid paintings, there must be three of *them*."

Chance's brow furrowed. "By why Fort Sumter? That made the news, for Pete's sake."

"Seems like *your* visit was personal." Hi's expression was deadly serious. "Speckman obviously holds a grudge. But the mess out at Sumter was a public announcement."

"Oh man, that's bad." Shelton's fingers found his earlobe. "We can't have some rogue group of Virals acting the fool all over town. They'll get caught. Then what happens?"

"I think it's a warning." I felt a rock in my gut. "And not for everyone. Just for us."

"Why say that?" Shelton squeaked. "We don't even know these people!"

I frowned. "Red eyes in the dunes, remember? For some reason, these Virals targeted me."

"And me," Chance said softly.

"If *they* get caught . . ." Hi's eyes rounded like dinner plates. "They could spill the beans about *us*."

No one spoke as the harsh truth sunk in.

These red-eyed Virals weren't just an annoyance, or a mere curiosity. They were a threat to our safety.

"So what do we do about it?" Chance drummed his fingers on the table. "And I do mean *we*. Can the five of us now agree we're in this together?"

All heads swiveled toward the bench.

A tense moment stretched. Finally, Ben nodded. "In this *one* thing, we are."

"Capital!" Hi slapped his hands together. "I can already feel the love. But Chance asked the billion-dollar question—what next?"

Ben rose and strode for the bunker's entrance. "We go to Fort Sumter, obviously. *Sewee*'s down in the cove. We can be there in ten minutes."

Shelton stiffened. "What? You mean right now?"

But Ben was already crawling outside. In seconds, his sneakers disappeared.

"He's nuts, right?" Shelton's gaze darted from face to face. "We don't need to see the vandalism in person. What's the point? There'll be dozens of photos online by tomorrow. The cops might still be around!"

"Doing what?" Hi scoffed. "Guarding a stone wall? There's nobody out there after sunset. Law dogs aren't just gonna sit beside a tagged rock all night long for no reason. They've got a union to prevent that kind of thing."

"He's right," I said.

"Who is?" Chance asked.

Shelton gave me a hopeful look.

"Ben."

Shelton smacked the table, grumbling under his breath.

"Shelton does have a point, though," said Chance. "Why go see the markings firsthand? We risk getting blamed for committing the crime."

"Damn right." Shelton slumped in his chair. "Guilty people always return to the scene of the crime. Don't y'all watch *Law & Order*?"

"*SVU* or original?" Hi asked. "Because I've got casting issues with—"

"If *they* return," I interrupted, "we might catch them. But I'm not counting on that."

I gathered my thoughts as best I could. "It's the words they used. *One territory, one pack.* That was meant for us alone, right? Which makes me wonder if there's something more. Some additional message other people might not pick up on."

Chance pursed his lips in thought. "Like some sort of clue?"

"More like a challenge." My tone grew frosty. "These jerks seem to think they own the city. They've been on Morris Island. They went *inside* your mansion." I pointed out the cannon-slit window. "Fort Sumter is practically on our doorstep."

The recitation gave me shivers.

What else did these people know about us?

Outside it was full dark, but floodlights ringed a hunk of rock rising from the dark ocean waters. Fort Sumter loomed in the harbor mouth, less than a mile from where we sat.

"I'm sold." Hi pushed himself up from his chair. "We can shoot over and take a look while the place is deserted, then bounce. Easy peasy, Japanesey."

Chance nodded, rising to his feet.

We all looked at Shelton, who rolled his eyes. "Like my vote matters now."

Hi patted his back. "If it makes you feel better, your vote's never mattered."

"Hilarious." Shelton rubbed his face. "I hope my parole officer finds you as funny."

I sprang up and hurried for the exit, stopping Chance with a hand on his shoulder. "Give me a second alone with Ben. He's still worked up, probably needs a few minutes to decompress."

Chance's expression soured, but he held back.

Hi fired a shooter my way. "Good idea. We need him mission focused. Roger dodger."

Shelton covered his face with his hands. "Enough already."

Slipping out into the warm night air, I scanned for Ben, but there was no sign. So I took the narrow path downhill to our secret anchorage below—surrounded by outthrusts of rock, the tiny bay was completely hidden from view by sea.

My friend was aboard *Sewee,* untying his vessel from an ancient sunken post.

"Ben?"

No response.

I slipped off my shoes and waded to the runabout. Pulled myself up the tiny ladder. Found Ben's hand waiting at the rail. He effortlessly hoisted me into the boat, maneuvering my weight like it was nothing.

I sometimes forgot how strong Ben was. How warm his hands could feel.

Ben released me. Went back to coiling line.

"Are you okay?" I immediately realized it was the wrong thing to say.

"Of course I'm okay." Gruff. Distant.

I stood watching him, unsure what to say next. Unbidden, the image of a bench sprang to mind. The two of us, huddled close. Me crying in his arms.

I felt blood rush to my face, was grateful for the concealing darkness.

"No one expects you to like Chance," I said finally.

"Good." Not looking up. "Because I don't."

Another awkward silence. Then Ben huffed, "You like him enough for both of us."

I straightened, surprised. Was *that* what was bothering him? Jealousy?

Why would Ben be jealous of Chance? After everything that spoiled boy had done to me?

Did Ben think I was some ditz? That my memory reset with every pretty smile?

Am I?

I felt a nervous twinge in my stomach. Felt it grow.

Ben. Jealous. Because of his feelings for me. The issue would not simply go away.

"Ben. I . . ." Words failed. My face grew hot.

How could I say he was being silly, without acknowledging what lay underneath?

Ben's hands stopped moving. He stared at the deck, his long black hair fanning around his face. He sucked in a breath, as if on the verge of something.

Footsteps echoed from above.

Gravel rolled down the trail as Hi lumbered into view. "Permission to board, captain?"

Shelton and Chance followed, an excited wolfdog bouncing at their heels.

Ben turned away, dropping into the captain's seat. "Granted. Let's get going."

I watched him, hoping he might look at me. Give some sign of what he'd been thinking.

Ben's hand spun. The engine fired to life.

"Everyone grab a life jacket" was all he said. "And somebody help the dog."

CHAPTER 6

Sewee's motor purred as we eased out of the hidden cove.

A full moon shimmered in the black, cloudless sky, providing more than enough light to see by as we slid across the glass-like water. Ben kept the running lights off. Dangerous—massive container ships traversed the harbor day and night, and our little boat wouldn't survive a collision—but it wasn't a good night to advertise an illegal trip to the national monument.

Which lurked dead ahead.

A stone's throw from Morris Island, warning lights announced our destination: Fort Sumter. The shadowy, man-made hunk of rock guarded the entrance to Charleston Harbor, silent and implacable, a medieval fortress out of step with modern times.

Ben cut the engine. As we drifted, I scanned the weathered battlements, alert for any sign someone might be home. Coop uncurled at my feet, rose, and stretched.

A tense minute passed. My body relaxed a fraction.

No sound. No movement. The island appeared to be empty.

"Hiram?" I said.

He needed no further prompting. "The Civil War's first battle happened right here. Federal troops were holding Fort Sumter when South Carolina seceded from the Union in 1861, and they refused to hand it over to the Confederates. So the surrounding fortifications—almost certainly including our own bunker, by the way—blasted it with cannons and mortars for a day and a half. Eventually the soldiers inside gave up and sailed away. I'm pretty sure the only casualty was a horse."

Chance ran his fingers along the starboard rail. "Delightful."

Shelton piped up. "When the fort was operational, nobody could enter the harbor without facing these cannons. Sumter was the linchpin of Charleston's harbor defenses, with Morris Island and Sullivan's Island protecting its flanks. A tough nut to crack. The Union tried to take it back twice, and failed both times."

"Great history lesson." Ben restarted the engine and nosed *Sewee* toward a small pier jutting from the rocky shoreline. "Skip ahead to something useful."

Hi spoke before Shelton could steal his thunder again. "Fort Sumter is an artificial island—seventy thousand tons of granite, stacked on a sandbar." He pointed up at the thick stone battlements. "The building is a giant brick pentagon. The walls are sixty yards long and five feet thick, and rise fifty feet above the waterline. The fortification could house nearly seven hundred men, and had over a hundred big guns arrayed in tiers."

I gazed up at the gloomy fortress. "And now?"

Hi looked surprised. "What? You've never been? This *national treasure* is like a thousand yards from your house. You could *swim* here."

"It's on my list," I said defensively.

Ben snorted. Chance gave me the side-eye. Even Coop's glance seemed reproachful.

Well, excuse me.

Hi shook his head like a disappointed father, but continued. "There's a big museum downtown where you catch the ferry, and a smaller one out here. But, honestly, not much else. The outer shell surrounds that one building and a grassy courtyard. No frills, just massive walls facing the water, lined with cannons to rain death upon passing boats."

"Those wolf-head jokers could've tagged anywhere," Shelton said. "All the walls inside look the same, but the fort isn't big. We should find the message without any trouble. What we're supposed to do then . . ."

I didn't respond. Because I didn't know either.

But my gut was certain: there was something out here for us to see.

Something intended for Viral eyes.

"We won't know until we get there." Chance steadied himself as *Sewee* kissed the dock. "No point worrying about it now."

Hi and Shelton scrambled over the rail and secured the lines. Chance presented a hand to Coop, then carefully lifted him onto the dock. Coop danced a few steps, shaking out his limbs before stretching into a perfect Downward Dog. Ben climbed out next, turned, and reached a hand back for me.

A deep, suffocating silence enveloped our group as we snuck toward shore. The fort loomed overhead—a massive, intimidating stone monolith dominating the tiny islet. I tried to picture men living and working on this desolate rock, day after day. Couldn't imagine it.

We exited the pier onto a short, rocky beach. A tidy brown sign announced: FORT SUMTER NATIONAL MONUMENT. HOURS: 10:00 A.M.–5:30 P.M. Oh well.

The path led to a sally port in the side of the fortress secured by massive steel doors. I examined them for any sign of electronic surveillance, found none.

"I doubt they alarm the entrance," Hi whispered. "This place is as isolated as it gets, and there's nothing valuable to steal in the outer tiers."

"Just avoid the building in the middle." Shelton, back pressed against the rough stonework. "That's Battery Huger, built during the Spanish-American War. The museum's inside it."

"We'll stick to the battlements," Ben said. "That's where the vandals struck anyway."

I waved Shelton forward. "You're up."

Shelton nodded reluctantly, dropping to a knee and removing his lock-pick set. "These locks are fossils." He worked quickly, inserting the fine tools, then moving his fingers clockwise with precision. In moments I heard a sharp click.

Shelton rose with a nervous smile. "Might as well not lock this at all."

I whistled for Cooper, who had strayed down the beach and was snuffling everything in sight. Chance swung the door open and we slipped inside.

We entered a low-ceilinged chamber supported by bulky brick columns. Archways on both sides revealed a line of similar rooms stretching in both directions. There was no rear wall, allowing a clear view of open grass and the smaller building in the fort's center.

Hi pointed to the oddly shaped structure dead ahead. "Battery Huger. You can walk right over it to the opposite side of the courtyard, but I don't know about security."

"Let's circle the outer wall." Ben peered through the archway to our left. "Work around to where the flagpoles are. I saw them on the news report, so the graffiti must be somewhere nearby."

"Lead on." I didn't have a better plan.

We snuck through dusty chambers composing the lowest tier, passing rows of cannons facing out to sea. In the last compartment, a narrow staircase led up to the fort's second level. A white chain was stretched across the opening.

"Out of bounds," Hi whispered, "but that should lead to the top of the wall."

"You know I hate heights," Shelton groaned.

Ben chucked him on the shoulder. "Come on, I'll carry you if you get scared."

"Real funny." Shelton pushed his glasses up his nose. "Until we plummet to the rocks."

Reaching the second level, I spotted another flight of steps.

After a short debate, we decided to climb. The upper catwalk was the quickest route to the other side of the fortress. Reaching the highest section, we walked along the top of the outer parapet, six dark profiles outlined against the moon for anyone to see.

Hi moved easily, seemingly unconcerned. Shelton followed close behind, arms outstretched, Ben whispering encouragement at his shoulder. Chance came next, then me. Coop brought up the rear, showing zero concern.

I refused to acknowledge the fifty-foot drop to the rocks below.

Reaching the next juncture, I blew out a relieved breath.

Hi was waiting where the wall sections met. "We just crossed the left face. Ahead is the right. Once we reach the next section, the ground rises to meet the wall and we can stroll down to the courtyard."

Everyone nodded, anxious to get down from the apex. Thankfully, the next section was easier—an interior roof connected to the catwalk, creating a wide, flat walking space. Crossing it quickly, we hopped to a grassy hill sloping down to the flagpoles.

We'd made it to the opposite side of the fort. Now to locate the crime scene.

Hi rubbed his chin, then pointed to ground level. "Let's check the storerooms in there. I'm guessing one of those walls."

It didn't take long to locate.

Ahead, a low passage burrowed into the junction where two massive exterior wall sections met. At the tunnel's far end, yellow police tape crisscrossed the entrance to a windowless, fortified chamber, likely once used for storing ammunition.

Inside, a bank of lights had been erected, facing a flat stretch of the dugout's rear wall. Long orange extension cords snaked back toward the museum. Even in the darkness, I could see paint streaking the ancient bricks.

Beside me, Coop voiced a nervous growl.

My heart kicked up a notch. "Fire up those halogens."

"Hi-aye, captain." Hi jostled the setup until he found a switch.

Harsh white light flooded the room.

Three wolf heads glowed in the artificial brightness.

"Black and white, with red eyes." Chance rubbed his chin. "This matches the sign they left at my house exactly."

Shelton ran a finger over the closest image. "Did they *carve* these things?"

Squinting, I saw it too. The wolf heads were aligned in a row, composed of jet-black paint bordered by pure white lines. Yet beneath the paint, delicate accents had been chiseled directly into the bricks. Teeth. Whiskers. The ghostly outlines of ears and snouts. Though roughly gouged, the engraved details gave the depictions a certain raw artistic appeal. A wraithlike flair.

Excepting the eyes.

Those were messy blobs of a brilliant scarlet. No lids. No pupils. Harsh. Unblinking.

Something clicked.

"Eye color," I whispered, trying to pin down the thought. "It means something specific."

Chance rubbed his cheek. "How so?"

"These wolves have red eyes," I said slowly, piecing my theory together, "just like the ones on your sign. I think they represent our adversaries. But your statue—a Claybourne—had its eyes *blackened*. With a note calling you 'traitor.'"

Shelton snapped his fingers. "They were casting Chance out! From their red-eye pack!"

I watched for a reaction, but Chance simply shook his head. "They broke into my house just to kick me out of their club?"

"Are you sad?" Ben taunted.

"Makes a sick kind of sense," Hi mused. "That was an insult; this is an announcement."

"Hell of a medium," Shelton muttered. "Next time just start a Facebook group."

The crude tableau was deeply unsettling. It felt both vague and intensely personal. The lines were rough, yet precise. The first impression was of slapdash vandalism, but a closer look revealed an artist's touch. Everything in proportion. Each drop of paint precise within a larger context. All exactly as intended.

"'One territory. One pack.'" Chance crossed his arms as he read. "What does it mean?"

The words were engraved above the canine images. Long, deep cuts, meticulously scored into aging brick, then painted white.

An icy fist squeezed my heart. Without thinking, I patted my leg for Cooper, then knelt and wrapped him in a hug. He panted in my arms, eyes bright.

Hi whistled. "Whoever did this spent a *lot* of time and energy."

"It's a warning." I no longer doubted my instincts. "They're claiming dominion."

"Over what?" Shelton waved a hand around the room. "Fort Sumter? They can have it."

I shook my head. "I'm guessing more."

"Fort Sumter is the gateway to Charleston," Chance said slowly. "The rock that guards the harbor."

Hi nodded, frowning at the wall. "It's like staking your claim on the Statue of Liberty. Fort Sumter is more than just a place, it's symbolic of the whole city."

Shelton glanced from face to face. "So what are they saying?"

I looked to Ben. Found him watching me.

Ben cracked his knuckles, eyes hard as granite.

"It means we're at war," he said.

CHAPTER 7

W e need to bail," Shelton urged.

"We barely got here." Hi reached into his pocket. "Let's get some pics."

"There'll be plenty online by now," Shelton grumbled, but he pulled out his iPhone as well. In moments the two were tapping away from various angles.

I stepped closer to the gruesome mural, circling slowly to avoid the cameramen as I studied our adversaries' handiwork. The wolf heads had been gouged with clean, violent strokes, then coated with three different paints. Red. Black. White.

Abruptly, Coop growled. Teeth bared, he began pacing the chamber, cutting back and forth in sudden, jerky motions. I tried to ruffle his bristling fur, but Coop skipped out of reach, halting to snarl at the wall.

"I'm with Coop." Shelton nodded toward the entrance. "We should get out of here."

"We need samples." Reaching into my pocket, I removed a Swiss Army knife and three plastic stoppers I'd brought specifically for this purpose. With delicate strokes, I peeled off flecks of each paint color and placed them into the receptacles. Then I knelt and examined the shards of brick at the foot of the wall.

"This was cleverly done." I rose, wiping my hands on my shorts. "Whoever created this has the fine motor skills to chisel quickly and efficiently, even crouching in the dark. Does it seem like something Speckman could've pulled off?"

"No," Chance said. "Will's a lot of things, but an artist isn't one of them."

"I'm not seeing anything new in person," Shelton complained. "Wasted trip."

"Then it's time." Chance's voice carried a trace of eagerness.

"For what?" I asked.

"We didn't come out here for the same view as the police." Oddly, Chance glanced at Ben, who nodded curtly. "If there's something for us to see," Chance continued, "some message from whoever did this, it's going to be—how should I say it?—for *our* eyes only."

His meaning was clear. "You think we should flare."

"Of course." Chance was surprised by my hesitant tone. "Why else would we come here? If other Virals put in the effort to craft this . . . whatever it is, then we need to examine it from our unique shared perspective."

"He's right." Ben scowled, then kicked at the floor in frustration. "Let Chance and me know what you find."

Chance squinted at Ben, confused. "Come again? I'll take a look for myself, thanks."

"You can't." I understood Ben's irritation. "You both flared already, during your stupid pissing match in the bunker. It'll be a while before you can access your powers again. Take it as a lesson in self-control."

Ben's face reddened, but he held his tongue.

Chance's head swung between Ben and me. "What are you talking about?"

"Flaring is like drawing water from a shallow well," I explained. "Once you drink, you have to wait for the reservoir to refill."

I didn't mention the few times we'd managed to flare in quick succession, mainly because I didn't fully understand myself. I knew it required extreme stress, and unusual circumstances, but the exact trigger remained a mystery.

Best not to confuse the newbie while he was still learning.

Chance, however, was looking at me like I was crazy. "Um, no."

He squeezed his eyes shut. Shuddered.

When his lids opened, Chance's irises burned fiery red.

The rest of us stared, dumbstruck. Then we closed like jackals.

"How'd you do that?" Shelton demanded.

"Back-to-back flares?" Hi snapped his fingers, incredulous. "Just like that?"

Ben's face was a mask of poorly concealed envy. No, more than that. Hunger.

"What?" Chance seemed startled by our reactions. "You can't do that?"

"No." My thoughts churned as I met his smoldering scarlet gaze. "At least, not on command. It *has* happened before, but no one has mastered the trick."

To be able to touch my powers at any time, unrestricted . . .

I understood the yearning in Ben's eyes.

Then I felt a stab of fear, like being dropped into a deep, dark pool.

"If Chance can flare at will—" I began.

"Then these wolf-head loons probably can, too," Shelton finished, tugging his ear. "Great."

Chance fidgeted, uncomfortable with our scrutiny. "I told you—the parvovirus strain I created wasn't the same as Karsten's. Obviously, since my eyes turn *red*. We don't know what all the differences may be."

Hi poked Chance in the shoulder. "Well, that's a pretty big one."

Chance didn't notice. He'd frozen in place, and was staring over Shelton's head at the rear wall. "We can discuss the finer points later. Right now, you should let the wolf loose. Because it turns out I was right."

I spun, following his line of sight. "What is it?"

"You'll see." Chance's eyes remained glued to the wolf-head mural.

That was enough for me.

I flipped the switch.

SNAP.

The power burned through me, like sticking a fork in an electric socket.

Sweat slicked my skin. My heartbeat thundered. When finally able to breathe again, I gasped at the painting. "Holy moly."

"Oh hell." Shelton pocketed his glasses, one hand covering his mouth. "That's not good."

There was another engraving above the first. Invisible to the naked eye—chiseled with no more than a whisper of pressure—was a second message only a flaring Viral could see.

I read the words out loud.

"'We see you. We know you.'"

Scratched beside the last letter was a vertical line topped by a rectangle on its right side. Inside the rectangle was a tiny triangle.

"They know everything," Hi whispered. "About us. About our powers."

I nodded grimly. "We're the only ones who could read this message. Or would even think to look for it. And they have the advantage. They know who we are. What we are."

"And we don't know a damn thing about them." Ben's non-glowing eyes narrowed on Chance. "This is all your fault, Claybourne."

"Enough with that!" I scolded. "We need to focus on finding these people."

"This here." Shelton hurried forward and tapped the rectangle design at the tail end of the hidden message. "What is it? It looks like the mast of a ship."

"A trademark?" Hi suggested. "Like their calling card, maybe?"

"They're messing with us." Ben punched his leg, frustrated he couldn't see the markings. "Taunting us. Making sure we know they have the edge."

"Not a mast." Wheels were turning. "Something more . . ." I straightened, sudden insight snapping me to attention. "Hi, you said there's a flag monument here?"

Hiram's eyes popped. "Of course! There are six flagpoles on the parade ground. I bet—"

"Lead the way." I snagged Coop by the collar and pulled him toward the exit.

Chance killed the lights as we hurried outside. Moonlight bathed the courtyard, narrowing my golden eyes. No sound but the sea. No movement. A bouquet of scents assailed my nose. Crumbing mortar. Wet stone. Damp mold. I tasted rain and salt on the sultry night air.

For a moment, the place felt deserted. A lonely atoll somewhere deep in an endless ocean.

The flagpoles stood at the bottom of a short slope. We gathered by their footings and peered up the long metal shafts. Five were empty, banners stowed for the evening. But something limp hung at the top of the sixth.

"Hiram." I made a "get it down" motion with my hands.

Hi exhaled theatrically. "Okay, but this is how horror movies start."

"I'll do it." Chance grabbed the slender rope, untied a double knot, then slowly lowered the object, one pull at a time.

My heart raced as I watched it descend.

Was a worst-case scenario unfolding before my eyes?

For the first time, our darkest secret lay exposed.

Someone knew we were Viral.

Not suspected. Not wondered. *Knew.*

And we have no idea who.

I kept my panic in check. Pushed away all thoughts of getting caught. Of being studied like rats in a laboratory. Men in white hazmat suits, holding me down, prodding me with needles until the wolf emerged.

Breathe, Tory. Breathe.

I felt pressure on my palm. Looked down. Ben's fingers had curled around mine.

I didn't pull away, surprised at how much I relished the contact.

No. More. I squeezed his hand tightly, hoping he might squeeze back.

Then Coop bumped into me from behind. Startled, I dropped Ben's hand, and it quickly slid away. Unsure what to do, I reached down and scratched the wolfdog's ears.

Coop whined, glancing up at the fort's outer wall. He nudged my leg a second time.

"What is it, boy?"

I knelt, but Coop danced backward. Then he turned and trotted up the slope. At the top of the wall he froze, gazing out over the waves. My flaring ears picked up his second whimper.

I was about to follow when Chance spoke. "Got it. Who wants first look?"

Chance was holding a yard-square piece of heavy canvas. Shelton, Hi, and Ben each snagged a corner and the four boys stretched it out between them.

Shelton's tongue clicked. Hi made a choking sound. Chance muttered under his breath.

Ben's voice was acid. "Yeah, I'd say that's a challenge."

The boys were holding a crude flag. A hole had been cut into one corner to attach it to the flagpole. On its face was a stylized triangle—three familiar wolf heads, equidistantly spaced, connected by straight black lines. Two short sentences ran across the top:

Can you find us? Come out and play.

Below the triangle were two additional words in all caps.

THE TRINITY

"What the hell does that mean?" Shelton squawked.

"It's what these Virals call themselves." Adrenaline rocketed through my body. "We were right—there are three of them. Three wolf heads. A connected triangle."

"A new pack, gunning for us." Ben scowled at the coarse fabric. "Stupid name, too."

Hi looked up suddenly. "Hey, what's *our* pack name? We should definitely come up with one. I'm kind of excited about this."

Shelton dropped his corner in disgust. "Why hang a stupid flag? Why come out here at all? How could they know we'd take the bait? That we'd flare and find their dumb taunt. That the police wouldn't see it. That's a whole lot of risk for absolutely nothing!"

"Um, guys?" Hi's voice cracked slightly.

I tore my eyes from the canvas. "Yeah?"

Hi was scanning the tiered walls surrounding us. "Just remembered. I kinda saw the flagpoles when we crossed the catwalk. I wasn't flaring or anything, but the moonlight's pretty strong. I, uh . . . I didn't see anything hanging then."

Shelton's face twisted. "What do you mean? We're holding this flag right . . ."

Everyone froze.

Coop. He's uneasy.

I whirled, searching for my wolfdog. Spotted him atop the wall, staring at the ocean.

"Coop!" I whistled. "Here, boy."

Coop looked over his shoulder, then returned his attention to the waves.

Bad thing. Coming.

The sending shocked me.

Coop's voice, echoing smoothly inside my head.

Beside me, Hi and Shelton flinched as one. They'd caught something, too.

"Was that *Coop*?" Shelton hissed. "Did he say 'bad thing'?"

"A bad thing?" Chance squinted at Shelton, confused. "Wait, Coop is talking?"

Chance hadn't caught the message, a fact I filed away for later consideration.

Frustration pinched Ben's features. "What's going on?"

"The wolfdog is spooked," Hi whispered, dropping to a crouch. "Now I am, too."

No more talking, I sent. *The Trinity may be here.*

But Chance couldn't hear me. "The Trinity may be here," he warned. "Right now."

I hustled a few yards upslope. *Coop! Come, boy.*

Coop's head whipped toward me. He yapped twice, then looked back out to the sea. A spike of agitation traversed the bond we shared. Unnerved, I raced up to the wall's edge.

"What is it, boy?"

Then my flaring eyes picked out a black speck floating just above the horizon. As I watched, mystified, the shadow crept toward the harbor, leaving a trail of wake but making no sound.

"What the . . ."

I tried to make sense of what I was seeing.

Despite its stillness, the object was advancing quickly.

Movement nearby. The boys had climbed to join me.

I ignored them, straining my flare senses, trying to decipher the puzzle.

"I don't like this," Hi said in flat voice.

"What's that sound?" Shelton whispered. "You guys hear?"

"Sssh!" My ears finally picked up something—a steady metallic thrum, like a sword slicing through air.

The answer came in a flash.

"Helicopter." It made no sense, but nothing *else* made sense. "Someone is flying a black helicopter over Charleston Harbor at night."

"One that doesn't make noise." Hi took a shaky step backward. "And appears to heading right for this pile of rocks."

The chopper grew larger as it approached the island at an angle. Then it banked.

There could be no mistake. It was coming straight for us.

"*Go go go!*" Ben started shoving people back downslope.

I grabbed Coop's collar and pulled him after me. We broke into a wild sprint, down the hill and across the parade ground.

"This way!" Hi pointed to a metal staircase leading up and over Battery Huger.

We raced up the steps, crossed the central building's flat roof, then hurried down an identical set of stairs on the opposite side.

As my foot hit the ground, an alarm began to wail.

"I told you the museum had security!" Hi moaned.

Too late for that. We sprinted for the sally port and the pier beyond. Outside the walls, I ducked instinctively as the helicopter passed overhead, virtually noiseless, with no lights or visible occupants.

Chance crouched down beside me. Coop growled, but I shushed him.

I grabbed Chance's arm. "What's going on? Who is that?"

Chance shook his head, motioned to *Sewee* bobbing fifty feet ahead.

We streaked across the dock to the runabout. Coop leaped aboard, then scrambled to the stern and gazed westward. The rest of us vaulted the rail in a disheveled throng. Hi and Shelton frantically untied lines as Ben dove for the captain's chair. Chance paced the tiny foredeck, face pale, focus turned inward.

I hurried astern to where Coop still watched the sky.

The helicopter was banking, coming around for another pass.

"Oh man oh man oh man . . ." Shelton's hands shook as he worked the last knot. "It's after us! Why would a stealth chopper be after us?"

Hi barked a nervous laugh. "Maybe they've *really* increased park security."

"Quiet!" Ben sat behind the wheel, lights off and engine dead.

We watched the helicopter pass overhead, slow, and then stop, hovering in midair twenty feet above the slender patch of open ground on the opposite side of the fortress.

Coop snarled menacingly, back stiff and tail extended. I couldn't have agreed more.

"Is it going to land?" Chance spoke aloud, unaware he was doing so. "Right now?"

"Let's not find out." Ben turned the key and spun the wheel, churning away from the dock. We ran blind across the harbor, fleeing toward Morris Island. I couldn't shake the feeling of eyes on my back.

As Fort Sumter disappeared behind us, two simple questions rattled in my brain.

Who was in that helicopter?

What did they want with us?

PART TWO

CHASE

ATTENTION: DIRECTOR WALSH ["EYES ONLY"]

FILE STATUS: TOP SECRET [LEVEL 5]

CASE: #34687 (AKA—PHOENIX INQUIRY)

FILE TYPE: INTERVIEW TRANSCRIPT

DATE: APRIL 12, 2014

SUBJECT(S): GOODWIN, ANTHONY ("AG")

PRINCIPAL INVESTIGATING AGENT(S): J. SALTMAN, B. ROGERS

INTERVIEWING AGENT(S): J. SALTMAN ("JS"), B. ROGERS ("BR")

INTERVIEW LOCATION: WINFRED COLEFIELD STATE MEDICAL INSTITUTION

INVOLUNTARY, LEVEL 7—MAXIMUM SECURITY

COLUMBIA, SOUTH CAROLINA

ADDITIONAL NOTE(S): SUBJECT GOODWIN IS CONFINED TO A PSYCHIATRIC

FACILITY (DIAGNOSIS: PTSD), PENDING TRIAL FOR VARIOUS STATE AND FEDERAL

CRIMINAL CHARGES. DURING THE INTERVIEW, SUBJECT GOODWIN REFUSED TO

ANSWER QUESTIONS UNLESS ADDRESSED AS "THE GAMEMASTER."

TIME: 10:47 AM

JS: Mr. Goodwin, we'd like to discuss your dealings with a young man from Charleston named Chance Claybourne.

[PAUSE; SUBJECT NON-RESPONSIVE]

JS: Mr. Goodwin? Could you—

AG: Gamemaster.

JS: Excuse me?

AG: My name is The Gamemaster.

JS: Right. Sure. Okay. So . . . *Gamemaster,* please tell us the nature of your relationship with Chance Claybourne.

AG: There is none.

JS: I don't understand. You don't know Mr. Claybourne? Never had any dealings with him?

AG: The boy means nothing to me. He was never part of The Game.

[PAUSE]

BS: But Chance Claybourne *was* involved in the events leading to your arrest. Are you saying—

AG: Claybourne interfered, and for that he'll pay. They'll *all* pay, in time, I can assure you. But Claybourne is barely an afterthought in the grand scheme of things. An interloper. He was never part of the challenge.

[PAUSE]

JS: What do you know about his friend Victoria Brennan?

[PAUSE]

JS: Uh, Mr. Gamemaster? Did you hear my question?

[PAUSE; SUBJECT NON-RESPONSIVE]

JS: You're staring down the barrel of some serious charges here. We *might* be able to help with that, but if you don't cooperate—

AG: What do you want with her?

JS: That's our concern. Just tell us what you know.

AG: I know that you're an imbecile. You and your silent friend, standing over there in the corner. I know that Tory Brennan cheated The Game. I know that she and her little pissant friends belong to *me alone.*

JS: You say Brennan cheated your game. How?

AG: *The* Game. The greatest intellectual construct this world has ever seen. A cunning test of brains, stamina, and will. One meant to purify. To find a champion. To anoint a leader for the dark times ahead.

JS: Right. Sure. And Tory Brennan won this game?

[BACKGROUND NOISE][SUBJECT VISIBLY AGITATED]

JS: Take it easy! Keep slamming fists and you'll land right back in solitary!

AG: She cheated! They all *must* have cheated! No gang of island brats could be *worthy* enough to defeat my masterpiece! Far better challengers have tried and failed.

JS: Fine. Fine. You're a prophet; she's a cheater. But *how* did she cheat? What's so special about this girl?

AG: Not just her. All of them. Hiram Stolowitski. Shelton Devers. Benjamin Blue. There's something unclean about them. They do things a person shouldn't be able to.

JS: *What* things? What did they do? Be specific, man!

[PAUSE][SUBJECT VISIBLY AGITATED]

AG: They moved too fast. And their *eyes*. I swear they glowed like . . . like . . . demons in the night. It's as though they can speak without words. The four of them circled me like beasts. [BACKGROUND NOISE] I'm a trained soldier! I know what an ambush looks like!

JS: Take it easy, now.

AG: They tracked me like . . . *predators*. The rain was . . . lightning blinding my eyes . . . wind gusting, knocking me down, but *not* those monsters. [GIGGLES] And that damn wolf that follows her around! I swear the girl *TALKS* to it!

JS: Sit down!

AG: They came from everywhere! EVERYWHERE!

[BACKGROUND NOISE][SUBJECT RESTRAINED BY AGENT ROGERS]

AG: Captain, I'm hit! IED, left side! I lost Houser in the market, and—

BR: Grab his—help me hold him, damn it!

JS: I'm trying!

BR: He's having a flashback, or—

[BACKGROUND NOISE][FACILITY PERSONNEL ENTER INTERVIEW ROOM]

[SUBJECT REMOVED BY FACILITY PERSONNEL]

[INTERVIEW SUSPENDED FOR TWO HOURS]

TIME: 12:51 PM

JS: This is your last chance, Gamemaster.

AG: [LAUGHS] You think you intimidate me? I served three tours in *hell.* I took a pound of C4 to the chin in Ramadi. Looked the devil square in the eye. Compared to pissed-off insurgents, you two are pussycats. [PAUSE] Who do you work for, anyway? What anonymous branch of our federal government has questions about a fifteen-year-old girl?

JS: That's not your concern.

AG: Of course not. You know what? I *despise* people like you. Fake soldiers, running black-ops crap like this, hiding from the public, using tax dollars to hunt our own citizens. Pretending to do some greater good, when all you're in it for is the dirty work. I know you, Agent No Name. I worked with men *just* like you, in the darkest alleys of the world. You people are what's ruining this country.

JS: Tell us what you know, Goodwin. What you saw. I'm all out of patience.

AG: Two men in black suits. No names, no badges. Just questions.

JS: We're done here.

AG: I'd never tell you bastards *anything*. Ever. Tory and her friends belong to *me,* do you understand? They violated something far greater than whatever your faceless shadow agency spends its time scheming about. Those kids cheated *The Game*. They broke rules I spent *years* devising. For that, they are mine, and mine alone.

JS: You're a nutjob.

AG: [GIGGLES] You realize they'll eat you alive, don't you?

JS: What's that supposed to mean?

AG: You think those kids don't have teeth? Oh, they do, Agent No Name. I know firsthand. They can *bite*. Those brats overcame all my obstacles. Defeated every trick, every puzzle. Every trap I set for them. Even to *cheat* The Game is a stunning accomplishment. [LAUGHS] They'll tear you fools to pieces.

JS: We can handle ourselves, thanks.

AG: Think what you like. I underestimated them, too. And look at my reward!

[AGENT ROGERS TAKES OVER THE INTERVIEW]

BR: That's right. You'll be living inside a box for the rest of your life. Claybourne and Brennan put you there. Forever. This is your one chance at revenge. Why not help us?

AG: Because you're fools, whoever you are. Whatever murky outfit you work for. You're not up to the task. That's my cross to bear, and I'm looking forward to it.

BR: Good luck with that.

[BACKGROUND NOISE]

BR: We'll learn what we want to know. Whatever secrets are out there, they can't hide from us. *Nothing* can hide from us.

AG: [WHISPERED] Be careful what you wish for.

BR: What's that?

AG: I have nothing else to say.

[END TRANSCRIPT]

CHAPTER 8

I paused before a pair of massive wrought-iron gates.

Morning sunshine knifed between ancient oak trees lining the sidewalk, having just crested the high stone wall surrounding Bolton Preparatory Academy. The air was warm, humid, and filled with chirping songbirds. Typical Charleston in late May.

Idyllic. If your nerves aren't completely frazzled.

Doves cooed in the branches overhead, as if discussing the merits of my school uniform. I watched them ruffle feathers and bob their heads, enjoying the distraction, unable to keep nervous fingers from pawing through my hair. For a crazy moment I wished we could trade places. It'd be nice having nothing but seeds to worry about.

"We staying out here today?" Hi rubbed his chin as if considering the proposition, his Bolton Prep blazer flipped inside-out with the lining exposed. "Mr. Terenzoni might not be willing to yell his lesson plan out the window."

I blew out a frustrated breath. "It just feels like we're wasting time. We should be looking for the Trinity. Who knows what they'll do next?"

"Education is important, Brennan." Hi bobbed his head toward the gates. "And besides, we won't get to investigate so much as a ham sandwich if our parents find out we cut school. I'm all out of excuses these days."

Shelton hitched his backpack higher onto his shoulders. "Headmaster Paugh is still pretty steamed about the whole kidnapping debacle. Don't think he's not watching us. That man would love to send us packing like he did Ben."

It was true. Bolton's prickly administrator had never wanted Morris Island kids at his prestigious academy. He'd opposed our LIRI scholarships from the beginning, though not publicly. The old fart would love an excuse to "purify" his institution in favor of more traditional, blue-blooded clientele.

"I know." Irritation edged my voice. "I'm just picturing our next seven hours, and I'm already out of patience." A quick glance around, then I stepped closer to Hi and Shelton. "This is serious. The Trinity are the first people to know about our powers."

"I'm well aware." Shelton reached for an earlobe. "It gives me the shakes."

Hi shrugged. "At least they're Viral, too."

Shelton's head reared back. "You think that's a *good* thing?"

"Better than the alternative." Hi tapped his temple. "Whoever the Trinity are, they need to avoid detection as much as we do. They could become lab rats, too."

Shelton nodded slowly. "Mutually assured destruction. That's something, at least."

My lips twisted into a grimace. "But they don't seem to understand what 'low profile' means. And these idiots apparently have a problem with us."

Hi flapped a hand. "Newborns. Always thinking they know everything!"

"Can you get serious for one minute?" Shelton jabbed a finger into Hi's chest, eyes jittery behind his sparkling lenses. "We've gotta find this crew and . . . and . . . I don't know. Shut 'em up. Or something."

"Unhand me, sir!" Hi brushed Shelton aside. "Although you make a good point. Well, no, actually. You make a terrible point, but it illuminates a good one."

Hiram's eyes found mine. "What *do* we do when we find these clowns?"

The bell rang.

Fortuitous, since I had no answer.

I sighed, then squared my shoulders. "Let's just get through the damn day."

○   ○   ○

Ella tapped my tray, then pointed to hers, the other hand covering a mouthful of Little Debbie snack cake. "Wan thum?"

"I'm good." My eyes narrowed with disapproval. "You know how processed that stuff is, right? You're basically eating chemicals."

Ella nodded seriously, lips smeared with crumbs. "Ith terrbul."

"Goofball." I turned back to the chicken Caesar salad Whitney had prepared the night before. It was typically delicious. Maybe she should become a cook?

In a fancy French restaurant. In France. Far, far away.

"What's that smile about?" Shelton asked good-naturedly, his first words since sitting down for lunch. Wildly uncomfortable around Ella, he usually stayed clammed up.

"I just had a *wonderful* thought."

Then I felt bad. Whitney wasn't going anywhere, and she really was trying. She'd learned to make this salad specifically for me after overhearing I liked it.

I needed to be more charitable. More accepting of other people's faults.

But a girl can dream, right?

"I like thinking about things, too," Hi blurted. "Big time."

I pinched the bridge of my nose. Ella had the opposite effect on Hiram—whenever she joined our table, he'd start talking and couldn't stop, and it rarely made sense.

"I don't even need a thinking cap," Hi continued, his hazel-brown eyes widening slightly with an intuitive awareness that he was making a mistake. "I'm anti-headwear on general principle. Never would've made it in the fifties. Hats tend to ruin the 'do, if you know what I mean. Except at temple, of course. But that's *God's* hat I'm wearing in there, and we don't argue with the big guy."

Hi laughed overloud at his own statement, then dropped his head. "Fedoras are cool, though."

I stared at Hiram in awe.

What a pretty girl can do to boys. Amazing.

"Fedowas *aw* coo." The last snack cake filled Ella's mouth.

At that moment Jason Taylor entered the cafeteria. Spotting me, he hurried to join us.

My hand lifted in a wave. Froze halfway as I noticed who was with him.

I wasn't the only one thrown.

"What's Jason doing with Madison?" Shelton eyed the pair like they were incoming smart bombs. "They a thing now?"

"You didn't hear?" Ella took a swig of her Coke, then leaned in conspiratorially. "They showed up at Khalid's party together last weekend." She flashed a mock-stern look at me. "The one *you* no-showed, I might add."

"Sorry. Something came up." Since Chance's bombshell about a new supervirus, I hadn't been much of a social butterfly.

Conversation ceased as the duo arrived. I put on my fake smile. After months of practice at home on Whitney, it was virtually bulletproof.

"Hey guys," Jason said in greeting. He's a big, muscular kid, with classic Nordic features—pale skin, ice-blue eyes, and snowy, white-blond hair. The only thing missing was Thor's hammer. Jason's a good-looking guy by anyone's account, and well-liked by everyone, but that morning his usual easy grin was noticeably absent.

Jason's gaze flicked from Ella, to Shelton, and then to Hi, before landing on me. "Got a second, Tory?" His hands worked, as if he could barely contain something.

Totally out of character. There are tree sloths more uptight than Jason Taylor.

Madison practically hid behind Jason's shoulder, anxiously twirling her long auburn hair. She flashed a meek finger wave, but didn't speak, her eyes finding the floor.

I suppressed a sigh. Nothing would ever make Madison comfortable around me. I'd done plenty enough to ensure that.

"Um, okay." My head tilted slightly. "Alone?"

He nodded sharply. "I think that'd be best. Outside?"

"Sure."

Hmm. Something's up.

The pair spun and beelined for the door, leaving me to hurry after. As we exited the cafeteria, Madison's fingers slipped into Jason's hand. He squeezed them tightly.

My eyeballs nearly burst.

What!?

An uncomfortable feeling curdled my gut.

Logically, this shouldn't have bothered me. I'd been politely deflecting Jason's advances for the better part of a year. He was a great friend—one of the few people I could count on outside my pack—but there was no spark. No magic. No tingle in the toes. And it had pained me to let him down so often.

If he'd finally set his sights on another, it could do wonders for our friendship.

But . . . *Madison Dunkle*? She's rich. Spoiled. Pampered. Entitled.

Could a girl *be* more different from me?

Lost in thought, I was nearly clubbed by the swinging door. Catching it awkwardly with one palm, I stepped out into the courtyard. Jason and Madison were waiting beside a stone bench facing Bolton's small pond.

The same bench where I'd spied on Chance and Madison weeks before.

When I tried to read her mind, and she noticed. And freaked.

The memory stung. I'd always felt bad about it.

What I'd attempted that afternoon—to force my way into Madison's head—was abhorrent. Disgusting. A violation. I understood that now. In a way, I owed Madison a debt, despite all the horrible things she'd done to me. When you boiled it down, I'd been pretty terrible right back.

Life is too short for petty jealousies.

My steps slowed.

Is that what I was feeling? Jealousy?

And what did they want to discuss privately?

I jerked to a halt.

Dear Lord, they don't want to talk about them dating each other, do they? Like they feel the need to tell me or something? Please no. I'll die.

Shrugging off shivers, I approached and waited, feeling decidedly uncomfortable.

Jason spoke first. "Sorry for being so cryptic, but it's hard to get you alone, and what Madison needs to tell you should be kept between us."

Blood rushed to my face. "No, really. I appreciate the thought, but you guys don't—"

"Someone's asking questions about you," Madison whispered.

That stopped me cold. "What? Me?"

She nodded, glancing around to make sure we were alone. "You and Chance."

My mind reeled. One hand rose to my forehead as my pulse took off like a speed skater.

"Who would be . . . Why would anyone . . ."

I flinched. *The Trinity. They're researching us!*

Then a second thought crashed into the first.

Madison must've spoken to one. She can help me track them down.

"I don't know who they are." Madison nervously smoothed her plaid skirt. "Or what . . . information . . . or whatever . . . that they might've wanted about you."

I watched her closely. She wouldn't meet my gaze.

Madison had always suspected I was different. She'd experienced things that scared her.

I could tell she was thinking of those things now.

Her eyes flicked up to meet mine, then quickly dropped again.

I crossed my arms. Not aggressively, but not welcoming, either. I knew she was dying to know why someone would inquire about me, but this was a road we simply couldn't go down.

"Not my business," Madison blurted finally, her face flushing scarlet.

She looked to Jason, who nodded encouragingly. It seemed to lend her strength.

Madison took a deep breath, then continued in a stronger voice. "I was horrible to you last year. Your friends, too. It was stupid, and mean, and I regret it. You've been nothing but nice to me since I joined the soccer team, and you didn't have to be. I want to repay the favor. So I told Jason what happened, and he thought you should know."

I had a thousand burning questions. What came out first surprised me.

"Why *did* you join the team?"

"And leave the Tripod of Bitch?" A wry smile appeared on Madison's face. "I needed a change. I got tired of spending all my time with people who don't respect me. Or maybe even *like* me. Ashley and Courtney—" she actually shuddered, "—they're not real friends. To them, everything is one big competition. That or a joke. I'm sick of it all. Done with them." Her voice cracked. "I thought, maybe, if I was part of something else, like the team, people might forget how awful I've been. Might actually like me. I was good at soccer when I was kid. Always liked it. I only quit because Ashley said it wasn't cool, and . . . and . . ."

Madison sniffed loudly.

Oh my God, she's going to cry.

Impulsively, I reached out and hugged her. Her. Madison Dunkle.

For a few beats, she silently shook in my arms.

In my wildest dreams, I would never *have thought . . .*

Madison abruptly pulled away, perhaps feeling the same. I noticed Jason watching, an unreadable expression on his face. What could he possibly be thinking?

Enough. There are bigger issues at play.

"What did the person look like?" I prodded gently. "The one asking about me."

Madison ran a finger under each eye, then cleared her throat. "There were two men, both in black suits. One was maybe late twenties. In good shape, but he wore sunglasses the whole time so I didn't get a great look at his face. Buzzed blond hair. Oh, and he had a fresh scar on the side of his face, like somebody had slashed him. But the other guy did all the talking. He was older, like my dad's age, with gray hair and an eighties mustache. Bad teeth."

My head was shaking on its own. This didn't sound right at all.

"They weren't younger? Maybe college age?"

"Not even close," Madison said firmly. "They acted like they were on official business or something. It was creepy. The creeps cornered me outside my house when no one else was around, and the blond one kept scanning the block to see if anyone was coming."

The more she described, then less sense it made. "What did they say?"

"Mustache guy said they needed to ask me some questions privately." Madison snorted, hugging her arms tightly. "Strange men in suits, wanting to take me somewhere alone? Not in this lifetime. I said no and started to walk away. That's when he mentioned Chance. Then you."

An icy feeling crept through my limbs.

Flashbulb images.

A black helicopter at night. Cages. Masked scientists holding syringes and clipboards.

"What'd you tell them?" I demanded.

"Nothing!" Madison's palms flew up. "I didn't say jack, I promise. I dug out my phone, told them to get out of my way or I'd call the police. I was terrified they'd stop me, but after exchanging a glance they stepped aside and let me pass. I bolted up the block, then looked back. They were gone."

"What's this about, Tor?" Jason wrapped an arm around Madison and began rubbing her shoulder. She melted into his side.

The twinge returned.

Stop it already. Did you think he'd follow you around forever?

I told Jason the truth. "I honestly don't know."

Then I reached out and squeezed Madison's hand. "Thanks for telling me. I mean it."

She gave me a tentative smile. "Anything for a . . . a friend, right?"

I tried the concept on for size. Realized it agreed with me.

My grin matched hers. "That's damn right."

○   ○   ○

"Welp! That's the ballgame." Hi covered his face with both hands. "We're as good as lab rats now. Dibs on the cage closest to a window."

"Stop joking!" Shelton snapped, his foot tapping incessantly as we huddled by my locker. "This is serious. The freaking Men in Black are on our tail!"

Hi dropped his hands. "I *wasn't* joking. We're in trouble."

Ben's voice floated up from my fingers. "This is all Chance's fault."

I glanced down at the iPhone cupped in my palm. Ben scowled back angrily as he huddled against a wall somewhere at Wando High. I was risking confiscation—Bolton's draconian cell phone policy outlawed all use during school hours—but this simply couldn't wait.

"Chance is playing some kind of double game," Ben swore. "He knows way more than he's telling us."

I nearly shook the phone in frustration. "These men were asking about *Chance,* too. He's not with them. We need to find out who they are."

"Claybourne is hiding something," Ben insisted stubbornly. "I know you sense it, too."

"I'm with Ben."

My glare whipped to Shelton, but he didn't back down.

"We've always been careful with our secret," he said. "But a few weeks with Chance being Viral, and suddenly it's all black helicopters and CIA spooks on the streets. Coincidence?"

"They're right, Tor." Hi cracked his knuckles as he spoke. "The only thing that's changed lately is Chance. He's gotta be the source of this, though it might not be his fault."

"Or Speckman," I countered reflexively, though their logic was starting to take hold. "He's Viral, too. Maybe the Trinity caught the attention of . . . of . . ." my hands worked uselessly, "—whoever these agents work for."

Hi's face was skeptical. "How could the Trinity dime us without getting caught in the same net?"

I didn't answer, temporarily out of arguments.

"Listen to reason, Victoria," Ben scolded from my iPhone. "Chance has been shady from the beginning. He's holding back."

A second, longer pause. Students streamed back and forth in the hallway behind me, unaware of the tension surrounding my locker.

"Crap."

They were right.

Chance must know more.

I slammed a fist against my locker. "Right after school."

"Finally!" Ben shouted. "I'll beat it out of him if I have to."

"No." A cauldron of anger began simmering inside me. "I'll talk to Chance alone."

"Fine by me." Shelton shirt-wiped his glasses and stuck them on his nose. "I'm happy to pass on that meeting."

Hi shrugged. "Your call."

"If you think I'm not—"

I hung up on Ben before he could finish.

"Just Chance and me." I let the fury boil, heating my skin from within.

If he's playing me again . . .

"He's going to tell me *everything*. Once and for all."

CHAPTER 9

We met beside the flat, still surface of Colonial Lake.

I'd given him little choice. A text that reads: **On my way to your office. We are meeting RIGHT NOW!** leaves no room for debate.

Chance had replied immediately: **Not here. Outside. I'll come to you.**

I didn't know why his office wasn't acceptable, but the detail didn't concern me.

I wanted to know what Chance was hiding. I was going to find out.

After last bell, I hurried off campus and strode down the concrete embankment on Ashley Avenue. I scanned the benches bordering Charleston's cherished tidal pond. Man-made, shallow, and occupying a full city block, Colonial Lake is a favorite gathering spot for dog walkers, baby strollers, and ducks. On any other day, the place would've made me smile.

I spotted Chance seated at the northwest corner of the lake. He wore an expensive-looking gray suit and silver aviator sunglasses. Something about his posture seemed . . . resigned. Chance was leaning forward, elbows on his knees, hands clasped before him.

He saw me approach but didn't wave, his expression suspiciously neutral.

Ben was right. He is *hiding something.*

"Tory." Nothing more.

"Chance." I chose to remain standing, forcing him to look up at me. An awkward moment stretched.

Arrrgh. Fine.

I hate losing a test of wills, but I *did* demand the meeting.

"You're keeping something from me."

Blunt, and to the point.

A ghost of a smile curled his lips. "Why would you say that?"

I crossed my arms. "Because two weirdos in black suits are asking questions about us."

The smile vanished. "Where did you hear that?"

My head tilted. "Does it matter? You're clearly not surprised."

For a moment he didn't respond. Then, "No."

Chance leaned back against the bench, exhaling a tired sigh. "No, I can't say that I am."

I threw my hands up, furious. "What the hell, Chance? Why are you still keeping secrets? I thought we were in this together!"

"Oh, we are." He grimaced slightly, before schooling his face. "More than you're going to like, I'm afraid."

I actually stamped a foot. "Then talk!"

Chance's sardonic grin returned. "Will you at least sit? We can ditch the theatrics. I'll tell you what I know."

I considered refusing out of spite, but relented. Dropping down beside him, I reached out and snatched the shades off his face. "Go. Spill."

Chance looked me dead in the eye. "We're in serious trouble."

My breath caught despite myself. With afternoon sunlight filtering through his thick black hair—bathing his chiseled cheekbones, chin, and nose—Chance's attractiveness smacked me full in the face. I sometimes forgot how beautiful he was.

A perfectly formed human male. If he wasn't such a jerk.

Focus Focus FOCUS!

Deep breath. "Why are we in trouble?"

"My office has a leak."

"A leak?" I frowned. "What does that mean?"

His eyebrows rose. "It means, *someone* has been talking about my experiment."

I sat back, thinking. "It must be Speckman."

Chance grunted. "So I thought, at first. But it makes no sense. Will is infected, too. He faces the same dangers from exposure as the rest of us."

Thoughts pinballed in my brain as I tried to make sense of things. "But why would they ask about *me,* then? I've got nothing to do with Candela."

"You haven't told me who was asking," he countered pointedly.

"Because I think you already know."

Chance said nothing. I gave him a level look, to no effect.

"You are *the* most frustrating . . ." I paused to shake off my annoyance. Then, in even, measured tones, I summarized what Madison had told me.

Chance's jaw tightened as I spoke. "This is worse than I thought. If these agents—whoever they are—have gone so far as to track *Madison* down . . ."

He didn't need to finish.

But Chance hadn't answered my question. "Still, how could these sidewalk interrogators know *my* name? I wasn't part of your supervirus project."

"That's how I know there's a leak." Chance sounded matter-of-fact, but he was staring across the pond with a grim expression. I could tell something troubled him deeply.

Which frightened me badly.

"I don't think Will Speckman is responsible," Chance said finally. "I have . . . personal files. Kept separately from the parvovirus experiment. Only those documents mention either you or Madison."

I straightened. "You have *files* on me?"

He breathed a low chuckle. "A few, yeah. What can I say?"

Then Chance blasted me with eye contact a second time.

"You've always intrigued me, Tory. I might be a little obsessed."

A hot flush crept up my neck and invested my cheeks, no doubt accentuating every freckle on my face. I had to look away.

What did he mean by *that*?

I could feel his eyes on me. "I've been recording everything about you for months," Chance continued. "What you do. Where you go. Who your friends are. At first, I did it because I knew you Morris Islanders were hiding something. And I was right."

"Doesn't give you the right to spy." Spoken weakly, still totally thrown.

"Debatable. I think I had a right to know why I went crazy."

My mind raced for a response. A way to regain control of this encounter. But Chance didn't leave an opening.

"After being infected, I began to understand." His casualness felt forced—I could tell this conversation was important to him. "Suddenly the four of you made . . . sense. Your actions became, if not rational—I still can't fathom why you stick your noses into everything—then at least understandable. So I wanted to know every detail. I felt a . . . connection."

Chance's voice sharpened in a way I can't define. "You became all I could think about."

I felt pressure on my wrist. Glanced down.

Found his smooth, warm hand covering mine.

My eyes rose, rounding with terror. Chance was looking right at me.

"You're *still* all I think about."

What. Is. Happening?

My breath came fast and furious. Every nerve went on high alert.

But I didn't move my hand. Not one inch.

Chance pulled away first, intertwining his fingers in his lap.

My skin tingled where his fingers had touched mine. For a hot second, I considered grabbing his hand back, but the notion made me jibber with panic.

Tripping over Chance Claybourne, again?

A voice in my head began scolding me, recounting every time Chance had betrayed me. Every lie he'd told. Every trick he'd used to manipulate my feelings.

Hell, I was sitting there *right that second* because he hadn't been honest.

I shoved my emotions into a box, locked the box in a trunk, and kicked the trunk under a bed inside a closet. Then I swam back up from the bottom of a lake.

When I spoke, the words were firm and clear. "We should focus on what to do next."

"Of course." Chance rose and pushed his sunglasses back into place, as if the last thirty seconds had never happened. "I can handle my own office. I've *been* handling it, actually. That's why I didn't bother you with my suspicions."

Arrogant, irritating boy!

Heat infused my voice. "No more secrets, Chance. No lies, no sins of omission. You go ahead and *bother* me next time. If you want to be a part of our pack, you need to understand the rules. Virals don't lie to one another. We don't mislead one another. We tell the truth."

Chance snorted. "Like Ben did?"

A hot spike of anger. "You leave—"

His hand chopped the air to cut me off. "You're right. I'm sorry. My mouth sometimes runs ahead of my brain. I won't mention it again."

"I'm serious, Chance. Total honesty, from this moment forward."

He flashed a million-dollar smile. "I promise."

Why am I not reassured?

I took another cleansing breath. "Who are these men asking questions?"

"No idea." His palms rose as my expression darkened. "I don't know. Really. They seem to be conducting some sort of covert investigation. Likely for a shady government agency."

I shivered despite the temperature. "The helicopter."

Chance nodded grimly. "You don't see those in the private sector."

Facts began linking in my brain. "Those same men might've tracked us to Fort Sumter. But how? We went on a whim, straight from the bunker."

"Don't jump to conclusions," Chance chided, dusting his jacket sleeves. "Maybe the spooks were tracking the Trinity instead, or were simply investigating the damage under cover of darkness."

"The Trinity?" My eyes narrowed. "But you said Speckman wasn't the leak."

"I don't *think* it's Will," Chance answered smoothly, sunlight reflecting off his lenses. "But until we're sure, let's not discount any possibility. I'm still half convinced this is some rival pharmaceutical outfit, looking to steal corporate secrets. It's happened before."

My turn to be skeptical. "Do most drug companies own stealth choppers?"

"I didn't say it was my *top* theory," Chance huffed.

Then, abruptly, we both laughed. Some of the tension dissipated.

I'd never felt more paranoid—not since the first days of my sickness from the supervirus. Unknown Virals rampaging across the city. Secret agents prowling the streets. The situation bordered on surreal. If you can't laugh then, you're already dead.

"I'll find out who's screwing me at work." Chance's voice hardened. "I still own the damn company. Time to track down the cockroach going through my trash."

From the look on his face, I pitied the one he discovered.

But that left the bigger issue unsettled. "How do we figure out who these agents are?"

Chance shrugged, his tone still frosty. "We wait. Hope they pop up somewhere we can anticipate. What else can we do?"

I nodded, rising and smoothing my skirt.

Not a satisfying answer, but I didn't have a better one.

"You have the paint flecks from Fort Sumter?" I asked. "The canvas flag?"

"Being analyzed as we speak, along with samples scraped from my statue. Shouldn't take long."

"And Speckman?"

"Him, we find." Chance straightened his tie in the manner of someone concluding a routine business meeting. "Gather the others and meet me at CU's administrative building in an hour."

I bristled at the curt instruction. "Dorm room check?"

Chance nodded. "Will is the key to finding the rest of the Trinity. I'm worried this might hit close to home."

That surprised me. "How so?"

"Speckman only left Bolton two years ago. He was very popular."

A glance at his watch, then Chance strode past me down the sidewalk.

Like it never even happened.

Maddening, infuriating, impossible boy!

"What does that mean?" I shouted at his back.

Chance raised a hand. A black BMW pulled from an alley a block away.

Of course he didn't walk. It was eight whole blocks.

Chance paused with the door open. "When things go bad for a normal person, what's the first thing they do?"

Huh? "What?"

"They find their friends."

Chance slipped inside and closed the door, never glancing back.

CHAPTER 10

Ben was last to arrive.

He parked his beat-up blue Explorer beside Charleston University's main building on Coming Street. A no-parking zone, but Ben never took that seriously. I was sure that one of these days we'd return to an empty curb and a note from whichever towing company to contact. Hopefully not today.

Ben sauntered up the steps, nodding to Hi, Shelton, and me, while pointedly snubbing Chance. "Sorry. Got tied up at Wando."

Chance returned the cold shoulder. He'd changed into his "casual" clothes: pressed Brooks Brothers pants, a crisp blue button-down shirt, and brown patent-leather loafers. All that was missing was a clapboard sign saying YUPPIE.

Hi, Shelton, and I still wore Bolton Prep uniforms, though we'd ditched our jackets and ties in the Explorer. Ben was sporting his standard black-and-denim look. As a group we surely stuck out, but it couldn't be helped.

"We'll canvass the dorm." Chance spoke directly to me. "See if any classmates remember Will spending time with someone in particular."

"Should we use code names?" Hi popped up from the steps on which he'd been sitting. "Of course we should. Inside, refer to me as Rex Condor."

Hi winced in surprise as Shelton smacked the back of his head. "*You?*"

Shelton shrugged. "Had to be done. Ben's too far away."

Ben gave Shelton a thumbs-up. My eyes rolled skyward.

"Game faces, guys." Adopting my no-nonsense posture. "Speckman is Viral. He must be part of the Trinity. And he could be responsible for our creepy new fans. We need to find him ASAP."

"These black-suit dudes are no joke." Shelton's voice dropped to a whisper. "We gotta think on that more. MIBs sniffing around are way more serious than everything else combined."

I'd filled in Shelton and Hi while we waited for the older boys to arrive. They'd slumped down on the steps with matching horrified expressions.

I'd updated Ben by phone as he drove over from Mount Pleasant, wanting him to hear the news without Chance present. He'd been furious, though he'd kept his comments to a petulant "I told you so!"

I'd made Ben promise not to cause trouble. He'd agreed—grudgingly, but I'd take what I could get. Yet I knew that pot would boil over again eventually. Ben's distrust of Chance was bordering on pathological.

Which is why I wanted to get the group moving. "Which dorm, Chance?"

"Coker. This way."

Bypassing the admin building, we cut across a magnolia-dotted courtyard. CU is beautiful in spring, with flower-lined walks and shady arbors brightening the downtown campus. That afternoon students were outside in force, tossing Frisbees, playing guitars, or just napping in the shade. College life looked pretty relaxing to me.

Reaching a side street, we turned toward the residences. Chance led us to a bulky brick structure surrounded by pink dogwoods. "This is Coker. Will's room is on the fourth floor."

We caught a break—a long-haired boy carrying bongo drums was exiting the front door. He held it open with a friendly wave as we scurried inside.

"People need to respect security more," Shelton grumbled as we crossed the flyer-strewn lobby. "The school issues key cards for a reason."

"You think that dude-bro cares?" Hi pressed the elevator button. "He's probably on a gummy bear hunt. He'd let you nap in his room if you asked."

We rode up four floors, then Chance led us down a carpeted hallway to the last room on the right. He knocked. Waited. Knocked a second time.

Shelton pushed his glasses back up his nose. "Looks like nobody's home."

"Doubtful." Chance hammered the door a third time. "I know Will's roommate."

I stood beside Chance, struggling to contain my impatience. Down the corridor, a few doors opened. Heads stuck out. One guy in a baseball cap watched us for a long moment before ducking back out of sight.

"Come on, Cole." Chance raised his fist for another assault.

Abruptly, the door swung inward. A skinny kid with a wispy mustache stared over the threshold, headphones around his neck, *Call of Duty* paused on a TV behind him. Greasy potato chip crumbs covered his Bob Marley T-shirt. He seemed bewildered by the crowd outside his dorm room. A distinctly herbal scent wafted from inside.

"Yo?" Then, recognizing Chance, his expression soured. "Oh, Claybourne. You again. What is it this time, man?" The boy glanced from face to face. "Who's the glee club?"

"Cole Gordon." Chance's nose crinkled at the overpowering odor. "I had a feeling you might be home. I'm still looking for my associate."

Cole shook his head. "Haven't seen Willie, bro. He's, like, *gone.*" He made a wobbly, sweeping hand gesture for emphasis. "His parents are looking for him, too. They came by for his stuff, said Willie sent them a postcard from NYC or something. He totally ditched out. Ain't coming back."

Chance rubbed his mouth, thinking. "Has anyone else been looking for him?"

"Naw, just you, man." Cole stroked his struggling peach-fuzz facial hair. Glancing behind him, I saw an unmade bed, a dozen empty Hot Pocket boxes, and concrete walls covered by movie posters and tribal art. "I mean, his girl came by, but that was like—"

"His girl?" I asked sharply.

Cole squinted at me. "Well, yeah. Black hair, super hot. Really, really mean. Don't think she's a CU student, though. I only saw her on weekends. I think she's, like, younger or something. But I never talked to her much, because she said I—" air quotes, "—'lack manners' and 'don't smell good.' Whatever."

Chance had tensed noticeably. "Black hair? When was this?"

Cole scratched his greasy hair. "I dunno. A week, maybe? Like I said, she never talks to me, so I don't pay much attention. She came by asking for Willie, I said he wasn't around anymore, then I never saw her again. That's it. End of story."

Chance considered a moment, then grunted. "All right." He turned from Cole as if the boy ceased to exist. "Let's check the hall. See if anyone knows more than this guy."

As an eye-rolling Cole closed his door, we divvied up rooms along the corridor. I chose a section including the boy in the baseball cap. Something about his reaction stuck with me.

"Let's meet by the elevator when we're done," Hi said. "I want to hit that taco truck over on Market Street. Starving." He clomped down the hall, a reluctant Shelton on his heels.

"Those foods trucks are nasty," Shelton grumbled.

Hi snorted. "Nasty good."

Chance knocked on the closest door while Ben took the next one down. I worried about leaving them alone together, but there's only so much policing a girl can do.

As I approached Ball Cap's room, a devilish thought occurred to me. Weighing its merits, I decided the risk was worth it. So before I could second-guess, I took out my sunglasses and slid them into place.

We were asking questions of strangers. People of unknown trustworthiness.

I have a certain skill in that area.

It'd be a pity not to use it.

SNAP.

The flare opened smoothly, as they had for the last few weeks. Following the initial jolt—fire, ice, an electric sizzle—my senses sharpened to preternatural acuity.

My eyes picked out hidden flaws in the grain of the wooden door before me. I could hear Chance and the others up and down the hall. Breathing. Knocking. Asking about Will Speckman. Then a smack of fetid, musty stench assaulted my nostrils, wafting from the communal bathroom two doors down.

Every muscle tingling with caged energy. I felt alive. Vibrant. Had to resist an urge to cartwheel down the hallway. To shout with the pure joy of my powers unleashed.

I *flared*. An indescribable feeling.

I cracked my knuckles and was overly careful knocking.

Didn't want to smash the door off its hinges.

A dry-erase board on the wall proclaimed this the domain of Jordan

Heffernan. At first there was no answer. Odd, since I knew someone was inside. But a second round of pounding did the trick.

Heffernan jerked open the door, irritation crimping his pimply face. "What?"

"Excuse me," flashing my flirtiest smile, "would you happen to know—"

"I haven't seen Will Speckman." He kept one hand on the knob, leaning awkwardly, as if ready to slam the door in my face at any moment.

So much for seduction. And he already knew my question.

I forged ahead in a more businesslike tone. "When did you last see him?"

Heffernan frowned at my follow-up query. He straightened, his entire body screaming reluctance as a thumb began unconsciously drumming against his pant leg. "Two weeks. Maybe three."

This guy seems nervous. Why?

Because he's lying.

But I had to be sure.

I leaned forward and took an experimental sniff.

Heffernan backpedaled a few steps, eyes widening. "Did you just . . . *smell* me?"

I didn't answer. How could I? It's not a thing people typically do. Plus my nose was busy unwinding a bundle of aromas and sorting them into categories.

Of all my pack, only I have this ability.

While flaring, my nose can identify emotions. Impossible, but true.

A host of scents billowed from Heffernan—old pizza, Clearasil, string cheese, sweaty socks. I ignored those, focusing on a sour tang lurking underneath.

My nose scrunched in distaste.

Anxiety.

I was right.

Heffernan eyed me like a wary zookeeper. "Are you having a fit or something?"

"You haven't seen Will Speckman?" Inhaling through my nose. "That's what you're saying?"

"No, already!" He retreated another few steps. "You're weird. Why are you wearing sunglasses?"

I ignored the question as a denser stream of odors flitted through my brain. Dry paper. Muddy shoes. The earthy muddle of a long-dead fern plant.

And something else just below the surface. Weak, but growing stronger by the second.

A salty, acrid stink, like hot garbage.

Deception.

Pants on fire, Heff Dawg.

"You're lying." Calmly spoken. "Why?"

"What? No I'm not." He shuffled his feet, a sickly sweet fragrance taking over the room. "This is nuts. You're seriously freaking me out."

Worry.

Interesting.

I crossed my arms and shrugged. "I'm not leaving until you tell the truth."

Heffernan's voice grew shrill as he pointed to the door. "I don't have to take this. Get out of my room!"

"Make me."

Shadows knifed across the walls. I didn't turn to look.

I could sense Chance and Ben were now standing in the doorway.

"This guy knows something," I announced. "But he doesn't want to share."

The appearance of two guys at my back seemed to change the dynamic for Heffernan. His shoulders slumped, a dull, stagnant odor washing over me.

Resignation.

He's gonna talk.

"I promised not to say anything," he mumbled at the floor.

"Not to say what?" Then, as the boy continued to waffle, "Look, man, we don't mean Speckman any harm." *I don't think.* "We just need to talk to him. Straighten something out."

Pretty accurate. As far as it went.

The fight leaked from Heffernan completely. With an audible sigh, he dropped onto a ragged two-seat couch. "Will came by three days ago. Said he needed to borrow my camping equipment. Sleeping bag, tent, et cetera. Said he was bugging out, and didn't want anyone to know where, not even his parents. We used to hang a bit, me and Will, and I never use that stuff anyway. So, sure, why not?"

"This was three days ago?" My mind raced as Heffernan nodded. Speckman had visited him shortly before breaking into Claybourne Manor. "Was he alone?"

Heffernan looked away.

Ben's voice arrowed from behind me. "Who was with him, friend?"

Softly spoken, but edged with menace.

"I don't know," Heffernan snapped. "Some chick. And somebody was waiting by the elevator, but I didn't get a look." When no one moved, his hands flew up as he squawked in an exasperated tone. "That's all I know, I swear! Now, would y'all please buzz off?"

The Trinity. It must be.

So close! But only this wastoid had seen them.

In the end, we were still nowhere.

Unless.

No. No no no . . . okay, yes.

We needed to know.

Closing my eyes, I pushed my thoughts outward, piercing the black space I've come to think of as between minds. I recognized the close presence of Ben. Knew Hi and Shelton were behind him in the hallway.

Those three were easy—minds as familiar to me as old jeans. I noted another vibrant consciousness close by, and knew it to be Chance. His mind had the same glow—the same unique pulsating pattern as my Viral packmates—yet humming to a slightly different rhythm.

Like, yet unlike. I filed the observation away for future consideration.

Other vibes buzzed at the edge of my perception—people down the hall watching TV, talking on the phone, one pair doing something I quickly veered away from—but I focused on a fuzzy tangle of thoughts, ideas, and emotions directly before me.

Respect his privacy. As much as you can.

"Look," Heffernan was saying, clearly nervous we hadn't left his room yet, "I don't know anything else. Me and Willie were friends, but it's not like we shared our deepest secrets with each other. I already told you—"

I brushed my consciousness lightly against his.

He stopped dead, eyes rounding.

An image coalesced in my mind. A boy. A girl. But I couldn't see their faces.

She's wearing something familiar . . .

Heffernan's hands shot to his head. "What the hell?"

Not good enough. I need to see.

I attempted a second contact, but his mental defenses had been triggered. Steel walls slammed into place around Heffernan's mind. I recoiled, nearly sick from a sudden, crushing slap of vertigo.

SNUP.

"Blargh."

My knees buckled.

Hands gripped my shoulders. One, Chance. The other, Ben.

Heffernan popped to his feet, unsure what was happening but *very* sure he didn't like it. "Y'all get out! Now! Or I'm calling security, I mean it!"

I spun, steadying myself. Found my face close to Ben's.

He raised an eyebrow. I nodded.

"Thanks for your time." Ben ushered me through the doorway.

Chance closed Heffernan's door, and the five of us hurried down the hallway.

Ten steps to the elevator. Forty seconds down. Twenty paces to the lobby doors.

Outside, I made it ten yards before collapsing on the grass. Dry heaves wracked my body as I tried not to lose my lunch.

The boys huddled around me, shielding my body from easy view.

A last round of gasps cleared my head. I was able to stand unaided.

"So you did it again." Shelton pressed both fists to his head, trying to keep his voice calm. "I thought we ruled that move out of bounds?"

"Had to." Spitting a mouthful of bile. "That guy saw the Trinity. I know it."

"Remind me not to watch any shows you miss," Hi quipped, attempting to lighten the mood. "Downloading fools like a DVR."

Ben smacked his head without looking. Hi barely reacted.

"Did it work?" Ben asked.

I tried to piece together the image I'd stolen. "Speckman was here. With a dark-haired girl, but I couldn't see her face."

Then it hit me. "But I *did* see what she was wearing."

Chance frowned. "It wasn't a Bolton Prep uniform, perchance?"

I gaped at him. "Yes! Plaid skirt pattern number three. I have two in my closet. How did you know?"

"Not mind-robbing like you, I promise." He smiled to lessen the sting, but his eyes were serious. "No, I have an idea who this person might be."

"Who?" Hi, Shelton, and I spoke at once. Ben waited silently, jaw clenched.

"His ex-girlfriend." Chance sighed. "Tory, at least, is acquainted."

At that moment a face popped into my head, fitting the image I'd taken from Heffernan's mind. My hands flew to my mouth.

"Oh no."

CHAPTER 11

"Ashley."

My stomach knotted as I spoke the name.

"Could be." Chance scraped a hand through his hair. "She and Will dated off and on for a year. When I heard Cole's description, Ashley was my first thought."

Ashley Bodford. The nastiest of the Tripod.

And now, possibly, Viral.

My stomach unknotted, but only to drop through my shoes.

Shelton eyed me cautiously. "Did you . . . *confirm* . . . it was Ashley who came here?"

"Yes." Then I stopped myself. "Well, no."

I tried to sharpen the image, but it remained hazy. The faces kept slipping away, like smoke though my fingers. "Honestly, I'm not sure. He was definitely picturing a girl in a Bolton Prep uniform. After Chance's hint . . . I *thought* I recognized Ashley's face. But now I wonder."

Was it really her? Or did I see Ashley's face because Chance planted the idea?

Please let that be the case.

Even a mile from school, the thought of Ashley Bodford's shark-like

smile made me shiver. She'd been playing at friendship for a few months—
her and that ditz Courtney, two girls I had *zero* in common with—but
I'd never felt comfortable in her presence.

Something in her eyes. The lilt of her voice. The way Ashley would
talk past me—almost *through* me—as if she didn't expect or need my
response.

The whole thing never sat right. Not for an instant. It felt like a prank
waiting to happen.

*And if Ashley's part of the Trinity. If she's behind these brazen
challenges . . .*

"We need to nail this down." I began pacing the sidewalk, thinking
out loud. "But how? Confront her? Corner Ashley somehow, and get
her to confess?" One hand came up. "But what if she *isn't* part of the
Trinity? She'd learn our secret for no reason."

"I once read a book on hypnosis." Hi flared an eyebrow and waggled
his fingers. "We could pry open Ashley's mind. Examine her darkest
secrets. Get her to stop being completely awful to everyone all the time."

Ben tapped his lip, as if deep in thought. "Do you need another head
smack?"

"Come at me, 'bro." Hi bounced on the balls of his feet and beat his
chest twice. "I'm ready this time. Can you *smell* what the *Hi* is—"

Hi cut off abruptly, gawking at something over my shoulder as the
color drained from his face. Moving woodenly, Hi elbowed Chance,
who was standing beside him checking email.

"Claybourne." Hi tried not to move his lips. "Gray stone building.
Ten o'clock. Who's that on the roof?"

Chance's head snapped up. He squinted, then his eyes rounded. "I
see two."

"Two what?" Shelton spun like a top. "Virals?"

"Don't all look at once!" Chance hissed.

Too late. Ben and I had also swiveled to see.

I spotted them immediately—a pair of men in dark clothing, peering down from atop the adjacent building. One held a camera. An instant later they ducked behind a parapet.

"You see that!?" Shelton's voice cracked as he backed up a few steps. "Spies! Spies are spying on us! Oh hell!"

A hand gripped my shoulder. Ben. He pointed up the street, to a black sedan idling at the mouth of an alley two blocks away. As if on cue, xenon lights blazed to life. Tires squealed as the car lurched into the road and swung toward us.

"Move!" Chance pulled me in the direction of the admin building. "Back to Ben's car!"

For once, no one argued. We bolted along a path leading back to the courtyard.

Behind us, I heard brakes screech, then car doors open and slam shut. *The surveillance pair getting in? Or riders getting out?*

I had no intention of finding out.

We bombed across the common and reached Coming Street. Ben clicked the doors and we scrambled into his Explorer. Something was blocking the windshield. I jumped out and snagged it, then fought down a fit of nervous giggles.

"Parking ticket, Ben!" Tossing it on the floor mat as I slammed home my seat belt. "Told you!"

"Bill me." He shifted into drive and stomped the gas. "Hold on."

We shot down the block, then swerved left onto Calhoun Street. Speeding east across the peninsula, Ben's eyes darted to the rearview mirror. Once. Twice. Three times.

"Anything?" I checked the side mirror. Saw nothing.

Ben shook his head, still death-gripping the wheel. "I don't think they followed."

Hi's voice sounded from a tangle of arms and legs in the backseat. "Because we lost them, or because they didn't try?"

"How would I know?" Ben snapped.

"If they were watching us at all." Chance righted himself and shoved free of Hi's sweaty limbs. "Those guys might have nothing to do with us."

"Oh, right!" Shelton snatched off his glasses, breathing hard. "We find out that shady government types are interrogating folks about you and Tor, and then some *other* random dudes just happen to be hanging out on a nearby rooftop, snapping selfies. And that town car that came barreling out? What was *it* doing?"

"I didn't say they *weren't* spying on us," Chance growled. "I just said they didn't *have* to be. They could be surveyors."

"Surveyors who bugged out the moment we spotted them?" Hi gave him an incredulous look. "That seems reasonable to you?"

"Fine." Chance jerked the ends of his sleeves back into place. "Whatever."

Ben steered onto the James Island Expressway, taking the bridge across the Ashley River and heading toward Folly Road. Traffic thinned. Five sets of eyes monitored our trail.

No black sedan.

"Wait." Chance sat upright. "I don't live out here."

"Call a driver, your majesty." Ben smirked as he drove on without pause. "This line has only one stop—Morris Island."

Chance shook his head, muttering something under his breath.

Ben's grin widened.

Ben parked in his usual spot and killed the engine. The sun was setting, painting the western sky in a staggering array of oranges, pinks, and purples. I stumbled out, still shaking off the surge of adrenaline that had accompanied our headlong flight.

Chance closed the back door, then stood with his arms crossed, a look of annoyance on his face. "Does this place even have an address?"

Hi yawned and stretched, rotating his arms in wide circles. "Tell them to find where the sidewalk ends, then keep going. We're the neighborhood at the end of the world."

"Helpful."

Chance began dialing, but I motioned for him to stop. "We're all here, so let's decide what to do next. I can't be the only one thinking time is short."

"We didn't learn much." Shelton shirt-wiped his glasses, then popped them back onto his nose. "Ashley Bodford knows Will Speckman, and she *might* be Viral, but we can't say for sure. And it's not like we can just ask her. Also, some creepy suit-wearing dudes may or may not have been following us today. Can't ask *them,* neither."

"The girl with Speckman goes to Bolton," Hi pointed out. "That's something, at least."

Ben grunted, but otherwise kept quiet. My eyes found Chance.

"We have to confront Ashley," he said. "I see no other way. And maybe finding the Trinity will help unmask whoever else is watching us."

I agreed. When you only have one lead, that's the one you follow.

Headlights flashed across the parking lot. A second later Kit's 4Runner appeared, waited for our garage door to rise, and pulled inside.

"Let's talk more tonight," I whispered quickly. "I'll set up a video chat, and—"

"Tory?" Kit's voice floated on the calm evening air. "That you, kiddo?"

"Yeah." *Ugh. Go inside.* "Hey."

Footsteps approached. I could make out my father's skinny frame in the dying light.

"I just want to give you a heads-up." Kit nodded toward the boys, then did a double take upon spotting Chance among them. "Claybourne. It's been a while. Didn't know you came out this way."

"Sir." Chance extended a hand, which Kit shook. "Just stopping by."

"We crossed paths at the library," I said quickly. "Chance is interested in a book Shelton mentioned, so he hitched a ride out here. His driver is coming to get him, but it might take a while. Okay if he waits at our place?"

"His driver. Right." Kit chuckled. "Not a problem. I'll have my butler take care of you."

Chance feigned a laugh at my father's lame joke.

Please, please go inside.

Kit refocused on me. "I came over to tell you—you'll need to feed yourself tonight. I've got a pile of work to do and Whitney's at her bridge club."

"Okay." My curiosity got the better of me. "Something wrong?"

"Too many morons in the world." Kit's lips curled into a frown. "Some day-tripping yahoos visited Loggerhead Island this morning and stirred up trouble. Smashed things, made a mess. Now I have to write a dozen incident reports for the environmental commission. As if I don't have enough to do."

Shelton's eyes narrowed. "Smashed things?"

Kit nodded tiredly. "They took out the wolf-pack feeders. Painted hooky symbols on a few trees, which got the monkeys all riled. H-troop bolted their territory in the northern woods and won't go back. You wouldn't *believe* the howling."

Kit yawned, apparently missing the electric tension that had infused our group.

"What hooky symbols?" I asked, as casually as possible.

"Triangles." Kit snorted in disbelief. "Big black-and-white triangles all over the place, and a red-eyed dog face on one of the feeders. Like these bozos were taunting Whisper's pack. People can be such idiots."

My eyes flicked to Chance. Then Ben. No one needed to say it.

The Trinity.

On Loggerhead.

"Anyway, I'll be in my office for the next few hours. Whitney won't be back until late, so eat whatever you can find."

"Okay." Struggling to keep my voice calm. Then a mad impulse. "I may go out for dinner instead, then. I mean, *we* may. The five of us. That okay?"

Kit waved as he turned for home. "Fine. Have fun. If it's pizza, bring me some."

He walked into our garage. I waited impatiently for the door to close.

"Damn it, Tory." Shelton was already tugging an ear.

"You heard him."

"But why go out there?" he whined. "Just to see more pictures?"

Hi tapped Shelton on the temple. "Use your head, dummy."

"Well, I don't understand either," Chance complained. "I'm not going home now?"

Ben snapped his fingers. "The camping gear."

I nodded, impressed. "Exactly."

Realization dawned in Shelton's eyes. "You think Speckman's still out there. Maybe all of them."

"Why else would he need the gear?" My voice sped up as I spoke. "And why hit Loggerhead Island, the one place besides Morris we're most connected to? A place where we'd *definitely* hear about their handiwork."

"It's a challenge," Ben growled. "They want us to come."

Chance and Hi muttered their agreement. Even Shelton conceded the point.

My fists found my hips.

"I say, game on."

CHAPTER 12

Sewee wound through the sandbars surrounding Morris Island.

Cooper crouched beside me in the bow. The wolfdog didn't love boats, but I wanted him along. Another set of eyes in the darkness.

Ben nosed the runabout clear of the shallows and set course for Loggerhead.

What will we find out there?

Oddly, I felt calm.

My hair fluttered in the breeze as we rode the ocean swells. A nearly full moon lit the sky like a paper lantern. A postcard night for poems and soft dreams.

Shelton and Hi were in the stern, watching for any sign we were being followed. Though Ben was busy piloting, I noticed an occasional glance over his shoulder.

Yet I was confident.

The Trinity had made a mistake. These new Virals were too impulsive, too eager to prove something. They'd given away their position. Soon we'd know who they were.

That would level the playing field.

And, hopefully, restore order.

Chance sat across from me, a bemused expression on his face. "You guys do this often?"

"Do what?"

He waved a hand. "Spontaneous, dangerous, gut-based midnight treks."

"Ah, those." I scratched behind Coop's ear. "Yes. Yes we do."

Chance snorted. "Must be exhausting. I hope they're actually out there. I've got a meeting in the morning, and would hate to lose a night's sleep over nothing."

That dampened my enthusiasm.

What if the Trinity *weren't* still on Loggerhead?

Doubts crept in. Upon reflection, borrowed camping equipment wasn't much to go on. Yet I'd cajoled my friends into a tiny boat speeding out to sea.

We reached the midway point, where, ever so briefly, land dropped from sight in all directions. That moment always gave me a chill, but it went double tonight. I had a sudden jolt of perspective: how small our vessel was in the wide, wild Atlantic.

This is necessary. We need to solve the problem.

But misgivings had taken firm root.

The Trinity weren't even our biggest concern. Not anymore. My mind flashed to grim-faced men in dark suits, staring down from above. An unmarked sedan careening over downtown streets.

Deal with what you can. Table the rest.

Baby steps.

So I watched the eastern horizon. Minutes ticked by, then a smear of black separated itself from the shadows. Moonbeams reflecting off the waves provided just enough light to see.

Beside me, Coop's ear perked. He began to whine.

I closed my eyes, listening. Teased out a discordance over the whirring motor.

Hooting monkeys. Lots of them.

"The troops are flustered," I called back to the others. Chance began rubbing his hands together. Ben nodded, then dropped *Sewee* into a lower gear as we approached shore.

A thin silver line appeared dead ahead. Chile Beach. Named for its sinuous shape as it ran along the western edge of Loggerhead, its loose white sand stretched back a dozen yards to the island's dense interior forest. LIRI old-schoolers called it Dead Cat Beach—because of a yowl the surf made as it slid over the rocks—but that night another sound predominated.

Howling. Loud and outraged.

Ben steered south, hugging the shoreline as he aimed for Logger-head's lone dock—a thin concrete span jutting into the island's natural harbor. Here, silence reigned. No lights burned.

Security is tight at the LIRI compound itself, but not at the landing. No cameras. No fences or gates. Loggerhead Island's isolation—and its absence from most maps—provided the greatest part of its protection.

Someone found it anyway. And now we'll find them.

"No other boats," Chance noted glumly.

"The Trinity wouldn't dock here." Ben slowed to a crawl as we drifted closer to the pier. "Not if they're trying to avoid detection. There's shallow water all around Loggerhead. You can anchor in a dozen places and simply wade ashore. We do it all the time."

Hi and Shelton grabbed tie ropes and vaulted onto the dock. After quickly securing bow and stern, they helped haul the wolfdog over the side. Coop hit the ground running, scampering down the pier and into the woods before I could so much as whistle.

"Where's the dog going?" Chance whispered, voice edgy.

"To find his family." I took the hand Ben offered, and he pulled me up. "Cooper was born out here. He always checks in with his mother's pack first thing."

Chance shook his head. "I thought he was going to help."

"He'll be back. Now let's get moving."

We hustled up a steep rise, then along a beaten-earth trail leading toward the LIRI facility. Shadowy woods closed in around us, swallowing our group like an inhaled breath. I heard swishing overhead, knew monkeys were shifting through the canopy, tracking our progress and passing warnings to one another.

Hi halted at the first junction. "I'm no monkey scientist, but the troops definitely seem discombobulated. They're tweaked."

I peered up into the murky branches. "No doubt. Something has them riled."

"It's way too dark in these woods." Though flat toned, I recognized an undercurrent of excitement in Ben's voice. I knew what he was asking. And agreed.

"Light 'em up."

SNAP.

The world spun, then shifted to hyperfocus.

My brain was bombarded by sensory input. Muscles throbbed and tingled.

I paused, gathering myself. Slowing my pulse and respiration.

Then I couldn't help but smile.

I could *feel* my packmates. Closing my eyes, I visualized the lines connecting our minds. Knew the exact location of each.

Somewhere across the island, I sensed Coop stalking through the brush, intent on surprising his older brother. He paused a beat, then howled in joyous recognition. Coop was always happiest when I unleashed the wolf.

Ben stood a pace to my left, flexing and unflexing his fingers. Satisfaction billowed from his mind. No one enjoyed flaring more than he did.

Shelton was pocketing his now-unnecessary glasses. Then he cocked an ear, straining to hear every rustling leaf.

Behind me, Hi spun in a circle, eyes blazing as he scanned the forest for trouble.

I could even sense Chance. There was no bond between us, but I could feel his presence. Foreign, almost alien. Yet somehow familiar at core. Like an identical jigsaw puzzle, but with the pieces cut differently and switched all around.

Opening my golden eyes, I found Chance's red ones locked onto me. The intensity of his gaze made me shiver. Then he looked away, just missing the scarlet flush that infused my cheeks.

Some things never change.

Shaking off jitters, I tested my pack's connection.

Hello, boys.

Yo. Hiram.

Here. Ben.

Still not cool. Shelton.

Sister-friend. Coop, far away.

I glanced at Chance. Raised an eyebrow.

Jaw clenched, he angrily shook his head.

Can you hear me, Chance?

His expression didn't change. He was clearly trying, and just as clearly failing.

Finally, Chance gave up. "Nothing."

I nodded, disappointed but not surprised. "Let's head to Tern Point, where the feeders are. Then we'll walk up Turtle Beach. If we haven't found anything by the time we hit gator territory, we can—"

"Sweet Jesus!" Chance stumbled, gripping the sides of his head.

I grabbed an arm to steady him. Surprisingly, Ben hooked the other. The older boy slumped between us, trembling in our hands. "Chance?" I hissed. "What's wrong?"

His scarlet eyes were wide with shock. "I can't hear *you* in my mind. But I hear *them*."

Shelton snagged his earlobe and yanked. "What do you mean, them? Like, *them* them?"

Gripping Chance by the shoulder, I forced eye contact. "You can hear the Trinity?"

He nodded dumbly. "Kind of. Like a radio playing in another room. Weak, but it's there."

"Naturally." Ben dropped Chance's arm. "Since you're in *their* pack, not ours."

Shut it, Ben. I gave him a warning look. *Not here. Not tonight.*

Ben looked away. *Fine.*

"Oh, snap!" Hi lifted two thumbs-ups. "We've got a wiretap!"

Chance was trying to gather himself. "I can't hear what they're thinking, if that's what you mean. The connection is too . . . too . . ." He struggled for words. "Flimsy. Too tenuous. Like I'm listening to a butt-dialed voice message. I'm not sure . . ."

Chance quieted for a long moment, periodically shaking his head.

You think he blew a fuse? Catching my eye, Shelton nodded discreetly at Chance. *Don't forget, he was crazy before. Like, nuthouse loco.*

Maybe he gets satellite radio, too. Hi tapped his temple. *We owe it to ourselves to check.*

He's one of them. Ben's denunciation was laced with scorn. *I say we leave him in the woods.*

Enough! I glared at the boys. *Chance and the Trinity caught the same strain of parvovirus. Just as we did, from Coop. It makes sense that he's on their . . . channel. Wavelength. Whatever.*

He is wolf. Coop's sending arrowed through the ether and landed in my brain. His message had the tone of a grade-school lesson. *Pack can change. Wolf is wolf.*

Chance was glancing from face to face, no doubt aware he was a topic of silent debate.

Who knows? Perhaps he could feel it.

"I'm not crazy." Chance blew out a breath. "I can sense their communications, but can't hear the content. And I get the impression they don't know I'm listening. But if I push too hard—like trying to actually read their thoughts—I'm certain they'll detect me. Shut me out for good."

"Then what's the point?" Ben challenged. "You can't help at all."

Chance spoke through gritted teeth. "Would you like to know exactly where they are?"

Before anyone could answer, Chance pointed to the right-hand path. "That way. Maybe three hundred yards. All three of the bastards."

Jackpot.

Hi, Shelton, and even Ben nodded at once. I hadn't realized I'd sent the thought.

Smiling coldly, I gestured down the trail.

"Lead the way, Claybourne."

CHAPTER 13

"Do you see it?" Chance whispered.

"Yes." I was annoyed by having to speak, but with Chance there was no choice.

Of course I saw it. We were crouched side-by-side at the edge of a tree line, flare-eyes blazing. With my powers unleashed, the moonlit clearing before me sparkled like Christmas.

A tent had been erected beside an ancient oak in the meadow's center. To its right, three folding chairs surrounded what looked like an unlit camp stove. Pale yellow light leaked from inside the shelter, but no people were visible.

"I can . . ." Chance squinted, as if straining to listen. "I hear them . . . inside my head. Three voices. Muffled. But I can't see their faces. I don't . . ."

Then Chance's eyelids snapped open, red fire spilling from his irises. He pointed to the middle of the clearing. "There. I'm sure of it."

"Okay." I glanced at my packmates, huddled a step behind me. *Ready?*

Shelton was bouncing on the balls of his feet. *Tory, do you realize where we are?*

I frowned. *What? Where?*

Hi jabbed a finger dead ahead. *That is the clearing, Tory! Where it all started. This is where we found Katherine Heaton.*

My breath caught. Memories came flooding back.

An angry monkey. The weathered dog tag. Our midnight dig.

Discovering a young woman's bones.

Before the supervirus. Before the sickness. Before everything else that occurred.

We'd uncovered a grisly murder in this exact spot.

Emotions roiled through me, unexpectedly intense.

We'd been in this position before.

Stalking these woods in the dead of night. Trying to solve a mystery. *Full circle.*

And not just us. Ben's voice boomed inside my brain as he glared at Chance's back. *Don't forget, your buddy Claybourne was here that night as well. He and his henchmen, chasing us through the forest with guns.*

Ben's rancorous sending shocked me. Mainly because it was true.

My eyes darted to the boy crouching beside me. Was Chance playing us again?

Ben certainly thought so. *We're relying solely on him. I don't like this.*

Shelton fidgeted behind me, his thoughts oozing suspicion as he rattled off points. *Chance claims he can hear the Trinity. He brought us here all by himself. But what are the odds they'd come to this exact place on their own? A random field that's only important to us, on an isolated island almost no one knows about.*

Ben's eyes narrowed dangerously. *A place he knows as well as we do.*

Chance turned, sensing another hidden conversation. "What's going on?"

Accuse him. There was nothing playful in Hi's tone. *See what happens.*

"You're working with them," I blurted, watching Chance closely. "The Trinity."

"What?" His eyebrows climbed his forehead. "Of course not! Why would you say that?"

"Remember this place?" I hissed. "I certainly do. I can still feel the bullets zipping past my head."

Chance spun back to face the clearing. Froze. "Sweet Jesus."

He whirled, startled me by grabbing one of my hands, his fiery gaze brimming with intensity. "Victoria Brennan, I'm not lying. I don't know why the Trinity came to this spot, but I had *nothing* to do with it."

Ben edged closer. My hand rose to stop him.

I stared into Chance's glowing red eyes. He didn't flinch. Didn't look away.

Chance's voice grew plaintive. "I'm with you. I swear it."

After a long moment, I nodded slowly. "Okay. I believe you."

Don't be stupid! Ben's anger surged through our bond. *I thought you don't believe in coincidence?*

"I *don't* believe in coincidence," I said aloud, removing my hand from Chance's and focusing on the tent. "There's an explanation. Right out there."

Ben seemed ready to argue further, but Shelton intervened. *Let it go, man. We've got no choice but to trust Chance tonight. We're in too deep.*

I heard Ben shift behind me. *Hiram? Back me up!*

Hi mentally shrugged. *We'll ask plenty of questions later. I promise.*

Ben's thoughts were scorching. *Fine. For now.*

I reached back to squeeze Ben's arm, but he pulled away. Oh well.

"I hear them again!" Chance was staring into the clearing. "It's coming from the tent."

"One person?" I whispered, scanning for any sign the tent was occupied. "Or all three?"

"I'm not sure. My sense is vague." He aimed a finger at the blue nylon dome beside the meadow's lonely tree. "But it's definitely that direction."

I rolled my shoulders, trying to ease tense muscles. "Options?"

Bull rush. With action imminent, Ben was all business. *Straight in. See what we catch.*

Could work. I sensed Hi weighing options. *They don't know we're here, and we've got the numbers advantage.*

Careful! Shelton cautioned. *We all thought this was some kind of challenge. That means the Trinity* wanted *us to come.*

True. But perhaps we moved quicker than expected. Not everyone prowls the dead of night.

Virals do.

I made the call. "Chance and Ben, rush the tent. The rest of us will circle, keeping watch." I turned, caught the attention of both older boys. "We want to corner them. Identify the other two members of the Trinity. Get answers. That's it for now. Understood?"

Ben nodded impatiently. *If they play nice, I'll play nice.*

"I'm not looking for a fight," Chance assured me. "I share a bond with these three, obviously. Hopefully . . ."

He didn't finish. Didn't need to.

None of us knew what was about to happen.

I gave the clearing a last scan. Took a deep breath.

Go.

We fired from the trees in silence. Streaking across the field, we reached the tent in seconds. Ben didn't hesitate, grabbing the zipper, ripping it upward, and charging inside. Chance was a heartbeat behind him.

The light inside the tent disappeared. I felt a stab of panic from Ben.

I froze, unsure what was happening.

"Whaa!" Chance grunted. I heard a dull thud, followed quickly by another.

A flash of pain touched my mind.

Back! The force of Ben's sending rocked me. *Trap!*

"Ben!?" I shouted, abandoning stealth. "Chance!?"

"Don't come inside!" Chance yelled, his voice strangely muffled. "We've fallen into some kind of hole!"

Tiger pit! Hi grabbed one of the tent's nylon walls and pulled.

The stakes held. I moved to help while Shelton turned his back to mine, trying to watch everywhere at once. A few more tugs ripped the tent from the ground.

We stepped back, stared down in shock.

Chance and Ben were tangled at the bottom of a ten-foot pit. It was a miracle neither had broken their neck. Ben winced as he worked an elbow. Having gone in first, he appeared to have gotten the worst of it, though blood oozed from a gash on Chance's cheek.

Suddenly, Chance grabbed his head with a grimace. "I can hear them clearly now! They're taunting me." His jaw clenched. "I'm such an idiot! They led me here like a child. Now they . . ."

Chance's eyes rounded. "Get back, Tory! They're right above—"

His whole body jerked. Chance made an unnatural sound, then his eyes rolled back. I watched in horror as he slumped against the wall of the pit, face slack, drool spilling from his mouth.

"Chance!"

Then his warning registered.

My eyes shot to the branches overhanging the campsite.

Three sets of red eyes glared down at me.

A cold voice hissed from above.

"Hello, cousins. Glad you could make it."

Backpedaling, I noticed a crisscross pattern blocking the moonlight.

No time to cry out. I dove to the side just as the cargo net released, trapping Hi and Shelton underneath. Then I scrambled to my feet, trying not to panic.

The largest shape dropped from the tree.

When it stepped forward, I recognized Will Speckman.

He sneered at me, a tall, sturdy boy with dark brown hair and heavy eyebrows.

"You must be Tory."

My eyes darted back to the branches, but even flaring I couldn't make out the other two hiding in the shadows.

"What happened to Chance?" First question I could think of.

Speckman shrugged, red eyes sparkling with amusement. "Not sure, honestly. We shut him down. He'd been spying on us, so we had to nip that in the bud. Then again, I guess it's not really spying if we *let* him hear. But that's over now."

"Get me out of here!" Ben snarled from below. "You've got ten seconds."

Shelton and Hi had stopped struggling with the net, and were listening to every word.

Speckman laughed, eyes never leaving me. "Don't worry, someone's coming for you."

The hair on my arms rose. "What do you mean?"

Speckman ignored the question. "Honestly, I thought you guys would be better than this. You've had so much more time to practice. But I guess your virus was the weaker strain. Which is why you have to go."

I felt a tingling in my subconscious, but ignored it. "Who's coming, Will?"

"Charleston is a one-pack town, Brennan. Ours." He swept a lazy hand toward his companions lurking in the tree. I stared hard, but still couldn't see their faces. "Sorry, but this is how it has to be."

"What are you talking about?" The tingling became an itch. I was too distracted to notice. "You're not making sense. What's wrong with Chance?"

Speckman's expression hardened. "No wolf should abandon his pack."

Then the itch exploded inside my head, pushing all other thoughts aside.

Sister-friend.

Coop's sending thundered in my mind.

We come.

I smiled. Felt a surge of adrenaline.

"You made a mistake, Will. You didn't catch us all."

He snorted. "You're gonna stop us, alone?"

Leaves rustled behind me.

Speckman's gaze flicked over my shoulder.

"Alone?" I barked a laugh. "Guess you haven't met the extended family."

A heavy form burst from the bushes.

Coop exploded past me, a gray blur followed closely by two others. Polo and Buster—Coop's dad and brother—shadowed my packmate as he buzzed Speckman's legs, snapping his massive jaws. The canine trio formed a moving circle around their quarry, teeth bared and fur bristling.

Speckman's eyes popped, but he recovered quickly, lashing a booted foot at Buster as he padded by. "You think these dogs scare me!?" Speckman darted forward and swung a fist at Polo, but the wolfdog nimbly leaped aside.

A deep, low growl split the night air.

The noise echoed across the clearing, sending shivers up my spine.

The circling canines halted, sitting back on their haunches and watching Speckman with luminous golden eyes.

Speckman froze, the first trace of fear pinching his features.

I didn't turn. Crossed my arms. Arched an eyebrow at my adversary.

I knew who had arrived.

Whisper stalked from the shadows, silently gliding to my side, her gleaming eyes pinned to the red-eyed Viral before me. A full-grown gray wolf, her head rose well past my waist. She paused, as if in judgment.

Then Cooper's mother bared her teeth at Speckman with unmistakable malice.

Flaring ears amped, I heard sharp intakes of breath from the pair in the branches. Scarlet eyes shot toward each other, then back to the angry, bristling, terrifying alpha wolf crouching beside me.

Whisper growled a second time. I felt it in my bones.

"Whoa. Take it easy." Speckman tried to watch all four animals at once. "Can't you guys take a joke?"

Hi giggled beneath the heavy cargo net. "You're dog food, bro. Shouldn't have messed with the lady's feeder."

Movement inside the hole.

"Blue!" Chance barked in a strained voice. "On my shoulders."

Shelton had wiggled his upper body free of the rope prison. *Cooper! Little help!*

My wolfdog glanced over, then trotted to Shelton's aid.

Buster and Polo inched toward Speckman, tightening the noose. The tall boy jab-stepped at one, then the other, sweat glistening his forehead. But his eyes never left the wolf.

"Call them off!" He raised his hands. "I'll talk. I have information you need!"

Fur bristling, tail erect, Whisper stepped closer to Speckman.

A rough, primal message crackled inside my head, more image than words.

Pack. Protect. Fight.

Not yet, my friend. A moment.

Whisper growled a third time, but halted.

Moment. Only.

Thank you.

We came to *corner* the Trinity, not rip them to shreds. But could I call off Whisper even if I wanted to? She didn't seem interested in negotiation. Likely didn't understand the concept.

"What information?" I pointed to the snarling wolf at my side. "Talk fast. She doesn't take orders from me."

One of Ben's arms snaked from the pit. With Shelton death-gripping his collar, Coop dragged my skinny friend free of the net. Hi had given up trying to escape and simply watched the action, hands propping his chin, a little boy absorbing Saturday morning cartoons.

Speckman opened his mouth to speak, then seemed to think twice. His head tilted like a bird's. Then his body went still, his face curiously blank.

Something's—

Two thumps sounded in the darkness.

My eyes shot to the branches, found them empty.

Look out!

Shadows darted at Buster and Polo. The two dogs scampered back, yipping in pain and surprise.

Speckman spun and ran for a break in the circle.

Whisper was quicker.

Moving faster than thought, she bounded forward and knocked Speckman from his feet. A massive paw dropped onto his back.

Speckman screamed in terror.

Everyone froze. Ben. Shelton. The two dark silhouettes at the campsite's edge. Even my canine allies. My hand shot out, though I was too far away to intervene. *Whisper, no!*

The wolf crouched over Speckman's prone form. He tensed, but wisely didn't move. I could see Whisper's hot breath misting the back of his exposed neck.

Enemy.

Yes, I sent. *But we can't hurt him.*

I added a series of images. A flood of people on Loggerhead. Traps set for her pack. Her family being taken away in cages.

Leave him to us.

Whisper hesitated, teeth bared, eyes gleaming.

Everything teetered on the brink.

A stab of light arrowed from the sky, knifing across the clearing.

My head jerked up in surprise. I glimpsed spinning black rotors against a bright moon. Then a familiar low hum broke the stillness.

"The helicopter!" I screamed.

The spotlight found me. Blinded me. Rooted me to the ground.

The chopper circled, its powerful beam never straying from my face.

My legs locked in terror. I couldn't move.

SNUP.

My flare vanished with a rush of lost energy, wobbling me.

Whisper peered skyward, startled by this strange intruder.

Speckman took advantage—flipping to his back, he flexed his legs and kneed the wolf in her chest. Whisper howled and leaped aside. Moving like quicksilver, Speckman barely rose from all fours as he fled into the forest.

Twin shadows followed at his back.

The Trinity, slipping through our fingers.

I stared, frozen, as the helicopter hovered directly above me, its spotlight zeroed on my bloodless face.

A length of black rope thumped to the ground beside me. Then another.

Then Ben was there, grabbing my hand and dragging me away. "Tory, run!"

The wolf pack scattered into the trees. Shelton dragged Hiram free of the cargo net, then the two boys pushed it halfway into the hole for Chance to climb.

But I was still mired in quicksand, hypnotized by the merciless light.

Finally, my flight instinct kicked in.

Clutching Ben's hand, I raced for the trees.

CHAPTER 14

Overhead, monkeys screeched and scattered.

Down below, I ran.

Panicked, legs hammering, I pounded through the undergrowth.

Who was that?! How did they find us?

Shapes loomed in the dark. Trees? Bushes? Without my flare power, I couldn't tell.

Heart thumping, I barreled forward in a dead sprint.

A branch snagged my shoulder and I nearly fell, saved only by Ben's hand around mine. He steadied me, a solid silhouette in the otherwise featureless dark. A shaft of moonlight caught his eyes, which had reverted to their normal dark brown.

"You okay?"

I nodded, ignoring the pain radiating from my shoulder.

Something heavy crashed through the underbrush beside us. I froze. Made no sound.

It could be any of them!

Suddenly, I was pummeled by a wave of déjà vu so powerful it nearly dropped me to my knees. This same wild flight. From the same clearing. Only a short year ago.

Life can be crazy sometimes.

"We have to keep moving!" Ben hissed.

"Go!" Gritting my teeth from the ache in my side. "Back to the boat."

Ben nodded, squeezing my hand as we scrambled through the ghostly woods.

Where were Hi and Shelton? What about Chance? Did he manage to get out of the hole?

I felt a flash of guilt at leaving him, but saw no other choice.

The Trinity were somewhere in these trees, too. Bastards. Had they tipped the agents?

I refused to acknowledge the implications of that helicopter.

The black ropes, landing in the clearing.

Faceless killers could be fanning across the island right now. Could be anywhere.

They found us again. How?

I mouthed a prayer of thanks that we'd formed a contingency plan. Meet back at the boat, if possible. If not, make for the temporary landing near Tern Point. Ben loved to fish there. We all knew the spot.

So I trailed Ben through a dense glade, never letting go of his fingers. I sucked in deep breaths. Flaring had wrung me dry. Always did.

Now I can't reach the others. Can't send a message. Damn it.

We were in trouble.

No doubting it anymore.

Packed earth thudded beneath my sneakers.

"The path," Ben whispered. "We're not far from the dock."

"Good job. I just hope the others were as lucky."

Ben nodded. Together we snuck down to the trail junction, then hurried toward Loggerhead's pier. I spied our vessel from the top of the rise, and my spirits sank. "Empty."

I sensed Ben shrug in the darkness. "Better than loaded with MIBs."

"True. What should we do?"

Ben thought a moment. "I say we go ahead and move *Sewee* to Tern Point. When the others get here, they'll know what to do, even if the boat being gone scares them a bit. That way we don't stand around exposed. The chopper could circle back here at any time. We need to move *Sewee* somewhere they won't look."

All good points. "Okay. But let's be careful—this would be an excellent spot for a trap."

"I know," Ben muttered, ear-tucking his hair. "It's what I'd do."

Moving as quietly as possible, we snuck downslope and along the dock. While I untied lines, Ben jumped aboard and fired the engine. I kept every sense on high alert, straining for sounds of pursuit, a glimpse of our friends, or the return of that damned invisible helicopter you couldn't hear coming. I cursed the loss of my flare powers, knowing how inferior normal human senses were.

But no one appeared. Nothing flew overhead. I wasn't sure whether that was good or bad, but Ben was right. We needed to move the boat. The dock was too hot a location.

As Ben eased *Sewee* oceanward, bushes shook along the cliff face.

A pair of red eyes appeared. Stared down at me.

I opened my mouth to shout for Chance, but the greeting died in my throat.

A second pair of scarlet orbs appeared by the first. Then a third.

Not Chance.

The Trinity had come to watch us depart.

Something brushed against my mind. A cold touch that sent shivers all over.

That almost felt like a sending. A Viral touch, but not one . . .

With a start, I understood. Slammed my defenses into place. The feeling vanished.

But I knew the score.

The Trinity had been picking at my thoughts.

I felt a groundswell of anger, unlike anything I could recall. These stupid, reckless *children*. Flaunting their flare powers. Playing games. Drawing attention!

They risked everything, for all of us.

I nearly screamed at the watchers, before remembering that more dangerous foes were prowling Loggerhead Island that night.

Instead, I gave them the only salute I could think of.

Two middle fingers. Held high for emphasis.

The six fiery orbs winked out at once. Hopefully, they'd died from affront.

Ben eyed me sideways as he maneuvered from shore. "What in the world are you doing?"

"Those red-eyed jerks were on the cliff," I spat, then immediately felt silly. "All I could think of."

Ben made an odd huffing sound I couldn't interpret. For a shocked second, I thought he was furious with me.

"Nice work, Victoria." Ben couldn't hold the laughter inside. "That oughta do it!"

I flinched, surprised by his reaction. Ben, cracking up at a time like this?

He had such a full, honest laugh—I wished I heard it more. Infectious, too. I couldn't help joining in, though mine came out in a low *Beavis and Butthead* cackle. Which made Ben howl even more.

In an instant, we were both in stitches at the absurdity of my one-finger salutes. At the insanity of the evening. At everything. Tears wet my eyes as *Sewee* bobbed over the surf, circling the southeast corner of the island. It was a release I desperately needed.

Ben ran a hand through his hair, then sighed deeply. "I love it," he snickered, steering *Sewee* through the breakers, keeping our speed to a crawl so the engine made less noise. "I love you, sometimes."

Abruptly, his good humor cut off like a guillotine. Ben's body went rigid. I felt a wave of panic roll from him, as if he'd accidentally triggered a nuclear bomb.

I experienced a parallel stab of distress. My stomach lurched into my throat, and not because of the rolling ocean swells.

Did he just . . . what did he mean when. . . .

Oh crap.

Ben's eyes darted to me, then shot back to open water. Even in the semidarkness, I saw a flush of red steal up his neck and into his cheeks.

I shifted uncomfortably in my seat. Shifted again. Debated going over the side.

Did he really mean to say he . . . loved me? Like, for real?

The awkward moment stretched longer than any event in human history.

He said "sometimes," which is a definite qualifier. I love Chinese food "sometimes."

Mouth opened as I searched for words that might defuse the tension. Came up with nothing. I felt trapped in a nightmare. Balanced on a beam a hundred feet off the ground. Sinking underwater in a sealed car, with no idea how to get out.

Ben's lips parted, then worked soundlessly, as if he, too, sought to break the horrible awkwardness. A verbal retreat, or some way to reverse time.

Is that what I want? For Ben to walk it back?

A part of me was astounded by the chaos a single four-word utterance could create.

Ben gulped a breath, seemed to reach a decision. As his mouth opened a second time, all the adrenaline in creation poured into my system.

"I . . . I was just saying that . . ." He trailed off, then smacked the steering wheel with his palm. Ben squeezed his eyes shut, shaking his head sharply as if disgusted by the effort.

Ben turned. Blasted me with his full attention. "I meant it. I'm not going to act—"

A light flashed somewhere close by, killing the conversation.

"We've got company!" Ben killed the motor and power, leaving *Sewee* adrift.

"Another boat?" I peered skyward. "The helo?"

"Boat." Ben's knuckles whitened on the steering wheel. "I hope it didn't see us."

I heard the distant whine of an outboard motor. Seconds later, something huge passed overhead. The helicopter, its cabin dark, flew directly toward a cluster of lights bobbing in the water farther offshore.

"Crap." Ben's face knotted with tension.

He didn't have to say it.

The boat and chopper were clearly together.

Sewee rolled over another wave, drifting closer to the jagged rocks lining Loggerhead's southern coastline. I worried we might run aground, but Ben seemed unconcerned, so I kept the thought to myself. I focused on the lights appearing and disappearing with each passing swell.

"The boat's getting closer," Ben whispered.

Then a yellow beam stabbed directly overhead.

"Down!" I slid from the copilot's seat onto the deck. Ben slithered down beside me. We lay on our backs, shoulder to shoulder, watching the high-powered spotlight slice the air.

The engine sounds grew louder. I could barely breathe. The beam swept left to right, no more than an inch above the runabout's rails. I was sure we'd be spotted at any moment, and this time, there was nowhere to run.

Ben's breathing quickened. I felt his biceps tense against my shoulder.

The whine rose until I was sure the other boat was right alongside us. Voices carried across the water, low and indistinct. My mind raced, debating the merits of capture versus a night swim in the deep, dark Atlantic.

Then, slowly, the sounds began to fade. The spotlight danced above us one last time, then disappeared. In less than a minute, all was quiet once more.

I released a breath I didn't remember holding. Turned to Ben.

Found him looking at me, face inches from mine on *Sewee*'s deck.

Panic flared, white hot, paralyzing me as I lay beside him.

Our gazes met. I saw fear in his dark brown eyes. Indecision. Doubt.

Ben went rigid, his chest rising and falling like a bellows. Then something changed. His face relaxed, a small smile playing on his lips.

Before I could blink, his mouth covered mine.

We shared a breath. A tingle ran my spine.

For a moment, I lost all track of time and space.

Then I pulled back, breathing hard, unsure what either my mind or body were doing.

Ben's unsure look returned. Then vanished.

He pulled me near again, his lips melting into mine. Strong, calloused fingers stroked the side of my face. His smell enveloped me. Earthy. Masculine. Ben.

Fire rolled through my body.

So this is what it's like.

I broke away again, gasping slightly for breath. Reality crashed home.

I sat up and scooted a few feet away, rubbing my face with both hands. What was I doing?

"Ben, I—"

His hand rose to cut me off. He leaned against the bench, face suddenly serious. "I'm not going to pretend anymore. One way or another, I'm going to say how I feel." Ben snorted softly. "Make my case."

We sat still in the darkness, *Sewee* rocking gently, the scene dreamlike and surreal.

"You don't have to make a case." I stared at my shoes, had no idea where I wanted this conversation to go. "It's just, things are—"

"YO!"

Our heads whipped in the voice's direction. Ben scrambled to a crouch, scanning the silent bulk of Tern Point, as if just now recalling we were adrift at sea.

The voice called down again, suddenly familiar. "What, are you guys *paddling* around the island? I don't have a boat license, but that seems dumb."

"Shut up, Hi!" Ben shouted, with more heat than was necessary. Scowling, he slid behind the controls and fired the engine.

I scurried to the bow, as far from the captain's chair as I could manage and stay dry.

You've done it now, Tory Brennan. Better hope there's a life preserver somewhere.

A glance back. Ben was watching me, looking for all the world like he had more to say.

I quickly turned away.

Nope. Nope nope nope.

I needed some time to think about this one. Perhaps a decade?

"Where are we?" I asked, changing the subject.

Ben must've sensed that my "personal" shop was closed for business. "Just below the platform," he answered flatly. "I'll pull up to Turtle Beach." He nodded to a white-sand expanse twenty yards ahead.

Though I still couldn't see him, Hi understood. "We'll meet you down there. Shelton and me, I mean. Haven't seen Chance."

Damn it.

Where was Chance? Had he gotten out of that hole?

I thought back to those red eyes watching from the cliffs above the dock.

That couldn't have been Chance up there, could it? Not with members of the Trinity.

Right?

Ben's suspicions flashed through my mind. I shoved them away. In fact, I shoved everything to do with Ben away, my defense mechanisms firing on all cylinders.

As *Sewee* entered the shallows, Ben leaped into the surf and towed the runabout ashore.

Hi and Shelton emerged from the forest, looking relieved.

"Thank God!" Shelton never paused, wading out to *Sewee*, climbing aboard, and collapsing on the bench. His powers were doused. "I cannot tell you how tired I am of running through these woods!"

"Keep it down," Ben warned. "The chopper bugged out, but there's a boat, too."

Shelton straightened as Hi flopped over the rail. "Boat? What boat?"

"We think it's with the helicopter." I quickly explained what we'd seen at sea.

Then I thought of what had happened next, and my ears burned. I was sure the truth was plastered across my face, had either Shelton or Hi bothered to look.

But they were watching the trees.

"Hear that?" Hi whispered, no longer flaring either.

"Yep." Ben was still standing in waist-deep water. "Someone's coming."

Chance emerged from the forest, backpedaling slowly, hands above his head.

Oh no!

My blood turned to ice. I waited for black-clad soldiers to follow, guns trained.

Instead, three sinuous shapes stalked from the understory.

The smaller two scurried to flank Chance, forcing him to face the largest head on.

I was first to react. "Whisper, no!"

I vaulted into the water and struggled toward shore.

The pack didn't glance my way. They coiled, eyes locked on the trembling figure.

Things were about to get very, very bad for Chance Claybourne.

He threw a desperate look over his shoulder, eyes blazing with red light.

"Chance, snuff your powers!" I shouted, muscling a path through the shallow water. "Whisper thinks you're an enemy!"

As if on cue, Whisper growled. Exposed her gleaming white teeth.

"Oh crap." Chance waved his hands, as if trying to persuade the wolf to hear him out. "I'm with you! Promise!" His frame shook, then Chance dropped to a knee, hacking up a lung. "You see?" He wheezed. "No more flare!"

Whisper bayed loudly.

I was certain she was about to charge.

Then Cooper burst from the trees and planted himself between Chance and his mother.

My wolfdog growled deep in his throat.

Whisper paused. Cocked her head. Then she barked loudly and jabbed her paws.

Coop didn't budge. Barked right back.

Both animals fell silent. For a few heartbeats, time itself stopped.

Then Whisper sat back on her haunches. Yapped twice. Coop seemed to stand down as well. He trotted forward and licked his mother's nose. She nuzzled him back.

Chance hadn't moved a millimeter. "What's happening?"

Finally ashore, I trudged over and slapped Chance on the back, nearly causing him to jump from his skin. "Coop just vouched for you." My tone grew serious. "Don't make him regret it."

Chance lowered his shaking hands.

He nodded to Coop when the wolfdog glanced his way.

"No. No, I certainly won't."

CHAPTER 15

We rode back in silence.

Ben was in the captain's seat, busy navigating the tricky mass of sandbars between Morris and Loggerhead. Shelton and Chance huddled up front, watching for other ships. I sat on the stern bench next to Hi, with Coop curled at my feet.

Secretly watching Ben's back.

Though my eyes darted away every time he seemed about to glance over his shoulder.

He never did. The moment—*our* moment—had passed, whatever it was.

Would it come again? I knew it was my imagination, but I could almost feel the walls rebuilding inside him.

Was that what I wanted? To bury what happened with a shovel, and then bury the shovel?

I ran a finger over my lips, replaying the moment his touched mine. The memory was electric, like grabbing a power line. Shocking. Surreal. Yet I couldn't stop. I thought about it over and over and over.

Me. Ben. Together, if only for a few heartbeats.

Was *that* what I wanted? Was *Ben* what I wanted?

I knew he liked me. Had known for months—ever since his tearful confession the day of the hurricane.

My mood soured, remembering those fateful hours. Ben had betrayed the pack because of his feelings for me. He'd unwittingly put hundreds of lives in danger.

Why was I even thinking about this? Stolen kisses on a boat, while maniacal Virals were wreaking havoc all over Charleston. While a covert organization was shadowing our every move?

There might be a worse time to fall in love, but I couldn't imagine it. My breath caught.

Was that what this was? Love? I had zero experience in that area.

Infatuation? Sure. Look no further than my naïve flirtation with Chance last year.

I shifted uncomfortably.

Chance.

Another complication.

Determined to torture me, my brain switched to young Master Claybourne.

The two of us, together on a park bench. His hand clutching mine.

I shook my head, as if my mind were an Etch-a-Sketch I could wipe clean.

Chance had said things, too.

He was so much more direct than Ben. Confident. Self-assured.

For an instant, old fantasies roared back to life. Dating Charleston's most eligible bachelor. Hosting fab parties at Claybourne Manor. Every girl in the city jealous of me. I'd be Charleston's Princess Kate, on the arm of the city's most handsome and powerful scion.

Enough. You're ridiculous.

I'd thought boy trouble was Jason Taylor chasing after me. Seemed like kids' stuff now.

And suddenly Jason's with Madison. I'm still not sure how that makes me feel.

What a mess.

Chance. Ben. Jason.

Could three boys be any more different?

"Blargh."

I rapped both fists against my temples. Once. Twice. Thrice.

Hi gave me a sympathetic look. "Head lice?"

My eyes rolled. "You nailed it."

He nodded knowingly. "I have some of that shampoo at home. It's for my cats, but I can't see why it wouldn't work on you."

"Lovely."

The other boys didn't know anything. Quite obviously, neither Ben nor I had announced we'd semi-made out aboard *Sewee* while they'd been stranded on Loggerhead.

Would they figure it out? Intuit that something happened?

Ben's brooding silence wouldn't raise eyebrows—that was par for the course. But I was sure to crack at the first sign of pressure. Hell, at the first odd glance.

I've never been a good liar. Not to my friends, at least.

Sewee's vibration changed, snapping me from my thoughts. Ben slowed the runabout, nosing into a final stretch of shallow water approaching our island home.

I glanced at my watch. Was stunned to learn it was only nine thirty.

Kit and Whitney wouldn't even be suspicious.

Because you never lie, right?

Okay. Fine.

Beside me, Hiram half rose from his seat. "Hey, what's that?"

He pointed northward, toward the tip of Morris Island.

A soft red glow was building at the entrance to Charleston Harbor.

"What's that light?" Shelton called from the bow, motioning to the same area. "A cruise ship getting in late?"

Coop stirred. His nose lifted, snuffling the night air. Then his eyes swung to meet mine. Whining softly, he rolled to his feet.

"Those ships don't come on Wednesdays." Ben's voice was oddly flat.

Chance climbed up on the bow and rose to his tiptoes. "Red light. But hazy . . . like . . ."

Ben stiffened in his seat, color draining from his face. "Oh crap."

I scurried to his side. "What?"

Ben didn't answer. Instead, he slammed the throttle, gunning *Sewee* in a tight arc toward the strange glow. Chance's arms pinwheeled as the boat accelerated beneath him. He toppled backward onto Shelton, who heroically tried to break his fall.

"Ugh!" Shelton lay on his back, pancaked by the much larger boy.

Chance punched the deck, not far from where I'd lain beside Ben only minutes before. "What the hell, Blue!?"

Then Hi brushed past me, hurtling toward the bow. "No no no no no!"

Coop raised his snout to the sky and howled, low and long.

"Has everyone gone nuts?" Chance demanded, rising unsteadily and helping Shelton up.

I was about to agree when a harsh, acrid scent hit my nostrils.

Everything slammed into place.

"Fire," I whispered.

Instantly, I knew that wasn't the worst of it.

Ben nodded grimly. "On Morris. Near the harbor."

We rounded a large stone outcropping that forms the entrance to our secret cove.

The rock flickered yellow, orange, and red, reflecting a tower of flame behind it.

Dry heat licked my skin, sucking away the moisture.

My eyes rose.

An inferno was raging inside the sand hill.

Our bunker.

Burning like a bonfire.

Smoke billowed from the cannon slit overlooking the water. Tongues of flame danced along its edges.

"How?!" Shelton snatched off his glasses, wiped tears from his eyes. "Who did this?!"

"The spooks?" Hi had both hands on his head, eyes round as Frisbees. "Those freaking helo guys?"

"The Trinity."

I spat the words with all the hate I could muster.

Ben slammed the wheel, nostrils wide as he struggled to control his rage.

"She's right," Chance said softly. "This must've been their plan all along."

"We were duped." I swore bitterly. "Lured away from Morris so they could cut our legs from behind."

So stupid. We've been charging around like blind rhinos.

"All our stuff," Shelton moaned. "All that time and effort. The money!"

Ben punched the wheel a second time. "When I get my hands on—"

There was a rumble deep within the earth, followed by a deafening roar. As we watched, helpless, the sand hill collapsed in on itself. Dirt burst from all sides as the mound imploded in a *whoosh* of heat and flame.

"Back!" Chance shouted, coughing into a fist as dust blanketed our tiny vessel.

Ben quickly reversed course, scooting us farther out to sea.

But it was already over—the collapsing hill doused the fire, thousands of pounds of gravel and earth smothering the flames like a snuffed candle.

The damage was done.

Where our bunker had been, nothing remained but a smoking pile.

I tried to think. To reboot my mind. "Where are Karsten's parvovirus files?"

"My study." Chance tapped his chest. "All of them. Locked in a private safe."

One less worry, at least. "Any chance the solar array survived?"

"None." Hi gestured uselessly at the scorched wreckage. "It was outside the bunker, but *look* at that. The whole damn hill just fell into the mine shaft. It's a total loss."

I glanced at Shelton. "What about the hard drives?"

Shelton's face brightened an iota. "I back everything up wirelessly. Our files are safe."

"The mini-fridge is toast." Hi sighed deeply. "I had a sandwich in there."

I mentally inventoried the rest of our clubhouse. Computer workstation. Table. Chairs. Lamps. Doggie bed. And a back room full of hardware we couldn't afford to replace.

Our secret place. Our sanctuary. Our private Viral oasis.

The Trinity took it from us.

"How'd they find it?" I asked.

"How do you think," Ben spat. "Claybourne, of course!"

Chance spun, irate. "I never told anyone about this place. Ever!"

"They could've ripped it from your mind!" Ben fired back. "It's your fault somehow, I know it. You're connected to *them,* not us."

A look of uncertainty pinched Chance's face. "That's not possible. I . . . I don't—"

"Enough." Spoken quietly, yet they all stilled.

A fire sparked inside me. Grew to match the flames that had enveloped our hideout.

"Okay, then."

Eyes never straying from the smoking remains.

"We're going to identify these people."

Fingers curling into fists.

"We're going to hunt them down."

Fists slamming together.

"We're going to make them pay."

CHAPTER 16

I snuck through the front door.

Shooing Coop before me, I beelined for the stairs and the safety of my bedroom. I hoped to avoid notice for a few minutes—my clothes were dirty and smoke-tinged, my hair a tangled mess.

But it was not to be. Whitney swung from the kitchen before I could blink.

"Tory!" Smiling brightly, she smoothed her apron with manicured fingers. "I was just about to wonder what you'd gotten up to!"

Whitney winked to assure me she was joking, but the cloying attempt at humor annoyed me anyway. It made me want to actually tell her.

I was out on Loggerhead, fighting with another group of genetic freaks, when a black-ops military attack squad tried to capture me. Oh, and Ben and I made out on his boat. You?

I smothered the suicidal notion.

Mad impulses had stirred the pot enough for one night.

"Studying." The one line they always seemed to buy. "Practice test in a few days."

Kit emerged from the kitchen behind Whitney, a half-peeled shrimp dangling from his mouth. "Hey, kiddo."

Whitney punched his shoulder as he moved past us into the living room. "Those are *supposed* to be for tomorrow's potluck."

Kit grinned, wiping cocktail sauce from his lips. "Nobody's going to miss that one. Or his delicious friend."

Whitney aimed a finger at him, face stern, but then dissolved into giggles. Kit chuckled in unison, chomping the purloined crustacean.

God. Barf.

I mean, I get that old people are allowed to be flirty-silly, too.

But not in front of your own daughter, hey?

And . . . there was something else. Whitney's hands kept squirming, her eyes flitting between Kit and me. My father's foot was tapping incessantly. He'd walked to the couch, but made no move to sit.

As I nudged Coop toward his doggie bed, I watched them closely.

Tightness to Kit's eyes. Tension in Whitney's shoulders.

And yet, both were beaming. Their good mood was undeniable, just undercut with . . .

Worry? Excitement? Anxiousness?

Maybe they're drunk.

Kit had on a nicer shirt than the one he'd worn to work that morning. Whitney was wearing a designer sundress. Not uncommon for her, even this late in the evening, but the outfit combination was highly suspicious.

Suddenly they were standing next to each other, grinning like dopes.

I got a sinking feeling in my gut.

An ANNOUNCEMENT was coming.

Kit didn't waste any time. "Whitney and I have something to tell you."

Whitney put a hand to her chest. "At least let her get settled, Kit!"

"Sorry, can't do it." Kit gripped her hand, then turned to face me.

They *both* faced me.

Holding hands.

To tell me something.

All the blood in my body stopped flowing.

Kit wore a smile that stretched across the harbor. "I have asked Whitney to be my wife."

My stomach leaked through my shoes.

Whitney started clapping like a six-year-old. "And I said yes!"

It's happening.

It's really, really happening.

I don't think I moved a muscle. My brain shorted. My eyes locked in place. A corner of my mind agreed with Whitney. They really should've let me get more settled.

"Kiddo?" Kit seemed equally paralyzed. Grin cemented in place, he held Whitney's hand and watched me like a hawk.

His fiancée's hand. I'll have to get used to that.

I couldn't speak. The awkward moment stretched.

Three people, staring in silence across a tiny dining room.

Sensing the tension, Coop padded to my side. I ignored him. Ignored everything.

This is what Kit wants. This is what makes him happy.

He was here first.

"That's . . . that's . . ."

Don't blow this. Don't ruin the moment for your father.

"I'm really . . . very . . ."

Whitney took a small step forward.

Don't. Stop. I can't screw this up.

"Tory?" Whitney spoke softly and sincerely. "Please know that I love your father very much, and—" Abruptly she cut off, eyes widening in alarm. "Sweetheart, you're *filthy*."

Nose crinkling, Whitney reached for my mussed, tangled hair. "There's dirt on your sleeves, and I can smell—"

She'd crafted the perfect escape. Like a release valve forcing open.

"Mind your own business!" Batting her hands away. "Ben's car got stuck in the mud. Is that okay?" Laced with all the sarcasm I could muster.

A part of my brain understood what was happening, but those cells weren't driving.

"God, you're *always* butting in!" I stormed past them both, pounding up the stairs with Coop on my heels. "I don't need a replacement mother!"

And there it was.

I blew it after all.

My steps quickened, fleeing the horror scene I'd no doubt created below.

I waited for Kit to shout. For Whitney to start bawling.

Neither happened.

Which made everything so much worse.

Pushing Coop ahead of me, I slammed my bedroom door, then slid down its length.

Waited for the inevitable footsteps and knock.

That didn't happen either.

Coop hopped onto my bed, circled twice, then settled with his head on his paws.

Watching me. Disapproving, I was sure.

"Don't *you* start." A snivel. I was a slight push from becoming Niagara Falls.

Coop tilted his head sideways.

"Fine. I'm sorry."

I slammed a palm on the carpet.

No.

No no no.

Crazy thing was, I wasn't upset about their engagement.

Surprised? Absolutely. Secretly disappointed? Yes.

But I'd known this day was coming.

I'd feared it. Hid from the possibility. Hoped it might wait until after I'd moved out. But Kit and Whitney getting married would shock absolutely no one. It was time.

No, the anger was at myself. For acting like a spoiled brat. For being incapable of the simple human decency of congratulating two happy people.

For bringing the shadow of my mother into their moment.

The tears came then. Hot and fast, in a torrent unaccompanied by words.

I didn't want to think about Mom. Then hated myself for it.

If *I* didn't remember her, who would? I was all she'd had. *We* were all *we'd* had.

And what had I reduced Mom to?

A club to smash my father's happiness. To batter Whitney, who'd never even met my mother, and had been at Kit's side since before I'd appeared.

Sobbing, I curled into a ball. Shoved my face in a pillow. Coop's frigid nose pressed against my arm, and I gathered him in, too. He wiggled close, nestling his furry head in my chest.

We lay like that until the tears ran dry.

I have to fix this.

My phone buzzed, startling me. Wiping my eyes, I dragged it from my pocket.

Text message. Ben. **Can we talk?**

"Oh my God!" I rolled onto my back and covered my face. "I'm cursed!"

I replied before I could get inside my own head.

Not now. Busy. Talk later.

Then I waited, worried how Ben would take the curt blowoff.

No return message came.

Not good. Knowing Ben, not good at all.

I buried my face in Coop's neck. "How many things can I screw up in one night?"

Coop shook free, then paced over to the door. Looked back.

"Nuh-uh."

But he was right.

I rose, changed into PJs, and washed my face. Then, squaring my shoulders, I left the protective bubble of my room and descended to the main floor.

Kit and Whitney were sitting silently on the couch. The TV was off. They both straightened when they saw me.

I cleared my throat, worried that I might break down again. "I want to apologize."

With the first words out, the rest flowed more easily. "I shouldn't have snapped at you, Whitney. You couldn't have known about our flat tire."

Whitney shifted—quite obviously bursting with things to say—but held her tongue.

Kit watched me with kind eyes, a sad smile on his lips.

I took a deep breath, then continued, not looking at either of them. "I also shouldn't have said what I did about my mother." My voice caught, but I pushed ahead. "That was totally unfair. To both of you. I apologize."

"You don't have to apologize about that," Kit said immediately. "Not ever."

Whitney's eyes became glassy.

"You're wrong." A single tear leaked onto my cheek. "I do. And I want to congratulate you both on the happy news."

That was all I could manage. "Good night."

I hurried back upstairs, not hearing whatever they may have said in response.

My door closed a second time, and stayed that way until morning.

CHAPTER 17

I was out the door at sunrise.

I didn't want to see Kit or Whitney. Having barely survived the night before, I couldn't make it through a tense breakfast.

One problem: Mr. Blue's shuttle wouldn't depart for another forty minutes.

I couldn't loiter on the dock—in plain sight of everyone in the complex—so I opted for a stroll along the beach.

I considered going back for Coop, but decided not to risk it. Sorry, boy.

The temperature was already seventy-five, with the promise of more heat to come. Seagulls cawed overhead, riding the thermals in search of their morning meals. A stiff breeze swept the shoreline, flapping my plaid skirt and ruffling my hair. I tried to keep the sand from my shoes, but knew it was impossible.

My thoughts were stuck on my father and his fiancée. How terrible I'd been. Hopefully I'd made things better in the end, but I wasn't sure. I feared the memory of their engagement night would always carry a sour note.

Distracted by dismal thoughts, I didn't realize where my feet had taken me. The first whiff of charred wood caught me unprepared. Brought the here and now crashing home with a vengeance. A whole new set of worries engulfed me.

Massive ships were lining up to enter the harbor. Fort Sumter sat at its mouth, defiant, forcing traffic around it like an old man on a sidewalk. The ancient brick fortress shimmered in the early morning haze.

But on my stretch of beach, the topography had changed forever.

Where our bunker had hidden for hundreds of years, there was now only a blackened mound of scorched earth. The ground had slumped at least twenty feet—likely beneath the notice of a casual observer, but a gash right to my jugular.

No smoke rose—the cave-in had doused the flames, a small blessing that would reduce prying eyes. I'd worried the fire department might be called, or perhaps the Coast Guard. Anyone picking through *that* rubble would have questions for the Morris Island locals.

Thankfully, that seemed unlikely. With any luck, no one would investigate at all. Just one more unmarked Civil War fortification collapsing under the weight of decades. Happened all the time.

But I knew better.

My fury simmered now, rather than running wild.

Our bunker had been taken from us. I knew who did it, if not the specific individuals.

Next on my list.

Who were the Trinity? Why did they harbor such hatred for my pack?

We should be working *together,* not fighting. We had the same issues. The same problems. We were the only two groups in the world who could flare. A unique species on earth. This rivalry was more than foolish, it was dangerous. It had to stop.

But as I surveyed the rubble where our clubhouse once hid, I knew cooperation was no longer possible.

The Trinity had declared war. I planned to win it.

So find them.

I turned my back to the damage. Resolved. Determined.

Striding toward home, thoughts coalesced in my head. Questions cropped up. Theories formed. By the time I spotted the dock—and Shelton and Hi, waiting to disembark—I was damn near running.

◇   ◇   ◇

"Just think about it," I argued, words spilling out in a torrent. "That kid in the baseball cap is the only person we *know* has been in contact with at least two of the Trinity."

"True." Hi flopped onto a bench as *Hugo* pulled from the dock. "Though we're banking on a memory you stole from the guy's head."

Shelton took a spot next to Hi, eyes thoughtful behind his thick lenses. Ben had driven back to Mount Pleasant that morning, a logistical gift from the gods.

"He did act kinda suspicious when you confronted him," Shelton admitted.

"Exactly!" I began pacing, too wound up to sit. "And who just hands over camping gear to someone they might not see again? That stuff isn't cheap. Jordan's whole story doesn't add up. I think he's one of them."

"Seemed like a huge wuss, though." Hi squinted in the morning sun. "These Trinity jokers—one thing I *won't* call them is afraid. So far they've broken into Chance's magic palace, raided Fort Sumter, set up a freaking night ambush on Loggerhead, and torched our HQ. Does the wet blanket you interrogated in that dorm room really fit the profile?"

I wasn't dissuaded. "Maybe Speckman is the driving force. When we confronted Jordan at CU, he was cornered. Alone. Plus—if he *is* Trinity—he knew who we were! That we were Viral, like him. Could *flare,* like him. It's hard to be a tough guy when caught off guard by your enemies and outnumbered five to one."

Hi nodded thoughtfully. Shelton grunted, noncommittal.

"So what should we do?" Shelton asked.

"We're going back to that college." I flashed my fake "camera" smile. "We'll turn up the heat on that clown, and see if he melts."

○   ○   ○

When the bell rang, I sprang from my seat.

"Easy, girl!" Ella pretended to flinch. "Save those moves for practice."

"Sorry!" Shoving books into my bag. "Busy day today. And I won't be at practice again, unfortunately."

Ella frowned. "Coach Lynch won't like it. That's twice this week. You're a starter, in case it slipped your mind. We have a game Tuesday."

"I know." My guilty look was genuine. I hated lying to Ella. "Kit's being crazy about the SATs. He *insisted* I take this prep class. But it only runs a few more days."

Ella flapped a hand. "I'll handle Lynchie. I'll say you're having girl issues. I guarantee he won't dig any further."

I snorted, then squeezed her hand good-bye.

Shrugging on my jacket, I'd just cleared the room when I stumbled into trouble.

"Hey, Tor!"

Face-to-face with Courtney Holt.

Crapballs.

"Hi!" I kept moving, but worse was lurking down the hallway.

"There you are." Ashley stood with her arms crossed, an unreadable expression on her face. Her tone was oddly level, as if merely stating a fact.

Crap crap crap.

What had I said to Hi and Shelton about being cornered?

I spotted the two boys as they crossed the hall, watching with anxious expressions. I waved them on. This was my problem. I'd deal with it.

"Hello, Ashley." Voice just as wooden.

We moved down the corridor, Ashley and Courtney flanking me like prison guards.

My pulse quickened. I was hemmed in by the remaining legs of the Tripod of Bitch.

Ashley stayed close to my side, like a best friend about to share gossip. I wanted to stare into her eyes. Take her measure. Search for any sign she was what I suspected.

If Ashley was Trinity, she knew my secret. She'd been hiding in the branches of a Loggerhead Island oak tree less than twelve hours before. She could flare.

I carefully concealed my suspicion. At the moment, I had only one edge—Ashley didn't know I suspected her. I wasn't ready to give that up yet.

Not until I've identified all three.

Ashley flashed her perfect teeth. I imagined them stripping the flesh off her prey.

"How are you, Tory? I feel like we haven't talked in ages."

Still this odd play at friendship. I didn't know how to react.

"Yeah, been busy." I tried to edge away, but she stayed glued to my side.

"Still, it makes me sad." Ashley drew out the last word. Her lilting tone gave me chills. "Courtney and I want to know if you're free this weekend. We've got a shopping day planned."

"You *have* to come." Courtney smiled vapidly, fingers tugging at her tight cheerleading uniform. "We're getting shoes. Pedicures, too."

For a hot second I imagined Courtney as the third member of the Trinity, but quickly dismissed the notion. She was too dumb to be devious.

Ashley, however, was anything but.

"Don't say no." Ashley's shark smile never touched her dark, piercing eyes. "We'll talk more tomorrow. But you're coming with us. I *insist*."

She gave my shoulder a squeeze. Did I imagine her fingers pressing a little too hard?

"Um, okay. Sure."

What!?

"Perfect. Talk soon." Ashley strode away, her sleek, athletic form gliding between nervous classmates skittering out of her path. Courtney waggled her fingers at me as she followed, a loyal puppy hoping for a head pat.

I exhaled sharply. Noticed my hands were trembling.

What had I just agreed to?

I spun, intending to track down Hi and Shelton.

Madison and Jason were approaching from the opposite direction.

Not my luckiest class break.

I plastered on a smile, determined to plow through their attempts at conversation as quickly as possible. But, spotting me, the two stopped abruptly. Exchanging a hurried whisper, they ducked through the nearest open door.

But that's Mr. Edde's room. Not their class.

What was going on?

I walked to the door they'd entered. Poked my head inside.

Saw Jason and Madison exit through the door at the opposite end of the room.

I stepped back out into the hall. The pair was hustling away, having bypassed me neatly.

"What in the what?"

Jason *never* avoided me. Far from it. And Madison now claimed to be a friend.

Yet they'd clearly given me the slip. And knew I saw them do it.

A fresh set of suspicions wormed into my mind.

Ashley and Courtney had ambushed me, sure, but that wasn't overly strange. I'd never understood them, and this kind of thing had happened before.

But Jason and Madison . . .

I thought of every conflict between Madison and me.

Every cruel rejection I'd served to Jason, sometimes in public. Every unkindness.

But *Jason*? Surely not! He'd always been an ally.

An ally taken for granted. One who'd suffered because of you.

In Jordan's mind, I'd seen a girl in a Bolton Prep uniform. But had it really been Ashley? I tried to recall the stolen memory, but the details remained stubbornly fuzzy.

Was I certain the girl had black hair? Madison's auburn locks weren't out of the question.

Madison and Chance had been close. Very close.

Chance was Viral, and connected to the Trinity. Who but Madison made the most sense?

What if Ben's right? What if I'm being played a fool. Again.

"Blargh." And I meant it.

This was almost too much. I had no clue who to trust.

The bell rang, scattering my dark thoughts.

I hurried after my friends, worried I'd been suspecting the wrong people.

CHAPTER 18

I kept these new suspicions to myself.

So much for my policy of full disclosure, but I didn't want Hi and Shelton glancing over their shoulders for no reason. I needed more to go on than a hallway dodge.

There were dozens of reasons why Jason and Madison might avoid me, their new relationship topping the list. Madison knew Jason used to have a thing for me. Jason knew I'd had problems with Madison forever. The pair avoiding me wasn't hard to explain.

Still . . . it was the *way* they'd done it.

I couldn't shake a feeling that something was off.

When last bell pealed, Hi, Shelton, and I hustled off the grounds and toward Chance's office. Ben would meet us there. We had a lot to discuss. The Trinity. Our mysterious stalkers. The DNA tests that had seemed so important just days ago.

My personal life needs to stay out of it.

Yet I knew I couldn't put Ben off forever. Or Chance, for that matter.

My phone buzzed, causing me to jump. I dug it from my bag and read the waiting text.

Chance. **Good news. Get here ASAP.**

"What do you think it is?" Hi had shed his jacket and was working his tie loose, already pink-faced in the afternoon heat.

"Probably got fired," Shelton grumbled, shuffling along at Hi's side. "Or maybe he heard that Morris Island was just leveled by a tidal wave. Some kinda terrible news to match our luck."

Of all the Virals, Shelton was taking the bunker disaster hardest.

"Cheer up." Hi's shoulders rose in an exaggerated shrug. "Maybe he's ordering pizza, and wants to know what toppings I like. *Which are all of them.*"

Shelton pushed his glasses up the bridge of his nose. "I feel so much better."

We arrived at Candela just as Ben was parking. Without a word, he joined us as we crossed the street, snuck down the alley, and entered through the keypad access door. Nor did he speak as we rode up to the twenty-fifth floor.

Ben didn't even look at me. Was he angry? Embarrassed? Hurt?

Ugh! No time for this.

Chance was waiting at his desk, wearing a pink oxford shirt and khaki pants. He rose as we entered, shut the door, and then joined us as we took seats around the coffee table. "I have news."

We waited, expectant.

He looked at me. "I got lab results for the materials you collected."

My eyes squinched. "Which ones?"

Chance began spreading papers on the tabletop. "The paint chips. Flecks. Whatever. From the statue in my atrium, and the delightful wall art decorating Fort Sumter."

"Oh. Those." I couldn't help but feel disappointed. Had been hoping for more.

Chance sensed my lack of enthusiasm. "I think this might be pertinent. Look."

He arranged several documents I didn't recognize. The first showed an image of two columns, like long stains, leaking across the color spectrum from red to blue.

"These are chromagraph readouts," Chance explained. "Our lab examined the paint samples collected from both my house and Fort Sumter. What you see here is a visual breakdown of the molecular components of each substance."

"Pretty," Hi cooed. "But I'm not skilled in the art of identifying different paints from chromagraph readouts."

"First, look at the results side by side." Chance laid the two sheets next to each other. "The left one is from Uncle Milton's touch-up job. The right one is from the wall graffiti. Notice anything?"

I held them up. "They're nearly identical. The hues in these readouts match."

Chance sat back with a satisfied smile. "The Trinity used the same paint in both places."

"Awesome," Ben deadpanned. "And useless."

Chance flashed a superior smile. "If I stopped there, then yes. But I didn't."

He flipped through the file, then slapped down a second set of documents. "I ran the chromagraph results through a spectrometer."

Ben just looked at him. "And that is?"

I jumped in. "A machine that identifies materials by measuring properties of light over a portion of the electromagnetic spectrum."

"Ah." Ben rolled his eyes. "Of course."

Shelton spun a finger in the air. "Can we get to the point?"

Chance tapped the closest page. "Paint is a chemical, and each brand and type is typically patented. I should know, Candela owns several. The chemical properties of most commercial paints are recorded, and can be cross-referenced for comparison."

"Like with cars!" Hi was nodding excitedly. "There's something called the National Automotive Paint File. Since the 1930s, police and the FBI have been cataloging samples of paint finishes used on vehicles. They've got tens of thousands on record now. Any fleck left at an accident can be run through the database, and investigators can find the make, model, and sometimes even the year of the car in question. Pretty dope."

"Great," Ben said sarcastically. "So, as long as the Trinity hit your statue with a Chevy, we're in business. Did they drive out to the island fortress, too?"

"Don't be silly." Chance laughed, his good humor seemingly unshakeable. "As I said, the compositions of most paints are cataloged. So I ran these results through *our* database."

He leaned back and put his hands behind his head.

"And?" Shelton asked finally.

"Next page."

Suppressing a groan, I flipped the sheet. Scanned the first paragraph. "Three matches. Black. White. Red."

"Military issue." Chance sat forward, eyes alight with excitement. "The paint used by the Trinity is *expensive*. An outdoor, rust-resistant formula that wears extremely well. The brand is used almost exclusively by government contractors. I couldn't locate a single civilian retailer of the stuff anywhere in South Carolina."

Ben shrugged. "So they used special Uncle Sam–approved paint. Who cares? They probably *stole* the stuff."

Damn. He's probably right.

Chance's smile widened. "Perhaps. But I didn't stop there. Remember the canvas flag?"

"With the fugly wolf-head trio?" Hi shivered. "Yes I do."

"On a hunch, I had its fibers tested with a microspectrophotometer."

Shelton's chin dropped. "Micro-spectro what?"

"You're just full of magical toys, aren't you?" Ben quipped, but his smirk vanished when I shushed him.

Chance continued as if he didn't hear. "A microspectrophotometer can tell if two pieces of fabric were colored by the same batch of dye, or cut from the same thread. Those results are in the folder, too, but I'll spare you. The canvas is also military-grade material."

"In what way?" I asked, a dark thought forming.

"It's designed for outdoor use. On a police boat maybe, or for covering military aircraft. I bet the Trinity found the canvas in the same place where the paint was being stored. Snatched them both."

"But none of that *tells* us anything," Ben repeated stubbornly. "It's useless."

"It's more than you had," Chance snapped, finally losing his cool. "What did *you* figure out today?"

"I didn't waste everyone's time," Ben shot back.

The two continued bickering, but I tuned them out.

Dots were connecting in my head.

I didn't like the picture being formed.

Jason Taylor's father was a detective with the Charleston PD.

The paint. The canvas. Items to which Jason might have unique access?

No. It can't be. You're grasping at straws.

And don't forget—all this information is coming from Chance.

Another dismal fact aligned with the others. I felt a twinge of panic, but kept it carefully concealed. I needed more information. Had to tread carefully.

"Chance?"

"What?" He carped, clearly annoyed that Ben was ruining his big reveal.

"You said Speckman was on the Bolton lacrosse team?"

"Year before last." Chance sat back with a huff. "He was good, a starter. Our third leading scorer, behind Jason. And me, of course."

Ben snorted. "Oh, of course."

"Did you guys ever hang out together?" I asked casually, then slipped in, "The three of you, I mean."

Chance shook his head. "I already told you, no. Will and I weren't close." Then, offhand, "He and Jason used to go fishing, I think. They both thought sitting motionless in a dinghy for hours, watching the water flow, was somehow entertainment."

"Better than some company," Ben muttered.

I tried to hide my alarm.

Jason and Speckman. Were they friends? *Good* friends?

You have to be *somewhat* close to share a boat with someone all day, right?

Abruptly, Chance seemed to realize something. His eyes slid to me, then quickly away.

I pretended not to notice. But inside, my temperature rose.

Chance hired Speckman. Speckman fished with Jason. All three played lacrosse together.

Madison connected to both Jason and Chance.

All four were linked.

It all fit, if you squinted hard enough.

Careful. Don't tip him off.

"It's not important. I'm just trying to get a picture of Speckman's social life."

Chance grunted, dropped the matter. "There's one other thing."

He walked to his desk, returning with yet another printout. "A symbol was stamped onto the canvas. It had nearly faded away, but the machines picked it up."

The image was gray, blurry, and smeared at the edges. But the subject was identifiable—a bird of some sort, framed inside a circle, gripping something cylindrical in it talons. I had no idea what to make of it.

"This has to be something specific," Hi declared. "Like a logo. Or a trademark."

I glanced at Shelton. Of all the Virals, he knew the most history.

He folded the page and put it in his pocket. "I'll see what I can find online."

I looked over at Chance, suddenly eager to leave. "Anything else? I want to go back to the dorm and squeeze that guy Jordan again. I think he's holding out."

I watched Chance for a reaction, but he surprised me by waving a hand. "Not today. We've got lots more to talk about. The other results are back as well."

Hi gave him a puzzled look. "Who shot who in the what now?"

"The DNA tests, Hi." Chance forced a smile. "Want to know what's wrong with you?"

JS: Mr. Iglehart, please explain—

MI: *Doctor* Iglehart.

JS: Excuse me, Dr. Iglehart. Please explain the nature of your relationship with Chance
Claybourne.

MI: Come again? What on earth are you talking about?

JS: How long have you worked for Mr. Claybourne?

MI: I don't *work* for— [PAUSE] Listen, I don't know who you are, but you've gotten
some bad information. I'm a veterinary biochemist. I'm employed by the LIRI institute,
out on Loggerhead Island. I'm a *highly* respected scientist, one of the leading—

JS: Dr. Iglehart, we know you've been taking money from Chance Claybourne. Do you deny knowing him?

[PAUSE]

MI: No. Of course not. *Everyone* knows the Claybourne family. Chance is the youngest, I think. He's one of the richest men in the city. But I don't see—

JS: We have records. You've received wires from a Candela account directly controlled by Chance Claybourne. Significant sums, actually. On at least three separate occasions.

[PAUSE]

JS: Does that jog your memory, Doctor?

MI: Um. Yes. [PAUSE] Could I get a glass of water?

JS: Later, perhaps. At first, we assumed this was run-of-the-mill corporate espionage. You funneling LIRI secrets to Candela. But these transactions smell a little different. They don't fit the usual pattern.

MI: *Whoa whoa whoa!* I never sold any LIRI secrets! We don't even *have* secrets! I've had my problems with Director Howard, sure—the man has no business running a petting zoo, much less a facility of LIRI's stature—but I . . . I would never! I'm a *respected* scientist.

JS: Then explain the payments. I hardly think Mr. Claybourne gave you thousands of dollars just to be friends.

MI: Chance . . . Mr. Claybourne . . . he needed . . . [PAUSE] He just wanted, shall we say, a set of eyes and ears on Loggerhead Island. A way to keep tabs on comings and goings. I kept him . . . informed.

JS: What, specifically, did he want information about?

MI: Not a *what*. A *who*.

JS: A person? Director Kit Howard?

[PAUSE]

JS: Doctor?

[PAUSE]

MI: Who are you guys, anyway? I haven't seen any IDs yet.

JS: If we show you those, know that the tone of this interview will change significantly. Is that what you want?

[PAUSE]

MI: The whole thing is so juvenile! No, I wasn't spying on Kit. Chance wanted me to watch the director's daughter. A schoolmate of his.

JS: A girl? Do you mean Tory Brennan?

MI: [CHUCKLING] Can you believe it? Here I am, a world-renowned veterinary expert with a half-dozen degrees, and scores of publications, and this spoiled rich boy wants me to spy on his high school crush.

JS: Yet you did so?

MI: I'm world-renowned, not overpaid.

JS: Did you know the girl was Director Howard's daughter?

MI: Of course. Kit Howard and I joined LIRI at about the same time. It was a smaller outfit back then, run by Marcus Karsten. I remember the month Kit's daughter came to live with him.

JS: You have a problem with Director Howard?

[PAUSE]

MI: Look. Kit Howard got lucky. He never should have advanced faster than I did, and he knows it. But the Institute went broke right when he had that fluke financial windfall, and suddenly Kit's the "Head Man in Charge." It couldn't have worked out better had he planned it. The smug little twerp has shunned me ever since. Feeling guilty, no doubt.

JS: What exactly did you report to Chance Claybourne?

MI: I'd tell him when Tory came out to the island. She and the annoying troop of boys that follows her around.

JS: What else would you tell him?

MI: What they did. Where they went. Those brats were always poking around where they shouldn't, even back when Karsten ran the place. And now, with Kit in charge? Ha! They're a menace.

JS: Did you ever notice anything strange about them?

MI: Strange? What do you mean? They're kids. All kids are strange.

JS: Did they ever act in a way that was suspicious?

MI: All the time. I caught them snooping in restricted labs. Messing with equipment in the A/V room. They seem drawn to anything that once belonged to Karsten. Which is just ghoulish.

JS: What things belonging to Marcus Karsten? Be specific.

MI: I don't know. I never saw anything directly. But it was . . . weird. Those kids *are* weird.

JS: Explain. This is important, Dr. Iglehart.

[PAUSE]

MI: I think they stole something. From LIRI.

JS: Why do you say that?

MI: I caught Tory in Karsten's private lab. For some reason the director had set up a hidden one, away from the rest of us, and tightly secured. Months later, after what happened, I caught the Brennan girl in there with one of the boys, using the computer. I'm almost certain they were reading research files. But that makes no sense.

JS: What files? Do you have copies?

MI: I don't know. And, no. Whatever Karsten was doing up there, he kept it off the logbooks. Probably illegal. He wiped those records before he died. Backups and hard copies, too.

JS: You think Tory Brennan may have those records?

MI: I. Don't. Know. I told Chance the same. That's it.

JS: Did you tell Mr. Claybourne anything else?

MI: No! And we haven't spoken in weeks. I consider our arrangement over.

JS: Did you ever notice these kids . . . moving oddly? Or maybe communicating in a way you couldn't explain?

MI: What? What are you talking about? [PAUSE] Seriously, who are you guys? Why all these questions about high school kids? [PAUSE] You know what? I think I *do* want to see some identification. And maybe speak to a lawyer.

JS: That won't be necessary. Thank you for your time.

[END TRANSCRIPT]

CHAPTER 19

Chance led us into the bowels of the Candela building.

Exiting a private elevator—separate from the main bank, plunging directly to below street level—we entered an empty lobby. The walls were white and unadorned, like something out of a sci-fi movie.

"Why didn't you mention the DNA result earlier?" I complained.

"Because we'd never have gotten to the other stuff." Chance approached a pair of hermetically sealed glass doors with SPECIAL PROJECTS stenciled on them in bold, black letters. He swiped an access card, input a ten-digit code, and then applied his thumb to a sensor. A light turned green and the entrance swished open.

We filed into a long, narrow corridor with metal doors lining both sides. I wondered how deep underground the facility burrowed.

Chance walked swiftly, outwardly confident, but his eyes flicked to each security camera we passed. I knew he had permission to access this level—he'd entered enough codes, and did oversee the department—but how would he explain *our* presence to any inquisitive coworkers? From the rigid set to Chance's shoulders—which he was manfully trying to hide—I think he was worrying about it, too.

Chance pointed to a room ahead on the left. Stainless steel door. No window. Another key code, another thumb scan, and the portal clicked open. Chance waved us inside.

The lab was the size of a small classroom. White paint. Antiseptic feel. Spotless floor tiles forming a square grid underfoot. Machines lined the chamber—serious, severe-looking pieces of equipment, humming with purpose and adorned by blinking lights. A waist-high metal counter was bolted to the wall sections between them.

Three workstations occupied the central floor space: one clear and empty, the next holding a locked file cabinet, and the last crammed with sleeping computer equipment.

"This is my private lab," Chance said. "As private as things get in this place, anyway. I ran the Brimstone experiment in here, with Will Speckman assisting."

"Bang-up job on that one." Ben, straight-faced.

Chance frowned, but didn't take the bait. "When I figured out what had happened, I destroyed everything associated with the project. Scrubbed the room. Incinerated the parvovirus samples. Wiped the company hard drives, even the backups. There's nothing left in the Candela universe to suggest Brimstone ever existed."

My heart sank. "Then how can we analyze what happened to us? Or examine the virus? You erased the baseline data."

"Not all of it."

Chance moved to the computer workstation, unlocked a drawer, removed a flash drive, and inserted it into the USB port. "I saved the most critical files on this drive."

Shelton stared hard at Chance. "You keep it in there? Locked in a drawer?"

Chance gave him an exasperated look. "On a secure level of a guarded building, behind three keypad access checkpoints. What would you have me do, Shelton? Keep it at my house? You saw how easily the Trinity got in there."

Shelton waved a hand, conceding the point.

"You said you learned something?" I joined Chance before the monitor. The others formed a loose circle around us as he typed.

"It's our DNA." A few more keystrokes, and the familiar human double helix appeared on the monitor. "Specifically, *this* set of chromosomes."

He tapped more keys. The image spun, zooming in on two glowing steps within the twisted ladder. "You all understand what DNA is, I assume?"

"Of course." I waved impatiently. "What did you find?"

"Wait." Ben's face reddened. "It's been a while since I took biology."

Surprisingly, Chance skipped the opportunity to needle Ben. "Our bodies consist of something like sixty trillion cells. Each one is specialized—to compose an organ, carry oxygen, make an enzyme, and so on. DNA is the instruction manual inside every living cell that tells it what to do."

"I know that much," Ben said. "Skip ahead a little."

I jumped in before Chance could reply. "DNA is a complex polymer organized into long strands called chromosomes. I tapped the monitor with a fingernail. "Humans have exactly forty-six chromosomes, arranged in twenty-three pairs and housed within the nucleus of every cell."

Chance pulled up a second image. "Chromosomes are divided into smaller parts called genes, which are the basic units of heredity. Genes determine ultraspecific things like how tall you are, your hair color, or whether you throw left-handed. Genes are also paired."

Hi nodded impatiently. "Kiddie stuff. How many chromosomes does a wolf have?"

"A gray wolf—known scientifically as *Canis lupus*—has seventy-eight chromosomes." I'd looked that up months ago, when we'd first suspected our infection. "Thirty-nine pairs—nearly double what a human possesses."

"Wait a sec." Shelton held up a bony finger. "Coop's a *wolfdog*, not a pureblooded gray wolf. His dad, Polo, is a German shepherd. Does that matter?"

I knew that as well. "Domesticated dogs—*Canis lupus familiaris*—and wolves share the same genetic blueprint—still exactly seventy-eight chromosomes for both. Though obviously, the individual genes are different."

Yet Shelton's point intrigued me—I'd never considered Coop's wolf-dog status in the supervirus context. "*Does* that matter?" I asked Chance.

Chance grunted, noncommittal. "Impossible to say. Who knows? Maybe Coop's hyperspecific genetic blend—gray wolf and domesticated German shepherd—was the key to the cross-species transference. Karsten's preliminary testing had indicated that mixing parvovirus strains simply couldn't result in a variant that was infectious to humans."

"Well, that was wrong," Hi quipped. "I should know."

"Very wrong," I agreed. "Karsten combined canine parvo DNA with something called Parvovirus B19, an innocuous strain that *was* contagious to people. Somewhere in that cocktail, his dangerous hybrid learned to hop the fence."

How exactly, we might never know.

Although it sounded like Chance had been trying to find out.

Typing rapidly, Chance opened a new program. "DNA molecules are made up of smaller units strung together like a train, called mono-mers, which themselves consist of a sugar, a phosphate, and a base. All DNA is composed of only *four* bases: guanine, cytosine, thymine, and adenine. G, C, T, and A for short. They pair as well—C only bonds with G, and A only with T—forming the rungs of the double helix. These four base pairs are the basis for all life on earth."

"Just four parts?" Ben scratched his nose. "In two possible pairings? That's all?"

"A strand of human DNA has approximately three *billion* base pairs,"

I replied. "Those pairs can be arranged in any order. The number of possible sequences is astronomical. More than eight *trillion* possible combinations arise from any two parents. That's why all people are different—we each have our own unique arrangement of base pairs."

"Okay." Ben nodded. "Eight trillion sounds like a lot."

"The relevant thing is—" Chance pointed to a new image on the monitor, "—only five percent of all human base pairs directly code for bodily activities. The other ninety-five percent are non-encoded, and don't seem to do much of anything. Whole sections of DNA appear to be nothing more than repetitive genetic information that no one understands."

"How is that relevant?" I asked.

"Because we don't know what happens if some of that dormant genetic material suddenly turns itself on." Chance gave me a level look. "Until now."

Before I could respond, he moved to the file cabinet atop the center workstation. More keys, another lock, then Chance began spreading files on the table.

We dutifully trooped over after him.

"Yes?" I said impatiently.

"I destroyed the samples I created," Chance said, shuffling through the documents. "And there are no similar records from Karsten—his tests never progressed to the point where he mapped the genetic sequence of his experimental virus. It escaped too soon."

"Sorry," I said. "I see a dog in a cage, I break it out. That's how I roll."

"Understood." Chance's eyes rose to catch mine. "But *our* DNA is locked inside every cell of our bodies."

I met his gaze. "The blood samples. You found something."

Chance nodded. "I mapped our DNA."

Hi thumb-tapped the edge of the table. "What, like, on Google?"

Chance chuckled. "Hardly. I extracted DNA from our blood samples using chemical agents to isolate and destroy white blood cells, break down the composite proteins, and release the genetic material. Then I cut the DNA into fragments to determine VNTR sequences."

Shelton blinked. "Did what now?"

"What process did you use?" I asked.

"Restriction fragment length polymorphism," Chance replied. "Then I separated the fragments by size using gel electrophoresis."

"Basic DNA fingerprinting." I nodded. "When did you learn to do all this?"

"After the mental hospital." He looked away. "You'd be surprised what you can accomplish when investigating whether or not you're crazy."

That stopped me short. *I* was the main reason he'd doubted his sanity.

Chance shook himself, then continued his explanation. "I transferred the DNA fragments to a nylon membrane, tagged them with radioisotopes, then ran them through radiography. And voilà—the DNA fingerprints you see here."

"I don't understand the words that are coming out of your mouth," Hi intoned.

"Just look." Chance spread out a number of pages, each with a DNA fingerprint pattern. "I won't lie—I didn't understand all of it either, but the computer did."

Chance stepped back from the table. "And according to the computer, we're not human."

"Come again?" Shelton reached for an earlobe.

"We have an extra pair of chromosomes." Chance's voice had dropped to a whisper. "They appear canine in nature, yet that doesn't exactly match, either. But whatever genes are contained in these foreign DNA segments, they've started some kind of chain reaction. Inside our cells, usually dormant base-pair sections are humming like cell phone towers."

Hi backed away from the table. "How is that possible?"

"The virus." I didn't need to see Chance's nod.

"I'm as shocked as you," Chance said. "These invasive chromosomes should've killed us."

"A virus can change our *species*?" Shelton squawked. "Good Lord!"

I spoke slowly, trying to piece it together. "A virus is an infectious agent that can only replicate inside another organism's cells. They're made of practically nothing—a section of genetic material, a few molecules to carry it, and a protein coat protecting it all. Some scientists don't even consider viruses to be alive—just inanimate DNA vehicles whose sole purpose is to inject foreign genetic material into host cells."

"*This* virus tricked our cells into incorporating its DNA, then vanished." Chance shook his head in wonder. "I can't find it anywhere. Not one single trace of the virus itself. But it's undeniable that we've been altered. The supervirus may be gone, but our DNA remains warped. I don't understand it at all."

I began to pace, thinking out loud. "Karsten said he inserted genetic material from canine parvovirus into Parvovirus B19, the innocuous human strain. That created Parvovirus XPB-19. Which *we* caught, while rescuing Coop."

"An outcome Karsten hadn't foreseen," Hi added. "And couldn't explain."

"Me either," Chance admitted. "When we first started, I never anticipated our strain becoming contagious. We were flying blind—I never knew exactly what DNA segments Karsten used in his experiment. We could only guess."

Chance looked away. I felt like he'd been about to say more.

I waited, sensing it wasn't something to press.

But when he spoke again, I was sure he'd changed topics. "The supervirus I created is different from Karsten's work. The genetic alterations in my cells are practically identical to yours, yet the manifestations are slightly dissimilar. My eyes glow red, not yellow. I can't reach your minds, but can connect with the Trinity. I don't have an explanation. And I destroyed all my samples."

Again, the slight hitch in his voice.

Was Chance holding something back?

Hi interrupted my thoughts. "Karsten thought our flare powers were a side effect—the result of genetic tweaks to the limbic portions of our nervous system."

I nodded, trying to recall Karsten's exact words. "He believed our brains had been altered, allowing for drastic hormonal changes. Wolf DNA mingling with human, transferring some of their unique abilities to us."

"And these tests prove it." Chance smacked the table. "We have canine DNA encoded within our cells. Dormant base pairs have suddenly gone hyperactive."

"So what does it all mean?" Shelton whispered. "What's the upshot?"

Chance ran a hand through his hair.

His voice became unsteady.

"The upshot is—we may not be done evolving yet. The mutations may not be complete."

CHAPTER 20

The Explorer's tires rumbled across the bridge to Morris Island.

Inside, silence reigned. Chance's revelations had taken the wind from our sails.

No one knew how to react, or what to do next.

We now had proof: canine DNA had infiltrated our chromosomes and scrambled our genetic code.

A stark conclusion was inescapable.

We Virals weren't fully human.

And I had no idea what came next.

A hot ball of anxiety was forming inside my chest. A familiar sense of helplessness crept over me. I could barely breathe.

What could I do, in the face of that kind of news? What could anyone?

Something. Anything.

Work with what you have.

"Stop."

Ben glanced at me, surprised. We were still navigating the dunes at the southern edge of the island, a few hundred yards from home.

"Stop the car," I repeated.

Ben shrugged, slowed to a halt in the middle of the road. It's not like there was other traffic. "What is it?"

"What Chance said," I began, half turning to address Shelton and Hi as well. "We can't let it paralyze us. We can't crawl into a shell and hide."

I met their eyes in turn. Didn't like what I saw.

My instincts had been right—the boys were experiencing the same feelings. I could see it in their dejected expressions. The discouraged set to their shoulders.

"I was just informed I'm a mutant," Hi grumbled. "Not my best day, ya know?"

I nodded. I did know.

"I mean . . ." Shelton raised a hand, then waved it ineffectually. "What do we do now? Do we just . . . you know, go on like . . . whatever? Act like we don't know? This is the worst."

"No, it's not." Ben spoke softly—hands on the wheel as he stared straight ahead—but his voice carried conviction. "We're not freaks. We're special. Lucky. I don't regret a thing."

"Lucky?" Hi ran a hand over his face. "Dude, Chance said we may continue to . . . evolve. Wolf chromosomes are tap-dancing inside our stem cells. How can that be good?"

Hi had voiced my own fears.

What good could come of this?

Nature is wild and full of variation, but she's also a stickler for order. The supervirus had shuffled the evolutionary deck. More times than not, that ended badly for the test subject.

Ben spun to face the group, his face knotted with intensity. "Do you really want to be *normal* again? Back to being just another schlub?"

Hi flinched, but said nothing.

Shelton reached for his ear. "You don't?"

"Not for a second." Ben glanced at me, gauging my reaction. "Y'all shouldn't either."

"You say that *now*." Hi shifted uncomfortably in his seat. "Sure, flaring is great. I love it every single time. But what happens if these powers turn on us? Or change into something else? Or worse, change *us*?"

Ben made a frustrated sound in his throat.

The conversation was veering from what I'd intended.

"We should deal with the things we can," I said. "What's in front of us, *right now,* that we can control. Let's shelve 'big picture' questions for another day."

"Okay." Shelton straightened, seemed to shake off some of his funk. "What's that?"

I answered without hesitation. "Find the damn Trinity. Nothing's changed on that score."

Hi perked up. "I'm guessing you have a plan?"

I nodded, then snapped my finger at Ben. "Turn this truck around. We've got unfinished business in the city."

○   ○   ○

"Let me do the talking."

I thumped the dorm-room door, ready to pounce on its occupant.

"You heard her, Benjamin." Hi gave our scowling companion a stern look. "No running your mouth like usual."

Hi ducked as Ben's palm swung for his head. "Too quick, son."

"Stop goofing around!" Shelton hissed. "This guy could be Trinity."

My foot tapped with each passing second.

Nothing. No answer. I pounded again.

Down the hallway, a door cracked open. When a scraggly head poked out, I recognized Speckman's roommate, Cole, staring down the corridor.

He rubbed his peach-fuzz mustache, eyes half closed, gripping a tube of cheddar cheese Pringles. "You guys know it's, like, nap time around here, right? I've got sculpting class in three hours."

I rolled my eyes, hammering Jordan's door a third time.

Rubbing his scalp, Cole shuffled out into the corridor. He wore a rumpled CU hoodie and dirty board shorts. Not much of a laundry man.

"Jordan's gone, bros." Cole wiped crumbs from his greasy sweatshirt. "He bugged out right after you jokers gave him the third degree. Said CU wasn't for him." He snorted. "Y'all are, like, the leading cause of dropout around here."

I jabbed my finger against the door, surprised. "He doesn't live here anymore?"

Yawning, Cole shook his head. "Some girl came by, and they got into a screaming match. Ruined drum circle. Then they left together. Hot chick. I would've left with her, too."

He smiled, exposing two rows of fuzzy yellow teeth. I suppressed a shiver.

"And he never came back?"

"Naw, he did once." Cole absently scratched beneath his hoodie. "Just to pack, though. I would've helped him, but, you know, I got a bad knee. Jordan said he was gonzo, but didn't say where. The same chick was waiting in his car." His face grew confused. "I don't get it, man. That *dude* has zero game, then suddenly he up and jets with a hottie? Meanwhile I can't *buy* a date."

"Makes no sense." Hi, face serious.

I pressed a fist to my lips, considering. "What'd the girl look like?"

"Hot."

Ben shifted his weight. I heard Hi chuckle behind me.

I choked back my mounting frustration. "Could you be more specific?"

"Oh, right." Cole rubbed his oily chin and squinted at the ceiling. "She had, like, nice hair. It was sorta . . . black? Or maybe brown. Not blonde, for sure. And she was kinda tall. But not really. Oh, and I think she wore a T-shirt. Could be wrong, though."

I stared at the useless witness before me.

What a moron.

"Can you remember anything else, Cole?" Catching his eye, I tried to urge the memory from his brain by force of will. "Anything at all?"

For a moment, Cole's face screwed up in thought, then it bloomed with contentment. "He said I could have his mattress. Solid dude, that Jordan."

○   ○   ○

Hi snapped on his seat belt. "Not everyone is college material."

Shelton shook his head. "I'm surprised that guy remembers to breathe."

I closed the passenger door, ordering facts in my mind. "Jordan was super nervous when we questioned him, then dropped out of school right afterward. We know he saw a girl in a Bolton Prep uniform when he loaned Speckman his camping gear. Then, later, he leaves campus with a girl."

"A *hot* girl." Hi tapped his forehead. "Don't omit crucial details."

I ignored him. "The question is, was it the same girl both times? Are Jordan and this mystery lady the missing members of the Trinity?"

Ben drummed the dashboard. "You think it's Ashley? Speckman used to date her, and she fits Jordan's memory plus what Cole just described."

My arms crossed. "Ashley's not that hot."

"Yeah she is." Shelton and Hi, in unison.

"We can all agree that Ashley is somewhat pretty." Ben, his face and voice carefully neutral.

"Pretty *hot*," Hi quipped.

"It might be her," I conceded. Through gritted teeth.

"What's the problem?" Shelton blew on his smudged lenses. "I thought Ashley was your prime suspect. Didn't you see her in Jordan's mind?" Then he shivered at what he'd just said.

"She is, but . . ." I trailed off, uncertain whether I should share my other suspicions. "I've been considering other possibilities as well."

A pause. I wavered, undecided.

"Well?" Hi extended both hands. "Out with it, Victoria."

You have to tell them sometime.

"Two other people might fit the evidence." With a sigh, I told them about Jason and Madison. How they'd avoided me at Bolton. I reminded them about Jason's fishing trips with Will Speckman, and his current connection to Madison. The Taylor family's easy access to government-issue supplies.

The only thing I omitted was Chance.

The question of his loyalty overshadowed everything, like a sickness, but I wasn't ready to light that bonfire. Not yet. Not without something concrete.

Hi was shaking his head before I finished. "I can't see it. Jason Taylor? He's always been so cool, and we've been through some stuff together."

"Not my boy Jase," Shelton swiftly agreed. "And aren't you tight with Madison now? Soccer sisters for life, or whatever?"

Ben, however, was less quick to dismiss. "The facts fit, though."

"Come off it, man!" Shelton waved a hand at Ben. "You've never liked Jason."

Ben's tone grew defensive. "So? The evidence fits, that's all I'm saying. Hell, *Tory's* the one saying it."

Hi began pulling on his hair. "But Jason's so nice to me. He calls me Hi-Rise. We play *Warcraft* together!"

I raised my palms to cut them off. "Everyone take a breath. I'm not sure of anything. I'm just pointing out . . . possibilities. Based on the evidence we have."

"So what's our move?" Shelton asked. "Are we focused on Jordan, and maybe Ashley? Or are we after Jason and Madison now?"

All eyes found me.

"I . . . I don't know."

A moment of tense silence. Then Ben turned the key.

Cruising back to Morris Island, no one said a word.

○   ○   ○

My laptop beeped an hour later.

Curious, I crossed to my desk, ruffling Coop's ears along the way. The wolfdog tracked me for a moment, then lost interest, eyes closing as he resumed his snooze on my bedroom floor.

A message from Shelton. He wanted to video-chat.

"Okeydokey."

I clicked the link and my screen split into quarters. The rest of the pack was already there.

Ben was still at his dad's place a few units down. He lay on their ratty old couch, laptop balanced on his stomach. Hi was in his room, already changed into Godzilla pajamas. Shelton was also bedside, but still dressed. And nearly bouncing with excitement.

"Found them!" Shelton's eyes twinkled behind his boxy black specs.

"Found who?" Hi pointed impatiently to his TV. "I'm watching *Catfish,* and they're about to meet in real life."

I felt a surge of excitement. "The Trinity?"

Shelton grinned ear to ear. "Yep!"

I experienced a moment of vertigo as Ben spun his computer, sitting upright and paying closer attention. "What? How? Where?"

Shelton blew on his nails, then buffed them on his shirt. "Which should I answer first?"

"All of them," Ben growled, "or I'll be down in thirty seconds to pound—"

I cut him off. "Just tell us what you've got."

"The symbol on the canvas flag. Hold up." Shelton began typing. An instant later, the image appeared in the corner of my screen. "I know what it is, and the shoe fits!"

"Keep going," I prodded.

"I scanned the image," Shelton explained, "then tried a Google search. No luck. It was too faded to make out." He flashed two rows of pearly whites. "But then I got lucky. My pops saw the printout sitting on my desk."

"Shelton!" Hi leaned in to his webcam. "How could you be so careless?"

"Relax." Shelton's grin never wavered. "There was nothing on it but the symbol. It's not like he could connect it to anything. He asked if I was joining up."

"Joining up?" Ben began gnawing his thumbnail. "That sounds military."

"Correctamundo." Shelton tapped keys as he talked. "I said, 'What do you mean?' And he's all, 'I didn't know you'd been out there before.' And I'm like, 'Out where?'"

Hi slapped his desk. "Yes, Shelton. Out *where*?"

Shelton lifted a finger dramatically, then pressed enter. A second, more detailed image appeared beside the faded one: an eagle, clutching a cannon in its talons, framed by a bloodred sun. The first symbol was clearly a washed-out example of the second.

"Nice work," I breathed.

"Pops is a military buff," Shelton explained, relishing the attention. "He recognized the emblem from one of his World War Two books. More importantly, he knew which ship it came from."

"Ship?" Ben, Hi, and I all spoke at once.

"What you see here is—"

Shelton paused, drawing out the moment. I could've killed him.

"The insignia of a United States Navy aircraft carrier. The USS *Yorktown*."

Silence. Then, bedlam.

Hi cackled. "That old hunk of junk?"

"I've been there!" Ben blurted at the same time.

"The *Yorktown* is just across the harbor." I actually pointed out the window.

"Think about it." Shelton clearly had. "The Trinity used *military* paint, and a piece of weathered canvas with a faded *Yorktown* insignia, a vessel that's been anchored at Patriots Point for decades."

"It's a museum ship," Ben added. "A national historic landmark. But she's been closed to the public for maintenance all month. I should know—I cruise by that monster every time I cross the harbor to Mount Pleasant."

Hiram's eyes rounded. "I bet there's paint on board, for upkeep and whatnot. The Trinity must've swiped the stuff from there."

"No!" I nearly shouted. "More than that! The *Yorktown* is *perfect*. Closed for weeks. Docked in the harbor. Massive. Empty."

I opened Safari and pulled up a Charleston map. "Consider the locations blitzed by the Trinity. Claybourne Manor on the peninsula. Fort Sumter in the harbor. Loggerhead Island just beyond. Our own bunker here on Morris."

Shelton slapped his desk. "All within easy striking distance from Patriots Point."

Recognition dawned on Hi's face. "They're using the *Yorktown* as a base of operations."

Ben's lips curled dangerously. "We know where the Trinity lives."

My smile was just as fierce.

"Let's pay them a visit."

CHAPTER 21

"Talk to me, Shelton."

Perched in *Sewee*'s bow, Coop at my shoulder, I gazed up at the massive superstructure dominating the harbor. We were idling a hundred yards out, dressed in dark athletic clothing. Our ninja gear, as Hi would say.

A glance at my watch. Two thirty a.m.

Of course we went that night. Even Shelton knew we would.

I wanted to catch the Trinity in the worst way. The boys did, too.

After the bunker, we had a score to settle.

But there were practical reasons as well. The Trinity had struck somewhere every night that week. To pull that off, they needed a launching point, or a place to rally afterward. The carrier was perfect. And late night might be the only time to catch them there.

Beside me, Shelton began reciting facts from his iPhone. "The USS *Yorktown* is one of twenty-four Essex-class carriers built by the navy during World War Two. Named after the famous Revolutionary War battle, she's almost nine hundred feet long and weighs twenty-seven thousand tons."

"A big girl." Hi whistled from the copilot's seat. "But still sexy."

We'd gathered as soon as everyone could sneak out. Then Ben piloted *Sewee* across Charleston Harbor to Patriots Point, a naval museum and park at the mouth of the Cooper River that served as the decommissioned behemoth's permanent residence. We kept well clear of the warship—nearing the park's marina, Ben killed the lights and pulled alongside the outermost pier.

"In 1975, the *Yorktown* was dedicated as a memorial on the navy's two hundredth anniversary." Shelton gawked up at the towering vessel. "Man, aircraft carriers are *huge*. They've had college basketball games on the flight deck." He paused, skipping ahead. "A radio station was housed inside her for a while, but that closed down. Now she's part of the maritime museum. There's a destroyer and submarine over here, too."

I scanned for any sign of people aboard. "Tell me about the ship itself."

"The flight deck is a hundred feet above the waterline, so we won't be climbing up. Don't fall off, either. Bad news." Shelton pointed to a cluster of inland buildings. "The park entrance is way over there. That fixed concrete dock has a series of ramps accessing the *Yorktown*."

Ben eyed the empty stretch of pier at the foot of the carrier. "Only way in?"

Shelton nodded with a frown. "Unfortunately, yeah. Anyone watching the ramps will see us come aboard."

"How many sailors lived on that thing?" I couldn't imagine the experience.

"When first built, over three thousand." Hi edged forward, anxious to show off what he knew. "And it held ninety planes, too. There's still a dozen different aircraft parked on the flight deck for tourists."

"Three thousand people?" I shivered. "Remind me never to sign up."

Hi snorted. "It wouldn't feel cramped. That boat has *five* acres of total space. She needs her own zip code."

Shelton grunted. "So how are we supposed to find someone inside?"

Coop brushed against my leg. As I reached down to scratch his ears, the answer hit me.

"Chance."

○   ○   ○

It took him an hour to arrive.

Ben fumed the whole time.

"We *don't* need Chance!" The fourth time he'd repeated the words. "He only gets in the way, when he's not tipping off the Trinity that we're coming!"

"Ben, look at the size of that monster." I shook my head at the scale of it. "If the Trinity really are holed up in there, they'll know the layout. We'd never be able to track them, even with Coop's help. But Chance might."

"Unless he just sent them a text message," Ben snapped. "Setting another trap."

I didn't respond. Wouldn't admit that the prospect worried me, too.

Could we really trust Chance? If he was working with the Trinity—or if they really could sense his thoughts—I'd given away our biggest advantage: surprise.

Taking a deep breath, I shoved those doubts aside. Having Chance along gave us our best shot at success. I had to trust he wasn't playing us.

How'd that go last time?

Finally, a black BMW rolled into the marina lot and parked. Chance stepped out, wearing his sheeny black tracksuit. He looked ridiculous and amazing at the same time.

I woke my phone and waved it overhead until he spotted me. Chance climbed over a locked gate as we hustled down the dock to meet him. As we passed dozens of vessels tied up for the night, I wondered which one the Trinity used. They had to have a way to travel between targets. Only a boat made sense.

Chance called out as we approached. "You guys ready?"

"We've *been* ready for over an hour." Ben walked past Chance, down the concrete quay leading to the *Yorktown* ramps. "Just don't get in the way."

"How about I toss you in the harbor?"

Ben stopped dead. "Excuse me?"

"Hey!" I whistled to get their attention. "Stop!"

I hurried between the two, Coop trotting at my side. Shelton and Hi hung back, sensing another blowup they wanted no part of.

"Ben." I pointed to the ground directly before me, my meaning clear.

He tensed, but, after the briefest of hesitations, stomped over. "What?"

I crooked a finger at Chance. "You. Here. Now."

Chance sighed dramatically, but complied.

I'd had enough of their bickering already. We didn't need any friendly fire on this mission. I was determined to stamp it out.

The two boys waited, eyes on their shoes, looking like fifth graders caught burning ants with a magnifying glass. I almost laughed at their matching sullen expressions.

"Not tonight." Without preamble, biting off the words.

Sensing my mood, Coop backed me with a low growl.

"On this trip, we will work as a team. No sarcasm. No fighting. No hesitation. We're going to trust one another. Got it?"

Chance looked suitably chastened. "Yes, ma'am."

Ben gritted his teeth, but nodded.

I gestured for Hi and Shelton to join us.

"Okay, then." I shook out my arms, preparing for the task ahead. "If the Trinity are aboard that beast, we'll have them cornered. We need to catch them and make them talk. Chance will track their thoughts. Coop will guard the ramps, blocking the escape route."

"And if they don't want to cooperate?" Ben asked, voice hard.

I matched his icy tone. "They don't have that option anymore."

Chance nodded, face unreadable.

Can I trust you?

Shelton shuffled his feet, wide-eyed and tugging one ear. Ben put a hand on his bony shoulder. "You stay close to me, okay?"

Shelton nodded, trying to psych himself up. "I took all that karate for a reason, right?"

I looked at Hi. For once there was no joke, just a firm thumbs-up.

Cooper pawed my leg. He was watching me, ice-blue eyes reflecting the moonlight. I had no doubt my wolfdog was ready.

My boys.

I felt a surge of love for each. Vowed to protect them as best I could.

But the Trinity needed dealing with. This crap had gone on long enough.

"All right, Virals." I spun to face the hulking vessel we were about to invade. "Time to take care of business. Light 'em up."

Eyes closed.

Mind unleashed.

SNAP.

We snuck down the pier single-file, like a string of ghosts. At the end of the marina we hopped a chain-link fence—security was laughably inadequate—and entered the museum park. The hardest part was passing an eighty-pound mutt over the eight-foot barrier, a sweaty task I let the boys handle.

"Just broke the law again." Shelton was crouched beside me in the shadows, eyes glowing like incandescent lanterns. "Thought we might skip a night, just for kicks, but nope!"

I gave him a level look. *No more talking, unless you need Chance.*

Hi-aye, captain.

We hurried past the submarine, then the old destroyer, closing in on the park's centerpiece. The *Yorktown* rose ten stories on my left, like an office block floating in the shallows.

Halfway down its length, the first metal ramp rose to meet the carrier's starboard side. My glowing eyes probed farther along the quay. I spotted two more ramps ahead.

I knelt, gripped Coop by the sides of his furry head. Looked directly into his eyes.

You stay here. Watch for enemies.

Coop shrugged me off, tilting his head and whining in obvious displeasure.

Go. Fight. Impressions rather than words.

I shook my head. *Hide. Watch. Alert the pack if enemies appear.*

Coop mewled again, but reluctantly settled down on his haunches. *Watch.*

"Good boy," I whispered. Then, to the others, *Sound off.*

This ramp should work, Ben sent. *It leads to a bulkhead door in the side of the ship.*

Eyes twinkling, Hi scanned the decks for any sign we were being watched. *No prying eyes. Maybe we'll catch these jerks napping.*

Shelton froze, eyes closed, a look of intense concentration on his face. After a few beats: *I don't hear anyone. Or much of anything, actually. This place is spooky.*

My turn.

I inhaled deeply, sifting through a bouquet of odors that poured into my nose. Algae. Seaweed. Motor oil. Wet metal. Chance's cologne. Nothing suspicious. No trace of other people. *All clear.*

"What are we waiting for?" Chance hissed, unable to hear our silent conversation.

"Nothing." Watch check—3:40 a.m. "Ben, lead the way."

The ramp began as a series of switchbacks that climbed five stories, then arced across the shallows to an entryway in the carrier's side. The flight deck hung another fifty feet farther overhead. Reaching the hatch, Ben pulled on its metal handle. To my delight, the door swung inward with barely a creak.

We rushed inside and shut the portal behind us. Found ourselves in utter pitch black.

Ben and Hi removed flashlights from their pockets and flicked them on. Twin beams cut the gloom, illuminating a narrow metal corridor. Pipes snaked along the ceiling and walls, flowing deeper into the mighty vessel.

Only one way to go. Ben crept forward with the light. I followed on his heels, with Shelton a step behind. Chance and Hi brought up the rear.

After a dozen yards, we reached an intersection. Ben aimed his beam down each passage.

I don't know. I could feel his mounting frustration. *They all look the same.*

I glanced back at Chance. "Sense anything?"

Chance went still, eyes glazing slightly as he turned his focus inward.

Seconds ticked by. No one moved, or made a sound beyond their own breathing.

Finally, he shook his head. "I can't hear them. They might not be here."

Shelton tapped my shoulder. I turned and met his gaze.

There's something to the left. He'd pocketed his glasses, and I could see the anxiousness in his golden eyes. *A noise, but . . . faint. I'm not sure what it is.*

Good enough for me.

Ben moved down the corridor with the effortless grace of a flaring Viral. We reached a stairwell. Suddenly, I could hear sounds, too.

Somewhere above us, a machine was humming.

There's light up there, Hi blurted inside my head. *Two levels up.*

Chance tugged my elbow, then pointed up the steps. "Light."

"I know." Chance's inability to connect was frustrating me. "Thoughts?"

"We're deep inside the ship," Chance whispered. "A good place to hide."

Ben spun a finger impatiently. *Let's go already.*

Fine. But be careful.

Ben led us up one flight, then a second. As we passed the first level, I thought I detected a familiar odor. The barest whiff of something stale, yet recognizable. I nearly stopped, but the scent disappeared as quickly as it came.

What was that? The aroma teased my mind, refusing to identify itself. Then Shelton tapped my shoulder, a questioning look on his face. I shook my head and moved on.

Reaching the second landing, the light source become obvious—a steady glow was leaking through the porthole of a closed bulkhead door. The humming sound emanated from within.

No one needed to say it.

In the next room, lights were on and the juice running.

Voices. Shelton's eyes rounded, then scrunched in confusion. *I think . . . it sounds like . . .* He trailed off, then shook his head in confusion. *I swear somebody's* singing *next door. What the heck?*

Chance tensed, one hand gripping his forehead. "I heard something! In my head." His finger jabbed toward the sealed opening. "There. In there."

Adrenaline flooded my system.

Okay. Shelton's sending was tinged with panic. *I got this. Let's bust 'em up.*

Hi started bouncing on his toes. *Remember, aim for the balls.*

Ben looked at me. Arched an eyebrow. *Ready?*

I rolled my shoulders. Squeezed my fingers into fists, then shook them out again. *Ready.*

Ben motioned for Chance to take point. Chance nodded, scuttled forward to crouch before the sealed entrance. Rising cautiously, he snuck a quick peek through the porthole, then turned and flashed us an A-okay. Ben blew out a breath. Then he strode straight ahead, spun the wheel to unlock the watertight portal, and yanked its bulky handle. The door swung wide, and the two fired inside.

I went next, temporarily blinded by the harsh light within. I sensed Hi and Shelton fan out behind me. The room was large—roughly twenty by twenty, the ceiling two stories overhead. A rusty catwalk circled halfway up, accessed by a narrow fireman's ladder.

An old-school boom box sat on a folding chair in the center of the room. Taylor Swift warbled from its battered speakers. "We Are Never Ever Getting Back Together."

My eyes searched the corners. Nothing. We were alone inside four bare, blank steel walls.

"What in the world?" Hi said aloud.

Ben walked over and shut the music off. Silence descended like a blanket.

Alarm bells clanged in my brain. My gut screamed a warning.

Then it hit me.

The smell from the stairwell. Salt and grease, just like—

I whirled, knowing it was too late.

The bulkhead door slammed shut with a thunderous clank. A rasping sound filled the room as someone spun the wheel, then metal struck metal as the lock engaged, sealing us inside.

Ben raced for the door, but it was pointless. "Damn it!" He pounded the steel barrier with inarticulate fury, cursing himself in his mind. "Let us out!"

"Again." Hi covered his face with both hands. "Twice we've been duped like idiots."

Shelton spun a 360, searching frantically for another way out. "How could they know we were coming tonight!?"

Ben grabbed Chance by the front of his tracksuit. "You said they were in this room!"

"He was right," a voice boomed down from above. "But only because I let him listen in."

My eyes rose to the catwalk.

Will Speckman leaned against the railing, his scarlet eyes brimming with laughter. "You guys charge around like bulls in the arena. That never works out for the bulls."

"You're locked in with us, Will." Chance nodded to the ladder accessing the catwalk. "Think you can keep us down here, all by yourself?"

Speckman gave a lazy smile. He wore a dark blue waffle-knit shirt, gray utility pants, and heavy black boots, like a hipster aiming for a soldier-of-fortune look. "There's another door on this level. And I'm not alone, either."

The portal at our backs. Speckman obviously hadn't sealed it himself.

The Trinity had trapped us again.

I thought of the salty odor from the stairwell.

The answer came to me just as another shadow joined Speckman on the walkway.

CHAPTER 22

Cole Gordon bro-hugged Speckman, smirking down at us from the catwalk.

A greasy carpet of potato-chip crumbs covered his brown T-shirt and wrinkled khaki cargo shorts.

"'Sup, dudes." Cole winked a blazing red eye, his former glassy, vacant look long gone. "Missed you at the dorm today. How come you don't visit anymore?"

Hi squeezed his lids shut. "We are the dumbest people alive."

I couldn't disagree.

Twice this punk had stood right in front of me, and played me like a violin. Belatedly, I remembered the tribal prints dotting Cole's dorm room. His sculpture class. How Chance said Speckman didn't possess the skill to create the wolf-head carvings at Fort Sumter. I cursed the tunnel vision that made me overlook the Trinity's resident artist.

Cole leaned his elbows on the railing with evident satisfaction. "Willie told me folks would come by looking for him. I didn't think so, but he was right. Like always."

"Where's Jordan?" I couldn't keep the sulk from my voice. "Off tonight?"

Speckman and Cole looked at each other, then burst out laughing. "Probably sleeping at his mom's house, dreaming of baseball stats or something."

I hesitated, thrown. "He's not Viral."

Speckman shook his head, addressed me like a particularly slow child. "No, Tory, he is not. Our other packmate prefers to remain anonymous for now."

My mind raced. Who was the third? At this point, I no longer trusted my instincts.

I'd been so wrong about everything thus far. So dangerously foolish.

An image strobed in my brain—the memory I'd stolen from Jordan's mind.

The girl in a Bolton Prep uniform. With Speckman, the day he borrowed camping gear.

Equipment used for the trap out on Loggerhead. She was there.

I took a shot. "I already know who she is."

Speckman chuckled. "I really doubt it, Tory."

Cole shook his head, scarlet eyes glittering. "She does *not* like you, though! Whoa boy! That'd be a catfight I'd pay—"

Speckman elbowed Cole in the ribs. "Nice going, dope. You just confirmed she's a girl."

A guilty look flashed across Cole's face, but it faded quickly. "Oh well. Still fifty percent of the population to guess from!"

So it's not Jason either. That's something, at least.

Which left Ashley or Madison. Suddenly, all the evidence tilted one way.

"Tell Ashley she can come out. It's time for this BS to end."

"Ah-ah-ah!" Cole waggled his finger theatrically. "No more hints."

I've had enough of this. Ben strode for the ladder, rage billowing from him in waves.

Shelton pumped a fist. *Get 'em, Ben.*

I wouldn't wanna be those guys right now, Hi sent. *They're toast.*

"Damn straight." Chance followed Ben to the ladder.

"That's close enough," Speckman barked, as Ben placed a foot on the bottom riser. "Another step, and we'll walk out and seal this door. How long would you like to stay in here?"

Ben's jaw clenched, but he took a step back. "Cowards."

Speckman shrugged. "Be a tough guy all you want. You're still dancing to my tune."

"We figured y'all out," Shelton yelled up at the insufferable pair. "Found this hidey-hole. You're not as smart as you think."

Speckman chuckled again. "Sure took your time. We left enough clues."

"How's *your* hideout doing?" Cole taunted. "Pretty toasty these days, eh?"

I had to choke back my anger. Ben felt close to losing control.

Hi spoke suddenly. "How'd you find our bunker? No one knew it was there."

Speckman clicked his tongue. "Same way we learned where you live. Where your parents work. Chance gave us all the answers."

"That's a lie!" Chance shouted, his finger jabbing upward. "I never told you a thing."

"Oh, not directly." Speckman drummed his hands on the rail. "But you're a little too casual with passwords around the lab. I hacked you, Claybourne. Not just the Brimstone documents you tried to hide. I saw that cute little file you keep on your crush."

Speckman leered down at me. "Chance has gigs of info on you. Some from spies, but much more from touching personal observations. All of it very, very . . . *intimate.* He even wrote about your bunker. I'd be impressed, if he wasn't such a stalker."

I stared at Chance, reddening from head to toe. Spies? Personal notes? What was he keeping in this file?

Ben snapped a dark look at Chance. "When this is done, I'm kicking your ass, rich boy."

Chance ignored him, glaring up at Speckman with undisguised hatred.

Then he turned and met my eye. "I started that file a long time ago, when I was still trying to figure out your secret. It contains information about all of you." His voice grew pleading. "You can't blame me—you guys spent a full year screwing with my head. I did what I had to do."

"I don't have a file on you," Hi muttered, crossing his arms. "Bad form, brah."

"Not cool," Shelton echoed.

"Well!" Speckman straightened, stretching his arms wide. "I'm guessing you guys have a lot to talk about. We'll leave you to it."

"So this was another stupid trap?" I shouted, stalling for time.

Cole nodded, tossing Speckman a languid high-five. "Thought you'd get here sooner. Honestly, I think my packmates overestimate your brainpower."

"Why, Will?" Chance peered up in honest bafflement. "What's the point of this? We're *all* Viral. We should be working together."

"Shut your mouth, traitor!" Speckman's cool slipped for the first time. "You turned your back on me. *Fired* me. Then you threw in with these Morris Island puppies. An inferior breed!"

"I didn't know you were infected!" Chance pointed to Cole. "I don't know *him* at all, or your mystery partner. How could I abandon you? And we both know why I couldn't keep you at Candela. You repeatedly broke company rules. It's not my own private kingdom."

Speckman pointed an accusatory finger. "*You* made the call. No one else."

"At first I was just mad," Cole added suddenly, scratching his patchy beard. "You and these island morons started the whole damn thing. Crazy viruses. Being sick for days. Thanks to y'all I turned into a freak."

Then he grinned wickedly. "Of course, I've come around now. Turns out, being Viral is the jam! But y'all need to pay the price, not my crew."

Price? What price?

Speckman nodded. "You brought the heat down on all of us, Chance. You were sloppy. So we're making sure that *you* take the fall."

A chill ran through my body.

What did Speckman mean?

My eyes flew to Chance. He wouldn't meet them.

Ben stuck his nose in Chance's face. "What's he talking about, Claybourne?"

"Get away from me." Chance shoved Ben in the chest.

Things teetered on the brink. Then three loud bangs echoed in the chamber.

Someone was pounding on the upper level door.

Speckman glanced at his watch, motioned for Cole to follow. "If it makes you feel better," he said, striding across the catwalk, "I think this whole thing is a waste. But better you than us. Cheers."

"Will, wait!" I tried to follow along beneath them. "Let's just talk, okay?"

"Sorry, no more time. Good luck!"

There was a loud clang, followed by the scrape of a hatch sealing shut. With mounting horror, I heard the lock thump into place. We were trapped.

Better you than us.

Suddenly, I guessed what Speckman planned.

Black helicopters at night.

Fort Sumter. Loggerhead. Places the Trinity had lured us.

Oh my God.

"Guys!" Hi's frantic tone grabbed my attention. "Take it easy!"

I spun to find Chance and Ben squaring off like prizefighters. Hi and Shelton were trying to calm them down, but the older boys were an instant from exchanging blows.

"Stop it already!" I screamed, startling everyone.

"We have to get out of here." In my strongest no-nonsense tone. "Speckman is expecting something to happen. I think I know what."

Shelton paled. "I'm not going to like this, am I?"

"No." Swallowing a lump in my throat. "I think the Trinity have been alerting those government bastards following us. Luring us places, and then tipping them to our location. They *want* us to get caught!"

"Somewhere dark and quiet," Hi breathed. "Off the grid. Oh God!"

"But why?" Shelton moaned. "That's just evil, man!"

I noticed Chance shift in the corner of my eye.

He knew something. I could sense it.

Another secret, unshared. I wanted to scream.

Interrogate him now, and Ben will lose it. You'll never get out of here.

So I pushed it aside for later. "We need out of this room, and off the ship. Suggestions?"

Everyone grew quiet, thinking furiously. Ben climbed to the catwalk and circled the room, then slapped the railing in frustration. "No way out. Not with the hatch sealed from the outside."

Abruptly, Chance's eyes bugged. He awkwardly waved his arms, as if trying to tune an antenna. "They forgot to shut me out. I can hear Speckman!" Chance closed his eyes, lips moving silently. When they reopened, a smile spread across his face.

Chance strode to the center of the room and kicked the chair aside, sending the stereo flying. Kneeling, he worked his fingers into a yard-square metal grate in the floor beneath it. Chance yanked the grillwork out and tossed it across the room.

Then he laughed in triumph. "Shouldn't have dwelled on your plan's weak spot, Willie!"

His red eyes locked on to my golden ones.

"Let's get them."

CHAPTER 23

I dropped through the opening.

Landed on a steel platform bisecting two giant turbines. Ahead of me, Ben and Chance were racing in the direction of the stairwell. A flashlight beam danced madly as they sped out of sight.

Hi crashed behind me in a heap, followed by Shelton a second later. I dragged both to their feet.

Free! Shelton's sending thrummed with relief. *Let's bounce. I hate this boat.*

More interested in revenge, I fired a message to Ben. *Cut them off at the stairwell.*

On it. He and Chance disappeared through a hatch up ahead.

They don't know we escaped. Hi handed me his flashlight. *Maybe we can turn the tables.*

We have to hurry. I was already moving. *The bastards might come right down to us.* By descending through the floor, we were only one level above the entrance ramp. Move quick enough and we could block their escape route.

The girl. Shelton's yellow eyes glinted in the darkness. *She's probably with the other two now.*

So come on already! I raced for the hatch, forcing them to sprint to keep up. *I won't let the Trinity slip away again. This ends tonight.*

In the next chamber, another murky passage stretched deep into the warship's interior. I ran as fast as I dared, flare senses probing the darkness. A single question repeated in my mind.

Ashley or Madison?

The last of the Trinity was female—Cole had confirmed it. I trusted Jordan's memory now, though I still couldn't make out a face.

With Jason no longer a suspect, Ashley made the most sense. I'd never trusted her, and she'd been Speckman's girlfriend. I had zero problem seeing her in the role.

But Madison had been tight with Chance at the time of his infection. She'd told me about the black-suited agents, but could've been lying, or setting me up for something else.

Ashley or Madison. Madison or Ashley.

In the end, it didn't matter. I was going to catch whichever bitch was hiding on this giant floating tub, and wring her damn neck.

Suddenly, I was nearly knocked off stride by a powerful sending.

Alert. Danger.

Coop!

I'd nearly forgotten he was guarding the pier below.

I slowed, concentrating on my connection to the wolfdog. *What is it, boy?*

The message was hazy and incomplete—canines don't focus on the same things people do—but the gist was clear: Another vessel was approaching the dock.

Who could it be at that hour? Drunken fisherman? The police? Park rangers?

Or was it much worse?

Speckman's words echoed in my mind: *better you than us.*

Shelton and Hi waited by my side, chests heaving, puzzled expressions on their faces. They hadn't heard Coop's message.

A crash up ahead. Shouts. Thundering feet.

Not a time for distractions.

Stay hidden, I told Coop. *Don't approach or interfere. Understood?*

I caught a surge of lupine frustration. *Hide. Watch.*

Shelton stared down the corridor. *What was that noise?*

Ben's voice exploded inside our heads. *They're in the stairwell! Speckman and Cole. We cut them off, but they tossed some junk down at us and fled up the steps.*

We're right behind you. Any sign of the girl?

No.

What kind of stuff are they throwing? Shelton. Nervous.

Come on. Hi pushed him down the passage.

Reaching the stairwell, I heard feet rattling the risers above me. I took the steps two at a time, frowning as we passed the room in which we'd been trapped.

We had to be smarter. Infighting was killing our effectiveness.

I halted on the catwalk level. The Trinity girl had been here, knocking on the portal.

Where was she now?

Shelton fidgeted, his eyes never resting in one place. Hi was breathing hard even with his powers unleashed.

I'm not built for climbs, Hi moaned in my head. *Let's find an escalator.*

Keep moving. I didn't know where the girl was, but Ben and Chance were racing into danger. We had to have their backs.

Three more levels passed in blur. Above us, something clanked.

New scents hit my nose. Tree flowers. Rain. Crisp night air.

A way outside.

The stairs ended with a short hallway leading to a narrow ladder. I saw a pair of immaculate tennis shoes disappear through the ceiling. "Chance!" I shouted.

His face popped back through the hatch. "What!?"

"Can you hear them?"

Chance shook his head impatiently. "No! They shut me out again. I have to help Ben!"

He vanished from the opening.

Hi was gripping his knees. *Oh good, a ladder. I was hoping our ascent would continue.*

We climbed quickly. Me. Shelton. Hi. Reaching the top, I blinked away bright moonlight, taking stock of our surroundings.

We'd reached the flight deck. Weak yellow floodlights burned at intervals, creating pools of light and dark. Open runway stretched before me, so different from the claustrophobic passages below. Vintage aircraft dotted the tarmac. Fighter jets. Helicopters. Even some sort of drone. I crouched in the shadow of the control tower, scanning the darkness, trying to locate my friends.

Ben?

Over here, by the Huey.

What's a Huey? But Shelton and Hi took the lead, hurrying across the tarmac.

On impulse I stopped short, grabbed the hatch, and flipped it closed, then spun the locking wheel. Metal screeched against metal as it sealed.

Then I raced after the boys, splitting a pair of nasty-looking fighters and circling a buglike helicopter. Beyond it was a bulkier version. Four silhouettes were dancing in its shadow.

No. Not dancing.

That's just what it looks like when flaring Virals fight.

I ran toward a jumble of grunting, grappling boys.

Ben snaked through a pool of light. Moving faster than thought, his fist slammed into Speckman's side. The red-eyed Viral stumbled backward, but quickly recovered, sliding left to avoid Ben's next blow.

My eyes darted right—Cole and Chance had locked arms, each straining to throw the other down. Then Cole slipped under Chance's guard, springing up like a kangaroo to knee him in the stomach.

Chance dropped to the tarmac, eyes bulging, but managed to roll away from Cole's kick. He popped up behind Speckman and shoved the taller boy with both hands, knocking him off balance. Ben pounced, grabbing Speckman in a vicious headlock.

"Say something smart now!" Ben snarled, his biceps squeezing Speckman's throat. "Not so tough without a catwalk to hide on!"

But Speckman surprised him, lunging sideways and toppling them both, then flipping to his feet like a cat. As Ben rose, Speckman punched him in the face, sending Ben back to the deck. I felt a painful jolt along the bond.

"You bastard!" I charged Speckman as he stood over Ben, one foot rising to stomp my friend's chest.

Hi got there first.

"*Bonsai!*"

Speckman looked up in time to catch Hiram's full weight squarely in his gut. Hi barreled over the Trinity's leader, driving them both backward and to the ground in a ragged heap. As I helped Ben to his feet, Speckman angrily shoved Hi aside, eyes blazing with scarlet fury. He snagged Hi by the shirt front and cocked a fist. "You're dead, fat boy!"

Shelton darted from the shadows and kicked him square in the ass.

Speckman fell forward onto his hands, momentarily stunned. Hi, Shelton, and Ben formed a loose circle around him, a flurry of sendings bouncing between them.

"Three against one, eh?" Speckman laughed harshly, wiping bloody spittle from his mouth. "Doesn't matter. You golden boys are the weaker breed. Come find out."

Ignore him. Ben eyed Speckman coldly as he shook off the cobwebs. *Let's work together and take this jerk down.*

Shelton and Hi nodded, silent, focused on their adversary.

Scuffling sounds behind me. I turned, spotted Chance fighting alone against Cole.

Chance needs my help.

Though smaller, Cole was wicked fast, bouncing around like a pogo stick and evading at every turn. Chance couldn't lay a finger on him. So I crept across the hardtop, sticking to the shadows as I soundlessly looped behind the greasy stoner.

Chance spotted me in the corner of his eye. He feinted left, forcing Cole to shift his back to me. I was mere feet away.

My lips curled as I prepared to pounce.

Never leave your tail exposed, friend.

Pain exploded in my abdomen.

The air whooshed from my lungs as I staggered sideways, caught completely off guard.

Something thumped the side of my head. Stars. Flashes of light.

I toppled to my knees, reeling, eyes glazing as a catlike form slunk from the darkness.

The girl.

She moved like smoke, cartwheeling behind Chance in the blink of an eye.

Cole nodded, as if hearing instructions in his head. He jabbed at Chance, forcing him to dodge sideways.

I tried to call out, but couldn't breathe.

The girl's foot connected with Chance's knee. He dropped with a howl.

I spied a flash of dark hair, bundled tightly.

Get her.

But before I could react, a blast of agony struck between my temples. Searing pain exploded inside my skull, as if my brain had been poked with a cattle prod. I spun, swinging both arms wildly, but to no avail. No one was there. The attack was on my mind.

I gasped, grabbed my head with both hands. A cold, alien feeling swept through me.

Fighting off panic, I glanced up. Cole was standing rock still, eyes half glazed, a look of intense concentration on his face.

Somehow, I knew the torment was coming from him.

Invisible hands rattled the doors of my consciousness. I grimaced, sweat drenching my clothes as I pushed back with all the mental energy I could muster.

He's trying to get inside. Trying to batter me from within.

Then the pain vanished as quickly as it came.

"I'm out of here," Cole blurted, backing from where Chance and I were sprawled on the tarmac. "This ain't my style." The shadow nodded, and the pair slipped away.

I rolled onto my stomach, trying not to puke. Chance was hunched over a few feet to my left, frowning as he worked his knee. He showed no signs of having beat back a similar attack.

What did that bastard Cole do? What powers were the Trinity playing with?

I shoved those thoughts aside as another fact crashed home.

My attacker.

How she moved. Her silhouette in the darkness.

I knew her. But with my head scrambled, I couldn't place it.

Never let someone behind you, right, Tory?

Cursing myself for being an easy target, I wobbled to my feet. The functioning part of my brain continued screaming.

The girl. You know her. You see her every day.

Ashley.

Even in the gloom, I'd noticed my attacker's glossy black hair. Her slender, sporty physique. The effortless grace of her movements.

I let her jump me. Now she and Cole are gone.

Someone grunted close by. With a jolt, I remembered the struggle behind me.

I turned to see Speckman knock Ben to the ground. He paused, panting, head on a swivel as he searched for Trinity allies. Finding none, he spat on the ground, then began to retreat toward the control tower. I tried to stop him, but the world was spinning beneath my tennis shoes. It was all I could do to remain upright.

Speckman wore an evil grin as he jogged past me. "Go help your puppies, golden girl. They don't look so good. Next time, remember to mind your betters." Then he disappeared into the gloom.

A voice groaned to my right. Someone was cursing softly. Still flaring, I spotted my packmates in the darkness and staggered over to them on rubbery legs. *Everyone okay!?*

Three against one, but it was clear who'd lost the fight.

Shelton lay on his back, a hand to his temple. *He moves so damn fast.*

Bastard. Ben was doubled over a few yards away, hacking and spitting. *He got lucky.*

Oh, no doubt. Hi struggled to one knee, wiping his nose. *All seven times he punched me were total flukes.*

I helped up Shelton, then Hi. We hustled over to Ben, but he waved us away, slapping the helicopter's metal hull in frustration.

Chance stumbled into the light, blood trickling from his bottom lip. "I'm fine, guys, thanks."

A spasm of guilt. "I was coming for you next."

The five of us stood in a ragged, panting circle. Pain and embarrassment fired up and down the bonds. We'd had the Trinity cornered, and gotten our butts kicked.

Speckman is strong. Hi was rubbing an abraded cheek. *Way stronger than us.*

"Out loud," I said. "Chance needs to hear, too."

"He's right." Shelton worked his jaw, checking to make sure his teeth were still in place. "We've horsed around before—and I know Ben's got more pop than me and Hi put together—but that guy?" Shelton shook his head. "I've never seen that kind of flare strength. That's next-level stuff."

"Will Speckman is nothing special." Ben's glare could cut diamonds, but I felt shame seeping through our connection. Could smell it on his skin. "He surprised me, but it won't happen again."

"Ben, don't." I remembered that twig Cole grappling with Chance. How fast my attacker had moved. "The Trinity may be stronger than us. They were infected by a different strain. We should consider the possibility that their flares are more powerful."

Chance glanced at me, then looked away.

"I'm telling you, it was luck." Ben refused to meet my eye. "Just give me another shot."

I didn't press the point.

We huddled in silence, each trapped in our own thoughts, listening to a dull sound echo over the water.

It took me a moment to recognize what it was.

Barking. Lots of it.

Coop.

Everyone's head jerked at once.

Better you than us.

Adrenaline poured into my bloodstream.

I turned my concentration inward. Found a fire alarm blaring, unnoticed.

Coop's bond thrummed with anger and fear. Unconsciously, my lips curled into a snarl.

An echo of pain hit me.

COOP!?!

CHAPTER 24

An image arrowed into my brain.

Men in black boots, pounding up the ramp.

Coop's sending was filled with rage. I sensed an ache in his side, as if he'd been kicked.

Enemies. Strong. Flee.

"Coop spotted men on the pier." Fighting down panic. "They're coming aboard."

"You were right!" Ben punched his open palm. "The Trinity are tipping the spooks!"

I was floored by their ruthlessness. The Trinity *wanted* us caught. Were trying to hand-deliver us into captivity. Why would they do such a thing?

My eyes darted to Chance.

Speckman said he knows the reason.

"What do we do?" Shelton whirled, searching for an escape route.

"The stairs are out," Hi blurted, his golden eyes wide with fear. "They'd cut us off like we did the Trinity."

"Over the side?" Chance suggested weakly. "Swim to shore?"

"We're a hundred feet up!" Shelton squawked. "We can't jump!"

My brain locked up, unable to formulate a plan. What about Coop? I couldn't leave him.

"Wait!" Something clicked. "The Trinity! They didn't use the stairs! We'd have heard them open the hatch."

I peered in the direction our enemies had fled. "They went that way."

Ben didn't hesitate, racing in pursuit. The rest of us followed on his heels.

We ran past the control tower to the still-sealed hatch. It was just as I had left it. I searched for another way inside the superstructure, but nothing looked promising.

Hi's voice thundered in my head. *They're down there!*

He was pointing to the south end of the flight deck, overlooking the marina. Moonlight framed three silhouettes. I took off down the runway, suddenly obsessed with seeing Ashley's face. Sick of shadows and guesswork.

As I watched, one of the forms simply disappeared.

I blinked to make sure my eyes were working properly.

A second shape vanished with a flip of dark hair.

Part of my brain jumped up and down, demanding I pay attention.

No time. I raced forward, determined to catch Ashley.

The flight deck ended dead ahead. There was nowhere else to run. But only Speckman stood there, glaring at us from beyond the stern guardrail. "Discovered your blind date early?" He shrugged, tightening something around his waist. A metal object glinted in his hands. "Doesn't matter, you won't escape their welcome party."

Before I could respond, Speckman did the unthinkable—waving impishly, he turned and leaped over the side.

We stood there, gaping in shock.

Hi's hand floated to his mouth. "Did he just . . ."

"Where are the other two?" Shelton warbled. "What's going on!?"

I ran to the rail. Saw Speckman's body falling to the dark sea below.

No. Not falling. Gliding.

I watched, baffled, as Will Speckman floated like an angel, drifting down to the marina dock a hundred yards away. My mind suggested all kinds of crazy answers.

The Trinity can fly. Will Speckman is actually a bird. Gravity has taken the night off.

Then I noticed a thin cable fastened to a rivet just below the railing.

"It's a zip wire."

Everything fell into place. Speckman's casual attitude as we approached. The harness around his waist. His missing packmates. As I stared down at the pier, three dark forms scurried into the marina and out of sight. The Trinity were gone.

My knees began to shake.

"We have to follow." I heard the shudder in my voice. "It's the only way."

"You're crazy!" Shelton lurched back from the railing. "We don't have any equipment!"

I grabbed him by the shoulders. "Those aren't hall monitors storming up here. Whoever is coming must be *bad* news. If they capture us, we might never be seen again."

Shelton flinched, retreating another step. "Stop talking crazy!"

"Tory's right." Hi peered over the edge of the runway. "We made it easy for them again. No one knows where we are right now. They could bag us up here and disappear. Who'd stop them?"

"We've done crazier stuff before." Ben grabbed the cable and shook it with both hands. "This line is solid, probably part of the anchoring system. We just ride it down."

"Ride *what*?" Shelton demanded, not giving in. "They took all the handlebars!"

Chance grunted. "We can't use our hands. Too much friction."

I spotted a stack of tarps to our right. "Look!"

We raced over, searching furiously for anything we could use.

My heart leaped. Beyond the tarps, a dozen braided ropes lay in messy pile.

"Perfect!" Ben grabbed five pieces—each roughly a yard in length—and passed them out. "Wrap the ends around your hands, and keep the line centered in the middle."

Hi laughed nervously. "Don't let go."

"Thanks." Shelton was sniffling quietly.

"You're still flaring," Chance added, trying to buck Shelton up. "It'll be easy."

A screeching sound filled the air. Someone was unscrewing the hatch from within.

"No more time!" I hissed.

"I'll go first." With a deep breath, Ben stepped over the guardrail. He crawled to the edge of the runway, where nothing separated him from a hundred-foot plunge to the murky water below.

I nearly threw up.

Arms trembling, Ben hooked a length of rope over the cable. Looped its ends around his palms. Gave a sharp tug. Then he cleared his throat. "Here goes nothing," he said in a cracked voice.

Ben stepped over the edge. Fell through the sky.

My hand shot sideways and seized Chance's shirt. He didn't notice, eyes glued to Ben as he mumbled, "*Come on come on come on . . .*" Hi and Shelton were hugging each other in terror.

It was over in moments. Ben zoomed down the line like a high wire expert. A dozen yards from the pier he let go, splashing into the marina shallows without a hitch. He surfaced quickly and swam over to the dock.

See? Ben sent, exhilaration pouring through the bond. *Easy!*

A clank behind us. The hatch, flipping open.

Who's next? I prodded, eying the empty flight deck at our backs.

Surprisingly, Shelton stepped forward. *I go now, or I'll never have the nerve.*

You can do this. Ben was watching from the dock, suddenly a bundle of nerves as he peered up at us. *I promise. I'll be with you the whole way.*

Shelton crawled over the guardrail, then edged slowly out to the line. He repeated Ben's routine exactly. Then, with a whimper, Shelton simply collapsed, allowing his body weight to drag him into space. I heard his mental scream as he sped down the cable.

Shelton released his rope on time, splashing down in nearly the same spot as Ben. *I'm alive!* he mind-screamed, even before surfacing. Then his head appeared and he scrambled for the dock. *Oh man, this water's disgusting! I think I got some in my mouth.*

Boots on the tarmac. I heard voices arguing somewhere close by.

I turned to Hi, who nodded, slithered over the railing, and slipped his rope into place. *I regret I have but one life to give. Because I'd prefer to have more lives.* Then he launched himself over the side.

Hi's terror arced through our bond like a completed circuit. He dropped faster than the other two, nearly failing to release his rope in time, splashing down less than a yard from the concrete dock. Seconds later his tubby form bobbed to surface, hacking and spitting. *Never a doubt!* he crowed, but his heart was pounding like a jackhammer.

I blew out a breath. That would've hurt.

Chance gripped my arm.

Footsteps, approaching fast.

Our eyes met. We didn't need telepathy. As one we vaulted the guardrail, scrambling to get our ropes in position without knocking each other from the ledge.

I was in front, balanced dangerously close to the drop. Chance wriggled and fidgeted close behind me as he tightened his grip. With every slight bump, I felt sure I was going over the side.

A flashlight beam slashed directly overhead.

Before I could react, Chance swung his legs up and wrapped them around me like a vise. "Don't worry! I won't let you fall." Then his bulk propelled us over the side.

A moment of weightlessness.

I choked back a scream, felt Chance's body go rigid against mine. Then we were falling, the wind whistling in my ears.

My rope caught the line with a jolt and dug cruelly into my palms. We slid down the cable like a bobsled team, moving faster than I could've imagined.

"Get ready!" Chance yelled in my ear.

The pier rushed up to meet us, looking hard and unforgiving.

"Let go . . . *now*!" Chance bellowed.

I opened my fists. In a double-cannonball, we dropped into the harbor.

Water flooded my nose. I kicked away from Chance, pulling for the surface. We came up side by side, Chance grinning like a Loggerhead monkey. "Not so bad!"

"A little warning next time!" Already swimming for the dock.

As Ben helped me from the water, I experienced a stab of panic. *Coop!*

My eyes darted down the concrete embankment. There was a security fence between us and the naval park, and dogs don't climb.

I slapped my head in self-recrimination. The boys huddled around me, but I waved them away, closing my eyes and reaching out to my wolfdog. *Boy, come!*

I waited, holding my breath, watching the restricted area beyond the fence where I'd asked Coop to stand guard. Painful seconds passed, then Cooper slunk from the shadows, studying me across the glassy channel of water.

I'm coming, boy! I'll climb over and—

Coop skipped back a few steps, then calmly launched himself into the harbor and began dog-paddling in our direction.

I started. "Oh. I see."

"That'll work." Ben dropped back into the water and waited.

Coop crossed the shallows with ease, allowing Ben to loop an arm around him as he neared the dock. Chance jumped in to help Ben lift the soggy wolfdog. As Hi, Shelton, and I dragged Coop from the ocean, I stole a glance back up at the *Yorktown*.

Lights bobbed on the flight deck. Muted voices barked orders. I felt eyes watching from above. Could feel their anger and frustration.

"Let's get out of here," I whispered, as Ben and Chance scrambled back onto the pier.

Like a flock of startled birds, we streaked into the night.

○   ○   ○

Sewee chugged across the harbor.

Coop had finished licking my face, and was curled up at my feet. Chance sat in the copilot's seat beside Ben, who was steering us toward home. Hi and Shelton were huddled in the bow, maniacally describing their zip rides to each other. It was nearly four in the morning.

I finally relaxed. We'd escaped again, this time against heavy odds.

Given the circumstances, I'd take it. Next time we'd be more prepared.

Shockingly, sleep threatened, but I fought back the urge. Relaxed my mind.

You know what you saw.

The thought jolted me upright. How long had I been ignoring it?

My shoulders slumped. My spirits sank. Almost against my will, I acknowledged a fact that had been lurking inside my brain since the fight on the flight deck.

Dropping my strongest, fiercest, most deeply imbedded mental

defenses, I let a frantic little voice step up to the microphone and un-
leash its terrible truth.

The third member of the Trinity.

I knew who the girl was.

With utter certainty, though I hadn't seen her face.

I mean, of *course* I did.

After all, she was practically my best friend.

Tears streaked down my cheeks. I barely noticed, shell-shocked by
revelation.

As we motored over the swells, a name escaped my lips.

"Ella."

PART THREE
CHAOS

ATTENTION: DIRECTOR WALSH ["EYES ONLY"]

FILE STATUS: TOP SECRET [LEVEL 5]

CASE: #34687 (AKA—PHOENIX INQUIRY)

FILE TYPE: SUSPICIOUS DEATH REPORT

DATE: APRIL 17, 2014

SUBJECT(S): FLETCHER, SALLIE D.; FLETCHER, CHRIS G.

PRINCIPAL INVESTIGATING AGENT(S): J. SALTMAN, B. ROGERS

NOTE(S): THE FIRST ATTEMPT TO INTERVIEW SUSPECTS CONNECTED TO THESE
DEATHS WAS UNSUCCESSFUL. SUSPECTS ARE BEING HELD IN A SECURE FACILITY
OUTSIDE INVESTIGATING AGENTS' CURRENT REACH WITHOUT ELEVATING
THIS INQUIRY TO PRIORITY LEVEL P-TSX-7. INVESTIGATING AGENTS AWAIT
AUTHORIZATION TO PROCEED.

NOTE TO FILE:

On October 21, 2011, at approximately 5:45 AM, Christopher Gerald Fletcher ("C.
Fletcher"), and his wife, Sallie Denise Fletcher ("S. Fletcher") (collectively "the
Fletchers"), were killed in a single-car accident on the Arthur Ravenel Jr. Bridge,
which connects the town of Mount Pleasant to Charleston, South Carolina. The
couple's 2010 Toyota Prius careened off the road near the Highway 17 interchange,
struck a concrete bridge abutment, and burst into flames, killing both passengers.

Though initially ruled an accident, the Charleston Police Department ("CPD")—in
light of subsequent events involving Phoenix Inquiry investigation target Victoria G.
Brennan ("Tory Brennan")—opened a homicide investigation on October 28, 2011. To
date, no one has been convicted of a crime in connection with the Fletchers' deaths.

The Fletchers were enrolled in a graduate program at Charleston University ("CU") and worked as assistant curators at the Charleston Museum at the time of their deaths. Investigating Agents have confirmed that, immediately prior to the crash, the Fletchers had close dealings with Tory Brennan (and her current associates)—both in person and by phone—of an unknown nature.

It is the belief of Investigating Agents that the nature of this unlikely association, and the Fletchers' deaths as described herein, directly relate to the subject matter of the Phoenix Inquiry. Therefore, we await further instruction and/or permission to proceed. [END SUSPICIOUS DEATH REPORT]

CHAPTER 25

I got there first.

Alone at the table we shared during first period, I waited for Ella Francis.

Shelton and Hi sat in their usual seats behind me, hiding bruises, fighting to stay awake.

Oblivious.

I hadn't shared what I knew about Ella yet.

Not aboard *Sewee* as we fled the *Yorktown,* nor at the Morris Island dock before we snuck back into our homes. I'd barely spoken ten words that morning.

I needed to confirm that Ella had betrayed me. Needed to look her in the eye.

Needed to know why.

Classmates streamed by the door. I spotted Ashley and Courtney strolling together, tensed when they stopped and peered inside the room. Maybe they wanted to press their shopping invitation again, but something in my posture must've warned them off. The girls simply waved and continued on down the hallway.

They were followed soon after by Jason and Madison. Madison

noticed my attention, flinched, and then smiled awkwardly. She gave Jason a quick hug before hurrying back into the corridor. Jason gave me the briefest of nods as he beelined to his seat in the back row. *What is it with those two?*

Ashley. Courtney. Jason. Madison.

Former suspects, all, but none were Trinity.

I barely noticed their discomfort. Focused wholly on my own.

Then she was there.

Ella bounced over to our table, smiling, looking beautiful, her deep green eyes twinkling with amusement. Her backpack thunked to the floor as she dropped into the chair beside mine. "*Ugh.* I got *zero* sleep last night. So looking forward to the weekend."

Ella flipped her waist-length rope of black hair my way. An old trick between us—I slapped the braid aside without even thinking.

"Did you read the whole section last night?" Digging into her bag, Ella pulled out a dog-eared calculus text. "Dullsville. Not that I thought polynomial approximations would be cool."

"I read it last week," I responded dumbly, totally thrown. Of all the scenarios I'd planned for, Ella pretending nothing had happened was not one of them.

"Always the studious one," she mocked lightly, tucking a stray wisp of hair behind her ear. "If only you treated soccer with the same diligence. Will you be at practice today?"

"What? No. I . . . I don't think so."

Ella shook her head. "Stupid SATs. Next week, then. I already told Coach Lynch that you weren't likely anyway, so you're covered. But I think he's at the end of his patience. Remember, we play Bishop England in four days."

"Right. Of course." *What is going on?*

I was prepared for Ella to be apologetic. Aggressive. Fearful. Pretty much anything but this. How can you ambush a friend in the dead of night, on the deck of a freaking aircraft carrier, then act like nothing happened?

I can safely attest to having no life experience to draw from on this one.

So I did the natural, unnatural thing. Played along.

Ella ignoring the elephant in the room left me nowhere to go.

Does she think I didn't recognize her? Even after she kicked me?

As if reading my thoughts, Ella glanced up. Met my gaze squarely for the first time.

For a split second, something lurked behind her eyes. The barest trace of . . .

Was it guilt? Suspicion? Or was it . . . defiance. A challenge.

Then she reached out and squeezed my shoulder, eyes soft with concern. "You okay, Tor? You seem distracted."

I looked away, my nerve folding like a deck chair. "No. I'm fine. Just . . . tired."

Ella snorted. "Maybe we should *both* get more sleep."

Up at the whiteboard, Mr. Terenzoni rose to begin his lecture. So I faced front, pretending to listen, and endured one the most uncomfortable hours of my life.

◇　　◇　　◇

Could I be wrong?

The question hounded me as I trudged to my locker, Hi and Shelton sleepwalking a few paces behind me. I asked myself over and over, but kept arriving at the same conclusion.

No.

I knew what I'd seen. It *had* been Ella who attacked me on the tarmac. Wish though I might to change that fact, I knew its truth. Once I'd recognized her profile, everything else slotted into place.

It *was* Ella Francis. I had zero doubt.

Ella had bolted right at the bell, claiming she had a doctor's appointment. She'd be gone for the rest of the morning. A small relief—I wasn't sure I could endure pretending I didn't know her secret.

Ella had physically attacked me. Was freaking Viral, with a grudge.

But why?

I couldn't figure it out. Nothing had ever come between us.

And how did Ella know Will Speckman? Cole? How did she catch the supervirus?

So many questions. No answers. Not even the cold comfort of having faced down my attacker. On whole, the day so far was a bust.

Which is why Chance's text caused me to groan out loud.

"What is it?" Shelton tensed at my expression. "I'm not up for another gang fight today."

"Chance has news. He wants to meet ASAP."

Hi waved the idea away. "I almost got caught sneaking in last night. My mother is suspicious—she wants to know why I look like I've joined an ice hockey team. I'm laying low. Mom said to be home right after school, and that's what I'm gonna do."

I turned weary eyes on Shelton. "You?"

"Not today." He shrugged apologetically. "I've slept thirty minutes in the last twenty-four hours. My head's still ringing from that beatdown. I need beauty rest."

"Okay." I ran a hand over my scalp. The boys had a point—I was sore head to toe, with a thousand bumps, bruises, and scrapes. "I'll go see Chance by myself."

"What do you think he wants?" Hi hitched his backpack, stepping closer so he wouldn't be overheard. "Does he know who karate-kicked him?"

Hi was referring to Mystery Girl. The Trinity's third member, whose identity the boys couldn't guess. I turned away, hiding my face. "Guess I'll find out when I see him."

○   ○   ○

I snuck away during lunch.

Though I'd told Chance to expect me after school, as the morning dragged I began to dread another encounter with Ella. She could pop into the cafeteria at any time, and my nerves couldn't take a second masquerade.

So noon found me knocking on Chance's office door. No answer.

Cursing myself for not calling, I slipped inside and closed it behind me. I had thirty minutes tops—hopefully he'd show before then, or the whole trip would be a waste.

I was debating a catnap on the couch when a folder on Chance's desk caught my eye.

Dark red. Sealed with tape. Stamped: "SECRET/PROPRIETARY."

Never above snooping, I drifted over for a look.

The tape had been sliced, saving me the trouble. Sinking into Chance's chair, I read the enclosed documents, eyes growing wider with each page. Then I nearly jumped from my skin as the door swung open.

Chance froze on his third step, sandwich in one hand, a Diet Coke in the other.

A hand rose to my chest. "You scared me!"

Chance glared at me in annoyance. "Because you're doing something wrong."

My finger tapped the open folder. "What is this?"

Chance set his lunch on the coffee table and approached the desk. Surprisingly, he dropped into a guest chair and waved me back into his own seat.

"You might as well know," Chance muttered, frowning at the file. "It's not like I meant to keep it secret. I just wasn't ready to advertise my intentions."

Sinking back down, I lifted documents at random. "Decoupling polymer bonds through biochemical agents. Viral genetic transference thresholds. The efficacy of recombinant protein therapy within cellular nuclei. Chance, what is this stuff? It looks like active research."

Chance nodded. "My last Candela project, since I'm sure to be fired when the board discovers how much money I've spent. I called in every favor I had to get it running. The researchers who wrote those reports think it's all theoretical. I've got separate teams assembled to produce the physical products—off-site firms, ones that don't ask questions. Each portion is being done blindly, like a drug study. Assuming we nail down a working formula, of course."

I scanned the papers as Chance spoke, growing more and more alarmed at what he'd set into motion. I'm no PhD, but I got the big picture. Knew exactly what Chance intended.

Glancing up, I found him staring at me.

"You're trying to counteract the effects of the supervirus," I whispered, even with the door closed. "Creating a serum to scrub foreign DNA from human cells."

"A new virus, to counteract the old." Chance didn't flinch. "I'm looking for a cure."

I was floored. "How?"

"Reverse engineering." Chance rubbed his neck, appeared to weigh how best to explain. "I've been lying to you. I didn't destroy *all* of the supervirus. Nor did I erase *every* record. I kept one set of files, which you've seen. And one sample."

His gaze strayed to a mini-fridge in the corner of his office.

My eyes bugged. "You've got to be kidding!"

Chance smiled sheepishly. "Where else could I keep it?"

I sat back, struggling to process this new information.

A cure.

The chance to counteract what had been done to my DNA.

A shot at a normal life.

I'd never considered the possibility before. How could I? I wasn't Chance Claybourne, with a family pharmaceutical empire at my disposal.

I'd daydreamed about telling Kit one day. Of my father, inspired to help, rededicating LIRI to fixing his only daughter. But those were silly fantasies. The most I'd ever really hoped for was for my body to stabilize. Some small peace of mind about the future.

But here was Chance, out of nowhere offering the possibility of a total reset.

I didn't know how to feel.

"Why didn't you mention this earlier? There's no reason to keep it secret from us."

"I didn't want to scare anyone. Through the course of this project, I've discovered a few things that disturb me." He looked away, seemed to steel himself. When Chance met my gaze again, his eyes were hard. "I learned two things I haven't shared."

I swallowed. Knew I wouldn't like what was coming next.

Chance held up one finger. "First, I know that my strain of parvovirus—the one that infected the Trinity as well—is more powerful than the one Karsten created."

My eyebrows rose. "What do you mean?"

Chance chose his words with care. "I was less careful to weaken the canine parvovirus than Karsten. Consequently, more of its DNA transferred into the hybrid strain. Last night, we saw an example of that difference."

Queasiness swept through my gut. "The Trinity's flares are stronger."

Chance nodded. "Mine as well. The second virus seems to have a more pronounced effect on the human limbic system, causing a greater release of hormones. The canine DNA is more active. We can flare more easily, and our powers are more intense."

This was bad. But I sensed worse was to come.

"And the second thing?"

Chance paused a moment before speaking. Finally, he leaned forward and spoke slowly. "My research indicates that a DNA exchange of this nature, once initiated, can't be stopped."

My gut turned to ice. "Speak plainly."

He smiled sadly. "I think our DNA—and I mean *everyone,* including your pack, me, and the Trinity—will continue to mutate, ultimately collapsing into an unsustainable state." Chance cleared his throat, then forced the last words out. "I believe our condition is terminal."

I always knew.

Long-held defenses collapsed.

For over a year, I'd worried. Nothing in life is free. People with superpowers only exist in movies. In the real world—in nature—99 percent of genetic mutations are fatal.

Why would being Viral be any different?

Chance confirmed what I'd always suspected. I understood why he hadn't said something before. Who wants to pass a death sentence along to friends?

"You're sure?"

"As sure as I can be. Which is why we need the antidote."

I dropped my head into my hands. Then slowly, quietly, began to cry.

I thought of Kit, losing a daughter he'd only just begun to know. Of Cooper, the first poor soul subjected to this horrible plague. Of my packmates, stuck in the same boat.

All because I stuck my nose where it didn't belong.

"Hey." Chance sounded surprised. "Hey, Tory. It's okay."

My head never rose. I was exhausted, demoralized, and bereft of hope. Reserves gone, I sobbed into my hands, releasing months of caged tension, a deluge of faded hopes and realized fears spilling from me in an ugly rush.

A hand on my shoulder. Another slipping around my waist.

Chance gently lifted me from his chair and lowered me to the floor, cradling my body like a child's. I sniveled, unable to control my emo-tions. He held me for what seemed like forever, stroking my hair, whis-pering soft words I didn't comprehend.

When the tears were finally spent, I pulled back, face streaked, look-ing and feeling like the world's biggest basket case.

Chance's face was inches from mine, his strong arms still wrapped around my shoulders.

Dark eyes. Dark lashes. I'd never seen a more beautiful man.

He lifted my chin in his hand. "I'm going to fix this. I'm going to cure you."

I don't know what came over me.

I launched forward, crushing my mouth against his.

Chance toppled backward, my weight hitting his chest as our lips met. Then he squeezed me tight, pulling my body closer.

An electric heat spread from head to toe.

Unbidden, my mind compared Chance to Ben. Chance was bolder, his entire bearing self-assured as he held me close. Ben had been fum-bling and hesitant. Chance hungrily devoured my kiss with an urgency I'd never felt before.

What is wrong with you!?! WHAT ARE YOU DOING!?!

I broke away. Scrambled back against the wall.

Chance sat up, confused. "Tory, it's okay."

"No. I . . . we . . ." I ran a hand through my hair, eyes widening at the thought of what Ben would say. Or do. "We can't."

"We *can*," Chance insisted, frustrated, one hand extending toward me. "We should!"

What is it with me and floors? The notion nearly sent me into hysterics.

Rising quickly, I hurried for the door. "I have to go. I'll call you later."

I fled the office before he could speak another word.

CHAPTER 26

I made it back to Bolton in record time.

Distracted, I walked right past the gate. Might've strolled on into the harbor had Hi and Shelton not been watching for me.

"Yo, Brennan!" Hi waved at me from where they lingered in the courtyard. "Get in here, quick. Headmaster Paugh is on patrol."

I slipped inside, joined them beside a bubbling fountain. Then my cheeks flushed scarlet.

Two make-out sessions in two days, with two different guys.

Should I track down Jason and take the Triple Crown?

"You okay, Tory?" Shelton edged closer, eyes worried. "Chance have bad news?"

For a moment, I didn't know what to say. Opted for a half-truth. "Chance had more lab results."

Technically accurate.

"He's still trying to figure out what's going on with our DNA."

Also true, as far as it went.

Shelton nodded, mollified. "I'm worried about these Trinity jokers. I've never seen anyone move that fast. Like ninja meth-heads."

"Tell me about it." Hi rubbed a purple blotch on his cheek. "Speckman's not much bigger than Chance, but his flare strength was through the roof. Next time, we need a better plan than shipboard wrestling after dark."

"True that." Shelton slumped against the stonework, rubbing his side. "My ribs are *killing* me. I just wish we'd spotted the girl. I didn't get a look."

Another fact I knew, but didn't share. The info I was withholding had begun to pile up. Made me sick to my stomach. I'd yelled at Chance for the exact same thing.

But I couldn't accuse Ella without proof. Things would get too crazy.

So get proof. Do something useful.

"I need to run by my locker." When the boys began to follow, I held up a hand to stop them. "Then I'm hitting the ladies' room. I'll catch up with you after."

They nodded, settled back down by the fountain. Began arguing about *Lost* for the millionth time.

Hurrying through the massive front doors, I headed for the cafeteria.

Ella would be having lunch.

It was time to force the issue.

○   ○   ○

She was eating alone in our spot. Taking a deep breath, I approached.

Ella spotted me halfway and waved. I waved back.

"Hey, Tory." Smiling sweetly, she kicked out the chair beside her. "Join the party."

I ignored it, circling and taking a seat across the table. "We need to talk."

"Oh? What's on your mind?" Her expression remained pleasant, but I didn't miss her narrowing eyes. Any final doubts died in that instant.

I looked her dead in the face. "You've got quite a kick."

Ella paused a beat. Then her lips twisted cruelly. "Of course I do."

She sat back, folding her arms over her chest. "I was less impressed with you."

My fist hit the table. I struggled to keep from shouting. "What the *hell*, Ella? Why?"

The smile vanished. Ella's emerald eyes glittered with malice. "Are you serious? You're asking *why*, after everything you've done to me?"

My mouth dropped open in genuine bafflement. "Done to you? What are you talking about? I—" a quick scan of the room to make sure we weren't being observed, "—*rescued* you. And nearly got killed in the process!"

"You're the only reason I was kidnapped in the first place!" Ella hissed. "Knocked out, and stuffed in a car trunk!" Her voice quavered. "Held in a pit for three days, by a psychopath, because of *you*."

Each word was a punch to my soul. Not least because they were true.

When the Gable twins had been abducted, I'd demanded the Virals get involved. During the investigation I'd shared some of my theories with Ella, inadvertently making her a target.

I hadn't known it would happen, but it did.

"You know I feel terrible about that," I said quietly.

"Oh gee, thanks!" Ella snorted without humor. "I'll cancel my therapy."

The surreal nature of our conversation washed over me. We were discussing a rain shower while lightning crashed down around us.

My voice dropped another notch. "Ella, how did you learn to flare?"

"Another disaster I have you to thank for," she spat. "You're a *disease*, Tory Brennan."

I brushed the insult aside, though I knew it would hurt later. "I don't understand."

Ella looked away. "Why should I tell you anything? I'm surprised you figured out this much."

It was my turn to lean forward. "We're in this together, Ella. You and the rest of the Trinity. Me and my Morris Island pack. Even Chance. We're *all* Viral."

"We're in it all right," Ella replied coldly, "but *not* together."

I nearly slapped my forehead. "How can you say that? We have to help each other!"

"Like you and Chance do?" Biting a thumbnail, she flashed a mocking smile. "He hasn't told you the whole story yet. It's obvious with every word you say."

I tried to keep my voice steady. "What do you mean?"

Ella watched me silently, then shook her head. I could tell she wouldn't answer.

I stared at her, stunned by the ugly transformation in my friend.

Ella smiled slyly, taunting me. "Who were you guessing? Ashley Bodford? Tripod becomes Trinity, eh? That was Will's bright idea, but I thought it'd be funnier if you suspected Jason and Madison. So I tricked them into avoiding you, told them their relationship made you *extremely* uncomfortable. You *really* needed space. Worked like a charm."

I gaped. Fumbled for words. "How . . . how did you became Viral?"

Ella shrugged, as if we were confidantes at Sunday tea. "I met Will Speckman a few days after our . . . incident. We went to the same counseling center." Ella rolled her sparkling green eyes. "Will has his own issues—talk about paranoid!—but he was *super* excited about his new job assisting the great Chance Claybourne. I was curious, but he wouldn't talk about their little project. Said the work was too important. Top secret. Life changing. Yada yada yada."

Ella rubbed her arms, eyes growing distant. "I never took his boasting seriously. But I learned my mistake pretty quickly, didn't I? And you should've seen Will after he got fired."

My shoulders slumped. "So you were infected by Speckman."

"Or his charming roommate," Ella chirped with false gaiety. "Who knows? Cole caught the virus soon after Will. I wasn't infected until weeks later, after my time in that cell. Will still can't figure out how, not that it matters anymore."

I felt sick. "I'm so sorry, Ella."

She continued as if I hadn't spoken. "I was puking for days. If Will hadn't talked me through it—hadn't been there to explain what was happening . . ." She shuddered. "I'd have gone to a hospital. Gotten tests run. Ended up in a cage."

Her eyes found mine. No warmth there. "Will had already transitioned, you see. He and Chance were trading notes, so Will already knew the score. Knew how to protect me. How to guide me through the changes. He'd done it once with Cole already."

Speckman and Chance spoke? When? How often? What did Chance tell him?

"Did anyone else get sick?" My mind reeled at the implications.

"No." Ella waved my question away, seemed irritated by her own compulsion to answer me. "The three of us went camping for a weekend. I didn't know his jackass roommate was coming until after I got there. Then I got sick, way out in the woods. Will must've suspected the supervirus immediately, because he kept us there an extra day. When I recovered, they showed me what they could do. What *I* could do."

Flaring. I crunched numbers in my head. Ella had gained control over her powers much sooner than my pack. Cole and Speckman as well. Chance, too, now that I thought about it.

Ella must've read my thoughts.

She leaned across the table, her voice dropping to a dangerous purr. "Yes, Tory. We learned quickly. We're stronger and faster than you and your friends. Whatever Will and Chance cooked up, the second batch had more kick than the original."

Ella winked, but not in friendship. I barely recognized my friend, sitting across from me with a spiteful glare. She'd borne this secret for weeks. Hid it from me every day. The depth of her scheming astounded me—to meticulously plan my downfall with such dedication, all while flawlessly pretending to be my best friend.

She torched my bunker.

With growing dismay, I realized how deep a grudge Ella must carry.

I chose my next words carefully. "I'm very sorry for what happened, Ella. All of it. And, yes, it was my fault. I thought you understood that I couldn't have foreseen how events would play out, and that I did everything possible afterward to make things right. I guess I was wrong."

Ella flinched the slightest bit. Her eyes found the tabletop.

I pressed ahead. "I've been Viral for over a year, with only the Morris Island boys to share it with. It's been a blessing and a curse. I'm sorry you got dragged into this situation, truly. But my hope is that we can all work together, and get past this silly feud. There's a bigger threat out there."

That the Trinity seemed to be working *with* that threat, I left unsaid.

Ella hesitated, eyes glazing as her focus turned inward. Then she shook her head sharply, as if dismissing a foolish notion. "Like I said, you don't understand. My pack needs to protect itself. That means you guys have to take the fall."

She half rose, lifting her tray. "Don't cross me again, Tory. You won't like what happens. Your crew dodged Will's stupid traps, so that nonsense is over with, but don't come running to us for help. I won't pretend to love what's happening, but your pack deserves to pay the bill, not mine."

I grabbed her arm. "Deserves *what*, Ella? What's going on? Who is chasing us?"

She pulled away with a condescending headshake. "You see? Clueless."

I popped up and shouted at her back. "Who was on the *Yorktown* last night?"

Ella called over her shoulder without turning.

"You should really talk to Chance."

◇   ◇   ◇

After school, I told Shelton and Hi everything.

I apologized for holding out, then spilled my guts. About Ella. Her warnings about Chance. Every last suspicion I harbored. Even Chance's dire prediction about the supervirus.

I was tired of keeping secrets from friends. Had my fill of betrayal.

It was time to lean on the people I trusted most.

Except the kissing stuff, of course. I wasn't crazy.

"We gotta tell Ben." Shelton sat on the curb, looking shell-shocked. "He deserves to know, too."

"But *delicately*," Hi advised with a wince. "Might take some finesse."

"Terminal?" Shelton looked at me with frightened eyes. "Is Chance sure?"

"No." I dropped down beside Shelton and clasped his hand in mine. "He's *not* sure. And he's working on a cure as we speak. Don't worry— one way or another, we're going to be fine. I promise."

Shelton nodded. Some of the tension left his shoulders.

"Let's get to the marina." Hi removed his blazer and tossed it over one shoulder. "We'll call Ben and tell him to drive over to his dad's place, then hammer out a plan."

"Should we invite Chance?" Shelton asked.

Both boys looked at me.

"Not this time," I said. "Tonight's meeting is Morris Islanders only."

I glanced down Broad Street. Not five blocks away sat Claybourne Manor, the largest private residence in the state. Home to Charleston's richest bachelor.

A boy with secrets.

A boy I'd kissed just hours earlier.

I'm done being played, Claybourne.

"Next time we see Chance," I vowed, "we'll have the upper hand."

CHAPTER 27

For the first time in forever, I went straight home from school.

I was dead tired. No sleep the night before, then Chance. Then my showdown with Ella. All my reserves were gone. I needed a nap in the worst way.

So of course it didn't happen.

Coop tipped me off as I walked through the door, greeting me silently and glancing over his shoulder. Kit and Whitney were sitting in the living room.

Great.

Spotting me, they practically jumped. For some reason I was sure they'd been arguing.

"Hey, kiddo." Kit rose, conjuring up a smile, hands locking behind his back. After an awkward moment he sat back down. "Just the person I wanted to see."

"Kit, I don't . . ." Whitney glanced at me, then down at her lap. She'd gotten better at not inserting herself into father-daughter discussions, but this felt different somehow.

I was too exhausted to play along. "Out with it."

Kit started. "What do you mean? I just wanted—"

Dropping my bag, I knelt to scratch Cooper's ears. "Guys, this is becoming ridiculous. You're getting married. I support that. But the silly dance we do every time you need to tell me something I might not like? It's tired. *I'm* tired."

"Then we can discuss this another time," Whitney said firmly, standing and shooting Kit a pointed look. In that moment it occurred to me that I'd never really seen her angry with my father. Was this what it looked like? If so, good for her.

But delay was not a solution. "No, it's fine. Just say what you want to say."

Kit took a deep breath. "How would you feel about moving?"

I blinked. Felt the walls close in around me.

"Not far!" Kit added in a rush. "I'm not talking about leaving Charleston, or anything drastic. But lately I've been thinking—maybe we need a home with a little more space?"

I started to breath again. "More space?"

Then it hit me. My eyes found the ceiling. "You mean Whitney's townhouse, in the city."

Their exchanged glance was all the confirmation I needed.

"I take it the repairs are finished."

Whitney nodded, her posture rigid. I could tell she was worried I'd explode.

As a lump built in my throat, I tried to think rationally. "Your place has like, what, four bedrooms? Each with its own bathroom?"

Another quick Whitney head-bob. Her tone was neutral, but tight with tension. "The square footage is roughly double that of here. My address is a short walk to Bolton Prep."

Kit moved to her side. "The only thing that would change for you is those long boat rides. No more ferries across the harbor. More neighbors, more things to do. We'd live like normal people for a change."

Something about the word *normal* broke the dam.

"No more best friends next door." My voice caught. "No more wolf-dog either, right? I doubt Cooper is welcome downtown."

Kit stepped toward me, hands extended. "Tory, honey! It won't be that—"

Beside him, Whitney stamped her foot. "No!"

I flinched, startled by Whitney's outburst. Kit looked at his fiancée in total surprise.

Fat tears had gathered in her eyes. "This was a *bad* idea, Kit Howard." Whitney's hand chopped the air. "In the last year, Tory's dealt with enough change for any *five* girls! She has friends out here, on Morris Island. Her own space. We are *not* going to uproot her to some place she's never even *seen* before, simply because it's more convenient for us!"

I'm not sure who was more stunned, Kit or me.

"It'd be more convenient for everyone," my father replied weakly. Honestly, I'm not sure he knew how to react. "We're not trying to—"

Whitney cut him off, speaking forcefully, as if the matter was settled. "We will rent out my townhouse for the next few years. By then, Tory will be off to whatever college is lucky enough to have her, and this won't be an issue. But she does *not* have to move now." Then her voice practically cracked. "And no one is taking that dog away from her!"

I stared at Whitney Blanche Dubois. The Blonde Bimbo. My father's annoying gal-pal, turned unwanted roommate, turned future stepmother.

Try as I might, I'd always regarded her with just a hair short of contempt.

But I'd never seen *this* woman before in my life.

Almost reflexively, I opened my mouth to argue. Quickly shut it. Whitney had laid things out exactly as I would've. So I stared at the woman, totally taken aback.

Kit seemed just as rattled as me. "I mean, if that's what everyone wants." He snorted a nervous laugh. "Hey, being totally honest, I *love* living out here. It's close to work, lots of quiet and fresh air, no traffic, or—"

"Kit!" Whitney gave him an exasperated look, then nodded toward me.

"Yes." I cleared my throat, blinking back a deluge. "I mean, I'd prefer to stay here, like Whitney said. If that's okay with everyone."

"Perfectly." Whitney lifted her palms and flapped them to each side. "It's all settled, then. No need for anyone to worry another *instant* about this issue."

"Yes, of course!" Kit blurted, quickly looping an arm around his future bride's waist. "This is my fault. Dumb idea. Don't give it another thought, Tory."

I sighed with relief.

Of all the things I feared, being separated from my pack topped the list. Especially now, with our world gone crazy. The people I could trust were dwindling fast. I couldn't move away from the ones I counted on most. Not now.

Sure, I could've made things work downtown—though none of us liked it, we'd been dealing with Ben's move for months. But I didn't want to.

I needed my friends close.

And Whitney, of all people, seemed to know it.

Something thawed inside me. Not a drastic, thunderous change, but a . . . softening. The first spiderweb cracks in a shell I'd maintained for longer than I could remember.

Impulsively, I stepped forward and hugged Whitney. "Thank you."

I caught a flash of surprise in her eyes before they closed as she squeezed me back. Then I pulled free, feeling my own emotions roil.

No one could ever replace my mother.

But that didn't mean I couldn't let others in.

My eyes misted. "I'm glad you're marrying my father."

Whitney's hand rose to cover her mouth.

I turned and fled upstairs, Coop nipping at my heels.

Whitney's cloudburst of gentle sobs echoed in the room behind me.

CHAPTER 28

I slept the next six hours straight.

Awoke groggy and disoriented. A glance at my clock revealed it was already 10:00 p.m.

Outside my window, a waning moon hung in the cloudless sky, lighting the sand hills a silvery gray. Blinking away sleep, I hunted for my iPhone in the folds of my comforter.

Seven texts and four missed calls. No voice mail.

Ben. Hi. Shelton. Chance. I'd slept through every one.

I sat up and rubbed my face. Heard Coop snoring at the foot of my bed.

A thousand things had happened that day. A few didn't seem real.

Had I really made out with Chance? *Gawd.*

What a . . . moment? Nightmare? Betrayal? Revelation?

I didn't know. Was afraid to probe my feelings on the subject.

Blargh.

And Ella was freaking Viral—she'd *admitted* it!

My mind reeled at the implications. How long had she been playing at friendship, while secretly plotting my downfall?

I felt a moment's regret for having told Shelton and Hi, but swiftly quelled it.

No more secrets in my pack. Not *relevant* ones, anyway.

Then I remembered my encounter with Whitney. Shook my head in wonderment.

That memory, at least, wasn't laced with frazzled nerves or a tinge of regret. A concord between me and Kit's fiancée was long overdue. I was glad we'd found common ground—a way to make peace with the inevitable. Though I knew one hug didn't magically fix everything.

Still. Baby steps.

I swung my feet to the carpet, unsure of my next move. Another phone check—the alerts were hours old. I worried the boys may have made decisions without me.

Thinking logically, I plotted my next moves. Contact Hi and Shelton first, and plan how we'd tell Ben about Ella's cryptic comments. Once Ben was in the fold, we had to corner Chance somehow, and find out what Ella's warnings meant.

But my strategy was already stale.

I got an immediate reply from Shelton: **BEN ALREADY KNOWS. NOT HAPPY. MEET US OUTSIDE IN FIVE.**

"Yikes."

◇   ◇   ◇

"I'll kill him." Ben white-knuckled the steering wheel.

I rolled my eyes for the fifth time. "We don't know what he's holding back yet."

He scowled, eyes on the road. "We know enough."

Ben sped across the bridge to Folly Island. Since it was Friday night, I still had two hours before my curfew. An ice-cream-run cover story had satisfied our parents, so we'd piled into the Explorer in T-shirts and shorts, intent on a very different destination.

"How many times has Chance claimed he told us everything?" Ben fumed. "Three? Four? But it's never true!"

Can't argue with that.

I glanced at Shelton and Hi in the backseat. Both avoided my eye. Unable to reach me earlier, they'd decided to call Ben and tell him everything. Frankly, I was amazed he hadn't driven straight to Claybourne Manor.

"Are we sure he's home?" Hi asked.

I shook my head. "I didn't want him to know we were coming. If Chance isn't there, we'll try his office. He must be at one or the other."

"Unless he's meeting the Trinity," Ben muttered. "Or government agents."

My teeth ground in frustration, but I moderated my tone. "Look, I get that Chance hasn't been truthful. I'm as pissed about that as you. But we don't know what he's keeping from us. Or why. And he's obviously not working with the Trinity, after what they did on Loggerhead and the *Yorktown.*"

"He *knew* the virus was dangerous!" Ben spat, jerking a rough right turn. "He's been talking to the Trinity. And he definitely knows something about these shady bastards chasing us. But what does that jerk tell us? Nothing we can't *force* out of him. You learned more from Ella in five minutes, and she's been working against us for weeks!"

I bit my tongue. Every word was true, but it wasn't the whole picture. Chance hadn't withheld anything that could hurt us.

Yet.

But what did Ella mean? What did Chance know about our pursuers?

"What are we gonna do about Ella?" Shelton poked his head between the front seats. "It's not the same as with Speckman, or that dope Cole. We see Ella every day. She's your freaking teammate, Tor."

And my best girlfriend. Or was.

Ella's betrayal was too fresh for me to have fully processed my feelings.

But I knew it'd hurt when I did.

"I'm officially terrified of that girl," Hi pronounced, watching dimly lit rental houses streak past as we drove through the town of Folly Beach. "She messed with my head *before* I knew she was a ninja-kicking flare master. Now? I don't stand a chance."

"I'll handle Ella," I promised. *Somehow.* "She gave me the impression that the Trinity were backing off. For the moment, let's concentrate on Chance."

"With pleasure," Ben said.

There was a sudden slapping sound, followed by Shelton's voice squeaking in my ear. "Ow! Why you grabbing me, man?" I turned to see Hi staring out the back window, one hand latched on to Shelton's arm.

"Oh crap," Hi whispered.

"Let go of me!" Shelton griped.

"Hi?" I tried to follow my friend's line of sight.

"That black sedan from the other day?" Hiram's eyes remained glued to our trail. "The one that chased us across CU's campus? It's behind us. *Right now.*"

My head whipped to Ben, who was scanning his mirrors. "Two back?" he asked tightly.

"Yep." Hi had rotated all the way around in his seat to keep watch. "I noticed a town car parked in the cul-de-sac near our bridge. Now it's on the move. It's gotta be them."

Shelton twisted for a look, his lenses flashing in the streetlights. "How can you be sure?"

"Xenon headlights. They're bright as hell." Hi shot me a worried glance. "Plus, you guys recall a lot of black sedans idling out here on a Friday night?"

I tried to pick out the vehicle in the side mirror. Squeezed Ben's shoulder. "Can you lose them?"

He nodded tightly. "At the highway interchange. No way these stooges know Lowcountry back roads."

The tension rose as we rolled down Folly Road, heading toward the bridges accessing downtown. Ben turned onto the James Island Expressway, keeping his speed normal.

"Still following." Hi pawed at his wavy brown hair. "Always exactly two cars back."

"We'll see about that." Ben accelerated, pulling away from a Volvo station wagon directly behind us. Seconds later, xenon lights flashed in our rearview as the black sedan passed the slower vehicle, keeping pace.

"Okay." Ben almost smiled. "Here we go."

Abruptly, he swerved onto the exit ramp for Harbor View Road. Thumping the gas, Ben propelled us toward a stoplight a quarter mile ahead.

"It followed!" Shelton called anxiously. "Staying right on our tail!"

Ben turned left at the light, then wheeled an immediate right into a small neighborhood surrounded by tidal basin on three sides. "This street is one big circle." He sped around the circuit, crossing the center stripe to take the racing line. "I bet they don't know that."

Tires screeched behind us.

Our shadow, dropping any pretense of stealth.

Ben reached the neighborhood entrance again and turned out, eyeing the rearview.

After several beats, the black sedan emerged in pursuit.

"Damn." Ben gritted his teeth and nodded, as if accepting a challenge. "Guess I'll have to step things up a notch." He stomped the accelerator, firing back up onto the expressway.

"Still on our butts!" Shelton warned. He and Hiram were on their knees in the backseat, gripping headrests as they watched out the back window. "Dig a little deeper into your bag of tricks!"

"Will do," Ben snarled.

We crossed Wappoo Creek, approaching the downtown bridges, but Ben surprised me by taking the next exit. A hairpin turn, then we roared down a deserted lane toward the tangle of roads near the banks of the Ashley River.

Hi started to chuckle, apparently guessing Ben's plan. "Good call. It's Thunderdome down here."

We passed two secluded highways heading into the city, then veered onto Wesley Drive. The town car shrank in our mirrors as it struggled to navigate the knotted roads.

Ben turned left, then right, never slowing as he caromed down the one-way streets. Then he killed our headlights and snuck up an un-marked ramp onto the Savannah Highway. Rejoining the flow of traffic, he flipped the beams back on and casually drove across the river.

"Still on us?" he called back to the other boys.

"Nope." Shelton flashed a thumbs-up. "Those jokers are probably riding a drive-through lane, or stuck in a car wash."

"That was inspired." Collapsing down into his seat, Hi saluted our driver. "Nice work, sir."

Ben tapped a finger to his forehead. "I try."

We reached the peninsula. With a satisfied smirk, Ben turned into the tight warren of streets composing South of Broad.

My own smile faded as I recalled our destination.

Time to see Chance.

CHAPTER 29

Chance didn't seem surprised to see us.

"Come on in, then." Swinging the door wide, he pointed to the far end of his cavernous entrance hall. "Let's discuss things in my study, okay?"

An ironic smile tilted his lips. "I'm sure you remember the way."

"Fine." I strode briskly into the foyer, determined to control this encounter.

We'd parked three blocks away, hoping to catch Chance unawares and throw him off balance. Obviously, we hadn't accomplished our goal.

The iron gates had parted as we approached. No guards manned the security booth beside the driveway. And the front door to Claybourne Manor was opened by the heir himself.

Strange, all of it. But I held my tongue, not wanting to get sidetracked.

Wrapped in shadows, the glittering hall stretched deep into the house. Priceless art lined the walls, interspaced by shimmering mirrors, family portraits, and pedestaled busts and statues. The chandeliers overhead were larger than I was.

But I refused to be awed by the opulence of Charleston's most famous private home.

Been there. Done that.

We had business with the owner.

Ben scowled at Chance as he followed me inside. Hi and Shelton came last, gawking like tourists as usual. They'd been there before, but it's hard to be blasé about such a spectacular building. The mansion is a registered historic landmark, with forty rooms, two dozen fireplaces, sixty bathrooms, and the fifty-foot entrance hall leading to a domed atrium.

Ignoring the hand-carved woodwork and graceful crown molding, I strode down the corridor like a soldier girding for war. Carpet gave way to marble as I reached the atrium, with its paint-covered statue of Milton Claybourne. Starlight poured through the stained-glass dome three stories overhead, bathing the chamber in soft, angelic light.

I was surprised Chance hadn't cleaned up the Trinity's handiwork. He must've read my mind as we walked to a wide staircase hugging the wall. "I thought it best not to disturb evidence. Though I guess it doesn't matter any longer."

"No." I gave him my levelest look. "It doesn't."

Chance nodded glumly. "Come."

Odd. I haven't told him about Ella yet.

On the second floor, Chance led us across a lushly carpeted hallway to a pair of massive oak doors. The study beyond looked the same as last I'd seen it. Floor lamps cast a warm yellow glow across the expansive chamber. The ceiling rose twenty feet overhead, with scarlet drapes adorning floor-to-ceiling windows along the rear wall. Towering bookcases lined the other three boundaries, with a wrought-iron catwalk circling the room ten feet overhead, accessed by a spiral staircase in the corner.

In the room's center, a giant mahogany desk faced four overstuffed leather chairs surrounding a wagon-wheel coffee table. Beyond the seating area was a yawning fireplace, its logs removed, the heavy flagstones swept clean for the summer. A hand-stitched Persian rug covered the floor.

The study occupied a huge swath of the manor's second floor, so large it practically had an echo. A chamber built for mighty men, designed to intimidate.

It's not going to work on me.

"Have a seat." Chance waved toward the chairs. A stack of folders rested on the coffee table, along with a slim metal box.

Shelton and Hi ambled over and plopped down.

Ben and I remained standing by the door, annoyed at how easily Chance was dictating the encounter.

"You think this is a social call?" Ben growled.

"We know you've been lying to us." I crossed my arms. "It stops now."

"Not *lying*. Just not revealing everything." Again, the wry smile. "A practice you have some experience with."

My ears burned, but I ignored the barb. "Last we spoke, you said no more secrets."

Chance lifted both palms, as if in surrender. "Please. Just sit. I promise to put everything on the table. There's no need for this to be confrontational."

I hesitated, glancing at Ben. He was breathing hard, his fingers curled into fists. For a hot second, nonsensically, I thought of kissing him on *Sewee*'s deck. Being wrapped in his arms. His warm breath on my cheek.

Blood rushed to my face. I shook my head to dispel the memory.

My eyes found Chance, who was watching Ben as if he were a stray dog of unknown temperament. The image of us rolling on his office floor entered my brain. My cheeks turned three shades darker.

For God's sake, Tory. Get it together!

"I'm not your enemy, Ben." Chance spoke softly, but firmly. "Let me prove it."

At first Ben didn't respond, his hands clenching and unclenching. Then he strode to an empty chair and sat. "Talk. One last time."

I took the remaining seat, hoping my blushes had gone unnoticed.

Now was *not* the time to daydream.

Chance surprised me by settling down on the floor by the hearth. After fumbling with the folders and box for a moment, he looked up. He seemed almost relieved. "I'm going to tell you everything. But first, I want you to understand that I never really lied."

"Garbage," Ben barked automatically.

"I've held a few things back," Chance acknowledged, his face honest and open, "but I've never told you something that wasn't true. I just want that out there before I start."

"Okay, Chance." I gestured for him to proceed. "You've made your point. Now explain what's going on. Who's chasing us? Why?"

"We need to go back further than that." Chance shuffled the files, selecting the oldest-looking one. "As you know, after our first few . . . adventures, I spent time at a mental institution."

I shifted uncomfortably. We were a large part of the reason for that.

"I don't mention that to make you feel guilty." Then he chuckled softly. "Although I hope you do, at least a *little* bit. Regardless, I need to explain my state of mind when this all started."

Hi was listening intently, chin on one fist, as if Chance were a master storyteller about to perform. "When *what* started?"

"My investigation into you four." Chance stroked the battered folder with a thumb. "Soon after my release, I found this file in my father's private safe. The project notes of Dr. Marcus Karsten, of the Loggerhead Island Research Institute."

My eyes widened. "The originals?"

Chance nodded. "Based on where I found this, I knew the experiment was illegal. And I was certain you guys were tied up in it somehow, though for the life of me I couldn't understand how. I must've read these pages a hundred times before I found the link."

Pieces fell into place. "Cooper."

Chance tipped an imaginary cap. "I put together the following facts. One: The supervirus was contagious. Two: The test subject was stolen. And three: Tory had a wolfdog of unknown origin." His gaze turned inward, as though he sifted through painful memories. "I *knew* there was something different about you. I'd seen it myself on several occasions."

Shelton leaned forward. "If you knew all this, why'd you restart the experiment?"

"Bad timing." Chance shook his head. "I didn't put those things together at first. By the time I realized the new virus was potentially dangerous, I'd already run the first trials. Assisted by an old friend from high school named Will Speckman."

"So you infected yourselves." Ben shook disgustedly. "Two dopes, playing at scientist."

Chance didn't take offense. "I don't know when it happened. Or how. It must've been early, when we first combined the parvovirus strains using a quirk in Karsten's notes. That was before I had proper protocols in place. I've checked extensively, and no one else who worked in that lab has been infected."

"You're sure about that?" Hi demanded. "We don't need a citywide Viral outbreak."

"One hundred percent certain," Chance answered firmly. "Only four people went into that room, and the other two techs are fine. Trust me on this point. My inquiries were . . . thorough."

"But what about the people Speckman contacted afterward?" I countered. "He obviously passed the virus to Cole and Ella."

"He *couldn't* have." Chance sifted through the remaining files, then jabbed one with his finger. "I've tested every conceivable viral property.

The bug Will and I created simply cannot be passed through the air. Nor can it spread through physical or surface contact. Ella and Cole were infected in some other way."

"Wait!" Ben shot to his feet. "We never told you Ella was part of the Trinity. Yet you didn't bat an eye when Tory just said her name!"

The air in the room froze. All eyes found Chance, including mine.

Surprisingly, he laughed. "You think I don't know why you're here?"

Ben took a step forward, but I held up my hand. "Ben, sit down."

He shot me a furious glare.

I didn't flinch. "We're getting the whole story, right now. After that we can . . . decide."

Ben muttered something under his breath, but did as I ordered.

Chance continued as if the outburst hadn't occurred. "I got a call this afternoon. Guess who?"

My expression soured. "Will Speckman."

Chance nodded. "Very good. After cursing me for a traitor—*again*—he told me the Trinity were done with us, and that we were on our own." Chance eyed me curiously. "He also recapped your showdown with Ella in the cafeteria. I won't deny being shocked. Ella Francis? Honestly! I did *not* see that coming."

"You didn't know Ella was Trinity?" I watched for any sign of deception. "Tell the truth."

Chance didn't evade my gaze. "No. I first learned it from Will, this afternoon. You must've figured it out some time earlier, and decided not to share." He winked. "I forgive you."

"Watch it," Ben warned. "Tory's not the one—"

"He's right," I conceded grudgingly. "I put it together on the boat ride home from the *Yorktown,* but wanted to make sure. I'm sorry, everyone. I should've told you sooner."

Hi waved my apology away. Shelton frowned, but nodded.

Ben lowered into his chair, his expression dangerously close to a sulk. "How many friendly chats have you and Speckman had behind our backs?"

Chance took a deep breath. "A few. But they never led to anything. Speckman just likes taunting me. He's still angry I let him go at Candela."

"You fired him." Shelton shrugged, as if that explained it. "No wonder he's mad."

"What was I supposed to do?" Chance leaned back against the fireplace, his dark eyes brimming with annoyance. "He became totally unreliable. Plus, I had to bury the project before people found out what I'd done. That meant erasing the files, destroying the samples, and, of course, eliminating the outside staff."

I bit my lip, thinking. "Did you know Speckman was Viral when you shut things down?"

"No." Chance's expression soured. "I thought I was the only one."

"Okay." Hi sat up straight, began ticking fingers. "Speckman caught the superbug. Later you fired him. Result: he's pissed. That all tracks. But how were Cole and Ella infected?"

For a few beats, no one spoke.

"I have a guess," Chance said quietly.

We waited.

Chance examined his fingernails, seemed uncomfortable with what he was about to suggest. "As I said, the Brimstone virus doesn't infect through the air, or even by casual human contact. It's actually a tough bug to transmit." He paused. "But it can be ingested."

I blinked, uncertain what to make of Chance's statement. Then the answer hit me.

My hands shot to my mouth. "No!"

Chance nodded grimly. "I think Will infected Cole and Ella on purpose."

Hiram half rose from his chair. "Holy sh—"

"Who would do that!?" Shelton blurted. "That's crazy!"

"Will may *be* a little crazy." Chance shook his head. "He was weird in the lab, always asking strange questions. Poking around where he shouldn't have. Will was *really* upset when he lost the job. Made some threats. Frankly, I was glad to be rid of him."

I shuddered. "If Speckman did that, he's a monster."

"No argument here," Chance said. "But I'm almost certain I'm right. At first I couldn't explain Cole's and Ella's accelerated incubation period—they cycled through their sickness much faster than Will and I did. But a direct viral dose, concentrated and ingested, is the most likely answer. Will must've stolen Brimstone samples soon after he discovered his Viral condition, but before I fired him. A tight window, but it was there."

Despite everything, I still thought of Ella as a friend. For someone to *intentionally* infect her with an illness was unconscionable. That went for Cole, too.

"When did you first suspect this?" I asked.

"A few days ago." Chance anticipated my next question. "When I got the lab results, and learned the mutations hadn't stopped."

Ben sneered. "When you found out your science project might kill us."

"*Might.*" Chance rose, began pacing before the fireplace. "As I told Tory, I'm not positive about anything. But I'm reasonably sure the cellular evolution will continue. And that's dangerous, obviously, unless we have an antidote."

His eyes strayed to the metal box sitting on the coffee table.

He didn't destroy all of the samples.

A synapse fired in my brain. "You already have it, don't you Chance?"

His eyebrows shot up, then he smiled ruefully. "Nothing slips by you, does it?"

Shelton popped up, pointed a shaky finger at the box. "There's a cure for being Viral in there?"

"Sweet Lord," Hi croaked, staring at the container.

Ben slapped his armrest, glaring at Chance. "We don't *need* a cure!"

"You may!" Chance shot back. "Your virus was different from my mine, but the results are nearly identical. My experiment used the same viral ingredients, and followed the same process as Karsten's. And my research shows we face the probability of future mutations. How do we know those changes won't kill us all?"

Ben looked away. "I'll take my chances."

"Go ahead, then." Chance pointed at me. "But you don't decide for her."

"And you do?" Ben snarled.

I shot to my feet. "Stop it, both of you!"

Eyes locked, Ben and Chance continued to stare each other down.

I placed a hand on Ben's arm, felt his muscles tense at my touch. "We haven't even gotten to the heart of this yet."

"Very true." Hi squirmed in his chair. "What about the Men in Black chasing us?"

Ben shrugged me off, remained standing with his arms crossed.

Shelton and I retook our seats.

Chance hadn't budged from the hearth. "Tell me what you know."

"No, Chance." My voice grew hard. "Not this time. Explain why Ella thinks you know something about our pursuers. Now."

His shoulders slumped. "I *may* be responsible. Possibly."

Ben grunted, but I waved him silent. "What does that mean?"

Chance's voice grew wooden. "You know how Will claims to have hacked my files? Even my private ones?"

I nodded, hiding my embarrassment.

"Someone else did, too." Leaning forward, Chance snagged a blue folder from the pile. "A few weeks ago I ran a system check, and discovered that another unknown user had accessed the Brimstone files. My private document had been opened as well."

My heart skipped a beat. "The agents."

Ben bristled. "Meaning, they know almost everything."

Chance nodded unhappily. "I kept everything but Karsten's research in that database."

Hi raised a hand. "Question. Why would a secret government agency break into your computer in the first place? Are you Batman? Because if you are, that could score you some much-needed points right now."

Chance rubbed his eyes, responded in a weary voice. "I think they were looking for something else. Lately I've discovered that my father was involved in dozens of shady deals like his one with Karsten. I think someone was investigating Candela, and stumbled upon Brimstone by accident."

A flash of insight. "Will Speckman is a disgruntled former employee," I said, wincing at the implications. "Perhaps agents approached him like they did Madison, and he cooperated."

"That's my guess." Chance ran a thumb along his eyebrow. "Maybe Will got scared, and thought the suits were after *him*. Or maybe he tipped them anonymously, trying to throw them off his own scent. In any case, he clearly sold me out at some point."

I thought of the last few nights. Three traps, each intended to deliver us to our stalkers.

Goose bumps puckered my arms.

This is bad.

"So everything *is* your fault." Ben smiled coldly. "I knew it."

Chance waved a tired hand. "Whatever makes you happy, Benjamin. But let's not forget, if you guys hadn't royally screwed with my head months ago, none of this would've happened. And now I'm Viral, too."

"Not our kind of Viral."

"Would y'all quit!" Shelton ripped off his specs. "I just wanna know who's chasing us!"

"I don't know *who* they are," Chance swore. "I just know they're out there."

"We were followed *today*." Hi jabbed a finger into his palm. "On the way *here*. Our fan club was watching the Morris Island bridge, which means they know who we are, and where we live."

"How long before they just snatch us up?" Shelton whispered.

"And what about the Trinity?" Hi said. "Their flare powers are stronger than ours. Not fair."

"No they aren't," Ben seethed, irritably tucking his hair behind his ears. "Not in this lifetime."

"We need some kind of edge." An idea was slowly forming in my head. "A way to catch the Trinity off guard, and convince those morons to work with us. Or to at least stop screwing us."

Chance opened his mouth, but the words never escaped.

Every light in the room died at once.

From downstairs came the shriek of breaking glass.

CHAPTER 30

Everyone froze.

"What was that?!" Shelton hissed in the darkness.

Footsteps swept past me.

A whirring sound. Followed by a low hum.

Fluorescent track lighting flickered to life above the study door.

"We lost power." Chance had crossed to a small LED touch panel built into the wall beside the entrance. A red light was blinking on its face. "The manor has a backup system, of course."

"Something broke." Hi's finger shook as he pointed at the door. "Out there, in the house."

"You've got a cat or something, right, Chancey?" Shelton was tugging an earlobe double-time. "Mr. Whiskers likes to knock over vases?"

"No." Chance cracked the door and stuck his head into the dark hallway. After several tense seconds, he closed it with a thud. Chance turned the massive lock, sealing us inside, then hurried to a bookshelf in the corner of the room.

As the boys and I huddled beside the chairs, uncertain what to do, Chance began fiddling with a painting bolted inside the towering cabinet.

"I don't like this." Ben strode to a window and looked outside.

I rushed over to Chance, who was tapping a keypad cunningly hidden within the picture's gilded frame. Brigadier General Harold Barnabas Claybourne glowered at me from its oily surface.

My heart raced. "Chance, what is it?"

"The motion sensors are blinking." A catch released and the portrait swung outward, revealing a security monitor behind it. "We may have visitors."

Hi and Shelton joined us, peering over my shoulder. Ben stayed by the window, squinting down at the gardens below.

Chance called up an image of the main foyer.

Four men were crouching in the darkness.

As I watched, stunned, the quartet crept down the entrance hall in standard two-by-two formation, hand-signaling with military efficiency.

"Oh crap." Hi's voice cracked.

Shelton grabbed Chance by the shoulder. "Tell me there's another way out of this room."

Chance was staring in disbelief. "The alarm didn't sound. How is that possible? This system cost a *fortune,* and it's failed twice! I reset everything when I let you guys in, so—"

"Chance!" I waved a hand in front of his face. "There's no time. Where are your guards?"

"I dismissed my team weeks ago." With a look of morbid fascination, Chance watched the intruders steal through his residence. "I was sick, and had to hide my condition. Then I started practicing my flares at night. I assumed that my *Colombian-drug-lord-rated* security system was more than enough protection."

Adrenaline flooded my system. "Not against these guys."

"Oh man." Shelton locked his hands together on the crown of his head. "That's *not* the Trinity. You think those town car dudes followed us here?"

"Impossible." Ben had moved to a second window. "We lost them across the river. They must've come for the lord of the manor."

I looked at Chance, who shrugged. "Does it matter?"

The four men reached the atrium and gathered by the stairs. Each wore night-vision goggles. Two carried devices I couldn't identify—held two-handed, the objects resembled snub-nosed shotguns, but appeared to be made of plastic.

Hi began slowly backing from the door. "They're *right* outside."

"Relax." Chance shook his head, as if just returning to the present. "This study is my safe room. Don't be fooled by appearances—that door is steel reinforced and magnetically sealed. It'd take a missile to knock it down."

Chance yanked open a drawer below the painting, exposing a gleaming equipment board. "These windows are bulletproof and welded to their frames. There's a trunk line providing power, along with a dedicated com link that runs through the manor's foundation. I don't know how these bastards got inside without tripping the alarm, but we can hole up in here while I contact the police. They can't—"

As he spoke, the lights on the equipment board went dead. With a dull clack, the halogens above the door winked out, leaving us in near-total darkness.

"So much for that theory," Ben hissed.

"What's that sound?" Shelton, somewhere to my left. "I think it came from the doorway."

"The magnetic seal disengaged." Chance's voice was tight, though I couldn't see his face. "We can slip away through the corner window. There's a fire escape attached to this side of the house. I know how to disengage—"

Look out!" Ben dropped to the floor just as a spotlight split the air above his head. The megawatt beam cut across the room before vanishing as quickly as it appeared. Ben crawled over to where the rest of us crouched before the cabinet. "At least two more men in the garden. Can't go that way."

Chance cursed.

"Keep thinking, bro!" Hi's voice had risen several octaves.

Suddenly, I felt an odd tingle in my brain.

Bloodred eyes flared to life beside me.

Startled, I stumbled backward, barging into someone behind me. Hi yelped a complaint about smashed toes.

"They're coming." Chance ran to the coffee table, grabbed the folders and metal box, and returned to the cabinet. "But they won't find what they're looking for."

He opened the lowest cabinet door, revealing a large safe.

A pair of golden eyes ignited behind Chance, quickly followed by two more sets.

Chance knelt, input several numbers, then mashed his thumb against a fingerprint scanner. The safe opened soundlessly. Chance dumped the folders inside, and was about to add the box when he paused. Reconsidering, he shoved it into his pocket. Then he shut the safe and closed the cabinet door.

Bang. Bang.

The doorframe shook.

And I was late to the party.

SNAP.

My powers roared free like water bursting through a dam.

Fire. Ice. Pain. Pleasure.

The room sharpened. My body tingled. Telepathic bonds slid into place.

Familiar voices echoed inside my head.

So we're gonna fight? Shelton squeaked. *That can't be a good idea!*

No other choice. I could see Ben clearly now—moonlight leaking through the windows was bright sunshine to my flaring eyes. He flexed his arms, reveling in the added strength our canine DNA provided. *They'll get through that door, whatever Chance says.*

Terrified, I tried not to panic. *Wait. Think.*

"Do you have a plan?" I whispered aloud to Chance.

Metal clanked against metal outside the door. It sounded like something was being assembled in the hallway. I could practically *see* Chance's mind racing behind his scarlet irises.

They haven't said anything, Shelton whined. *Why haven't the agents tried talking to us?*

They're not here to chat. Ben's sending sizzled with fury. *They want us. Period.*

Sweat coated my body.

Ben was right.

We had to escape, or we might never be seen again.

"The book nook!" Chance snapped his fingers. "There's a way!"

A mechanical whine erupted in the corridor. The timbre changed abruptly, then the study door began to shake.

"Come on!" Chance arrowed for the spiral staircase in the far corner. "I've got a trick they couldn't possibly know about."

The clamor grew as we climbed up to the catwalk. I glanced at the door—the heavy lock was bouncing and rattling. The spotlight returned, nearly blinding me.

"We don't have much time," I whispered, inanely stating the obvious.

Capture. Incarceration. Experimentation.

Awful possibilities danced through my mind.

What would they do to me? To us all?

Would I ever see Kit again? Would my father ever learn what really happened?

I felt a stirring in the pack mind.

Somewhere, Coop was howling.

Ben wrapped his fingers tightly around mine, brown eyes fierce, his thoughts a maelstrom of anger and worry. He was only thinking of me. Getting *me* away. Keeping *me* safe.

Ben was ready to die for me.

Chance halted before a battered case halfway down the wall. He began pulling on books, muttering to himself as he shoved each one aside.

They won't get you, Ben promised abruptly. I felt his determination flowing through the bond, mixed with love and desperation. He really would give his life to protect mine.

Ben. I—

Hey, save me, too. Hi was dry-washing his hands as he stared at the study door. *I'm not itching to be a lab rat either.*

Shelton mentally shivered. *How's about we all escape? That work?*

Then Chance howled in triumph, tugging a worn volume that refused to budge. "This is the one! *The Count of Monte Cristo.* It's been years since I came up here. Almost forgot."

Gripping the book by its spine, he jerked it to the right. Something clicked.

The bookcase swung inward.

Beyond was a narrow passage roughly five feet high.

"Follow me." Shoulders hunched, Chance crept inside.

We jammed in after him, Ben closing the case behind us with a soft clink. I caught a last glimpse of the study door, which was nearly shaking off its hinges. Our pursuers would break through in moments.

The passage was short, wood-walled, and windowless, making it hard to see even with flare vision. One turn, then I caught a whiff of humid night air. We stumbled into a small, sparsely appointed room. A single cabinet. Two chairs. One table. The hidden space had a cabin-like feel, with cedar walls and a hunting scene tacked up for decoration. A round, shuttered window provided the only ventilation.

There was no other way in or out.

"Great-grandfather's reading room." Chance wiped sweat from his forehead, then squeezed his pocket to be sure the metal box was still there. "Really just a place to drink whiskey with his buddies during Prohibition. Not that anyone would've arrested *him*—Mathias Claybourne was the biggest bootlegger in South Carolina. He just liked the secrecy of it all."

"Super." Hi was eyeing the passage. "But what happens when those GI Joes find the only way in?"

A freaking dead end, Ben cursed bitterly. *At least in the study we could've fought.*

My heart sank. I agreed with Ben. This was a trap.

"We'll be long gone." Chance pointed to the manhole-sized window. "There's a ledge outside that circles the second floor. Ten paces to the left, a gutter accesses the roof. We climb up, then cross to the other side of the house. There's an orchard there. We use the trees to get down."

Shelton gave him a flat look. "You serious?"

Chance nodded. "I've done it before. When I was nine."

The floorboards shook. A loud crash rumbled down the passage.

Shelton closed his eyes, listening hard. Then he waved frantically. *Voices on the catwalk!*

Chance didn't need to hear the message. He grabbed the shutter and yanked. Once. Twice. Wood groaned, then the entire frame came loose in his hands.

Chance set it aside and waved us close. "I'll go first. Just follow me, step where I step, and everything will be fine."

"Get on with it." Ben shoved a chair below the opening.

Chance vaulted up and deftly slipped through the porthole. Ben motioned me next. Mimicking Chance's movements exactly, I slithered through the opening and dropped onto the narrow ledge outside.

I took a moment to get my bearings. We were balanced on a two-foot-wide toehold between the second and third floors of Claybourne Manor. Below was a leg-breaking drop to a brick patio. Chance had sidestepped a few feet down the ledge to make room. He pointed ahead to where a gutter climbed the length of the building.

I inched toward Chance, making room for Hi, who wobbled precariously as his feet touched down. He righted himself with a shaky smile and followed. Shelton came next, hugging the building for dear life. Ben was last out, watching our backs as usual.

Chance reached the gutter and scurried up. At the top, he swung a leg onto the slate roof, then waved me forward. Gripping the metal gutter, I was relieved to see rungs along one side. Ascending was easy, and Chance practically lifted me over the side.

The others had no problems either, though I could hear Shelton's mumbled prayers with every step. Once we'd gathered on the roof, Chance led us across the massive structure, everyone hunched to reduce our moonlit profiles.

The night was deathly silent. Our pursuers didn't seem close by.

Then we hit a snag. Chance reached the section of roof he'd been aiming for, but there wasn't a tree in sight.

"Where are the trees?" Shelton hissed.

"Ha." A sick look twisted Chance's face. "So. Funny story. I just now remembered—we had the orchard bulldozed five years ago to build a koi pond."

I looked down. A dark blob rippled below, ten feet from the side of the building.

Ben slapped his forehead. "How can you be such an idiot!?"

"I'm not the damn gardener!" Chance shot back defensively. "Do you have any idea how big this estate is? I can't keep track of my own freaking *laundry,* much less—"

"Guys!" Hi was pointing back across the roof.

Flashlights.

Oh no.

"We're toast." Shelton's voice cracked. "How'd they find us so fast?"

I was peering over the side. "Koi pond, you said?"

Chance nodded without comprehension.

Hiram's eyes sparkled with golden light. "How deep are those things?"

Chance straightened, red eyes narrowing as he spoke. "Hector can stand when it's completely filled, but only barely. He's six two." A pause. "Give or take."

Ben grabbed Chance by the shoulder. "Think, damn it!"

Chance shoved Ben away. "The deep end is closest to the house. It's big for this type of feature, but that's all I know about koi ponds. I didn't design the stupid thing!" He snorted hysterically. "I thought I still had an orchard."

"We're three stories up." Shelton did the math as he spoke. "Five or six feet deep? That's a neck breaker, for sure. And it's, what, ten feet out to the water?"

"We're flaring." Ben peered over the edge, then took a few steps back, legs bouncing. "Virals are stronger than others."

Another light joined the first pair. White beams began scouring the roof, creeping in our direction.

We were cornered. And Shelton was right—the fall was too high to risk.

My mind froze, refusing to function as the flashlights tracked closer and closer.

These men were relentless. Merciless. They'd put me in a steel box.

I verged on panic.

A gust of air blew past me.

Here goes nothing. Ben launched himself from the building.

BEN!

For the second time in two nights, I watched in horror as Ben sailed through the air. His arms pinwheeled as he dropped toward the shimmering inkblot below.

Ben hit with a thunderous splash and disappeared beneath the water. Heart in my throat, I willed him to resurface.

Ben! Ben, are you okay?!

My bond with Ben grew fuzzy. Tenuous. Then it broke altogether.

Frantic, I unleashed a swell of love for Ben I didn't know existed. All my hopes and cares burst outward. In a split second, I bared my soul.

The water rippled.

I never knew you cared.

Ben's head emerged, our connection thrumming stronger than ever. He dragged himself from the pond, spitting and hacking. I watched him roll to his back and flash a thumbs-up.

It's deeper than Chance thought, Ben sent. *Hector must be a tall dude.*

I was about to tell Chance when a flashlight beam fell squarely on me. Shouts echoed across the roof.

Chance barked another strangled laugh. "Just like the *Yorktown*, eh? Let's get wet."

I looked at Shelton, who covered his face and screamed. Then he retreated a few steps.

Holy crap. Shelton shot forward and leaped over the side.

Boots on the slate behind us. No time for delay.

How wide is the pond!? I mind-screamed at Ben.

Maybe ten yards. He replied. *Why?*

Good enough.

I glanced at Hi, who nodded, eyes wide. "You jump, I jump, right, Tory? Like *Titanic*."

Chance was watching the approaching lights. "They're almost on us!"

Hi and I raced back from the edge, dragging Chance between us. "Together, on three!"

Chance pulled the metal box from his pocket and gripped it to his chest.

"One."

Footsteps closing in.

"TWO."

Harsh breathing, mere steps away.

"*THREE!*"

We charged forward. Fingertips brushed through my hair.

As one, we launched into space. The fall was terrifying, but short. I barely had time to register the craziness before my head smacked the hard, inky water.

Sour liquid filled my mouth, nose, and ears. I was slammed sideways, then my chest hit bottom. The air rushed from my lungs. For a moment, I couldn't think, couldn't move. My mind gibbered in panic. Underwater, chest burning, I couldn't tell up from down.

Hands dragged me upward. I broke the surface gasping. Chance and Hi were pushing me toward the edge of the pond. I wiggled out, body tingling with elation.

But there was no time for celebration.

Lights arced down. Rooftop voices called to allies on the ground.

"This way," Chance wheezed, still clutching the box as he led us deeper into the grounds. Down a trail, across a rock garden, and through a false hedge brought us to the ten-foot wall bounding Chance's property. We hurried to a locked gate. Ben punched a sequence into metal keys above the knob.

The gate sprang open. We fled into the night.

CHAPTER 31

I sprinted for three straight blocks.

We fled through Charleston's richest neighborhood—across hidden backyards, over spike-capped fences, and down quiet nighttime streets. At one point a pair of Rottweilers gave chase, but a sharp glance from our glowing eyes sent them scampering to their doghouses.

In under two minutes, we stumbled up to where Ben's Explorer was parked on Water Street. Panting like draft horses, the five of us piled inside.

"What are you doing?" Ben yelled at Chance. "Get out!"

"And go where?" Chance was wedged between Hi and Shelton in the back, still gripping his precious metal box as he searched for a seat belt. "Those men are inside my house!"

"Not my problem, Claybourne." Ben jerked a thumb over his shoulder. "Hit the road!"

"Ben, stop it!" I scolded. His glare shifted to me. I'd never seen him this angry, but I wasn't in the mood for macho nonsense. "We can't just leave Chance in the street. And we have to hurry if we're going to catch them!"

All eyes shot to me.

Chance stopped moving. "Excuse me?"

"What?" Shelton squawked. "Catch *who*?"

"I think you have it backwards." Hi was watching the street for any sign of pursuit. "You see, *we're* the ones running for our lives, and *those* guys are—"

"Swarming Claybourne Manor," I interrupted. "But they won't stay there for long. This time *we* are going to follow *them*."

"Nope!" Shelton shook his head vehemently. "Nope nope nope!"

"What do we know about surveillance?" Hi pointed to his gleaming eyes. "And I think a car packed with fire-eyed monsters might get noticed by professionals."

SNUP.

I shook off a wave of dizziness. Choked back the acid taste in my mouth.

"You guys, too," I rasped. "Hi's right. Flaring at night, we stand out like a pack of werewolves."

One by one, the others powered down. Ben last, of course, and not before muttering a string of four-letter words. He hated losing his edge, even when necessary.

"Just listen." Wiping sweat from my forehead. "Whoever those soldiers are, they won't try to follow us tonight. They missed, and they know it."

"How can you be sure?" Shelton's hand crept up to his ear.

"Think about the times they've made a move," I said. "Always at night, and only when we've isolated ourselves."

Chance barked a laugh. "My mansion is hardly isolated."

"It's big, and surrounded by high walls." I spoke with an urgency I didn't quite understand. "Claybourne Manor was a great place to bag us without being seen. But we blew their plan by escaping from the roof. Your neighbors must've heard the commotion, or seen the lights. They'll call the police, or at the very least take a look. Which means those MIBs better disappear as fast as we did."

"The discretion of my neighbors might surprise you," Chance replied, "but you have a point. Good, then. Let them slink back to whatever hole they crept from. We survive to fight another day."

I slammed a fist on the dash. "Even better, let's find the damn hole."

Hi arched an eyebrow. "Pardon?"

Ben understood. "They'll be in a hurry." He fired the Explorer's engine. "Disorganized after missing us. They'll need to regroup. Form another plan. That assault team will hightail it back to their base of operations."

Ben pulled onto Water Street, all but abandoned at the late hour. He took a left on Church, then a sharp right into an alley leading over to Meeting. Killing the lights, Ben rolled to halt near the end of the narrow lane. "If they haven't left already, they'll come this way."

"This is crazy," Shelton hissed. "They followed us here. They know your ride, Ben!"

"He's got a point," Hiram's eyes were glued to the cross street before us. "This might be tempting fate a bit more than is healthy."

Chance dismissed Hi's concern. "They won't expect being tailed by a bunch of punk teenagers they just chased off a three-story building."

I checked my watch. Eleven fifteen p.m.

My curfew was at risk, but that didn't even rate.

Had we returned in time? These operators were quick, skilled, and motivated. Without our powers, we'd never have escaped them.

And they just saw what we can do. With their own eyes.

If these goons were hunting Virals, we'd announced ourselves with fireworks.

I shivered. What if next time they dropped the stealth?

All the more reason to follow them. We could be running out of time.

Seconds ticked past. I grew certain they'd already flown the coop.

Then a town car rolled past. Seconds later, a black van followed.

I squeezed Ben's shoulder. "It's them." He nodded, allowing a few beats to pass before turning on the headlights and easing onto Meeting Street.

Shelton thrust his face between Ben and me. "Why the beams, man?"

"We're driving through downtown Charleston on a Friday night," Ben said calmly. "No headlights might stick out a bit, don't you think?"

"Solid point." Shelton's head retreated.

We followed in silence, as if worried our voices might carry to the vehicles ahead. Despite the confident talk, I knew how risky this was. I prayed my guess was correct. That these men wouldn't dream we'd have the guts to turn the tables on them.

Ben kept far enough back to avoid detection while not losing the trail. Neither vehicle turned as we rolled through the heart of the city, heading north up the peninsula. There our quarry surprised me, merging onto Interstate 26. Miles piled up as we sped north, inland, away from our usual stomping grounds.

Traffic was light, but not so sparse that we stood out. The car and van were a hundred yards ahead, traveling the speed limit. Ben stayed several car lengths back, driving slower than he usually would. As we entered North Charleston, I began to worry the spies were heading all the way back to Columbia.

Hi sat forward in his seat. "How far do we dog these guys?"

Chance, Ben, and I all spoke at once. "As far as it takes."

"Jinx." Shelton scratched the side of his nose. "But let's be real—if we're not home by midnight, Tory, Hi, and me are shark bait."

Movement in the lane ahead.

"Look!" I pointed to the left. "They're exiting. Onto Dorchester Road. Ring any bells?"

Everyone shook their heads.

"So they *are* local," I said. "We can handle Lowcountry bullies, right, guys?"

"*Based* locally." Ben's gaze never strayed from the taillights ahead. "I doubt they're stationed here all the time. Probably flew in just for us."

Then Shelton gasped.

I spun in my seat. "What is it?"

"Oh man." He squeezed his forehead. "I know where we're going."

Chance gave him a skeptical look. "Seriously?"

"I-526 is up ahead," Ben called out. "Signs for the airport. That your guess?"

Shelton frowned. "Ten bucks says we go right by."

He was right—we zipped past the exit and continued north. Traffic thinned as we entered a forested area, then a large sign glittering in the Explorer's headlights.

"We're here," Shelton mumbled glumly.

"'Joint Base Charleston,'" I read aloud. "What's that?"

"Only the largest military base around." Shelton crossed his arms. "Air force, navy, marines, you name it. The guys that attacked us are probably SEALS. Could kill us all with a pack of dental floss."

But the car and van drove by the base's main entrance, then zoomed past a smaller gatehouse beyond it. I was about to question Shelton's guess when the vehicles abruptly slowed, then turned onto a small, un-marked gravel road leading into the woods.

Ben tensed, uncertain what to do. Then he flicked off the headlights and followed.

"Oh God," Shelton breathed. "There's no mistaking what we're up to now."

"Only if they see us," Ben replied, but he began chewing his thumbnail.

We stayed well back as we traveled a winding road, ready to U-turn and flee at the slightest inkling we'd been spotted. My anxiety rose with each rotation of the tires.

We were in the middle of nowhere. Easy pickings once again.

Brake lights ahead. Ben slowed, then stopped.

The van's high beams lit up the car it was following. The passenger had gotten out to unlock a rusty gate while the driver punched a code into a keypad.

Lights strobed around both vehicles, shockingly bright in the gloom. Then they rumbled forward, pausing only to collect the man outside, who'd relocked the gate and was hustling back to the sedan. Both vehicles disappeared around a bend.

"What was that?" Chance whispered. "The flash, I mean."

"Cameras." I tapped my bottom lip, thinking furiously. "Some kind of security."

Ben looked at me. "I think this is as far as we go."

I nodded, then had a crazy idea.

Before anyone could react, I opened my door and hopped outside. "I'll be right back."

"Hey!" Ben shouted, but I was already sprinting toward the gate.

Twenty-five yards. Fifty. Seventy-five yards. One hundred.

I was puffing hard by the time I reached the barrier.

Rusty, faded sign. Rickety metal gate. Department store padlock.

So why the fancy camera?

Sticking to the shoulder, I slunk forward another dozen yards to where the road veered sharply. Peered down the gravel drive into a shallow dell just ahead.

My breath caught.

A sleek, low-slung building swarmed with uniformed men. Light poured from every window as I counted a half-dozen cameras bolted to the eaves. The area hummed with purpose, hyperactive even at this late hour.

I turned and ran back to the Explorer. Diving back into the passenger seat, I waved for Ben to get going, wheezing from back-to-back headlong dashes.

As Ben spun a circle, I finally caught my breath.

"Well?" Hi demanded.

"There's an army down there." Failing to keep a tremor from my voice as I described the scene. "The sign said, 'Department of Defense—Homeland Security. Trespassers will be shot on sight.'"

Ben punched the gas, racing back toward the highway in near total darkness. Reaching pavement, he flipped on the headlights and sped in the direction we'd come.

Back toward Morris Island. Our parents. Our homes.

But to safety? Who knew anymore.

There was no longer any doubt: Government agents were after us.

Had tried to capture us. Perhaps even kill us.

As we tore down the empty highway, one question kept looping in my brain.

Who were we really dealing with?

CHAPTER 32

B en pulled up to the Candela building.

He shifted to park, but didn't kill the engine. Then he waited, not speaking, both hands on the steering wheel. The message was obvious: Ben wanted Chance out. Now.

Rolling his eyes, Chance tapped Hi's shoulder. Hi nodded, opening the door and exiting so Chance could escape the middle seat.

"Thanks for the ride." Chance's voice dripped with sarcasm.

"Any time." Ben was equally insincere.

Chance couldn't go home. What if agents still watched Claybourne Manor? This was the next best thing. Big, well-lit building. Twenty-four-hour security. Public location. Chance even had a couch in his office. A part of me was actually jealous.

He's safer here than on Morris Island.

The thought drew a shudder. This evening was a game changer, I was sure. But to what extent? How soon? Was I safe in my own bed tonight? Were any of us?

We had to hope rules were still in place.

We had to hope these men wouldn't take us in our homes.

They came for Chance. Was that different?

Hi was re-buckling his seat belt when a thought occurred to me. "Wait."

Ben tensed. "We're very late, Tory. Like, grounded-for-days late."

I waved his comment away, trying to capture an idea forming in my head. "We're missing something. We're forgetting about the Trinity."

Hi wearily rubbed his eyes. "I thought they were done harassing us?"

Shelton sighed. "We should return the favor."

"They won't try again." Chance was standing on the curb, one hand still on the door. "Will's smart enough to know we won't fall for another trap."

"No, no." I made a hushing gesture, trying to fit pieces together. The boys fell dutifully silent. Finally, "What I mean is, the Trinity are connected to our stalkers. They've tipped off our location at least three separate times. How?"

No one had an answer.

"We need to talk to them." I opened the passenger door. "I think I know how."

Ben scrambled from the driver's seat. "Where are you going?"

Watch check. Eleven forty-five p.m.

First I had a parent issue to deal with. I needed more time.

"Be quiet for a sec." I called Kit, practicing lines in my head.

He answered groggily on the second ring. "Yello?"

"Kit!" Voice cheery. "It's me. I'm *so* sorry leaving this until the last minute, but can I stay over at Ella's tonight? We're super close to her house and I lost track of time."

I ignored my companions' startled glances. Who else could I use? Ella was my only close friend that didn't live within fifty feet of me on Morris. The only plausible sleepover spot.

"Tory." I sensed Kit sitting up in bed, no doubt checking the clock. "This is the definition of last minute, kiddo. I thought you were out with the boys? You know, your dog was acting crazy earlier. Darn squirrels."

Another pause. Whitney spoke in the background, but I couldn't make out what she said.

"Are Ella's parents home?" Kit asked finally.

"Oh yeah. But I think they're asleep. Do you want her to wake them?"

Please no.

A big sigh. "No, that's fine. But how about a little warning next time, hey?"

"Thanks, Dad." I knew Kit liked when I called him that, which made me feel guilty for doing it. "Won't happen again, I promise. Bye!"

"Hm-mm. Bye." The line went dead.

I shoved my phone back into my pocket. Turned. Found all four boys staring at me.

"Not good," Hi whispered.

"I don't know *what* you've got planned," Shelton began, the color draining from his face, "but I can't pull that garbage with *my* parents. I'm already gonna catch—"

"You guys go home. Ben, take Shelton and Hi." I nodded to the hulking, black-windowed office building behind me. "I think I know how to draw the Trinity out, but I need Chance's help to make it work. We can handle this alone."

Ben rounded the Explorer. "No way."

"What? Ben, you have to drive Hi and Shelton back, or—"

"So you can shack up with him!?" Ben's face was bright red, his eyes pinched in anger.

Before I could even fathom a response, Ben charged directly at Chance and shoved him in the chest. Caught off guard, Chance tumbled to the ground.

This time, Ben didn't stop. He jumped on Chance, fists rising and falling. I heard several dull smacks.

"Ben! Stop it!" I shouted, but was wasting my breath.

Then Chance grunted. His whole body spasmed. Moving faster than my eyes could follow, he caught Ben's fists in his hands. An instant later Ben went flying, landing hard and sliding down the sidewalk.

Chance rose, eyes blazing bloodred.

"Chance! No!" I raced to intercept, but he dodged me easily, nostrils wide as he lifted Ben by the shirt.

"I've had it!" Chance growled, hair mussed, tracksuit ripped, blood trickling from a cut on his forehead. "I never wanted this fight, but I'm done playing nice."

The analytic part of my brain marveled, even as my emotions ran riot.

Chance can flare at will. Twice in one night, without a thought.

The Trinity are stronger.

Dazed, Ben swiped at the air ineffectually, unable to defend himself. Chance crouched over him, fist cocked, his face a mask of fury.

Hands grabbed Chance.

"That's enough, Claybourne." Shelton hooked his skinny arms around Chance's muscular one, looking the older boy squarely in the eye. "Step away."

"Right now." Hi snagged Chance's other shoulder, no joke in his tone. "Let him go."

Chance bared his teeth, as if considering taking on all three. If he tried, I didn't know what would happen. Chance was flaring, rage directing his actions. He'd been attacked by Ben without provocation. Had every right to be furious.

Things balanced on a razor's edge.

I stepped forward. Placed a hand against Chance's cheek.

Fierce red eyes met mine. Softened the slightest bit.

I held his fiery gaze. "Don't. Please."

Chance's brow furrowed, then all emotion drained from his face. The red glow vanished as he released Ben and took a step back. Neither Hi nor Shelton let go, but Chance didn't lash out. "He's got to stop this" was all he said.

"I know."

I knelt beside Ben, whose senses were slowly returning. Abruptly, he registered what had happened. Shaking me off, he lurched unsteadily to his feet.

I tensed. Hi and Shelton still clung to Chance's powerful frame.

Ben turned roiling eyes on me. I was startled to see a tear leak from one corner.

I knew it had nothing to do with the fight.

"You can't." Ben spoke in a strangled voice. "Please. Not with him."

I stared. Stunned.

Shelton and Hi dropped Chance's arms, began a thorough inspection of their tennis shoes.

Chance turned and walked toward the alley.

With no idea what to say, I went with the truth. "Ben, I want to lay a trap for the Trinity. To pull it off, I need access to a Candela computer. I can only do that with Chance's help. That's why I'm going in there. The *only* reason."

Ben looked away. "Sure. Whatever."

He staggered toward the Explorer. Shelton stopped him gently and steered him to the backseat. Surprisingly, Ben didn't resist, climbing inside and closing the door without looking my direction. Shelton hurried around to the driver's seat and gave me a thumbs-up.

"Tell us your plan later," Hi whispered as he slid into the passenger seat.

Taillights.

They were gone.

○   ○   ○

Chance was waiting in the alley.

Neither of us spoke as he typed the code, opened the door, and led me to the elevator.

We were halfway up before he finally broke the silence. "I apologize."

"Don't. Ben hit you. He's the one wrong here."

Is he, though? Or did I push him to this?

The problem with never addressing your personal issues is that they don't get smaller.

Quite the opposite.

Chance gave me a knowing glance. "It's pretty clear why, though, isn't it?"

My cheeks flushed. "I don't want to talk about it."

Chance sighed. "Of course not."

Then, after an excruciatingly awkward pause, "Want to explain what you're doing here?"

The elevator doors opened to a dark and empty hallway. Not surprisingly, no one else was working the Friday midnight shift. "I'll show you. Come on."

Inside Chance's office, I walked to his desk and sat. "Take a seat. I want to see these secret files you've got squirreled away."

Chance froze in the act of moving a chair. "Which files?"

Oh. Right.

"The Brimstone experiment." Hiding my blushes. "Any file Speckman hacked."

"That'd be all of them." Chance grabbed his wireless keyboard and began typing. "First I have to disable the encryption."

Moments later, a familiar file tree appeared on-screen. "I've seen these. We stole this database from the aquarium months ago. That's what led us to you in the first place."

"Correct." Chance set the keyboard down and crossed his arms. Wedged in behind the desk together as we were, his forearm rubbed against mine. Goose bumps rose on my flesh.

He didn't seem to notice. "The Trinity have already seen these. So what are we doing?"

I inched away. Felt a moment's regret at the lost contact. "I want to plant something in the files. Bait for the Trinity to find."

Chance leaned back, gave me a speculative look. "Why?"

"A hunch." I rubbed my arms, attempting to settle tingling skin. "Speckman keeps tabs on you somehow. I suspect spyware. So, maybe, if we leave something *new* in here . . ."

"The Trinity will find it." A smile spread across Chance's face. "We can manipulate *them* for a change. Tory, that's brilliant!"

He squeezed my shoulder. Electricity ran down my spine.

"But what should we leave?" Chance stroked his chin in thought. A few days' stubble roughened his smooth, tan cheeks. It only made him look more rugged.

Focus.

"That's what we need to figure out." I began scrolling files, unsure what to look for. There were the Brimstone files, but those were technical in nature, and the project had been shuttered and erased. It'd be suspicious to suddenly alter one now.

Doubt began to creep in. Did the Trinity even look at this stuff anymore? Why would they? And what could we add that would draw attention, yet not give our scheme away?

Then I saw it.

A single file, in its own directory.

Tory Brennan.

Of course.

"This one." Voice taut. "They must check it."

Chance's forehead creased. "Why do you say that?"

"You located our bunker a few weeks ago, right?"

Chance nodded.

"And recorded that here?"

Another head bob.

"On the *Yorktown*, Speckman admitted that this specific file tipped him to the bunker's location." I grew excited despite the subject matter. *A file on me.* "He must monitor your entries. We can turn that against him."

Chance raked fingers through his onyx hair. "But I haven't added a thing since our fight with the Trinity. Why would I? Will *told* me I'd been hacked."

I shrugged. "Make a mistake. Change the encryption, here, right now, but not so well that he can't break it again. Trick Speckman into thinking you believe the file is secure."

Chance tapped the desk. I could tell he was warming to the idea. "This might work, but making it look plausible will take some time."

I raised an eyebrow. "Got other plans tonight?"

◇   ◇   ◇

"Okay." Chance sat back and blew out a weary breath. "Done."

I shook myself fully awake. Had been dozing with my eyes open. A glance at my iPhone revealed it was almost four in the morning. "Take me through it."

"I recoded the file, renamed it, then moved it to a different directory." Chance rubbed tired eyes. "Then I encrypted the new framework and buried everything in a shell application. To any prying eyes, it appears that I tried very hard to conceal this information."

I frowned. "Hopefully not too hard."

Chance wagged his head. "Will is good. If he looks, he'll figure out what I did, though it might take him a while to sort everything." He cracked a tight smile. "And the whole time he'll think I'm an idiot, swimming out of my depth."

I tapped my lip, testing the plan in my head. "All that work. Speckman should buy it."

"Oh, he'll buy." Chance spoke through a deep yawn. "But the question remains, what are we selling?"

I spun in my chair, surprised him by tapping the metal box in his pocket.

"That."

The corners of Chance's mouth lowered. "Ah. *That.*"

His reluctance surprised me. "We need them to come to us. What could possibly be more enticing than a cure for being Viral?"

"It's just . . ." Chance hesitated, as if searching for the right words. "Do we want to show our best card? Once they know about a cure, everything could change. They might consider us a threat again."

I shrugged, too exhausted to worry about it. "We don't have another card to play. If you've got a better plan to draw out the Trinity—to a place of *our* choosing—I'm all ears."

Chance sighed. "I don't. So what do we plant?"

"Write that you've finally produced an antidote," I instructed, thinking aloud, "but you're scared the Candela building is compromised. So you're storing it at a secret hiding place of mine."

Chance was nodding. "That should send them running into our arms."

The keyboard was sitting right before me. I lifted it and opened the Tory Brennan file. "I can make the entry. I'll just add a few lines at the—"

"No!" Chance snatched at my fingers. Startled, I dropped the keyboard and it clattered to the carpet. Chance dove to his knees to retrieve it, suddenly frantic. "Don't read anything! Those thoughts are private and I . . . I don't . . ."

By the time he popped up, I was staring at the screen.

The first lines seared into my brain.

Dear computer. We meet again.

Are you my only TRUE friend?

I'm opening this file because I'm obsessed.

Tory Brennan.

She haunts me, even as she ruins my once-perfect life. I can't fight it

anymore. That nosy, childish, prying, know-it-all little brat is perfect in
every way.

Damn her. I'm beaten.

I love her. God, but it's true.

Chance closed the file with a strangled grunt. Then he dropped the keyboard, burying his face in the crook of his elbow.

I stared at the now-blank screen.

I love her. He wrote, "I love her." Could that possibly be true?

"You weren't supposed to see that."

I couldn't speak. Didn't move.

My body was immobile. In stasis. But my mind ran like wildfire.

I'm staying here tonight. With him, in this office.

And he loves me?

I found my voice, if not the courage to look at him. "Did you mean that?"

There was an electric pause. Then Chance slowly reached out and cupped my chin.

Turned it to face him. Pressed his lips against mine.

Heat seared through my veins. I leaned into the kiss, tasting his lips, drinking in his smell. For a magical moment, I was lost in the connection of his mouth to mine.

Then a single image arrowed through my brain.

Ben, standing on the curb, eyes filled with hurt and pain.

I recoiled as if slapped, emotions bubbling inside me like a cauldron.

Shame. Desire. Guilt. Need.

Chance nearly slipped from his chair, the hungry look in his eyes quickly giving way to hurt. "What is it?"

"I . . . I can't. It's not right."

Chance sat back, sulking like a sullen child. "Because of me? Or because of him?"

"Both. Neither." My pulse raced. My lungs pumped like bellows. "I don't know."

"You don't know." He couldn't keep the acid from his voice.

"No. But I know *this* isn't right."

I met his eyes, afraid of what I'd see there. "Please."

He seemed about to say more, then caught himself with a rueful shake of the head.

"Fine."

Clearing his throat, Chance lifted the keyboard, reopened the file, and tabbed to the bottom. After pounding the space bar a dozen times until no text was visible, he turned to me with a neutral expression. "What would you like the entry to say?"

Speaking robotically, I told him my idea. He actually laughed.

"It's novel, I'll give you that." Chance began typing without further conversation.

Feeling decidedly awkward, I rose from the desk and walked to the couch. Sat down. Then lay down, to think. I felt like the walls of my life had morphed into fun-house mirrors. Everything was blurred, stretched, and sideways.

I needed a moment to myself. A chance to get my thoughts in order.

But I hadn't accounted for how tired I was. My exhausted nerves. The physical toll the day had taken on me.

Within moments, I was fast asleep.

NOTE TO FILE:

Investigating Agents attempted to contact and interview Lucile W. Gable ("Lucy
Gable") and Peter E. Gable ("Peter Gable") (collectively, the "Gable twins"), in
connection with the Phoenix Inquiry, but were unable to ascertain their current
location.

It is believed that the Gable twins had close and meaningful contact with Phoenix
Inquiry investigation target Victoria G. Brennan ("Tory Brennan"), immediately prior to
their disappearance.

Global PSA tracking and human intelligence sources, in combination, rate the Gable
twins' most likely current locations, in order, as being a) Bali; b) Fiji; or c) New

Zealand. Investigating Agents believe there is a high probability of locating said subjects.

Investigating Agents request initiation of priority search status and the implementation of DNA-signature location program INTUIT to track and locate the Gable twins. They are believed to have high-level intelligence directly related to Tory Brennan and her associates. Investigating Agents do not believe this request would compromise the secrecy of the INTUIT program or any other agency security interests.

[END SEARCH REPORT]

CHAPTER 33

A hand gently shook me awake.

Blinking away unsettling dreams, I found Chance standing over me.

"Up and at 'em, Sleeping Beauty. Your plan worked."

"Wha?" Not an eloquent rejoinder, but my mind was sludge.

Chance flashed a half smile. "It's nearly eight. We need to look presentable."

Somehow Chance had already cleaned himself up and changed clothes, and looked fresh as a daisy. If still upset about the night before, he gave no sign.

His words finally penetrated my still-waking brain. "It worked? You're sure?"

He nodded, moving across the office to his desk.

I rubbed a fist into each eye socket. Only then did I notice a fluffy fleece blanket covering my legs. Chance must've placed it there while I slept. The thought of him watching me sleep triggered an unexpected thrill.

Glancing around, I couldn't tell where Chance had slept. Maybe he hadn't, though I'd bet my life he'd snuck in a quick shower at some point. *That* thought sparked me fully alert.

"How can you tell?" I asked, digging out my iPhone with a twinge of panic.

Exhale. No missed calls, no messages.

No irate father hunting me across Charleston.

"This time I thought ahead." Chance was typing away, calm as a cucumber. "I crafted a little tell, should anyone open the file. Here, come look."

Like nothing ever happened. I'm down with that.

I rose, wrapping the blanket around me as I crossed the carpeted floor. I'd slept fully clothed, and the office was warm, but for some reason I was reluctant to discard the extra layer of protection. Chance often made me feel that way.

The hall outside was silent, which surprised me, until I remembered it was Saturday morning. Still, if someone walked in right now I'd probably die. Perhaps the blanket-robe was a bad idea after all.

Chance gave me an odd look, then tapped the screen. "I adjusted the document system to log an indicator every time this file is opened. Nothing that should've drawn Speckman's notice—just an added blip in the metadata."

I scanned the coded lines onscreen. "Those two *J*s?"

He nodded. "The program records a single *J* in the metadata for each time this file is accessed. From *anywhere*, internal servers or otherwise. According to this, my file was opened once early this morning, and again an hour ago. Will found it quicker than I'd have thought."

He spun his chair to face me. "The Trinity took the bait."

I swept tangled red strands from my face. My eyes slid to the slim metal box sitting on the desktop.

"Then let's reel them in."

○   ○   ○

Getting back to Morris Island was tricky.

Chance drove us most of the way, but I couldn't be seen with him. Kit's gullible, but not blind. If my father spotted me arriving home in Chance's BMW, after spending the night out, I'd never leave my room again.

Instead, we stopped at Black Magic Cafe in Folly Beach. I called Shelton. A stroke of luck—the boys were together, playing *Call of Duty* in Ben's rec room. I told them to come meet us for breakfast, on the double.

"You sure that's a good idea?" Shelton whispered. "We don't need another throwdown, and after last night . . ."

"It can't wait." Though, admittedly, I shared his concern. "Chance and I set something in motion that might attract the Trinity, but the timetable is short. So get Ben's head screwed on straight and hurry down here. Please."

Shelton snorted. "Oh, sure. Get his head on straight. No problem."

I hung up. Found Chance watching me.

"I'm not in the mood to get punched again." He stroked the left side of his perfect chin. "And I think we can agree Ben's not listening to reason."

"I'll handle Ben." Curt. "Let's just focus on our strategy."

Our breakfast arrived, and I set to with gusto. I was famished, sleep deprived, and wearing the same clothes as the day before. I didn't want to think about what I looked like.

But I was also charged up.

We had a shot at catching one enemy, to learn about the other.

For the first time in a week, I felt a degree of control. So I speared a turkey sausage link, imagining it was that dopey jerk Cole.

The Trinity liked playing games? Thought *we* were puppies?

I almost laughed.

We were Virals. My pack had accomplished things they couldn't even imagine.

The Trinity had no idea who they were dealing with.

◇   ◇   ◇

To say the meeting was tense is putting it mildly.

Ben and Chance sat across from each other at our table. Hi and Shelton flanked Ben, poised to grab our temperamental friend should he try anything rash. I sat next to Chance, hoping Ben wouldn't read anything into it.

"We have an opportunity," I began slowly. "A way to get the drop on the Trinity for once. But we have to work together."

Ben said nothing, dressed in his usual black tee and jeans. Arms crossed, scowl in place, he stared straight ahead at nothing. I wasn't 100 percent sure he was listening.

Hi drummed the table, wearing a yellow and blue tiki shirt that hurt my eyes. "So what's the plan?"

"We have something they want." I glanced at Chance, who nodded. "Last night, we laid a trap in the files Speckman hacked—the location of the Viral cure."

Shelton and Hi sucked in breaths. Ben shifted, but remained silent.

"Chance and I think the Trinity will come for it," I continued, then winced internally for grouping the two of us together. "If they do, it'll be today. This afternoon."

Shelton had on a lime-green polo and white shorts. He squinted at me, eyes serious behind his thick lenses. "Why today?"

"Because of where it's supposedly hidden." I told my packmates the message we'd planted. "We know Speckman saw the info early this morning. He won't be able to resist. So when the Trinity show up, we corner them. Try one last time to get them to cooperate."

"They won't." Ben, never looking my way.

Maybe Ella will.

But I remembered her eyes in the cafeteria.

"I think Ben's right." Hi slumped in his seat. "If they don't play ball, what then?"

My voice was cold enough to scare even me. "Then we do what we have to."

In short, curt sentences, I outlined my plan.

All eyes zeroed on me. Even Ben's. Hiram's face grew ashen. Shelton began vigorously tugging an earlobe. Chance gave me a considering look, as if seeing something for the first time.

I didn't flinch.

I remembered the alien touch I felt aboard *Sewee* as the Trinity watched from the cliffs. The mental assault Cole had inflicted on the *Yorktown*.

The Trinity were dangerous. Rabid dogs, roaming the city at night.

They'd attacked us. Trapped us. Tried to sell us to some twisted government agency.

And now they were running amok, messing with powers better left untested.

They had to be stopped. One way, or another.

"That's my proposal." I spoke quietly, but with iron conviction. "I need to know if you're in. And more importantly, *will you work together*?"

For a moment, no one responded. Then Hiram nodded, followed swiftly by Chance and Shelton, though the smaller boy swallowed audibly before doing so.

I looked at Ben, who was glowering at Chance. Then he closed his eyes and mumbled something to himself. When his brown irises reappeared, they were aimed directly at me. "Yes. For you."

"Good." I shrugged off a tingly feeling. No time for girlish nonsense. "Because this crap ends now. After today, there'll only be one Viral pack in Charleston. *Ours*."

CHAPTER 34

Bolton Preparatory Academy was deathly quiet.

Saturday activities had ended an hour earlier, and the campus was a ghost town.

Then footsteps echoed in the corridor. Three dark shapes slunk into view.

"This one." A lithe form with a long black braid rapped her knuckles against my locker. "But I don't know the combination."

Hello, Ella.

I could hear every word. Smell their breath. See the tiniest wrinkles in their clothing.

My eyes burned with golden light as I waited for our trap to spring.

I was crouched behind a classroom door not ten feet away, heart thumping in my chest. But my powers gave me comfort. Flaring, I felt confident, even against our stronger adversaries.

One of the shapes turned. I ducked and shielded my eyes, praying their radiance wouldn't betray me as I watched through the window. The boys were in position as well. Some more reluctantly than others.

The tallest figure snapped his fingers. "Cole, get this open. Now."

"Whatever you say, Willie." Grinning, Cole removed a wicked-looking hammer from his backpack. "I've got the perfect key."

Beside him, Ella shifted, her lips twisted as though she'd eaten something sour. "Why would they keep the cure in Tory's locker? Makes no sense."

Speckman shrugged. "The puppies thought no one would ever look here. And they'd have been right, if Claybourne hadn't written about it in his love diary."

Cole laughed like a hyena, but Ella's frown deepened. "Exactly," she pressed. "So why would he do that?"

Ella was no fool. I didn't like where her thoughts were headed.

I sent the signal. *Shelton, now.*

Reluctance oozed through the bond.

Cole spun his hammer in one hand, preparing to bash my locker to bits.

Now, Devers!

Bwhhhhhaaaaa!

My locker door flew open, startling the trio huddled before it. Before they could react, Shelton aimed a fire extinguisher at their faces. "Lights out, suckas!"

Shelton pulled the handle. The hallway disappeared in a cloud of gray and white dust.

Now! Go!

Doors burst open up and down the corridor. With a surge of adrenaline, I fired into the hallway and beelined for Ella, who was hacking into her fist a few yards away. Her eyes widened as I shoved her to the ground.

Speckman gasped and sputtered as Chance and Ben grabbed him from behind. Hi slid on his knees across the floor, arm-wrapping Cole's legs while Shelton rammed a shoulder into his side. Bodies went sprawling.

I tried to pin Ella, one hand fumbling for a zip tie in my pocket. I knew the advantage of surprise would only last a few more seconds. But the plastic restraint slipped through my fingers.

Ella's body quaked. She slithered beneath me like a snake, flipping onto her back and wedging her knees between us. I caught a glimpse of burning red eyes, then Ella launched me across the hall like a rag doll.

I hit the floor and careened into lockers on the opposite side.

For a moment, everything went hazy. I watched Ella flee deeper into the building.

No. Not again.

I glanced back at the boys, saw Cole jump six feet straight up in the air, shedding Hi and Shelton like flies. Behind him, Speckman dodged a punch by Ben, then grabbed his arm and launched him into Chance.

I lurched to my feet. Dove at Speckman's knees.

He sidestepped with ease, red eyes contemptuous as I tumbled past. Then Cole and Speckman ran after Ella. I turned, wobbling. My friends were lying like flotsam on the hallway floor.

Our ambush had been a disaster.

So strong. Hi rubbed the side of his head as he helped Shelton stand.

"You keep getting in my way!" Ben yelled at Chance.

"You can't take him alone!" Chance threw his hands skyward. "Work *with* me, Blue. For once!"

They're getting away. I took off after the Trinity, sending a message the boys couldn't hear as I revised my plan on the fly.

The hallway ended in a T intersection. Sniffing the air, I could tell the Trinity had turned right, toward the rear of the school. I sent another message, hoping I wasn't too late.

Ben appeared, puffing, at my side. *They* are *stronger than we are,* he sent grimly. I knew how much the admission cost him.

I nodded. *We need to fight smarter.*

Chance and Shelton caught up, with Hi just a step behind.

"We have to corner them." I spoke aloud for Chance's benefit. "But we can't take them by force alone. Not when they're flaring."

"What can we do?" Shelton's golden eyes crinkled with worry. "They've been Viral less than a month, yet we can't compete."

The answer hit me like a thunderbolt.

"Of course!" I almost smiled. "We've been going about this all wrong. We have to show these newbies what we've learned."

Before I could say more, riotous barking erupted from somewhere up ahead.

A message slid into my brain.

"Come on!"

I flew down the hall, then turned left. Up ahead, the Trinity were slowly backing away from an emergency exit. Speckman slammed the door with a grunt, cutting off the baying outside.

Thanks, Coop.

Beyond the portal, I sensed his doggie grin.

Spotting us, the Trinity bolted through a pair of double doors at their backs.

"The gym." Chance glanced at me. "They still padlock the corner exits on weekends?"

I nodded. "There's no other way out."

We ran to the double doors, opened them slowly. The gymnasium was crisscrossed with shadows, the only light streaking down from windows high overhead. Plenty enough for Virals, however.

The rafters were jammed with purple-and-white banners. Bleachers on both sides had been tucked to the walls, exposing an acre of gleaming hardwood. A sinuous griffin glared up from the center. Fire exits dotted each corner, closed and locked.

The Trinity stood at mid-court, arms crossed, smug expressions on their faces.

"Your dog isn't very friendly." Speckman's mocking tone carried across the hollow chamber. "You should teach him to respect his betters."

I actually laughed. "When he meets one, I'll let him know."

"The cure isn't here, is it?" Ella turned to scowl at her companions. "I *knew* this was too easy. They set us up, and we walked right into it."

Cole shrugged, cracking his knuckles with an evil grin. "Whatevs, man. These dopes want another beatdown, I'm game."

Speckman snarled at Chance. "We'll find it eventually. You can't hide the cure forever."

I took a few steps onto the court. "Why do you want it so bad?"

Speckman gave me a withering look. "Same as you. To trade."

His answer surprised me. "You think you can *buy* off those agents?"

"It's what they want." Speckman spoke as if I were a child. "They're after our research. If we deliver it to them, and don't cause trouble, they'll go away."

I shook my head. "What good's a cure without the virus it's designed to counteract? They'll want both, or at the very least a person who's afflicted. Which means capturing a Viral."

"Duh." Cole snorted. "Why do you think we set you up?"

My temper slipped. "You'd deliver us into cages? To save your own skins?"

My eyes found Ella.

At first, she met my gaze boldly. But then her head dropped.

"We didn't have a choice!" Speckman said hotly. "Agents were snooping into the Brimstone project. Chance was too sloppy, and we landed on their radar. Once that happened, there was only one way for this to play out. Someone *has* to end up a lab rat. Not. Me."

Ella's chin rose suddenly. "But that's not true anymore."

Cole and Speckman spun on their companion—one surprised, the other annoyed.

"If we *took* the cure," Ella said, her voice trembling, "there'd be no Virals left to capture."

My eyes popped.

So simple, yet a solution I'd never considered.

"Take the cure?" Speckman closed in on Ella, his expression livid. "What, you want to be weak again? A *victim,* again?"

"No." Ella shivered, hugged her body close. "Never that."

Speckman nodded sharply. "That's what I thought. Give up being Viral! Who would do that? No thanks."

I watched Ella. She'd been close to something, but I felt it slipping away.

"This is dumb." Cole scratched his greasy mustache. "There's no cure here, anyway. Nothing but a group of weaklings and a fight I'm looking forward to."

"Don't be so sure." I nodded to Chance.

Chance removed the metal box from his pocket. Held it aloft for everyone to see.

Speckman's eyes narrowed with pleasure. "Stupid to the bitter end, eh, Claybourne?"

He stepped forward and held out a hand.

"I'll take that. *Now.*"

CHAPTER 35

Everything happened quickly.

My friends and I were spread out in a line, blocking the only exit.

Speckman and Cole stalked across the hardwood, feral expressions twisting their faces. After a moment, Ella joined them, eyes hardening.

"They're talking to one another," Chance warned. "But they're lousy at it." Then he winced, one hand grabbing his forehead. "They just shut me out."

"We hear one another just fine," Speckman sneered. "Same as you."

My pulse quickened.

Was that the best they could do?

The Trinity oozed confidence, like cats approaching an injured bird. They had every right to feel that way. Experience had proven we couldn't stand against them.

But we knew more tricks than they did. Had overcome greater odds than this.

We'd faced down murderers. Kidnappers. Lunatics. Thieves. Had put our lives on the line a dozen times. Why should we fear three red-eyed kids who barely knew which way was up?

I sent a message to my pack.

They don't know how to work together. Time to show these jerks what we can do.

Closing my eyes, I slipped into my subconscious. Called forth the telepathic connections linking my friends and me. A flaming grid sprang to life in my mind—humming, glowing lines that bound me to each Viral, and them to me.

I focused on the connections, converting cords into conduits. Then I threw my conscious mind down each channel, widening and deepening the bonds.

There was a shock, like a plunge into cold water. The feeling of a bolt sliding into place.

I felt my mind merge with others.

Ben. Hi. Shelton. Me. And Coop, prowling outside the building.

My pack united in a way the Trinity couldn't imagine. Body and soul. My senses were theirs. Theirs were mine. Our thoughts became one.

When my eyes opened, the world had changed.

I watched the Trinity approach from four different vantage points.

Hi. Shelton. Take Cole down.

My instruction was barely complete when the two boys sprang forward. Speckman dodged left. Ella right.

Hi and Shelton struck Cole simultaneously, bowling him over backward.

"Get off me, you geeks!" Cole struggled to rise, but the smaller boys had him pinned.

Then everyone was moving.

Speckman tried to grab Hi from behind, but Hi spotted the move through Ben's eyes.

Hi rolled, releasing Cole's arm and popping up behind him. One hand free, Cole tried to punch Shelton, but a glance from me alerted my friend in time. Shelton ducked, then shoved the overextended stoner past him. Cole skidded across the hardwood.

Speckman turned just in time to catch Ben's fist across his jaw. The taller boy staggered backward, then spit out a mouthful of blood. "You'll pay for that one."

Speckman darted at Ben, catching him by the shoulder. But Chance slipped behind and wrapped an arm around Speckman's neck. Two sets of red eyes strained as Chance wrestled Speckman to the ground.

"*You're . . . not . . . stronger . . . than me . . . pal!*" Chance wheezed. "We're from the same litter!"

Speckman roared, then elbowed Chance square in the stomach. "I've *always* been better than you, Claybourne! Always!"

Speckman reached backward. Grabbed a fistful of Chance's hair. Pulled hard.

Chance howled, his grip slipping. Speckman was close to wrenching free.

Ben's knuckles connected with Speckman's chin.

Then again.

Then a third time.

I winced, but the older boy roared to his feet, knocking Ben and Chance backward. He staggered sideways, swinging his fists wildly.

A shadow darted at my back. Through Shelton, I saw Ella's foot arcing toward me.

I dropped to a crouch, felt a leg swoosh overhead. Popping back up, I rolled left, having seen Ella's next attack through Hi.

Her jaw clenched as I spun out of reach. She glanced at Hiram, then back at me. "How did you—"

My hand smashed across Ella's face, knocking her sideways.

Ella doubled over. I kicked her in the stomach.

Gasping, she collapsed in a heap. I was already turning to help my friends.

Cole had Hiram by the throat. Shelton was lying on his back.

I lunged at Cole. Spotting me late, he whirled as I threw a punch.

I connected with his ear, and we both howled in pain. Cole staggered, releasing Hi and grabbing his temple.

Hi wheeled. Slammed his forehead into Cole's face.

Cole let out a whimper, then dropped to the floorboards. The fire winked from his eyes.

Speckman's head whipped to where Cole lay crumpled on the hardwood.

Ben, now!

Ben sprang forward and snaked his arms around the taller boy. "Chance, help!"

Red eyes gleaming, blood streaming from his nose, Chance darted forward and punched Speckman in the jaw. The leader of the Trinity slumped.

Ben spun the taller boy, his golden eyes blazing with hatred. I felt a pulse of triumph as he pummeled Speckman with both fists.

Speckman's eyes rolled up as he fell.

Ben hit him again. Then again. Then again.

Ben, stop it! You'll kill him.

Good.

Stop it!

Ben stepped back and unclenched his fists. Then he spat in Speckman's face.

Chance clapped Ben on the back. I tensed, unsure what my packmate would do.

Panting, Ben held out a bloody fist. Chance bumped it with a weary sigh.

Tory, look out!

Too late, I saw what Shelton had.

Ella's fist connected to my side. Every liter of breath whooshed from my lungs.

I crumpled, and Ella jumped on top of me. She slapped me across the face.

"It's all your fault!" she hissed. "Getting taken by that monster. Becoming a mutant. These men hunting me. It's all because of *you*!"

Ella lifted my head, then slammed it to the floorboards.

The room spun. Ella grabbed my hair a second time.

Then froze.

A menacing growl rattled my bones. Set my teeth on edge.

Ella went deathly pale. Setting my head down gently, she slowly crawled backward, the red glow vanishing from her eyes.

I rose to an elbow, unsure what was happening.

Felt a giant pink tongue slather my face.

Sister-friend.

Great timing, boy.

I patted my wolfdog's furry side.

Then I rolled over and threw up on the hardwood.

CHAPTER 36

It was over.

Cole was sprawled out on the floorboards, unconscious, but Shelton and Hi had fun tying him up with jump ropes anyway. The two were loudly debating the most effective types of knots.

Speckman was sitting on the floor with his back to the bleachers. A dozen zip ties secured his wrists before him, giving him the appearance of a man at prayer. But the supplicant posture didn't touch his eyes, which radiated anger.

Chance and Ben stood a few paces away, watching closely.

None of the boys were flaring.

Nor was I. My powers had slipped away like an ugly rumor.

Which had me worried—the Trinity could call up second flares at will. We couldn't.

We had to hope they didn't know that.

Ella was cowering on her butt at mid-court. Coop stood beside her, providing his undivided attention. Sweat dampened Ella's temples. Fear clouded her flinty-green eyes.

"Um, Tory?" Ella's voice quavered.

I reached into my pocket and removed three zip ties. Raised a questioning eyebrow.

Her gaze flicked back to Coop, who bared his teeth. She nodded quickly.

I knelt and secured her wrists, being careful not to pull the plastic handcuffs too tight. For a terrible moment, I wanted to cry.

Ella was my friend. My *best* one, outside of the Morris pack.

I didn't want to tie her up. I wanted to *hug* her. But I knew those days were gone.

She blames me for everything. Nothing I say will change that.

"Come on."

After patting Coop's head I helped Ella stand, then walked her over to where Speckman was stewing against the bleachers. She went meekly, tears streaking her cheeks.

Cole came around, moaning as he struggled inside his rope cocoon. Hi and Shelton lifted him upright and perp-walked him over to his companions.

The Trinity were lined up on the floor.

They stared at us. We at them.

The same question was written on every face.

What next?

"Get the bag," I said to Shelton, loud enough for the Trinity to overhear. "And stick your head out the front door—make sure nobody called the police or anything."

Shelton hustled out of the gym. The rest of us crossed our arms and waited, trying to look intimidating. I was sure it wasn't working.

Ella kept her head down, avoiding my gaze. Cole's eyes darted everywhere. But Speckman stared back defiantly, a contemptuous curl to his lips. The sneer retreated somewhat when Coop settled down in front of him, fixing the boy with an unblinking canine glare.

Shelton returned, flashing a thumbs-up as he handed over my backpack. "All clear outside."

"We should hand them over to the spooks," Ben growled, following our script. "That's what they planned for us."

Cole squirmed inside his jump-rope prison. "Come on, man. Don't be like that. We're all Virals here."

Hi snorted loudly. "Oh! So *now* we're in this together? When we have you guys trussed like Thanksgiving turkeys, instead of the other way around?"

"We were just playing." Cole smiled weakly. "All in good fun."

"*My* favorite part was sliding down a support cable from the deck of an aircraft carrier," Shelton said sarcastically, shoving his glasses into place. "Good times! Lucky thing your plan to imprison us for the MIBs failed."

"We shouldn't have done that," Ella said quietly. "We shouldn't have gotten involved with those agents at all." She glared at Speckman. "This whole vendetta was stupid. We should've been working *with* them, not trying to ruin other Virals."

"This is *their* fault, Ella." Speckman gestured with his bound hands. "Tory and these morons got you kidnapped. Chance and his stupid experiment got us sick. They transformed us into monsters. Nearly killed us. You just gonna let that go?"

Ella flinched.

My temper boiled over. "I didn't get Ella kidnapped, you idiot!"

I closed my eyes, took a deep, calming breath. Then met Ella's troubled gaze. "I'm sorry you got caught up in that, Ella. I was trying to help other people. I feel terrible about what happened to you—I even risked my life to save you. But I'm not responsible. The bastard who took you is."

Speckman opened his mouth to argue, but I cut him off.

"And as for your sickness, you have Will Speckman to thank for that. Alone."

Ella looked at me askance. "What do you mean?"

"Don't listen to her!" Speckman shouted.

"She means," Chance interjected smoothly, "that you couldn't have caught the supervirus accidentally. It's not transmitted that way. The form Speckman and I created differs from the bug that infected Tory. It's not contagious through the air, or even by physical contact. The virus must be injected or ingested."

Ella looked from face to face. "What are you saying?"

Speckman began struggling with his zip ties, but there were too many to break. "Ignore them, Ella! They're trying to divide us."

I knelt before my teammate. Reached out and took her hand. "I'm saying, Speckman infected you on purpose. *Both* of you," I added, glancing at Cole.

"Liar!" Speckman shouted.

Chance glared at his former employee. "Will wanted a pack of his own, and was angry at me after losing his job. So he preyed on you two. His not-too-bright roommate—"

"Hey," Cole protested.

"—and a new friend from therapy, one who'd recently suffered a traumatic experience."

"A vulnerable girl," Hi added softly, "who could be manipulated into bearing a grudge."

Ella's eyes widened. "I . . . I never blamed Tory . . . not for anything . . . not until Will . . . The camping trip!" She shot a horrified look at Speckman. "The whole thing was a setup from the start! You bastard!" Tears spilled from her eyes.

My arms flew forward, wrapped Ella in a hug. I let her cry on my shoulder.

Cole half turned to face Speckman. "That true, man? You slip me that virus?"

Speckman looked away, didn't answer.

Cole stared at his shoes, then his eyes widened. "The *burrito*. That was the only time you ever bought me lunch. Not cool, bro."

Speckman seemed about to protest, then simply shrugged. "Fine. Yes. Do you regret it?"

"Not cool, bro," Cole repeated, but the hurt look quickly faded. "Naw, no regrets. Being Viral is freaking sweet. Who'd want to be normal when you can jump over walls?"

"You son of a bitch!" Ella broke free of me. Three steps brought her to where Speckman slouched. She kicked him in the ribs. "I trusted you!"

Speckman winced. "But you'd never go out with me, would you, Ella?" His tone was toxic. "You knew how I felt, but you just wanted to be *friends*. Just wanted me to listen to your sad story, over and over!"

"We were in therapy!" Ella thundered. "We weren't there to *date*."

Speckman's sneer returned. "Well, I made us close anyway, didn't I? We're a pack now. You can thank me later."

Ella answered with another boot to his side. I pulled her back.

"I never wanted this," Ella hissed. Then her voice broke. "I don't want this."

"Funny you should mention that."

Eyes slid to Chance. He was holding the metal box.

"I have a cure for being Viral." He opened the lid and removed a thin vial of green liquid. Five more doses were nestled inside. "Government agents are chasing us, and they want two things: Virals for experimentation, and this antidote."

He approached Ella with a vial. "Do you want a way out?"

Ella stared at the lime-green solution in Chance's fingers. Then her back straightened. "I do. My life has been crazy enough. I don't need this. I'm tired of being chased."

I nodded to Shelton, who removed a pocketknife from my bag and cut Ella's zip ties.

She smoothed her hair. Gave my hand a thankful squeeze.

Chance handed Ella the vial. "I reverse-engineered the virus. Just take this and drink. The serum is odorless and tasteless, and was extremely fast acting in mice."

"Mice. Wonderful." Ella cleared her throat, then turned to me. "Can you forgive me?"

"Already have," I replied, surprising myself.

It had taken me months to forgive Ben, and he'd been less culpable than Ella. But I now understood. Speckman had manipulated Ella during her darkest hours. She was a victim, too.

Plus, I wanted my friend back.

With shaky fingers, Ella took the vial from Chance. Removed the stopper. Tipped it back. Swallowed.

Nothing happened. No dramatic transformation, no violent reaction. Ella handed the empty vessel back to Chance. He swung to face the two boys tied up beside the bleachers.

"No chance, holmes." Cole began struggling with his makeshift bonds. "I'm not drinking that stuff. Viral till I die."

Speckman watched Chance like a rabid dog. "Don't come near me with that." Then he squeezed his eyelids shut. When they reopened, his irises glowed like volcanos.

Speckman ripped at his bonds, straining to tear through ten layers of plastic. But even Virals have limits. After a few moments, he collapsed in exhaustion.

But he wasn't done. Speckman fixed his sizzling red glare on me.

I felt a sharp pressure in my skull, as if my brain had been placed in a vise.

Beside me, Shelton reached for his temple.

Noticing his roommate, Cole closed his eyes as well. They popped open leaking fire. He squinted at Chance, who staggered and nearly dropped the box. A moment later, Ben grimaced in pain.

This was different from before. Without subtlety. A brute force assault.

The Trinity boys weren't trying to pick locks. They were trying to burn down our houses.

"It's an attack!" Chance spat through gritted teeth. "They're not trying to read our thoughts, they're trying to erase them!"

I felt a stab of existential panic. My instincts screamed in warning.

If I dropped my guard, my entire identity would be gone.

Speckman leered, enjoying himself. "You've never understood. Never accepted your inferiority. Even tied up, I'm too much for you. You brats share minds? Well, I can *break* them!"

The pressure increased. I felt my walls crumbling.

A growl cut the air.

The pain abruptly ceased.

I looked up.

Coop stood over Speckman, his jaws wrapped around the boy's throat.

Pure terror filled Speckman's scarlet eyes. He stiffened, not daring to move an inch. Cole was squirming away from Coop like an earthworm, the red light already gone from his gaze.

"Help . . . me . . ." Barely a whisper.

"Release your flare," I commanded, voice hard, though I was as nervous as he was. Coop's incisors were pressing into Speckman's flesh. A twitch of the wolfdog's mouth, and he'd be dead.

The scarlet glow vanished.

"Coop, heel."

To my infinite relief, Coop released Speckman and took a step back.

Then he barked loudly into his face.

A dark patch spread across Speckman's pants.

"Here, boy." I tapped my side. Coop trotted over and rubbed against my leg.

I rubbed his back, thankful beyond words.

Hi and Shelton grabbed Cole, who was attempting to wriggle across the gym. Setting him back against the bleachers, the two boys shared a flustered glance. Everyone knew how close we'd come to bloodshed.

I faced Speckman, who was struggling to control his breathing. "You might *like* being Viral, but you're not responsible enough for it. You're a menace. We'd hoped to somehow make peace, but it's clear that'll never happen."

I waved Chance forward. "That means you have to go."

"What are you saying?" Cole squawked. "You're gonna . . . kill us?" He watched Coop with terrified eyes.

"Shut up, you moron." Speckman had tensed like a cornered wolverine. "They don't have the guts to murder us in cold blood. Can't you see that?"

"You have a choice." Chance removed two more vials from the box. "Take the cure, now, or we leave you here for the agents."

"But I don't wanna be cured," Cole whimpered. "My life sucked before this. I'll be good now, I promise!"

"Sorry," I said, crossing my arms. "That ship sailed with the mind attack."

Speckman glared at me with contempt. "I won't drink."

My voice bubbled with irritation. "Fine! Enjoy the cages."

He laughed. "Cheer up, Cole. Haven't you been paying attention? This little girl doesn't have the stomach to play dirty."

"I'll do it. Watch me."

In response, Speckman dug his trussed hands into his pocket. A cell phone fell out, and he kicked it across the floor to me. "Go ahead. The top saved number. Those spooks came to interview Ella about you, even gave her a card. I don't know who they are, but they monitor that line."

He's so damn arrogant.

I picked up the phone. "Last chance, dirtbags."

Speckman rolled his eyes. "You're bluffing. Badly."

Cole seemed close to bursting, but he shook his head. "Willie's right. You won't call."

I unlocked the screen. Pulled up the caller list. Held my finger above the number.

My gaze locked on to my adversary's. Speckman didn't bat an eyelash. *He knows me. Damn it, but he does.*

I slammed the phone to the ground with a shriek, breaking it to pieces. Cole released a pent-up breath. Speckman just laughed.

I waved my companions into a huddle. Hi and Shelton trudged over, throwing angry glances over their shoulders. Chance began earnestly debating what to do next. Ben didn't say a word.

"Hey, jailors," Cole called in a singsong cadence. "Can I get a Mountain Dew?"

I shot him a baleful look. "Ella, can you give those jerks some water? There are bottles in my bag."

Ella nodded and rose. I returned to a whispered conversation with my pack.

"What are we going to do now?" Ben hissed.

"What else can we?" I whispered back. "We made our play."

Ella knelt beside Cole, whose arms were tied to his sides. She shoved a water bottle into his mouth. "You're such an idiot."

Cole looked hurt as he gulped half of it down. Ella threw the other bottle at Speckman, naked hatred in her eyes. He caught it deftly, even with his hands tied together.

"Thanks, sweetheart." Speckman winked.

I thought she'd go for his throat.

"Ella?" I called.

"Yes?" Without turning.

"Don't do anything rash, okay?"

"Fine." Ella poured more water down Cole's throat. "I hope you both choke."

"Love you, too." Speckman twisted open his bottle and knocked it back.

Ella stood, carefully smoothed her clothing, then reached over and slapped his face.

Oh, well.

Speckman tried to throw his bottle at her. It missed, rolled harmlessly across the gym floor. Hi raced to snag it, then tipped the container over. Empty.

I took my first breath in minutes.

A hand squeezed my shoulder. Ben, smiling from ear to ear.

Impulsively, I hugged him as Hi walked over and slapped fives with Shelton and Chance. Then Hi knelt and presented the bottle to me like a championship trophy. I ruffled his sweaty hair.

Ella's brow furrowed as she watched us. "What's going on? Have you decided . . . what to do with them?"

"It's all good!" Shelton crowed, breaking out the robot dance. "Game over!" Then he and Hiram started into an impromptu square-dance number. Ben even counted off the steps.

"Hey!" Ella stamped a foot, some of her old fire returning. "Explain."

"The naughty kids just needed a little help taking their medicine." Chance tapped the empty water bottle in my fingers. "All gone!"

Cole squinted at Chance, totally lost. "What? You've got meds?"

But I was watching Speckman. Saw his eyes nearly pop from his skull.

"No!" Chest heaving, he struggled with his bonds. "That's not fair!"

I laughed out loud. "Oh, we're discussing fairness now, Willie?"

Cole's face was still blank with incomprehension. "I don't understand what's happening."

"The water, you jackass." Speckman gave up the fight, utter defeat etched on his face. "They spiked it with the antidote." His voice broke. "We just drank away our powers."

"Oh." Ella gaped at the container she still held, then actually giggled. "Oh, that's good."

Cole stared at me, openmouthed. "Not cool, bro."

I flashed my biggest smile. Didn't feel a moment's sympathy for the lying, manipulating, bullying, terrorizing jerks.

Instead I dropped the bottle and wiped my hands.

"Gotcha."

PART FOUR
CULMINATION

CHAPTER 37

Speckman's sniffles carried across the empty gym.

We'd held the Trinity boys there for over an hour. Morbidly, I wondered what Headmaster Paugh might say if he popped in to work, and found Bolton Prep students and alumni holding one another hostage on school grounds. A wolfdog prowling his basketball court.

The ceaseless whimpering was grating on my nerves. After discovering he'd been duped into taking the cure, Speckman had morphed from a hard-ass to a quivering mound of Jell-O.

"How much longer do we wait?" I asked.

Chance glanced at his watch. "I don't really know. In trials, the antidote worked almost immediately, but that was on mice. I've no idea how long the process might take with humans." A guilty look crossed his face. "Obviously, I've never tested this serum on an actual person before. I just got the vials yesterday. They were manufactured by a black-market pharma outfit based in Singapore."

Hi slapped Chance on the back. "Well here's hoping it doesn't kill them!"

"Not funny," I scolded. We were playing with fire, but there'd been no other options. Speckman and Cole were dangerous. They'd forfeited the right to be Viral.

Assuming this works.

I snapped my fingers as a thought occurred to me. "Ella!"

Motioning Coop to sit, I hurried across the gym.

Her head rose as I approached. I'd simply asked her to stay, hoping she wouldn't force a confrontation. But Ella had just nodded wearily and found a corner to huddle in. She hadn't moved or said a word since.

"Ella?" I knelt and took her hand. She tensed, but didn't pull away.

"Come to tell me you're quitting soccer?" A weak joke, but I was glad Ella made the attempt. I was worried about her state of mind.

"We have to be sure the cure worked. Before we release Cole and Speckman, I mean."

Ella smiled wryly. "I'm not a prisoner, too?"

I shook my head. "Not at all. We trust you now. All of us. I . . . we understand how you were misled. How Speckman mistreated you. You can go whenever you want."

She sighed. "But you need to me try flaring, first."

I nodded. "You took the serum before the boys. If it worked on you, we'll know."

Ella rubbed a hand over her mouth, then slowly got to her feet. "I feel kinda funny. Light-headed. Chance's magic potion did *something* to me, but I haven't tried to touch my powers."

I offered my arm, but she waved it off.

Ella took a deep breath. Closed her eyes.

Ella's facial muscles tensed. For long seconds she stood, motionless, her forehead scrunched like a washboard. Then her whole body relaxed. When her eyes reopened, they were their normal, stunning green. "It's gone." Her voice broke. "For the best, I guess, but I feel like I've lost a part of me."

I wrapped her in my arms. She sobbed once, twice.

"I'm so sorry, Ella. Really." Inadequate, but there was nothing else to say.

"It's not your fault." Ella cleared her throat, wiping tears from her cheeks. "None of this was. I see that now. I hope we can be friends again. I don't expect you to—"

I crushed her with a second hug. "It's already okay. I promise."

This time, Ella squeezed back.

When we'd gathered ourselves—Ella mocking our "special moment" with her usual sarcasm—the two of us walked back over to the boys, who were studiously pretending they hadn't witnessed any of it.

"You're in luck, fellas." Ella pointed to her eyes. "No glow. I'm officially out of the mutant club. Can't say I miss it."

A lie, I suspected. But a healthy one.

Chance edged forward. Ella's back straightened at his undivided attention.

"We'll run tests later," he promised. "Dozens of them. I'll monitor your health for as long as necessary, and make sure there are no side effects. I won't abandon you. You're with us now."

Ella blushed to the roots of her glossy black hair. "Thank you, Chance."

Hmmm.

"Can we cut them loose?" Hi jabbed a thumb at Cole and Speckman.

"I guess we have to," I replied. "Not that they deserve it."

"Let me." Ben took the pocketknife from Shelton. "I almost hope they try something."

We approached our prisoners, who were slouched against the bleachers. Hi and Shelton tried to unwind the jump-rope straitjacket they'd tied around Cole, but in the end Ben had to saw through the lines. Coop watched, wary and ready.

Cole rose and backed up a few steps. "Like, thanks. You guys seem all right. Sorry about all the kicking and fighting."

Hi rolled his eyes. "Stay in school, Cole. Seriously. For a long time."

Confused, the scruffy boy simply nodded.

Ben knelt before Speckman, who'd finally stopped sniveling. He glowered at my friend with palpable loathing. "This isn't over, Blue. Not by a long shot."

Ben rocked back and crossed his arms. "You want free, or not?"

Speckman sneered, but held out his wrists. One by one, Ben sliced through the plastic cuffs we'd used to secure the Trinity's leader. As the last strip parted, both boys sprang to their feet.

Towering over the rest of us, Speckman clenched his fists.

Chance stepped forward to stand beside Ben. "Not a good idea."

In response, Speckman snapped his eyes shut. His whole body trembled. When his eyelids popped back open, red fire leaked from his irises.

Speckman laughed in triumph. My heart dropped. Coop crouched beside me, teeth bared.

The cure hadn't worked! We'd have to—

Speckman's smile vanished. He grabbed his temples. "No. No! NO!"

The scarlet radiance flickered, then died. Speckman dropped to a knee, straining with every muscle he possessed. Then he collapsed in a heap. One fist pounded the floor.

I took a breath.

"You took everything from me," Speckman moaned. "How could you?"

My voice was pitiless. "You gave us no choice, Will. You're not fit to be Viral."

"Come on, man." Cole tugged his friend's arm. "Let's bail."

Speckman allowed himself to be led toward the exit. But at the threshold he swung back to face us, malevolence twisting his features.

"You'll pay for this!" Speckman spat on the floor. "Somehow. I promise."

Then he shoved Cole through the doorway and was gone.

"I'm gonna miss that guy," Hi deadpanned. "He's got a lot of great qualities."

Ella tugged my sleeve. "I should go, too." Against all odds, she smiled. "Don't forget, we have a game on Tuesday."

I gave her one more bear hug. "Wouldn't miss it."

Ella waved to the others and, with a last glance at Chance, headed out the door.

I caught him watching her go.

Well, well.

Shelton's voice drew me back. "So now *we* need to decide."

"Decide what?" Ben asked, scuffing the floor with his shoe.

Shelton gave him a surprised look, then pointed to the metal box in Chance's pocket. "Whether we should take that serum ourselves."

His words sent a shockwave through my system.

The question was out there now, in the open. No more avoiding it.

"What!?" Ben's eyebrows rose in disbelief. "No way!"

"He's right." Ignoring Ben's incredulous stare, Hi pawed at his scalp. "Those agents are still hunting us. Last night, they stormed Chance's freaking mega-castle to bag a Viral. They're not gonna let up. We have to decide what we're willing to risk."

"I won't give up being Viral," Ben vowed stubbornly. "Not ever."

"Even if it means your freedom?" Hi countered. "Or your life?"

Ben was about to fire back, but Chance cut him off. "What about *her* life?" He snapped a nod at me. "Would you risk that?"

Ben paled, mouth working but words failing.

"How many vials do we have left?" Shelton asked. "After dosing the Trinity, I mean."

"Plenty." Chance flipped open the box and tossed the rightmost two vials aside. Those were fake—their original contents had been dumped into the water bottles. "I have two more full vials in here, and it doesn't take much to work."

My brow furrowed. "How can you know that?"

"I don't *know*," Chance answered peevishly. "Not for certain. But our clinical trials indicated that a small amount should be sufficient."

For a moment, no one spoke.

I stared at the green liquid. Torn.

Normally, I'd never have considered giving up my powers. But those storm troopers had changed the equation. Our secret was out, and the very worst ears had heard it.

We'd barely escaped them last time. Who knew what would happen next?

Is being Viral worth my life?

"Things have gotten too dangerous," Shelton said quietly. "I don't think we can wiggle out of this one."

Hi ran a hand down his face, then spoke through his fingers. "They'll put us in cages. Slice us and dice us."

Ben punched his thigh. Again. Then again, muttering and cursing. When he finally spoke, he was looking directly at me. "I don't want to risk . . . anyone."

Chance removed the last two vials. "Are we decided, then?"

My eyes found Ben's. He crossed his arms, fingers digging into his flesh. But he nodded.

I looked to Shelton, who removed his glasses to wipe his eyes. "Yes," he said weakly.

Hi next. He nodded, then looked away.

Chance was watching me. "I'm in if you are."

I swallowed. Thought of all the crazy things we'd done with our powers.

Scaling the Morris Island lighthouse. Roughhousing on Turtle Beach. Stalking through dark forests and swamps. Breaking into the Charleston Public Library. Running from the cops. Raiding tombs. Tunneling under the city. Swimming the harbor in the dead of the night.

So many wild nights. Dangerous situations.

All because we were Viral. Unique. A breed apart.

But it's not worth our freedom.

"We don't have a choice." Unshed tears stung my eyes. "We have to protect ourselves."

I extended my hand. Chance passed me a vial.

Fingers shaking, I pulled the stopper and held it to my lips.

Said good-bye.

Something bumped my leg. I looked down.

Coop was staring at me intently, eyes bright.

Other memories fired through my brain.

Cooper and me, trotting down the coastline. Wrestling on my bed. Hiking across Loggerhead Island. The two of us sitting alone, watching the sun set into Schooner Creek, our minds linked, our souls in harmony.

The wolfdog and I shared a special bond, unique to this world.

A strange, wonderful way to communicate. The unrivaled closeness of being pack.

I lowered the vial.

No way I was giving that up.

"I won't do it." I handed the serum back to Chance, then knelt and scratched Coop's ears. "I won't judge anyone else's decision, but I can't sacrifice part of myself. I couldn't live with it."

Ben smacked his hands together. "Thank God!"

"You're serious?" Shelton gaped. "This isn't like the other times. Men are *hunting* us!"

"Sorry, Shelton." Hi blew out a breath, looked relieved. "But I feel the same. This body's too sexy to go normal. I'm wolfman all the way. Pack for life, and all that."

Chance gripped Hi's shoulder, grinning sardonically. "Hopefully you'll let me in now. My original pack no longer exists."

"Lunatics." Shelton slowly shook his head. "You people are straight-up crazy."

I squeezed his skinny arm. "You need to decide for yourself, Shelton. We'll respect whatever you choose."

He took a step back. Visibly resisted grabbing an earlobe. "Why won't y'all see reason?"

"It's your call." Chance handed over one of the vials. "Do what you feel is right."

I caught and held Shelton's eye. "Trust your instincts."

Shelton looked from face to face, expression pained, before settling on the vial between his fingers. Several beats passed, then he rolled his eyes. "Oh, forget this. Like I'm gonna ditch my family."

Everyone cheered as he thrust the vial into my hand.

I looked at Chance.

He nodded. "If we're not going to use them . . ."

The whole group counted together.

"One."

"Two."

"Three!"

Chance and I dropped the vials and crushed them with our heels.

CHAPTER 38

W e're the dumbest collection of dummies ever to be dumb."
Shelton stared ruefully at the green puddles on the hardwood. "So how do we outsmart these government thugs?"

The million-dollar question.

"I don't know." It was time for total honesty, even if the truth was
scary. "It feels like things are escalating. Before last night, they'd only
tried to grab us in remote places."

"Places the Trinity had lured us." Ben shot Chance a black look.
"Red-eye schemes, working against the golden."

Chance met him glare for glare. "Those soldiers came for *me,* too,
you know. In my ancestral home, which I can't go back to now."

"My *point* is," I continued, "something changed. The agents lost patience, tried to kidnap us right from South of Broad. From freaking
Claybourne Manor."

Hi held up an index finger. "Which brings us to the point—will they
strike again? Are these jerks about to stop being polite . . . and start
getting real?"

Coop bumped my leg again.

I glanced down, found him staring at me with an expression I couldn't place.

"We should go to my office," Chance suggested, pacing as he thought. "The Candela building has airtight physical security. You can't possibly drag someone out of there without witnesses."

"And do what?" Shelton's hands rose, his voice sharp with irritation. "Live there forever? We have to go home eventually. You might have problems at your gigantic fancy mansion, but Morris Island is as remote as America gets. If these psychos *really* wanna bag us, they could burn down our whole damn neighborhood and nobody would notice!"

Goose bumps rose on my arms. Shelton was right. The agents missed at Claybourne Manor, but Morris Island was the next best thing. If they decided to capture us at all costs, nothing would stand in their way.

I went cold, imagining an attack on our sleepy little community. Our families as "collateral damage." *In today's top story, a freak gas explosion on Morris Island claimed the lives of . . .*

"Tory?"

I blinked. Found Hi watching me closely.

"You okay?" he asked. "You've got a strange expression on your face."

I didn't know how to respond. All of a sudden, I realized how hopeless our situation was.

We could never stop the men chasing us.

And they'd never leave us alone.

"We should split up," Chance said suddenly.

All heads whipped to him.

"Of course!" Chance grew animated as he spoke. "The spooks have only moved in when we're all together. They must be afraid of missing someone. One of us getting away, maybe feeling desperate enough, and . . . and . . . talking to the police. Or the FBI. Or the media, I guess."

"They already *did* miss," Hi pointed out. "Last night. And who could we talk to?"

"They know we can't tell anyone," Shelton said glumly. "We're trapped by our own secret. If we tell our parents we're being stalked by secret government agents, they'll laugh their asses off. Or have our heads checked. And if we *prove* it by showing them our powers . . ."

I tensed.

Was that the answer?

Was it time to come clean at home?

I imagined Kit's face, watching my irises ignite. Felt sick at the prospect. Would he flip out? Run screaming from his golden-eyed freak of a daughter? I didn't want to find out, but our options were nearly nonexistent.

Ben's acid tone crashed my train of thought. "Split up, eh Chance?" His neck flushed red, a sure sign he was losing his temper. "And let me guess, you and Tory would sneak off together, leaving us three losers to fend for ourselves?"

"Ben!" I barked. *Sneak off?*

"My office is the safest place!" Chance argued. "Shouldn't that be where Tory is?"

Ben got up in Chance's face. "Not if *you're* there, Claybourne. And we all know what you're really up to."

"You do?" Chance gave Ben a nasty smile. "You think you're up to speed, Ben?"

Ben's face blanched. "What's that supposed to mean?" His troubled gaze darted to me. "What's he saying, Tor? You can't *want* to go away with him again, right? It's not safe."

Chance scoffed. "Who appointed you her protector?"

My temper exploded.

"Enough!"

Both boys started in surprise. Coop inched closer to my side, eyeing them.

"Ben! Chance!" Biting off their names, I pointed to center court. "A private word."

Hi and Shelton began slowly backing away. "Yeah, um. No problem." Hi scratched his head, looking everywhere but at me. "You guys go and . . . like . . . chat. We'll, like—"

"We'll be over there." Shelton pushed Hi toward the far baseline. "You guys talk. Take your time." He snagged Coop's collar as they retreated across the gym. "Come on, boy." The wolfdog reluctantly went along.

I couldn't hold back any longer. "I have had *enough* of this crap!"

Both spoke at once.

"You can't trust this creep any farther—"

"I'm only trying—"

I actually stamped a foot.

"What makes you think I'm interested in either of you?" I practically shouted, too furious to mince words. "You bicker and fight like toddlers. And *now,* of all times! It's ridiculous!"

Twin sullen expressions soured their faces. I might've laughed, had the situation not been so deadly serious. So I kept blasting away. "I'm sick and tired of you constantly attacking each other. It's *exhausting.*" My breath came hot and fast, the words spilling out in a torrent. "So let me say this one time, out loud, so neither of you can miss it: *I'm not selecting a boyfriend this week.* And if I was, right now it sure as hell wouldn't be either one of you!"

Neither spoke.

I paused my tirade, nostrils flaring, my pulse firing a mile a minute.

Did I really mean that?

Chance was staring at his shoes, his expression that of a man falsely accused of crime.

Ben's face was wooden. He'd retreated into his shell, letting nothing show.

Worried I'd gone too far, I softened my tone. Held up a thumb and forefinger, only a millimeter apart. "We're *this* close to becoming a medical experiment. That's what matters right now. Nothing else. Don't you get that?"

They never got a chance to respond.

Two men in black suits stepped through the double doors.

Buzz Cut. Mustache.

Mustache smiled, exposing two rows of brown, crooked teeth. Buzz Cut's face was granite, except for an angry red scar puckering his cheek.

"Look out!" I shouted, but it was far too late.

In each corner of the gym, the emergency doors swung wide. Pairs of black-uniformed agents took up position at each exit, one man unarmed, the other holding the same odd, blunt-nosed weapon we'd seen the night before.

Shelton and Hi raced to join us at center court.

Ben squeezed his eyes shut.

"Ben, no!" I hissed, but my friend ignored me, straining silently as agents surrounded us.

Finally, he let out a ragged breath. "My flare won't come. Chance, it's up to you."

Chance looked at me. I could tell he was calculating in his mind.

Before I could react, Cooper fired from the shadow of the bleachers, charging Buzz Cut and Mustache with bared teeth. Growling viscously, he lunged at the startled agents.

Time slowed.

Mustache yelled something.

An agent ran forward and dropped to a knee, aiming his weapon at Coop's back.

"No!" I lurched forward, but Chance grabbed me and held me back.

There was an odd popping sound. The air seemed to warp in a straight line toward my wolfdog.

Coop's back arched. He let out a piteous whine, then crumpled to the ground.

"Let me go!" I pounded Chance's arm, trying to break free.

He held fast, squeezing me tighter. "You can't do anything for him!"

"Coop!" I blubbered, tears streaming. "You bastards!"

Mustache's gravelly voice cut across the gym. "You plan on coming quietly? Or do my boys get to use their fancy stun guns again?"

Stun gun.

I stared at Coop. Saw his chest rise and fall.

My knees nearly buckled with relief. I pulled away, meeting Chance's eye. "I'm okay."

As he relented, Ben stepped between me and the agents. "What do you want?"

"You know," Mustache said flatly, eyes hard beneath a spiky cap of thinning gray hair. He was doing all the talking; Buzz Cut had barely moved a muscle since entering the building. "And you have no choice."

Ben tensed. I could tell he was ready to fight, with fists alone, if need be.

So was I.

I straightened. Wiped away my tears.

Flaring or not, I wasn't going meekly into a cage.

But Chance grabbed my arm and spoke under his breath. "Do as they say."

Ben's head whipped. "Claybourne, you—"

"There's no time!" Chance hissed. "You have to trust me!"

I met Chance's gaze. His eyes pleaded silently.

"I have a plan," Chance whispered. "But we have to be awake to do it."

I nodded slowly.

I'd trust Chance. One last time.

Against every instinct, I stepped around Ben. Lightly pushed him back. Hi and Shelton watched with terrified eyes as I faced the agents and raised my hands.

"We surrender."

CHAPTER 39

The next minutes were a blur.

Agents closed in from all sides. Not a hand was laid on me, but it was clear resistance was futile. We were outnumbered two to one. They were armed. Our flares were spent.

Buzz Cut's face was an iron mask behind his reflective shades. Mustache simply pointed to a corner of the gym. His black-clad minions marched us toward the indicated exit.

Twenty yards to the doorway—its glowing rectangle of sunlight felt like a mouth set to swallow us whole. Afternoon beams blinded me as we were herded outside like cattle.

While his younger partner watched, aloof, Mustache barked orders. "Grab the girl's bag and that metal box. And bring the animal. It's mentioned in the file."

My temperature spiked as I realized our mistake. *So stupid. Again.*

Mustache had read Chance's records. That morning, Candela's document program had recorded two *J*s in the metadata. *Two* unauthorized viewings of his secret file.

We'd assumed Speckman had accessed the file twice. How wrong we were.

These bastards had also found our bait.

Mustache led us around a corner of the building. I obeyed meekly, barely able to process what was happening. Was this the last daylight I'd ever see? Would anyone ever learn what happened to us?

Once again, Ben's hand found mine. His eyes were helpless, and full of rage.

I grabbed the closest hand on my other side. Shelton gripped back. I saw Hi link fingers with Shelton, and the Morris Island pack became a human chain. Small comfort, but it was something.

Chance walked alone a few paces away, his face a mask.

We were hustled to a narrow service driveway behind the main school building. Agents were forming up beside three black vehicles: a familiar sedan and two windowless cargo vans.

The back doors of the each van stood open. In the first, I spotted three huddled forms.

Cole. Speckman. Ella.

The Trinity.

Ella's frantic gaze found mine. I could feel her terror. Shared it myself.

"We don't know anything!" Speckman shouted. "Honest! You don't want us!"

His pleas were silenced as the doors slammed shut.

I stopped dead, stunned by my own shortsightedness. How long had these men waited, closing a fist around Bolton's grounds as we fought the Trinity inside? In trapping the small fish, we'd drawn a much larger predator down on our heads.

Authors of our own downfall. I've been such a fool.

I thought of Chance's antidote, drying on the hardwood floor. Fought down panic. The Trinity should be safe—the serum had removed their flare powers. But what about my pack? What would these psychopaths find if they took us apart, cell by cell?

Mustache reached the second van and swept a hand inside.

This was *our* ride.

Was this the last thing I'd ever see? The dark interior of a kidnapper van?

Bolton's high perimeter wall blocked any view from outside. I considered screaming, but knew it was pointless. No one would hear me. Not here, not on a Saturday. This ambush had been perfectly planned and executed.

"Put the mutt in there." Mustache pointed to the black sedan. I watched in horror as two agents dumped Cooper into the town car's trunk.

"Don't you hurt my dog." My voice was low, and full of menace.

Mustache ignored me. "Will you get in quietly, or do you need . . . help?"

I glared at the older man, memorizing his pockmarked features. His thick ash-colored eyebrows and uneven teeth. I committed the ugly face to memory.

Fingers pressed into my back. Chance, face taut. "Just do it, Tory. Climb inside."

I nodded almost imperceptibly. What choice did I have?

Swallowing my fears, I climbed into the van without another word.

I had to trust Chance. It was all we had left.

Metal benches ran along each side of the van's interior. Nothing else. Hi climbed up behind me, his hands shaking badly. Together we helped Shelton inside. Ben came next, a ball of caged fury. His teeth were clamped, his jaw tight as a snare drum. I knew the only reason he wasn't fighting was me.

I looked back.

Chance was standing at the bumper, watching with sad eyes.

My heart leaped into my throat.

Chance made no move to get inside.

Oh no.

Ben's eyes widened. "I knew it."

I felt my walls collapsing. My mouth opened, but no sound emerged. I couldn't breathe.

He really did betray us. And I fell for it, all the way down.

Then Mustache thumped Chance on the back. "Get in the vehicle. Now." He signaled two agents forward as Buzz Cut watched impassively. "Or you'll get our special treatment."

Chance sneered at the crusty old man. Then he vaulted up into the van and took the seat across from me. I felt his temper simmering, but when he looked at me, I saw only pain.

"I'm sorry, Tory. This is all my fault."

The doors swung shut.

○   ○   ○

Miles rolled by beneath our feet.

I couldn't tell where we were going—our rolling prison was dark, spare, and windowless, stinking of gasoline and oxidized metal. A cracked light in the ceiling provided the only illumination. The benches were cold hard steel, bolted into place.

No one had bothered to cuff us.

Why would they? They've got nothing to fear.

I sat between Shelton and Ben. Hi and Chance rode the opposite bench. Our knees thudded together with every bump in the road, but no one cared. This was a funeral procession, and we all knew it.

Suddenly Ben's hand shot out, grabbing Chance by the arm. "Why didn't you fight? You can flare anytime you want!"

Chance batted his fingers away. "What did I say about touching me?"

Hi's hand replaced Ben's. "You said you had a plan. That's what you said!"

Shelton looked up, daring to hope. "You know a way out of this?"

Chance hesitated, then nodded. "Of sorts."

He leaned back against the side of the van. We rolled along in silence as Chance stared at a point above my head, seemingly lost in thought. Finally, I could wait no longer. "I don't know who these men are, where they're taking us, or what might happen when we get there. But I'm afraid this could be the last time we're all together."

Chance regarded me with the same sad expression as before.

I couldn't fathom what he was thinking.

"Back in the gym," Chance began slowly, speaking to the whole group, "I wouldn't have taken the cure. Even if you guys had. I don't want to lose what makes me different, even with the risks. But I drew these bastards to us, however unintentionally. This is my fault. I'm truly sorry."

"We trusted you enough to get into this van," I said quietly. "Tell us your idea."

Chance took a deep breath. Then he reached down and rolled up his pant leg. "They really should've searched us."

A small bundle was strapped to his left calf. Chance unrolled the gray parcel and pulled its Velcro flap. Five green vials were nestled inside.

Shelton lurched forward in his seat. "Is that what I think it is?"

Chance nodded. "I thought it prudent to have a backup stock, just in case. For emergencies."

"Exactly five vials." Ben's frown deepened. "More damn secrets."

Chance snorted. "I'd say this was a fairly smart one, wouldn't you?"

Chance's plan was obvious now. To escape this trap, we had to take the cure.

Make ourselves normal. Boring. Ordinary.

To regain our freedom, we could no longer be Viral.

Ben edged away from the bundle. "I . . . I still don't want to do it."

Shelton ripped off his glasses. "We're past that now, Benjamin! Look where we are!"

Hi began dry-washing his hands. "Will it work? We were infected by a different strain."

"It'll work." But I heard a tremor in Chance's voice. "The genetic response of our bodies was essentially the same for both viruses. This antidote negates those effects."

Hi looked at me. "What do you think, Tor? We're in a jam. I don't see another way out."

I stared at the vile green liquid. Hated it with every ounce of my being. I wanted to smash these glass cylinders to the ground, just like the last ones.

The serum would change me. Unmake me. I didn't want to let it.

But this time, there was no choice.

"I'll drink."

Hi nodded slowly, as did Chance. Shelton seemed almost eager.

"I won't do it!" Ben swore.

"We can't let them get the supervirus." Hi shivered as he spoke. "Ask yourself this—why do these government creeps want us in the first place? To make weapons, dummy! Viral *armies*. You want that on your conscience?"

"I want to see my mom and dad again," Shelton said. "I want y'all to see yours, too."

Ben jerked away. Punched the side of the van.

I put a hand on his knee. "We'll always be a pack, Ben. No matter what."

He didn't respond.

Suddenly, we all lurched sideways as the van made a sharp turn.

"Out of time." Chance looked from face to face. "Who's first?"

Shelton reached out a hand. Chance carefully unstoppered a vial and handed it to him. Tears leaked beneath his black specs. "Love you guys."

Shelton downed the liquid in one go. Chance handed the next vial to Hiram.

Hi flashed a shaky smile, then winked. "Cheers, eh? See you on the other side." He drank his dose in two swallows, then smacked his lips. "Tastes like cabbage."

Chance looked at me. I gestured for him to go ahead.

Chance held a delicate pipette close to his face, swirling its contents gently. "I wish I'd never found you," he whispered. Then he knocked the serum back.

Two doses remained. I looked at Ben. Knew he'd resist.

The van decelerated, took another sharp turn, then bumped onto an unpaved road.

I crossed my arms. "If you don't drink, Ben, then I won't either."

Ben's expression became hunted. Then he slammed a fist into his thigh. "Damn it." He glared at the floor, eyes narrow and face miserable. "You know me too well, Victoria."

Ben reached without looking. Chance handed him a vial. Ben closed his eyes, mumbled a prayer, and drank.

The van abruptly stopped. Doors opened and closed. Chance shoved the last dose into my hand, then gathered the empties and stuffed them back into his Velcro case.

I stared at the green liquid.

Keys rattled. Voices boomed outside the rear doors.

Everyone watched as I hesitated. The moment had come, yet I froze.

This isn't fair.

But when is life?

I lifted the slender tube. Opened it. Tipped it into my mouth. Swallowed the detestable liquid.

Then I smashed the glass to the floor, grinding it to dust.

CHAPTER 40

"Deny everything!" I hissed.

Chance shoved the Velcro case behind his belt, then whispered something to Hi, who nodded, grim-faced. Shelton inched away from the rear of the van, eyes wide behind his glasses. He backed into Ben, who put a steadying hand on his shoulder.

Everyone flinched as the metal doors swung outward. Mustache and Buzz Cut stood in the opening, the former smiling darkly, the latter expressionless.

"Let's go." Mustache waved us out, glancing at his watch. One by one we stepped from the van, blinking like moles in the bright afternoon sun. A chill passed through me as I took in our surroundings.

I knew the place. Had been there once before.

We were standing in front of the low-slung building near the military base. A single black-lettered sign above the entrance read: D.O.D. SPECIAL OPERATIONS ANNEX. The area hummed with activity—a half-dozen guards in nondescript uniforms surrounded the structure, casually holding weapons, eyes hidden behind dark sunglasses. The windows were reflective, blocking any view inside the building, but I sensed dozens more inside.

Behind me, a familiar gravel road wound up to the rusty gate I'd huddled behind the previous evening. There could be no mistake—we'd been abducted by our own government.

But what branch? What agency? For what purpose?

Who did these men answer to?

Hi's elbow found my side. "Look."

Beyond our vehicle was the second van. Doors open. Rear compartment empty.

Where had they taken the Trinity? Were we next?

I thought of Ella, kidnapped a second time. My heart nearly broke.

At that moment, a burly bald man in a spotless white lab coat strode from the facility. Red-faced and bearded, with a thick bull neck, he stormed up to Mustache while anxiously glancing skyward. "Are you insane?" he shouted. "Unloading outside, in broad daylight!"

Mustache showed the agitated scientist his wristwatch. "There's no sat coverage in this sector for another fourteen minutes, Dr. Keegan. We're deep in the woods, and this facility doesn't have an underground—"

"Just take them around back with the other three." Keegan was already retreating toward the building. "Do it now, before you're seen!"

Mustache watched him go, then spat on the ground. "You heard him. March."

No one moved.

Mustache grabbed Shelton's arm. Ben shot forward and shoved the agent aside, then stepped between them.

Buzz Cut turned. Straightened his tie. His face never twitched behind the dark shades.

But I could taste the impending violence. Sensed that Ben welcomed it.

Mustache straightened, his hands finding his pockets. "So it's like that, eh, boy? I wouldn't test my partner's patience, if I were you."

Soldiers turned our way. Things were about to get ugly.

"We'll cooperate." I motioned Ben back, speaking directly to Mustache.

"But there's been some kind of mistake. I don't know what you people want with us, but no one needs to get hurt."

Ben took a deep breath, unclenching his fists.

"Mistake?" Mustache laughed, buffing a pockmarked cheek. "I was on that rooftop, girl. I saw you kids fly. There's no mistake here."

Soldiers surrounded us, gripping their odd weapons. Fingers found triggers.

My gut screamed for me to run. Make a dash for the woods. Take my chances. But I had to remain calm, or the situation might turn violent.

Taking Shelton's hand, I started toward the building. He followed meekly.

I caught a covert glance between Chance and Hi.

What are they up to?

Mustache's strike team fell in around us, herding us to a dirt path running alongside the building that was hemmed in by trees on both sides. Mustache and Buzz Cut followed on our heels. I still didn't know their names.

The trail narrowed a dozen paces into the woods.

Behind me, Hi started coughing uncontrollably.

I glanced back. My friend was hacking into a fist, his chubby cheeks growing redder by the second. "I think I swallowed a bug," he wheezed.

Chance began pounding Hi's back, but this only made him cough harder.

"I've got asthma, too," Hi sputtered. "And gingivitis."

"What's going on?" Mustache growled. "No tricks, fat boy. This old dog knows 'em all."

The guards halted, uncertain what to do. Mustache pushed his way forward, knocking Chance off the path to reach Hiram's side.

Hi had dropped to a knee, body trembling, tears streaming down his face. "My sciatica!"

But I was watching Chance.

Saw a hand slip under his shirt, remove the Velcro case, and drop it into the pine needles.

Ditching any trace of the cure.

I looked away, trying not to draw attention to Chance.

Thankfully, Hi was laying down an Academy Award performance.

I cursed myself for crushing a vial inside the van, but quickly dismissed the concern. Even if the agents thought to look, there wasn't much left to recover.

The cure was gone. That's what had drawn them to Bolton Prep.

But what about the supervirus? What about our DNA?

Chance slipped back onto the path and resumed patting Hi's back. Almost instantly, the coughing subsided. Hi straightened, wiping his eyes. "Man, pollen is a killer this year."

Mustache grabbed Hi by the shirt and pulled his face close. Buzz Cut watched from the back of the group, reflective shades revealing nothing.

Hi stared back at the agent gripping him, afraid to blink. An eon passed, then Mustache grunted, releasing my friend roughly. "Let's get these kids inside," he barked. "I'm not getting chewed out again."

He shoved Hi down the trail toward me. As I caught him, I saw Shelton clamp Ben's arm with his own. The line lurched forward again. Another twenty paces brought us to a metal door in the rear of the building. Mustache pounded twice with the heel of his hand.

A security camera zeroed on his coarse face.

Locks clicked. The portal swung inward. Single file, we were forced inside.

Lambs to the slaughter.

○   ○   ○

I awoke in darkness.

Rubbed groggy eyes. For some reason, I was sure hours had passed.

My head pounded. Lifting a hand to my temple, I felt cool, filtered air tickle my side. With a sharp shock, I noticed the medical gown enveloping me. I wore nothing else.

I sat bolt upright, fighting a surge of panic. Flashes came back to me. A long, brightly lit corridor. Unsmiling men in white lab coats, carrying clipboards. Being forced into a tiny white-walled room.

My breath caught as more memories surfaced.

Ben. Shouting, punching, clawing his way toward me.

Soldiers tackling him, pinning his writhing form to the floor. Ben squeezing his eyelids shut, straining with every muscle. Yet nothing happened.

I remembered Hi diving onto the pile. Mustache grabbing my friend in a headlock, holding him down while a white coat stuck a needle in his arm. Bodies swarming over Ben until he finally stopped struggling.

Chance had kicked a soldier holding Ben in the face. Was that right?

I cringed at the next memory: a snarling flatfoot, shooting Chance in the back with the strange weapon they all carried.

Shelton. Screaming. Somewhere out of sight.

Silence. Solitude. Minutes ticking by in a locked room. Then a flock of white coats surrounding me. A long needle. Blue liquid. Burning cold running through my veins. My mind going soft, thoughts scattering. A door slamming shut, taking the light with it.

And now I huddled in the dark, with nothing but fragmented memories for company.

What day was it? Where was Coop? Would Kit have missed me yet?

The thought of my father brought fresh tears to my eyes.

I'd always known the risk of being Viral. Had feared this day might come. But I'd never really considered the implications. Never imagined not being able to say good-bye.

Now it was all I could think about.

If I'm still Viral.

I felt a surge of hope, though tinged with sadness. To save my life, I needed the cure to have worked. But the thought of never flaring again left a bitter taste in my mouth.

Know what tastes worse? Death. Imprisonment. Never seeing family or friends again.

Focus on what matters.

I had to hope my powers were gone.

There was only one way to find out.

I closed my eyes. Delved into my subconscious.

Sought the wolf inside.

Nothing.

No spark. No surge of power.

My pack was silent, my mind still and cold.

Whatever I'd been, it was gone.

Viral, no more.

I cried harder. The feeling of loss was overwhelming.

I hugged my knees. Felt broken. Lessened. Weak.

Lights flickered to life overhead, flooding the room in bright white.

I bolted to my feet. Would face what came next standing up.

The door buzzed. I palmed tears from my face as the portal swung open and the husky bald doctor from the driveway stepped inside.

Keegan. Mustache named him Dr. Keegan.

"What was that?" Keegan jabbed his clipboard at me. "What were you attempting to do?"

My eyes darted the room. Spotted a tiny camera mounted in the ceiling.

"You all do the *same* thing, at some point or another, if pressed hard enough." Keegan sounded at the edge of his patience. "Close your eyes. Tense. Is that how you force the change?"

My heart stopped. The change? And what did he mean by 'pressed'?

I kept my face blank. "I don't understand."

"Yes you do!" Keegan smacked the clipboard with his free hand. "I've led this inquiry for months. Spent more time and money than you could imagine." His bulk filled the room, anger radiating from his eyes like heat from a stove.

I didn't know how to respond. So I didn't.

"You dove off the flight deck of an aircraft carrier." Keegan thrust a stubby finger into the air, then another. "You jumped from the roof of a three-story building. Both times escaping totally unharmed! I am *not* wrong. The Phoenix Inquiry is not wrong!"

Phoenix Inquiry? What was that? How long had we been investigated? What did they know?

My mind raced. Sifting facts, compiling probabilities.

He wouldn't demand answers if he had proof.

The door opened behind Keegan. Two stern-faced men in white coats entered.

One held a very large syringe.

"Another blood test," Keegan explained, eyes hard. "We need to delve a little deeper. I've read the Claybourne boy's files. We've been watching Candela for years, and that led us to you. Did you know that?"

I did. But was past blaming Chance.

He'd sought answers. In his place, I'd have done the same.

The henchmen approached. I didn't shy away. To what purpose?

Instead, I offered my arm. Glared at Keegan as the needle sank into my flesh.

I hate you. I'll fight you when I can.

"That look!" The doctor snapped his fingers. "You're all the same, even the other group. Not one of you shows the proper fear. It's because you all *know* why you've been taken. You kids are more than you pretend."

Red blood flowed into the tube.

What story will you tell? What will you reveal to these awful monsters?

The pair stepped back, handing over my sample as they left the room. Keegan smiled darkly, pulling at his beard as he regarded me. "Think hard about how you want things to go from here, Tory. I know you're different. *Special.* I need to understand. To learn how it works. I can extract the information in a number of ways."

I crossed my arms to keep my hands from shaking. "You've made a mistake."

Keegan clicked his tongue. "No. I wouldn't have ordered your abduction in broad daylight if I had any doubt left. And soon—" he jiggled the vial of my blood, "—we'll have the proof we've been searching for. A power *our* nation alone must possess, before anyone else gets wind of it."

A weapon. He wants the supervirus as a tool for war.

Please, God, don't let my blood give it to him.

"Who are you?" It was the only question I really had.

"We're the sentinels that keep America safe." Keegan's eyes glittered portentously. "The last line. You won't find us on any organizational chart, but nations tremble at our footsteps."

He's a fanatic. And I'm completely in his power.

"People will look for us." I couldn't keep the quake from my voice. "Eight teenagers can't just disappear."

Keegan's face hardened.

"If the prize is great enough, anything can be arranged."

He turned and walked from the room.

CHAPTER 41

The wait was endless.

My eyes crawled the boundaries of my featureless cell—no windows, no decorations, no furniture beyond the hospital bed on which I sat.

Nothing to distract my thoughts. Nothing to provide comfort.

During the first hour I pressed an ear to the door, straining for the slightest indication of where my friends were being held. Where Coop had been taken. Eventually I gave up, returned to my sad little cot, and wrapped the flimsy medical gown tightly around me.

My last words to Keegan seemed hollow. These monsters *could* make us disappear. There were hundreds of ways to fake our deaths, if they even bothered.

No one knew we'd gone to Bolton Prep that morning. I doubted the agents had allowed themselves to be seen. If my blood came back Viral, who knew what they'd do? Eight lost teens might be worth the return, if they cared more about the virus than our lives.

A second hour slipped past. My anxiety grew with each passing heartbeat.

Outside these walls, where time still mattered, it had to be nearing sunset. Was Kit already looking for me? What would he do when I didn't answer my phone?

My eyes filled with tears, but I fought them back.

I wasn't beaten yet.

I wanted to go home. To have any shot, I had to keep it together.

Without warning, the door opened. Keegan stormed in, red-faced, a computer printout crumpled in one fist. Mustache and Buzz Cut entered at his back, faces impassive.

"What is the meaning of this?" Keegan shoved the paper under my nose, his nostrils flaring in anger. There was a wildness to his eyes that set my teeth on edge.

"How could I possibly answer that?" I replied.

"Your blood work!" the bald doctor spat. "Normal. Every measure within typical ranges. How did you do it?"

My heart leaped. Chance's serum worked!

Time to play the fool.

"I don't know what you're taking about!" I whined, letting my bottom lip tremble. "What's going on? Why are we here?"

Keegan slapped the printout onto the cot, causing me to jump. Mustache turned slightly toward Buzz Cut, who remained stoic. With their sunglasses still in place, I couldn't interpret the exchange.

"You *do* know!" Every fold on Keegan's neck quivered with indignation. "All of you! I'm not a fool. I didn't have you brought here on a *guess*! I have every research document from Candela's Brimstone experiment—Chance Claybourne developed a genetically tailored parvo supervirus, and he did so based on *you.*"

His eyes flicked briefly to the black-suited agents stationed by the door. "We have a dozen field reports detailing events and abilities that *cannot* be explained by normal human behavior. The file is an inch thick!"

I kept my mouth shut. My instincts were picking up on something.

Keegan seemed to be speaking for the benefit of Mustache and Buzz

Cut as much as me. Perhaps more. The burly doctor licked his lips, hands fidgety, eyes continually straying toward the two agents, as if to gauge their reaction. The pair merely watched, stone-faced, making no response.

Interesting. Who's really in charge here?

Keep up the act.

"Look, mister," I said in a shaky voice, hamming it up as much as I dared, "I have no idea what you're talking about. Are you saying I've got superpowers or something?"

Keegan's body stilled. Sweat beaded at his temples. "Show me your ability. Now. Or I'll dig it out the hard way."

This time I didn't fake the tremor in my voice. "Is that why you kidnapped us? To kill us? This is crazy! I'm just a kid!"

Mustache glanced at Buzz Cut, who continued to watch Keegan.

"I read Claybourne's files." Keegan's cheek twitched, a jittery hand rising to tug on his beard. "He talked about you at length. Things you and your friends did. The gleam that fills your eyes. You can't *lie* your way out of this! I want to see a flare. NOW!"

"Chance was in a mental institution!" I scooted back on the hospital bed until my shoulder blades touched the wall. I no longer doubted this man would hurt me. "He imagined those things. Ask him!"

"I did," Keegan answered, frustration dripping from every word. "For some reason he's covering for you. But I saw his research. I saw his notes."

"He's a deluded teenager, playing at scientist." I stole a glance at the black-suited duo, who seemed to be listening intently. "A spoiled, lonely rich boy, without any friends, who invented a crazy story to make himself feel important. Chance has serious problems. I've been trying to help him separate fact from fiction."

Improvised, but I kept going. These men hadn't seen Karsten's files, only the Brimstone experiment at Candela. If I could discredit Chance, they might begin to doubt.

"I'm not lying." I lifted the crumpled printout on the cot. "You have proof right there. My friends and I aren't some mystical group of fantasy creatures." Ignoring Keegan, I focused my attention on the agents by the door. "We're high school students. We have finals next month. I'm visiting colleges with my dad this summer." I released the tears I'd been holding back. "I want to go home."

"Liar!" Keegan snarled, snatching the paper from my fingers. "Very well. Blood tests aren't the only method at my disposal. I'll find what's hiding inside you, even if I have to *cut* the answers out, piece by piece."

My heart stopped. There was nowhere to run.

This man would *dissect* me to get what he wanted. And the ability he sought wasn't even there.

"You're insane," I whimpered. "I don't have magic powers. Please let me go."

Keegan shook his head, a dangerous glint to his eye. "Too late for that. You're *never* leaving here, Victoria Brennan. You belong to me now. You're my new favorite guinea pig."

A sweaty hand snaked forward and stroked my head. I recoiled in horror. "I'll find what I'm after, though you won't like how I do it. Despite all the setbacks, this project *will* succeed."

Buzz Cut turned to Mustache. Nodded once.

Mustache stepped forward. "That'll be all, Dr. Keegan."

Keegan spun, eyes narrowing. "What do you mean? One more day, surely. I can *prove* my theory. I can make this venture work! We'll open up the subjects and examine their stem cells, which can't be—"

"This way, Doctor." Mustache's voice was ice cold.

Keegan tensed. The printout dropped to the floor. His eyes darted the room.

For a crazy moment, I thought he might make a break for it.

What is going on?

"I . . . I can . . . the process is imperfect at present, but . . . but . . ."

Keegan trudged unsteadily toward the door, watching Buzz Cut intently. "Let me show you my research notes again. I'm not wrong here. We're a *hairsbreadth* away! Nothing else can explain the phenomena that—"

Mustache pushed Keegan from the room and followed close behind.

The door swung shut, leaving me alone with the ever-silent Buzz Cut.

He stared at me a very long moment, one hand cupping his chin.

I now understood who was in charge.

From behind the shades, I could feel his gaze boring into me. Could sense the weight of his judgment. The cold calculation of his thoughts.

I felt exposed. Helpless. Every lie I'd ever told was written in neon on my face.

But I endured his cold regard without flinching.

Knew my life depended on the next few moments.

"The roof." Buzz Cut's voice was surprisingly soft and high-pitched. "Three stories down, into a shallow pond."

"We were being chased."

"Chance Claybourne *did* create a supervirus. And a cure. He has files for both."

"He created a fantasy. A delusion centered on me. Chance doesn't know how to make scrambled eggs, much less a medical miracle. This is all a horrible mistake."

Buzz Cut's chin rose, as if evaluating my response. "Where are Marcus Karsten's files? We know he ran his own parvovirus experiment at LIRI. We believe you saw records. Were you involved?"

I bit my tongue, tried to look confused as I shook my head.

"You and your friends have a long list of enemies. An astonishing number, actually, for a group of teenagers. I've heard from many of them."

I forced a chuckle. "We can't stay out of trouble, that's certainly true. Perhaps that's what Chance first noticed. But we're not fairy-tale creatures. The proof is right in front of you."

I pointed to the printout lying on the tiles.

Buzz Cut intertwined his fingers behind his back. For another end-less moment, he regarded me without speaking.

Finally, he broke the silence. "Want to know what I think?"

I nodded, not trusting myself to reply.

"I think Keegan is right." Buzz Cut paced slowly across the room. "I think you caught a supervirus from this Dr. Karsten. I think the virus did something to you. I think you've been lying this whole time."

That's it. I'm done.

"Glass fragments on the floor of the van." His lips curled into the barest trace of a grin. "Not much, but I noticed. A small vial, perhaps? My partner should've searched you. Thankfully, I found the package Claybourne dumped in the woods."

Oh no.

"But what was *inside* those empty vials?" The smile broadened a trace. "My guess is the antidote. Probably the same substance we scraped off the basketball court."

I froze. Tried to keep the horror from my face.

Buzz Cut's smile vanished. "You took it, didn't you?"

I swallowed. What could I say that he didn't already know?

"That's why your blood came back clean," he continued, folding his arms across his chest. "You kids drank the serum while locked inside the vehicle. I'll wager you forced it on the other group beforehand as well."

My eyes dropped to the tiles. All our secrets, laid bare.

"I really wish you hadn't done that." The agent stepped closer to my cot. "Because now you're useless to me."

I finally found my voice. "What are you going to do to us?"

"We don't need you anymore, Tory Brennan." He spoke in a cold, dispassionate voice. "Any of you. We have Claybourne's files. Every step he took to recreate the supervirus. And we recovered a sample of the antidote. Not much, but enough. You and your friends tried to deny us these things, but we got them in the end. Now it's time to tie up loose ends."

"Please." My voice cracked. "Don't."

"A pity I never got to see you in action." Buzz Cut shrugged. "I was so looking forward to the show. Over the last few weeks, I've listened to a conversation between you and Claybourne at least thirty times. Typed the transcript myself. You know the one—when he first told you he could flare, that he'd infected himself, that his eyes burned red, not gold. That there were other Virals."

My blood turned to ice. *Checkmate.*

The agent smirked, his cruel mouth twisting with amusement. "Powers. Flares. Pack. It all sounded so . . . *exciting.* But now it's gone. From all of you. A pity, as I said."

Buzz Cut abruptly removed his sunglasses. Regarded me with sharp blue eyes.

Then he leaned close, his scarred face inches from mine.

The man terrified me, but I didn't look away.

I knew his next question would determine my life.

"Can you keep a secret, Tory Brennan?" he asked softly.

I nodded as my arms began to tremble. "If I must."

He smiled wide, showing perfect teeth. "I hope so. For your sake."

Then Buzz Cut spun and strode for the door.

A mad impulse took me.

"Sir?"

He paused. Turned.

"Please don't hurt my dog," I begged. "His name is Cooper. He's just a puppy."

Buzz Cut snorted, then left the room.

I gasped. Covered my face with my hands. Then shook uncontrollably.

Moments later, the door opened again.

A white coat entered, holding a syringe. He approached me warily, one eyebrow raised.

I met his eye. Extended my arm.

What else could I do?

CHAPTER 42

I awoke to a thousand pinpricks of light.

Blink.

Blink blink blink.

A soft breeze stirred my hair. My limbs felt weirdly disjointed, as if they didn't belong to me and I was merely borrowing them from someone else.

I was lying on my back. On grass, I realized, bolting upright in shock.

The tiny lights resolved into stars as my vision came into focus. Night sounds surrounded me. Frogs. Crickets. Rustling leaves.

Someone groaned to my left. I spun, spotted a lime-green polo shirt a dozen yards away.

"Shelton!" I scrambled to my friend's side. "You okay?"

He smacked his lips, hands absently searching for his glasses. I found them in his pocket and slipped them onto his nose. I abruptly realized I was wearing my own clothes again, as well.

I shivered, remembering the needle. Picturing those dead-eyed scientists dressing me.

The feeling of violation was total.

"My mouth tastes like death." Shelton sat up and rubbed his head.

Then his eyes widened. "Where are we? How long since . . ." He trailed off, no doubt remembering his own white-walled cell.

"I don't know." I scanned the clearing, but nothing seemed familiar. "But we're alone and outside, not strapped to hospital beds. That's an improvement."

Shelton rose on shaky legs. "Where's Ben and Hi? Chance?"

"Here," someone croaked. I ran toward the voice, found Hi slumped against a tree with his head in his hands. "Are we dead? Because if heaven's just a gloomy forest with you guys, I'm gonna be pretty let down."

"We're alive." I whirled, searching for any sign of the others. "I'll take it."

Chance stumbled into the clearing, hair a mess, one hand holding his side. He pointed back in the direction from which he'd appeared. "Ben's over there. He hasn't come to yet. I think they pounded him pretty good."

I fired in the direction Chance indicated, found Ben motionless beside a honeysuckle bush. Chance must've dragged him there from somewhere else, then folded his hands on his chest. Ben looked like a body lying in state, which twisted my stomach into knots.

"Ben!" I dropped to my knees.

His chest rose and fell. My heart resumed beating.

"I told you," Chance muttered behind me. "He's just been knocked around a bit."

Ben's left eye was swollen shut. He must've fought to the end. Of course.

"Stupid," I sniveled, cradling his head in my lap. I tucked his long black hair behind his ears. "Brave and stupid."

Ben stirred, murmuring words I couldn't understand. Then he whispered, "Tory."

Something melted inside me.

Hi and Shelton stumbled over as Ben began to wake. One eye opened, uncomprehending. Then Ben vaulted to his feet with a snarl.

"Easy!" I called. "We're alone."

Ben spun a ragged 360, stumbling on his feet. "Where are we?"

"Woods." Chance had been watching me. He shook his head, then pointed to a small trail to our right. "I saw something down there, but had to deal with Ben first."

Ben wobbled, dropping his hands to his knees. "What happened? Where's that fat jackass doctor?"

"I don't know." The memory sent a shiver down my spine. "But we shouldn't waste time finding out. Let's get out of here."

"I hear that!" Shelton bounded to the trailhead. "This way?"

I nodded. As good a choice as any.

The path led downhill and turned sharply a dozen yards ahead. The trees broke.

My breath caught, though I knew instantly where we were.

"Holy smokes." Hi stared, wide-eyed. "Is this the same place?"

Before us was the low-slung military building we'd been forced inside who knew how many hours before. We'd come up behind it, approaching the structure from the rear.

Except, it was barely a building anymore.

The windows and doors were gone. Every sign and fixture had been removed, every camera taken down. Even from the outside, the interior was obviously empty. No lights. Exposed girders. Abandoned hallways. Nothing but a windswept shell, its concrete bones crumbling and covered with graffiti.

"It's a ghost town." Shelton grabbed an earlobe. "Like the facility never existed!"

"They're gone," Chance said grimly. "Were never here at all."

The scale of the cover-up took my breath away. "No one here for us to accuse. Nothing to see. Zero evidence that a project ever existed."

"Assuming we were that stupid," Hi added. "Telling anyone, I mean."

I nodded, remembering Buzz Cut's final warning.

Not that it matters. They got what they wanted in the end.

Voices carried on the wind. I crouched, feeling a jolt of adrenaline as I prepared to flee into the woods. Then I heard a name I recognized.

"Ella!" I took off around the building.

"Tory, wait!" Ben hissed.

But I didn't, rounding the corner and sprinting up the gravel drive. I spotted the Trinity huddled beside a parked vehicle, trying to jimmy the door with a coat hanger. Impossibly, it was Ben's Explorer. Someone had moved it here.

I skidded to a stop. Cole spotted me and tapped Speckman's shoulder. The taller boy turned, then straightened abruptly, a wary look on his face.

Ella stood a few paces away. Recognizing me, she squealed in delight. We met in the middle of the driveway and wrapped each other in a hug.

"I was so worried," Ella blurted. "Is everyone okay?"

"Yes." I nodded to the others as they hurried into view. "You guys?"

"We're fine, too." Ella wiped her cheeks. "That bearded douchebag hammered us with questions, but no one talked. They took blood and I guess we passed." Her eyes found Chance, who was just then emerging from the woods. "Your cure must've worked. Thank you."

Chance smiled as he approached. "I pretended to be unhinged. Said I made everything up. Forged records to impress Tory. The doctor didn't believe a word of it, but I think the agents may have bought the act." He rubbed his jaw, grimacing slightly. "When they couldn't compel me to flare, the mood changed."

I looked away. Didn't want to tell Chance how wrong he was.

Not yet, anyway. Not there.

Ben stormed across the gravel. "Get the hell away from my car."

Cole raised his hands and backed off. "Just trying to get gone, man. This has been, like, the worst day of my life."

"Hope you're happy, Claybourne." Speckman tossed the coat hanger aside, bile dripping from his voice. "You killed off our powers. Ended a species."

"That's the only reason we're free right now," Ella scolded. "Show some respect."

I kept my mouth shut. Didn't want to think about not being Viral. Not yet.

Ben went face-to-face with Speckman. "You've got three seconds. Starting now."

The older boy glared at Ben. Didn't budge. Cole glanced at his companion uneasily.

Chance moved to Ben's side, followed quickly by Hi and Shelton.

Cole backed up another step. "Hey, dudes, I was just looking for a ride. But I can totally hike it out of here. No worries." He turned, began loping up the road toward the highway.

Ben spoke quietly. "No more flares, Willie. Just me and you."

"And me," Chance said.

"Ditto," Shelton and Hi said in unison.

Speckman's eyes slid down the line. Then he turned and spat. "Not worth the trouble." Moving slowly to show he wasn't intimidated, he followed after his roommate.

"Will?" I called.

He half turned. "What?"

"It goes without saying that we can't talk about this. Any of it. To anyone."

Speckman spat again. Nodded. Then he sauntered up the driveway.

"That gentleman has anger issues," Hi pronounced. "His mom didn't hug him enough. Or spank him enough. One or the other."

Shelton jiggled the Explorer's handle. "How are *we* going to get home?"

With a wince, I remembered Kit. Whitney.

What time was it? What *day* was it?

Out of habit, my fingers dipped into my pocket. Found my iPhone nestled inside.

"No way." I tapped the home button, bringing up the display. Saturday. Ten fifteen p.m. We'd been imprisoned for roughly nine hours.

"I don't believe it." Ben was staring at his car keys. "Right in my pocket."

One text message waited. Kit. I opened it with dread—how could I explain this one?

"'Okay, have fun,'" I read aloud. "Wait. What?"

I checked my outgoing messages. The phone claimed I'd texted my father three hours earlier.

Hi grunted, scratching his head. "Why does my mother think I'm at a movie?"

"They gave us a cover story," I breathed, incredulous.

"The spooks don't want us to get caught!" Shelton said excitedly. "Or anyone to know about this. Which means they're gonna leave us alone, right?"

Buzz Cut's words floated through my brain. *Can you keep a secret, Tory Brennan?*

"If we keep our mouths shut, I think it's over." I waved a hand at the ravaged building behind me. "What would we say anyway? We'd sound like those crazy people claiming to be alien abductees."

Hi froze. "You don't think they were aliens, do you?"

Ben smacked the back of his head. "Come on, dummy. Let's get home."

I smiled, bouncing across the gravel toward the Explorer. Then I stopped dead.

A thought I'd been avoiding broke through.

Cooper.

I spun and scanned the tree line. Then I yelled at the top of my lungs.

"Cooper! Here, boy!"

My panicked voice shattered the evening calm.

I waited, holding my breath, hoping for a miracle. Then I shouted again.

"Coop! Come on, boy!"

Ella reached for me, but I dodged her embrace. I ignored Ben's grimace, and how Chance looked away. Pretended not to see Hi and Shelton staring at the ground.

No. You're all wrong. You have to be.

I stuck fingers in my mouth and whistled. "Cooper! Coop! Let's go, boy!"

Seconds ticked past. Then minutes.

A voice inside my head began speaking calmly, telling me things I refused to hear.

He was a good dog. I gave him a better life. He was lucky to have met me.

I shoved the thoughts away like poison. Stepping closer to the forest, I cupped my hands to my mouth. "Cooper! Let's go, dog face!"

My voice broke. My chin dropped to my chest.

Then a bark echoed in the trees. My head jerked up as something crashed through the undergrowth.

A gray streak launched from the woods.

Coop's shaggy body bowled me to the ground.

Shouts of joy exploded around me. I heard high-fives and exhaled breaths. One person choked back a sob—pretty sure it was Hiram.

But I only had eyes for my wolfdog.

Tears spilled from my cheeks as I wrapped Coop in my arms.

His rough pink tongue skidded across my face.

For one moment, at least, everything was okay again.

CHAPTER 43

I awoke from a turbulent dream I couldn't remember.

Sat up in bed. Stared at my bedroom wall while my brain tried to process the day before.

Back home. Unharmed. Buried in my comforter like every other morning.

It didn't seem real.

Coop eyed me reproachfully from the floor.

I was startled by a snore to my left.

Ella. She hadn't wanted to be alone, even in her own house. I understood.

"Lost your spot, eh, dog face?" I tapped the blanket and Coop vaulted up, shoving his furry head into my arms. He sighed contentedly, stretching his legs and rolling over for a belly scratch. I complied.

Ella muttered something, but didn't wake. I knew she was exhausted.

As my head came fully online, conflicting emotions coursed through me.

Joyous relief.

I was alive. My friends and family were safe. Against all odds, we'd escaped a deadly trap. The target was off our backs.

Bone-deep sadness.

My powers gone. I'd never flare again.

The Virals were no more.

Ben had driven everyone back to Morris the night before, including Ella and Chance. With an eighty-pound canine in the mix, the ride had been a tight fit.

Kit and Whitney hadn't blinked when Ella and I stumbled through the door.

My father asked about the movie. Where Coop had been all day. Whitney wanted to know if we were hungry. Boring, mundane questions, offered with no understanding of what had just happened. The ordeal we'd survived. The loss I was nursing.

But that's how it had to be.

We'd mumbled sufficient responses, then trudged upstairs, wolfdog in tow. I'd lent Ella pajamas, both of us too tired to talk, even if we'd known how to put the last few days into words.

How do you apologize for something so massive?

How do you accept such an apology?

Instead, we'd simply shared another hug, then crawled under the covers. Sleep took me before my head hit the pillow.

Today's the first day.

Ella finally stirred. Her eyes slid open, green irises glinting in the morning sun. Then she tensed as the full weight of memory crushed down upon her.

I grabbed her arm. "It's okay! You're safe."

Recognition dawned in her eyes, followed swiftly by a tinge of guilt.

I plastered on a smile I didn't truly feel. Ella had betrayed me, but I'd experienced worse. She'd been badly used. Had experienced a second kidnapping horror to match the first. I couldn't hold a grudge.

Frankly, the idea seemed ridiculous. Everything was different now.

I just wanted my friend back.

Ella blew out a breath, wisps of her long black hair spinning skyward. "It's really gone, isn't it?" She didn't have to say what.

"I think so." Though I hadn't attempted another flare. Didn't want to try.

Ella winced, but her jaw hardened. "We should be thankful. That's what saved us, right?"

I nodded. "They let us go because we were useless. No virus. No proof. Nothing to possess."

Her eyes grew troubled. "Do you think they'll come back?"

I remembered a glance between the two agents. How Mustache had all but pushed the flustered doctor from my white-walled cell. The fear in Keegan's eyes. A hint of panic in his voice.

"They're done with us." I spoke with certainty. "Whoever those agents were, they closed up shop and blew town. They're gone. The bastards didn't find what they were after."

Lie.

Ella relaxed a fraction. "Thanks to Chance." I noted the warmth in her tone.

Another thought winged into my brain.

"My God!" Both hands found my face. "Chance is sleeping at Ben's place right now."

Ella giggled. "How did *that* happen?"

"It was the only way." I hopped out of bed. "Shelton's parents ask a lot of questions, and Mrs. Stolowitski can be a nightmare. But Mr. Blue barely knows when *Ben* is home, much less a guest. He's pretty hands off."

Ella snorted. "Let's hope Ben was hands off as well. Of Chance, I mean."

My stomach roiled. "We should hurry."

○   ○   ○

Fifteen minutes later, Ella and I were standing on the blacktop behind my town house, waiting for the others. Coop hung by my side for a minute, but couldn't resist chasing a group of squirrels into the dunes.

At the driveway's edge he looked back, tilting his head in a way I understood. I waved permission. Coop yapped once, then fired into the sand hills. He seemed unperturbed by the loss of my powers, wagging his tail as he raced across the sand, content as ever, as though nothing had changed between us.

Could he not feel their lack, as I did?

Perhaps that's best. Maybe we all should start to forget.

"You live in such a weird place." Ella watched Coop weave through the cattails and scrub grass. We both had on soccer shorts and Bolton Prep tees, but she wore them better. "This neighborhood feels like another world."

I smiled, shaking out my hair in the mild ocean breeze. "I love my island."

I did. Where others saw isolation, I saw . . . freedom. Room to breathe.

Once, living here had been a shock to the system. Some kind of sick cosmic joke.

Now, it was the only thing I wanted.

My life is good. It can still be great.

A door opened down the row and Hiram stepped outside. He stretched extravagantly, expanding his yellow smiley face tee and sweat shorts to their physical limits. "Hello, ladies!"

A moment later, Shelton emerged in a white polo and blue shorts. The boys bumped fists as they strolled over to join Ella and me. They seemed relaxed for the first time in days.

I peered down at the end unit. "Anyone seen Ben and Chance?"

"The BFFs?" Hi shrugged, then winced, one hand reaching to massage the opposite shoulder. I knew without asking that a needle prick hid beneath his sleeve. "They're probably making weave bracelets for each other. Or building a slam book."

Shelton shook his head, boxy black specs bouncing on his nose. "You won't be cracking jokes if they start throwing haymakers again. Next time, I say we just let them slug it out."

The last door opened and Ben and Chance walked out, both in faded jeans and black tees. Not surprising, since that was practically all Ben owned.

"Twinsies!" Hiram lifted his iPhone. "Stop! Let me get a pic."

"Do it and that's going for a swim," Ben warned. Chance just rolled his eyes.

"Boo!" Hi slipped the phone back into his pocket. "Years from now you're gonna wish we'd captured more memories."

Our circle became six. An awkward hush fell over the group.

Suddenly, I didn't know what to say. Where to start. What to avoid.

Ben's left eye was a mess, but at least the swelling had gone down. The purple bruise along Chance's jaw had begun to yellow at the edges. Everyone was banged up and sore—we'd survived enough fights to last a lifetime—but those two had taken the worst of it.

"Are you okay?" I asked them both.

"Fine," Ben said.

"I'll live," Chance answered at the same time.

Another long silence.

"Those agents," Shelton said finally, "they know where we live. How to find us."

"They're gone." Chance spoke with quiet certitude. "I convinced them I was delusional, and they only had my Brimstone records to go on. I never uploaded Karsten's files to a Candela server. The only copies are locked away in my study."

I looked down at my shoes.

The others obviously didn't know what Buzz Cut had told me.

Should I tell them?

"The fat quack mentioned interviews," Shelton pressed, oblivious to my discomfort. "They were digging through our past, like when they approached Madison. That's bad news."

"We've always been careful," Hi countered. "What could they learn? Some crazy stories, but those aren't *proof.* When our blood came back clean, I think they pulled the plug."

I opened my mouth, then closed it.

Ben tapped my shoulder. "Out with it."

I flinched. "What do you mean?"

"You're holding something back. It's eating at you, I can tell."

I sighed. Why spread the misery? But Ben had asked me a direct question.

"The younger agent," I began, "the short-haired one with the scar on his cheek? He told me some . . . bad things."

Everyone tensed, but no one interrupted.

Deep breath. "They found our empty vials. Both the one I crushed inside the van and the case Chance ditched in the woods. Worse, they found the serum we dumped out in the gym."

Chance grimaced. "Enough to collect a sample?"

I nodded.

Shelton sucked in a breath. Hi covered his face.

"What does it matter?" Ben turned to Chance, speaking civilly to the older boy for the first time I could remember. "They still don't have a live virus, and didn't collect our blood before we took the cure. I thought that was the key?"

"They can't work backward solely from the serum," Chance said slowly, thinking it through. "The antidote merely treats the Viral side effects—what happened to our DNA. It's not a blueprint for reverse engineering the supervirus."

"Great." Ella glanced from his face to mine. "Then they won't be able to make more Virals."

I shook my head sadly. "They have *all* your records, Chance. Every single one. They'll duplicate the Brimstone experiment exactly. Buzz Cut was gloating—with the antidote in hand, those monsters have both pieces in their possession. It's just a matter of retracing your footsteps."

But Chance was grinning from ear to ear. "Then they'll be frustrated a *long* time."

My eyes narrowed. "Explain."

"Brimstone didn't work." Chance laughed excitedly, running a hand through his tousled hair. "Not once. I had pages of methodology on file, but I couldn't get the protein coats to hold up. The supervirus never survived insertion."

I stared, uncomprehending. "But you made yourself Viral, Chance. It *did* work."

"Not until I cheated," Chance explained. "I went back through Karsten's notes and found the trick. I doubt even *he* knew what did it."

I waved a hand, demanding he continue.

Chance was happy to oblige. "When Karsten created Parvovirus XPB-19, he made a mistake. But that error was key." His face scrunched in thought. "How to explain?"

"The Cliff Notes version," Ben requested.

"Simply put, Karsten overcooked his sample." Chance clicked his teeth, as if uncertain where to begin. "First, the basics. Viruses are cultivated in a lab by using bacterial cells as hosts. Being smaller, a virus is injected—or injects itself—into a bacterial cell and use the host's nucleus and machinery to replicate. So you need a virus, a bacterial host, and a growth medium to keep the bacteria viable during the replication process. Follow me so far?"

Nods. Of varying confidence.

Chance formed a circle with his fingers. "I was using sixty-millimeter dishes, then heating the growth medium to Karsten's specified temperature. But it never worked. Either the host cells or the supervirus would inevitably collapse. After weeks of failure, I was about to give up, but went back to Karsten's records one last time. I discovered a note I'd never considered before. One day he'd run out of clean sixty-millimeter dishes, and substituted a hundred fifty–millimeter one instead. Curious, I checked his results log, and discovered that *this* was the sample that became infectious."

My eyebrows rose. "It was the freaking plate size?"

Chance shook his head. "Curious, I followed this trial through the records, and found something else. Karsten had tried to adjust the temperature to compensate for a larger dish. But he goofed. The computer printout showed that instead of being dialed up a mere ten degrees, as his notes indicated, he'd accidentally increased the temperature by *thirty* degrees."

Chance held his hands wide. "That was it. The crucial breakthrough. A significantly warmer growth-culture environment was the golden ticket. Suddenly, the bacterial host cells held together, and the virus was able to hijack them with ease. Karsten likely never knew why his experiment succeeded that one solitary time."

I blinked, struck silent. Such a tiny mistake, never recognized, had changed the course of my life. Then I snapped back to the present. "But isn't *that* in your notes, too?"

Chance slapped his hands together. "Nope. It was late when I found the discrepancy, and I didn't understand its importance. Will and I had been working all night. I didn't even share my theory with him—I simply walked over and jacked up the heat on our current batch."

"This is loony tunes," Shelton breathed. "So then what happened?"

Chance scratched his cheek. "The next morning we both noticed a difference—our medium had practically cooked. We took it out and examined it closely. It was misting slightly, and smelled terrible. I was about to chuck the dish when Will suggested we test it anyway."

Then Chance started, eyes popping. "We were so close to . . . never really took care . . ."

I grabbed his arm. "Chance, what?"

"That's how we got infected." His hands found his face. "Speckman and I touched the first sample while it was still simmering. We didn't use precautions. Maybe it got under our skin, or we inhaled hot particles somehow. But it's the only thing that makes sense."

"This heat thing?" Ben pressed. "It never got written down?"

Chance shook his head, still reeling. "We ran tests. The replicated virus held up. We cultivated a second generation through traditional methods. The trick to its origin was never recorded. I never explained it to Will, either."

I sifted the facts. Testing every possible permutation. Then I shot forward and crushed Chance in a hug. "Those thugs think they have the recipe, but they don't!"

The group exploded in cheers and high-fives.

We'd lost our powers, but at least those black-ops psychos hadn't acquired the formula.

No new weapon would terrorize the world.

It was something.

Shelton was nodding, looking relieved. "What about the Trinity guys?"

Ella snorted. "Don't worry about those morons. Speckman's a bully, but he's been declawed. Cole is just a dope. We created a cover story long ago, and I'm sure they'll stick to it. You won't hear from them again."

Hi shuffled his feet. "Has . . . has anyone tried?"

The mood died.

Ben looked away. Chance cringed, but shook his head. Ella and Shelton did the same.

A funeral pall settled over the group. In a way, it was appropriate.

My lips moved before I knew what would come out. "Why not one last time?"

Eyes found me. Then, slowly, everyone nodded.

I straightened, preparing myself for failure. "All together. On my count."

Everyone closed their eyes.

"One. Two. Three."

Plunging deep into my subconscious, I strained with all my being. Struggled to find that spark lurking at my core. The fire within me.

Nothing.

The power was gone. The light burned out.

My eyes opened.

The six of us glanced at each other. No golden glow. No red fire.

The serum had done its work.

"For the best," I croaked.

Nods. Shrugs.

What else was there to say?

Shelton pushed Ben lightly. "Remember when you couldn't flare without losing your temper? So Hi kicked you from behind to get you mad, and you threw him in the ocean?"

Ben snorted. "He deserved it."

"I was providing a service," Hi protested. "I recall Tory once trying to eat a mouse."

I pinched my nose. "Ugh, don't remind me."

Ella giggled. "One time Cole lost his flare while carrying a boulder. It pinned his leg for an hour."

Then everyone had a story. Our funeral became a wake.

The mood lifted as we swapped flare stories. It was cathartic. A way to say good-bye.

I caught Ben smiling at me. "I remember when Tory sniffed that mound of bird crap in the old lighthouse. I thought she'd vomit on the spot."

Chance laughed. "I *knew* she was too clever. Always with a trick up her sleeve."

The boys glanced at each other. Their smiles faded.

Something passed between them.

Abruptly, both looked at me.

I could see a question in their eyes. A resolve to see something through.

They talked. Oh God, they talked about me.

They're going to make me choose.

In a flash of dread, I realized I could delay this no longer.

With another jolt, I realized I didn't need to.

There was no point putting it off.

There was also no decision to make.

My eyes met a dark, intense pair staring back earnestly. Longingly. Fearfully.

I smiled. Even as my heart pounded.

Before anyone spoke, I stepped forward, legs shaking so badly I worried I might fall.

But my second foot successfully followed the first.

I walked over to Ben's side.

Slipped my hand inside his.

Squeezed for dear life.

Ben's eyes widened. He gasped quietly, his chest rising and falling.

I met his startled gaze. Smiled through my blushes.

A goofy smile split Ben's face, one I'd never seen before. His fingers crushed mine.

No decision to make.

Tearing my eyes from Ben, I looked at Chance, found him watching me with a glum expression. Then he sighed, a wry smile twisting his lips.

Chance nodded slightly.

Not one word spoken. Volumes exchanged.

The silence stretched, like a living breathing force.

Finally, Hi cleared his throat. "Um."

My face burned scarlet as I remembered our audience. Ella was gaping at me, a delighted grin on her face. Shelton looked like he might turn and run. Hi was rubbing the back of his neck, his face twisted in an uncomfortable grimace.

Still no one said a word.

This was the most painful moment of my life.

"So . . ." Hi drummed his thighs, eyes fixed to the pavement. "Right. A lot just happened there. Weirdly without anyone talking, but, um, yeah. So. Are we just gonna—"

"I should be getting home," Chance interrupted, glancing awkwardly at his watch. "Ben, can I borrow your car? I'll have my driver return it this afternoon."

"Huh? What?" Ben stuttered, staring at my hand as if he couldn't process what was happening. "Oh. Yeah. Sure." Incredibly, he dug out his keys and tossed them to the older boy.

Chance's eyes met mine. "Good luck with everything."

I could tell he wanted to say more, but didn't, pivoting and striding for the vehicle.

"Chance?" Ella called.

He half turned. "Yes?"

"Can you give me a ride?" Ella smiled sweetly, her green eyes sparkling. "I'm stuck, and we're practically neighbors."

Chance puffed up, a touch of his old swagger returning. "It'd be a privilege."

Ella crushed me with a quick hug, grinning wickedly. "Talk later, you sly devil." Then she hurried over to Chance. He opened the passenger door and helped her inside, then rounded the Explorer, a brighter look on his face.

Well, well.

"If he scratches my baby . . ." Ben tried to scowl, but it didn't take. He seemed relieved. And still hadn't let go of my hand.

I heard a shoe scuff the ground. Shelton and Hi were standing across from Ben and me.

Shelton took a deep breath. "So it's like that, huh?"

"Guys." I felt my stomach lurch. "I know this is weird. Ben and I, we—"

Hi's face was pained. "I don't even get a chance? No shot to say how *I* feel?"

My head jerked back. "What?"

"So it's all decided." Shelton sullenly kicked a rock, his voice resentful. "What does Ben have that I don't?"

I stared, openmouthed.

Hi dropped to a knee and pinned me with solemn eyes. "I can't hide it anymore, Victoria. You need to know the truth. *I* love you, too. Forever and ever. I want to be your sweet babushka."

My mind reeled. "Hi, I . . . I didn't—"

"I'm gonna wring your stupid necks." Ben's face was burning.

Hi burst out laughing, rolling away from his kick. I glanced at Shelton, who was trying—and failing—to hold it together.

"I love you, Tory Brennan!" Hi bounced to his feet, ready to bolt at Ben's slightest twitch. "Let me rub your supple feet!"

I covered my face with both hands. "Oh God."

"Shut up, Hiram." But Shelton couldn't keep the laughter from his voice. "We're just playing, Tor. Everything's cool. Cooler, now, honestly."

"I want to plan the wedding," Hi demanded. "I've got strong feelings about flowers and centerpieces, plus I'm willing to DJ."

Ben stared daggers at Hi, at his outer limits of embarrassment.

But he wouldn't release my hand.

I pulled Ben closer, suddenly comfortable doing so. "Thanks, Hi. You're the best."

Hi winked, still on the balls of his feet.

I caught movement in the corner of my eye. Glanced up.

Kit was standing at our kitchen window.

My face flamed scarlet.

Ben followed my gaze, then dropped my hand like a hot frying pan.

As Kit was gaping in shock, Whitney appeared at his side. Seeing us, she practically jumped, then she shook a finger under my father's nose as her mouth began working. Grabbing his arm, she dragged Kit out of sight.

At the last instant, I swear I saw Dad smile.

"Blargh." I covered my eyes. "Kill me now."

"Good luck with that." Hi nudged Shelton toward his garage. "Come on, hot shot. Let's give these turtledoves some space. I got a bootleg copy of *Grand Theft Auto V* in my room. Let's play before my mother finds it and kills me."

"My Sunday is suddenly wide open." Shelton pushed Hi back. "You still got those mini-pizzas? My mom never buys that stuff."

The boys jostled toward Hi's door, laughing and cracking jokes.

I turned.

Ben was right beside me, eyes scared.

He opened his mouth, groping for words, as Hi and Shelton disappeared inside.

I pressed a finger to his lips. "I know."

The tension broke. Ben leaned forward and closed his mouth on mine.

Warmth rolled through my body.

Everything else faded.

ATTENTION: DIRECTOR WALSH ["EYES ONLY"]

FILE STATUS: TOP SECRET [LEVEL 5]

CASE: #34687 (AKA—PHOENIX INQUIRY)

FILE TYPE: CLOSING REPORT

DATE: JUNE 24, 2014

PRINCIPAL INVESTIGATING AGENT(S): J. SALTMAN, B. ROGERS

NOTE TO FILE:

It is hereby recommended that the Phoenix Inquiry be officially closed. Investigating Agents have found no actionable evidence to support the existence of the target objective (see Weaponized Canine Parvovirus—Dr. L. K. Keegan), and no longer believe the investigation has operational merit. (See Phoenix subject lab results, Phoenix subject detention reports A-H, Brimstone Study lab trials, and Investigating Agent Field Note 31, attached to this closing report.)

Investigating Agents have 1) dismantled and removed Operational Field HQ CHARL-14 ("OFHQC-14"); 2) disbanded Special Medical Unit Phoenix; 3) reassigned Tactical Weapons Team Bravo and Vehicle Support Unit Baker; and 4) liquidated Research Director Dr. Lester K. Keegan ("Dr. Keegan") in accordance with Information Containment Protocol 51.A ("ICP 51.A-4.3")[1].

---

[1] Dr. Keegan was erratic and uncooperative during the latter phase of this investigation and determined to be unreliable for continued Level 5 security clearance. Given his direct knowledge of the Phoenix Inquiry and his irrational advocacy of the failed venture, the potential exposure to the Agency was deemed unacceptable. Therefore, Agent Rogers invoked ICP 51.A-4.3 at the time of the project's disbandment. The matter is thus closed and containment assured.

FINAL ASSESSMENT: The Phoenix Inquiry was without merit.

RECOMMENDED ACTION: Due to the sensitive nature of the associated detentions and medical testing, it is hereby recommended that all records pertaining to the Phoenix Inquiry be destroyed immediately.

[END CLOSING REPORT]

EPILOGUE

I crawled out of bed at sunrise.

Trudged to the bathroom. Snagged my toothbrush.

Monday morning. School day. Ella had already texted, reminding me to pack my cleats. We had a game that week, and I intended to play.

Life. Returned to normal.

I thought of Ben, and smiled as I scrubbed.

Not *completely* normal, but that part was okay.

Thirty minutes to get ready. My boyfriend would be waiting down by the dock.

Ben. My boyfriend.

Boyfriend.

Wow.

I swished the remaining toothpaste. Spat.

Wiping my mouth, I caught my eyes in the mirror.

They were green. Always would be, now.

A sob erupted from somewhere deep inside my chest. I choked it off.

No. I will not cry. If I start now, I might never stop.

I'd been given a wonderful gift, then lost it. Painful, but I was better for the experience.

Am I?

I dropped the towel. Gripped the counter with both hands.

Stared at the freckly, red-haired girl in the mirror. The one with sad eyes.

I spoke to her.

"What I've lost does not define me."

Just words.

"I am not less than I was."

Not true.

I trembled. Tears pressed at my eyelids.

My voice dropped to a whisper. "I'm still whole. I am *not* broken."

A lie. But necessarily said.

"I won't look back. Only forward. My life will go on."

As a shell, a remnant.

But this was required. Needed to be internalized.

Breathing deeply, I prepared for my first full day of not being Viral.

My head dropped.

I thought of Coop. Ben. Shelton and Hi. My pack, severed by cruel luck and worse men.

The sadness morphed to anger. White rage burned through my system.

I don't WANT to change.

Something clicked in my brain. Shifted. Reset.

My hands stilled.

Warmth surged through me.

Suddenly, I felt at peace. As if the pain had washed away, replaced by a quiet strength I'd never felt before.

My fingers began to tingle. An electric jolt traveled my spine.

Outside, Cooper howled.

I looked up at the mirror.

My breath caught.

A confident girl stared back.

Poised. Unbroken.

Her eyes smoldered with pale blue flame.

ACKNOWLEDGMENTS

Terminal was only possible through the wonderful support of Arianne Lewin at G. P. Putnam's Sons and everyone at Penguin Young Readers Group. You guys make it all happen. We are forever in your debt.

Our continuing thanks go to Don Weisberg at Penguin and Susan Sandon at Random House UK for supporting Tory and her pack from the start. And, as always, we are deeply in debt to Jennifer Rudolph Walsh and the team at William Morris Endeavor Entertainment. Thanks for keeping the Reichs boat afloat.

Finally, an emphatic and heartfelt thank-you to our loyal readers. You are the reason we get up in the morning, write all day and night, and limit our naps to reasonable afternoon intervals. Thanks for taking this journey with us and giving it a purpose.